CAPTAIN
of Industry

T0126161

KARIN KALLMAKER

Bella
BOOKS
2016

Bella Books, Inc.
P.O. Box 10543
Tallahassee, FL 32302

Printed in the United States of America on acid-free paper.

First Bella Books Edition 2016

Editor: Katherine V. Forrest
Cover Designer: Linda Callaghan

ISBN: 978-1-59493-491-9

Other Bella Books by Karin Kallmaker

Romance:
Love by the Numbers
Roller Coaster
Above Temptation
Stepping Stone
Warming Trend
The Kiss that Counted
Night Vision/The Dawning
Christabel
Finders Keepers
Just Like That
Sugar
One Degree of Separation
Maybe Next Time
Substitute for Love
Frosting on the Cake I and II
Unforgettable
Watermark
Making Up for Lost Time
Embrace in Motion
Wild Things
Painted Moon
Car Pool
Paperback Romance
Touchwood
In Every Port

Erotica:
In Deep Waters: Cruising the Seas
18th and Castro
All the Wrong Places
Tall in the Saddle: New Exploits of Western Lesbians
Stake through the Heart: New Exploits of Twilight Lesbians
Bell, Book and Dyke: New Exploits of Magical Lesbians
Once Upon a Dyke: New Exploits of Fairy Tale Lesbians

Dedication

The late Suzanne Corson of Boadecia's Books and all independent booksellers and reading advocates who put books in the hands of readers, one story at a time.

Twenty-seven, at last.

Seven alien civilizations, 792 large cups of coffee, 8 cans of Pringles, innumerable Goldfish crackers, bits of chocolate and 1,283 hours of ambient music were consumed during the writing of this book. No pictures of Della Street were harmed.

Special thanks to...

Kay Carney for her generous donation to the Golden Crown Literary Society (GCLS) and her inspired names "Laverne and Shirley" for Jennifer Lamont's formidable Girls.

Ann de Mooij for her generosity to GCLS and even more so for her patience.

KG MacGregor, Melissa Brayden, MJ Lowe, Polly Robinson and Erica Abbott for their support by both example and direct kick-in-the-pants. Polly (again) and Toni Whitaker for their Lego-based inspirations.

Katherine V. Forrest and Bella Books, who continue to make me better than I am.

About the Author

Karin Kallmaker has been exclusively devoted to lesbian fiction since the publication of her first novel in 1989. As an author published by the storied Naiad Press, she worked with Barbara Grier and Donna McBride, and has been fortunate to be mentored by a number of editors, including Katherine V. Forrest.

In addition to multiple Lambda Literary Awards, she has been featured as a Stonewall Library and Archives Distinguished Author. Other accolades include the Ann Bannon Popular Choice and other awards for her writing, as well as the selection as a Trailblazer by the Golden Crown Literary Society. She is best known for novels such as *Painted Moon, Substitute for Love, Touchwood, Maybe Next Time* and *The Kiss that Counted.*

The California native is the mother of two and blogs at Romance and Chocolate. Write to her at karin@kallmaker. com or visit at Facebook or @kallmaker on Twitter. More about books and writing at kallmaker.com.

A complete list of books by this author available from Bella Books: http://www.bellabooks.com/Author-Karin-Kallmaker-cat.html

When you purchase from the publisher more of your dollars reach the women who write and produce the books you love. Karin thanks you for your support of books for and about lesbians!

References to Characters from Other Novels

Selena Ryan and Gail Welles - *Stepping Stone*
Helen Baynor and Laura Izmani - *Roller Coaster*
Syrah Ardani and Toni Blanchard - *Just Like That*
Reyna Putnam and "the mathematician" (Holly Markham) -
Substitute for Love
Leah Beck and Jackie Frakes - *Painted Moon*
Sydney Van Allen and Faith Fitzgerald - *Wild Things*

ACT I

CHAPTER ONE

The twinkling party lights woven into the hedges and trees brightened the amber glow of the chardonnay that was no longer in Jennifer Lamont's glass. Droplets of wine shimmered in an arc away from her, and in each Jennifer fancied she could see snapshots from the A-list soiree that surrounded her.

In the nearest drop was the face of her ex, cuddling with the new love. The next reflected the swathed sculpture up for auction. The ribbon of shimmering wine just leaving the fluted mouth of her glass gleamed with a hundred eyes that had turned from their vivacious conversations toward her crescendoing cry of alarm.

There were at least seventy Beautiful People gathered in the expansive cliffside backyard of some Southern California Internet tycoon, and all of them were eager to talk about women in politics while they showed their support for breast cancer screening and research. All of them were now witnessing La Lamont falling off her five-inch Jimmy Choo heels.

A producer had bought the coveted, high-priced tickets for the opportunity to rub shoulders with some of the wealthiest and most famous women in the country. Jennifer had agreed to be arm candy because of the auction of the new Leah Beck sculpture. Even though it was midweek and she had a five a.m. makeup call in Los Angeles, she'd passed up sleep and gotten herself A-list dressed in a Michael Kors off-the-shoulder cocktail sheath. When her date—name to be forever cursed—had canceled at the last minute, Jennifer had demanded the address and made the drive to La Jolla on her own.

In the small pool of wine left in her glass, Jennifer thought she saw the white flare of at least one cell phone flash. Then the glass followed the wine arc across the terra-cotta patio and she had one final split-second choice: fall hard, fast, and then roll her face away from most of the probable witnesses and cameras, or windmill, flail, and try to stay upright. Which one would make the worst picture on SLY or Buzztastic? Which one would she prefer to explain on talk shows? Which one would look more like she had caught her heel between the flagstones—the truth—and less like she was drunk—the likely headline?

All the while the clay tiles rushed toward her nose and an increasingly urgent part of her brain screamed, "Protect your face!"

She twisted to take the impact on her side, threw her arms around her head.

Later, pictures confirmed that the back of her skull was a scant inch above the tiles. Not that most people looked at that part of the tableau. Instead, all eyes were on the wardrobe malfunction of the year—of two years, more accurately.

To her credit, her rescuer glanced only briefly at Laverne and Shirley in all their glory, then met Jennifer's panicked gaze. With one eyebrow arched she asked, "You get regularly scheduled mammograms, right?"

Jennifer scarcely heard the laughter from the partygoers near enough to have heard the question. White flashes from cameras didn't blot out the face of the woman who had caught her.

She knew the sardonic edge, the light blue eyes. She knew the strong arms lifting her. Not again, she thought helplessly. *Not again*.

CHAPTER TWO

Twenty Years Earlier

Eighteen, nineteen, twenty.

The elevator's faint *ping* coincided with the doors easing open to reveal concrete floors, exposed steel beams and tall, broad windows lightly frosted with snow. A red carpet runner led across the foyer to ceiling-high wooden double doors that stood open. Two of the other women in the lift let out a unison "ooh" at the sight of Central Park, and, across the treetops, the roof line of the Metropolitan Museum of Art.

But nobody moved until Jennifer stepped forward. A show runway or an entrance into a high-end society party—Jennifer Lamont walked and people watched her. Picking up the rhythm of a jazzed up "Holly Jolly Christmas" that poured through the doors, she strode along the red runner in a cloud of Shalimar. Her agent said she wasn't old enough to carry off the cologne, but tonight's designer hadn't specified scent or footwear, so she had chosen what she wanted.

Her client's Stormy Nights line of nightclub dresses and lingerie had led to the indigo hair color that had teens in New

York draining salons dry of similar shades. She was pleased that her stunning lion's mane hairstyle had led to a new nickname. She'd already been Baby Jennifer, Sweetheart Jen, Luscious Lamont. Now she was Hurricane Jennifer and she liked it. She liked it a lot.

Beyond the open doors she could see the chilly glass and steel of a lavish Upper East Side corner loft. Her gait deliberately long, she strode through the open doors, not deviating from her runway strut for another six strides. She paused, quarter-turned, treated the nearest server bearing a tray of champagne flutes to a long look and was pleased when he scurried over to offer one. Flashes popped.

Ninety percent of her job was done.

Her client, whose designs didn't live up to his ego, was the next to scurry in her direction. She dropped about half of her runway bearing, returned the air-cheek kisses and shifted to become his literal arm candy.

"You look divine!"

"How could I look anything else in your gorgeous clothes, Lucius?" The shadow they cast together in the long, last light of the setting December sun only magnified her height advantage, turning her additional eight inches into several feet.

They sipped champagne and began a circuit of the party. In spite of the bright holiday dresses and scattering of Santa hats on the guests, the room was sterile and cold compared to the old, tiny East Village apartment she lived in. This loft, mostly concrete and steel with an open-plan brushed stainless steel kitchen in the middle, lacked for personality until she saw that an enormous mural replica of *Starry Night* was painted on the ceiling. The real Van Gogh was one of her favorite paintings to visit at MOMA. The view across Central Park was indeed stunning and Jennifer would have liked to have lingered and picked out more landmarks, but she was being paid to be part of the scenery.

Halfway around the loft, after dozens of air kisses, her repetition of how wonderful it was to be wearing Lucius's divinely retro princess-cut cocktail dress with lavish rhinestone trim, along with darling lace ankle boots she "just grabbed out of the closet," was sounding only slightly tired to her own ears.

She was diverted from a tedious Lucius monologue by a server hovering in her line of sight, offering canapés and cheese.

He was cute enough—a twenty-something scrubby-shaved New York aspiring actor currently playing the role of waiter. She met his eager gaze, lifted an eyebrow at his outstretched tray and then deliberately looked down at the sewn-to-fit gown that molded her 38-24-32 silhouette.

He gulped and hurried away.

"Well done. Not a clue why he thought you ever ate anything," someone with a husky voice said in her ear.

"Oh, I eat." She didn't bother to turn around. "Every third Tuesday."

"Aren't you a little young for the champagne?"

That made her turn.

At five-seven, she was not used to having to look up at other women, especially when she was wearing four-inch heels. But the woman who had spoken to her was still an inch or two taller and a quick glance confirmed she was wearing flat-heeled, square-toed Steve Madden boots below a plain black custom-tailored men's suit and James-Bond-meets-Devo narrow tie. Light blue eyes stood out against a smooth tan that was the product of time in sunlight, not a salon booth. Sun was also responsible for the slight bleaching at the very tips of the short-cropped hair.

She wasn't going to admit she didn't like champagne. "A mentor told me that three months in Manhattan equaled a year in the University of Life. I came here a year ago when I was nineteen."

The light blue eyes lit up. "Oh, a math word problem. You're flirting with me, aren't you?"

The smug smile brought out a stiff one of her own as Jennifer answered with, "Do you want me to be?"

The smile deepened. "Anyone with a heartbeat wants you to be. So you're saying you're twenty-three in Manhattan years?"

"You're making me feel like a kid trying to sit at the grown-up table." It was not a feeling she had ever liked. After a slow, substantial swallow of more champagne she added, "It's all on the inside."

"And you don't look a day over twenty."

Being mocked always brought out Jennifer's bad side, but her bitchy response was squashed by the arrival of Lucius, who oozed, "Darling, this is our host, Suzanne Mason. The CEO of Connecks."

"Former CEO," Suzanne said. "Our stock was just bought out by AOL and I'm unemployed at the moment."

Unemployed and looking like a California surfer, Jennifer mused, and probably with millions of dollars to go with her bad-boy hair. "Everyone should be so lucky in their lack of work."

"Luck was a big part of it. Would you like to meet some people?" Long fingers lightly touched her free elbow.

Just like that, Jennifer found herself extricated from Lucius's grasp and blithely introduced to several pop singers, two Broadway rising stars and a cluster of aides to the mayor.

"Stop talking politics," Suzanne warned them, while Jennifer made a point of telling one of the Broadway divas how much she'd enjoyed her small but notable part in the revival of *Chicago*.

Just as she was about to ask if the starlet had a theatrical agent, Suzanne gestured at the prominent Christmas tree. "Who wants prezzies?"

In the resulting clamor Jennifer looked around her. There was nobody much over thirty, unusual for parties like this where she'd worn clothes for Lucius and other designers all the holiday season. Usually everyone was half dead and super serious, utterly focused on drinking the right thing from the right glass. At the last Lucius party there had been loud words over where the best seats at a play were to be had, and a whispered sharing of which of three kinds of saffron could be found at some Midtown grocer, if you knew to ask for it. She had found it wise to listen and otherwise be a moving statue. Sometimes people even assumed she didn't understand English and she let them think it rather than argue about whether it was a better view from Fifth Avenue facing west or Central Park West facing east—once you got above 74th Street and the fifteenth floor, of course.

She unwrapped the little package Suzanne pressed into her hands to find a cheap kazoo, and laughed outright as others joined in with a swing cover of "Jingle Bell Rock" playing on the stereo.

Suzanne stopped tooting her kazoo long enough to ask, "Afraid you'll mess up your lipstick?"

"I *am* working."

"Working?" Suzanne's gaze flicked to Lucius and back. The music segued to "Deck the Halls" and Lucius was joining in.

"You didn't think this was a date, did you? It's purely business." Suzanne blinked just enough times for Jennifer to hastily add, "I wear his clothes to parties, he pays me, and that's it."

"Oh, I get it. And you can't be untidy?"

"I can hardly ruin my look over a kazoo."

"You're right. A kazoo is a poor excuse."

Jennifer found herself being kissed soundly on the lips and released again before she could even react. Her Smouldering Rose Lancôme lip rouge now highlighted Suzanne's smile. Realizing that she was staring she hastily said, "It's not your color."

With a comfortable gesture at her suit and tie, Suzanne quipped, "You think?"

Behind her the kazoo band sang out, "Don we now our gay apparel!" and Lucius warbled, "Who's Don and how do I meet him?" With her employer distracted by the revelry, Jennifer let herself be drawn by Suzanne to the picture windows. The few patches of snow visible through the trees in the park were taking on a moonlit glow. Lights were popping out everywhere, including masses of green and red for the holidays—she couldn't hold back a pleased murmur.

Suzanne was sighing. "It's magical. I'll be sorry to leave it."

"You're selling?" Jennifer was disconcerted after a glance showed that Suzanne was looking at her, not the view. She was used to flirtation but not with a woman. The kiss had been surprising and nice and she couldn't think of a reason not to do it again. Except...she hadn't kissed a woman before. It hadn't occurred to her that she might enjoy it.

"I'm renting for now, and I don't think I have the right stuff to be a New Yorker." Suzanne crossed her eyes, earning a giggle from Jennifer. "I'm planning to get back to Silicon Valley by spring. That's where the next big thing will be and I will be there."

"New York has a lot to offer. The art. Theater. Food." She cleared her throat. "Fashion."

"Those would be your people?"

"Well, I'm trying."

"Succeeding, looks like."

"It's hard to tell if it'll last." She had studied the rise and fall of other models just this season alone. One had publicly voiced fervent disapproval of gay men, forgetting who she worked for and who dressed and photographed her, not to mention it was the Gay 90s. The more spectacular implosion had been the girl who apparently couldn't say no to alcohol and cocaine. Jennifer had taken note of how quickly both girls, once swimming in fawning followers and fashion reporter attention, had been wiped from everyone's collective shoe in a matter of weeks. "I'm going to make a confession—I have no idea what Connecks does. Or did."

"Neither does AOL, but they outbid Time-Warner."

Suzanne's cheerful wink combined with a cheeky smile left Jennifer with a disconcerting tingle south of her stomach. "How exactly does that all work?"

"I had an idea about how to more quickly and securely store a lot of data. I got some capital, built up a server farm run by my software and waited for a buyer."

"Like flipping a house."

Suzanne laughed. "I hadn't thought of it that way, but you're right. Except that I created the real estate, built the house, and then flipped it for a big profit. The employees didn't do too badly either."

The woman oozed confidence, and who could blame her, Jennifer thought. She was maybe twenty-six or twenty-seven, worth millions and had the brains to do it all again. "And to think all I've done is hit the gym, get dressed and walk up and down a runway."

Suzanne put the view to her back, hands comfortably tucked in her pant-front pockets. "I'm thinking that's not as easy as it sounds."

"If it were, anyone would do it." She shifted her shoulders, the right slightly higher than the left, and shook back her hair. She might not like champagne or know what half the little tasty things were that kept going by them on trays, but she had mad skills of her own.

She was satisfied by the heated look on Suzanne's face, and realized at the same time she'd never been given *that* look by a woman before, at least that she'd noticed. Hadn't wanted to see it before either. The kiss had been for fun, and they'd abruptly tumbled right past flirting. There was no air.

After glancing over the party, Suzanne said, "No, not everyone can do that."

"I don't know what you mean," Jennifer lied.

Twilight had finally eased into night and they were now reflected in the window. She'd grown up in a noisy house with one full-length mirror on the back of the bathroom door. Gazing at the picture the two of them made was part vanity, but it was also a now habitual check that the built-in breast shields and neckline were still where they were supposed to be, and that the static cling so common in dry falling temperatures wasn't ruining the line of the dress around her calves.

As her gaze ran up the long crease in the front of Suzanne's trousers, she knew it was more than aesthetic appreciation. Yes, she liked the way Armani looked on Suzanne and she flashed on an image of the jacket and tie draped over the end of her bed. Flustered, she asked, "Do you dress that way to make a point?"

The frown she got in answer made her regret even more the abrupt question. She'd clearly given offense.

"Maybe. If the point is that women can be exactly what they want to be. Would you have asked a man that question?"

"Sure." Realizing that Suzanne was on the verge of walking away, she brushed an imaginary hair off the nearest sleeve of her jacket. "You have to admit, it's not the norm."

"It is for me."

And when you've made millions before your thirtieth birthday, what's normal for you is exactly what you get to be, Jennifer thought. "Good for you. I have no idea what I'd wear, left to my own devices." She glanced down. "I'd wear these boots every day of the week, I guess."

"They're very fetching." Suzanne's body had relaxed again.

A chorus of "Santa Baby" rose from the kazoos, now clustered around the bar. Suzanne abruptly frowned at the sight of more arrivals.

"I apologize. It's someone I'd especially hoped would show." She met Jennifer's gaze and visibly swallowed. "Please don't leave without saying goodbye."

"I won't." The promise slipped out before she could think of anything coy.

She watched Suzanne greet a turtleneck-wearing man she knew she should have recognized. Some tech mogul, probably, and at least a decade older than anyone else at the party.

Lucius returned to her side and maneuvered them in that direction. "Jennifer, dear girl, if either of us married that guy we'd be set for life."

Her gaze flicked to Suzanne. "Lucius, dear boy, he's not my type."

CHAPTER THREE

For the next hour, she watched not one but two very cute blondes drape themselves on Suzanne. She also realized that nearly everyone there was probably gay. She was surrounded by gay men at photo shoots and in couture dressing rooms, but gay women not nearly as much. She'd assumed that high fashion didn't interest them, but the Givenchy and McQueen holiday gowns intermittently pressed up against Suzanne's hips proved her wrong. Suzanne seemed well-acquainted with both women. That or she didn't mind being used as a thigh napkin.

Which didn't stop Jennifer from looking over Lucius's head in that direction, or reduce the searing flare of desire she felt when she caught Suzanne looking back at her.

Lucius was enjoying himself, but at precisely ten p.m. he paused in his pursuit of the scrubby-cute waiter to tell her she was off the clock. She wasn't going to party until dawn on his dime, a fact she accepted. Normally she would have called for a cab and gone home. She had a photo shoot with a new photographer at eight thirty in the morning. She'd expected this party to be another midweek yawner.

She looked at Suzanne again, caught her looking back, again. This time there might have been even a hint of a plea.

Club soda on ice with a twist of lime looked sophisticated and wouldn't ruin her dress if spilled. The bitter taste made her grimace the same way people who loved their whiskey or gin did. One more locked-eyes exchange with Suzanne brought her all the way across the loft, skirting the cushions that had slipped onto the floor and the chairs askew from little cocktail party tables.

Blonde #1 received her most sincere smile of pure ice, perfected by studying her idol of grace and sophistication, Lauren Bacall. It had the instantaneous effect of loosening the talons gripping Suzanne's arm. Suzanne gave her a grateful look and completed her escape by turning her back on Blonde #2.

A welcoming gesture opened a path directly into the midst of the cluster surrounding Suzanne. "Can you finally enjoy yourself?"

That's when her boot heel caught on a chair leg, snagging her dress.

She felt the ping of popped stitches along her ribs.

The drink went left, Jennifer went right.

The dress stayed where it was.

She needed two hands to keep her face from smashing onto the concrete floor. She needed two hands to cover Laverne and Shirley.

Everyone nearby had been moving away from her arrival. Only Suzanne had been moving toward her. How the long arms got under her before she face-planted on the floor she never knew. Then she was wobbly but upright.

She used one arm to cover the girls, and her free hand to keep the dress from dropping farther than her hips, then found Suzanne's jacket draped over her shoulders. Clutching it close she realized the kazoo ballad had stopped and both blondes were giving her looks of pure delight.

"You're heavier than you look." Suzanne was laughing.

"You did not seriously just say that to me." She dashed her hair out of her eyes.

Suzanne flushed, but her merriment continued. "You're not expecting me not to have noticed..." She waved a hand toward Jennifer's chest. "The, umm, kit and caboodle."

Blonde #2 waved her Nokia at Jennifer. "Why don't I call you a cab?"

Lucius rushed up, overflowing with concern. "Is anything torn? Did the skirt catch?"

"How about a trip to the powder room to assess the damage," Suzanne suggested. "It's this way."

This is not happening, Jennifer thought. "I just caught my heel is all."

"There's a side panel stitch showing now," Lucius fussed.

The bathroom held the three of them without a problem. Suzanne reclaimed her jacket as Jennifer assumed strip position. She tried to ignore Suzanne as Lucius whisked the dress past her black panties and thigh-high hose to just below her knees. She stepped to the left as Lucius moved to the right, a familiar dance without a hint of modesty—until she realized Suzanne wasn't making any effort to avert her eyes.

"I don't see any damage," Lucius cautiously announced.

"I'm fine. Thanks for asking," Jennifer snapped. She caught Suzanne nodding. "Could I have a towel or something?"

Lucius let out a wail. "The side seam is popped! How could this happen?"

Because you're a lousy tailor, Jennifer wanted to say.

Suzanne slipped out of the room leaving Jennifer still without anything to use as a cover-up—the delicate little hand towels were less dignified than nudity. The little bag that had been dangling forgotten from one shoulder all evening was on the loft floor, no doubt, with her ID, lipstick and cab fare in it. It wouldn't even cover one boob, let alone both, and Lucius was useless.

A quick knock at the door led to Suzanne's reentry. She offered a wrapped package. "A gift from someone who doesn't know I prefer cotton. You're tall enough I think."

Silk pajamas, dark blue. Jennifer ripped the package open, shook out the pleating hooks and cardboard liner and pulled the top over her head without bothering with the buttons. Everything was going fine until she couldn't get her head through the collar.

"Hang on." Suzanne's cologne—something subtle and mildly woody—wafted under the pajama top. Jennifer felt fingers at the first button, then her head was clear. Her hair tangled on the collar and Suzanne's touch was gentle as she separated it. "Don't want to damage the extensions."

"I don't have any, but thank you."

"So this is all you?"

There was no air again. Her skin was both warmed and chilled by the silk. "All me."

She tried to tell herself that panting was unattractive, but desire was so loud in her ears that all she could hear was a low, thick pulse. I should be afraid, she thought, but she could see in Suzanne's face exactly what she felt.

With Lucius moaning over the dress, Suzanne offered wordless assistance with the pajama bottoms.

"I can take the boots off." Her own voice sounded far away.

Kneeling, Suzanne cupped the back of Jennifer's ankle and gently pulled the pajama leg upward while protecting it from heel snags. "It's okay, I've got it. Now the other one."

Looking down at the short-cropped hair and the Oxford shirt, Jennifer had only one thought: *I'm glad she's a woman.* She didn't know what showed in her face, but Suzanne looked up suddenly and swallowed hard.

Jennifer was glad Lucius was there and wanted him to go away.

Suzanne retreated to the opposite wall and Jennifer fussed with rolling up the waist so she wasn't walking on puddles of pajama silk.

A Frisbee fight using now-useless hourly America Online trial CDs had broken out by the time Hurricane Jennifer joined the party again. A little worse for wear and in loose-fitting Brooks Bros. silk pajamas, she avoided the flying discs and coiled up in front of the picture window. She sincerely hoped Suzanne would join her.

When a *Times* photographer took a photo of her mussed, yet comfortable look she asked for a courtesy copy to be sent to her agent, which was what she'd been told she should always do even though no one ever sent one. The photographer departed, happy with her scoop.

Suzanne brought her a drink and a plate with two crackers, a wedge of cheese and some strawberries.

Her jangled nerves settled with the food, but when Suzanne sat next to her she found it hard to swallow. Heat seemed to ripple through Suzanne's shirtsleeve and the silk, and it only made Jennifer crave more warmth. The blondes, it seemed, had given up pursuit.

"Thank you—for everything." Jennifer eyed the drink Suzanne had given her.

"Just club soda. The bartender said that's what you were drinking."

Thoughtful… "I wasn't drunk."

"I tripped on one of those damned things earlier, when they were setting them up."

"Photographers like to provide champagne during photo shoots, but I don't get it. They say it's for nerves." She thought of her father. "I don't drink on the job. I guess I'm getting used to the taste too."

"Where did you live before you got to Manhattan?"

She found herself telling Suzanne about King of Prussia, Pennsylvania, the Queen of Prussia College for Models and the big photo shoot for the first anniversary issue of *Glamour* that had paid off her school loan and made the deposit and first six months of rent in the East Village possible. Focusing on the joys and hazards of learning Manhattan she avoided mentioning her family and hoped Suzanne didn't think that was strange. That was all behind her.

It was after midnight when Suzanne declared it a "school night" and closed the bar. Jennifer turned down invitations to take her new fashion look out on the town and start a new rage. Lucius had departed with his poor little dress and suddenly, with the exception of the caterer packing up glasses and trays, they were alone.

I could never live in a place like this, Jennifer thought. Though the bedroom was tucked on the other side of the floor, around the corner from the dramatic open-plan kitchen, it had no door, no walls. There was no real privacy.

Small talk seemed dangerously complicated.

They were sharing the view again, agreeing that the winter moon seemed larger than usual, when Jennifer said, "I have an appointment at eight thirty in the morning that I can't miss."

Suzanne glanced at her watch, looking rueful. "Where do you have to be?"

"The shoot is in Midtown. I'm supposed to arrive with hair down, no makeup—they provide a stylist."

"Then I should get you home."

"I'll call a cab."

Suzanne was again looking at the moon. "You're not taking a cab alone, dressed like that."

"I'm all covered up," Jennifer insisted, though she didn't want the evening to end. "I am usually wearing less than this, and Lucius didn't provide a coat."

"Cheap bastard."

"His checks don't bounce. Which is why my agency keeps sending me out with him."

"I would think pneumonia would be against everyone's business interests."

"Hardly." Jennifer's laugh was rueful. "Models like me are a dime a dozen. There's always someone younger and more memorable."

Suzanne turned to give her a long, taut look. "You are not cheap. Or forgettable."

Around a now enormous lump in her throat, Jennifer said, "You'd be surprised."

"I hope I'm never so old that I forget this." With the lightest pressure, Suzanne ran the back of one hand over the silk covering Jennifer's shoulder.

She moaned, or thought she did. She wasn't sure. That she had no bra on was abundantly obvious.

A clatter of dishes startled them both.

"I should go."

"I'll see you home."

"It's not necessary." She rifled in her little bag as she turned blindly toward the door.

"After your appointment, what is your day like?"

"I'm free until two. From ten to two." Almost at the door, she realized she was running away.

"Then bring back my overcoat then."

"What coat?"

"The one I'm going to lend you. I'll be here."

The coat was a long, men's camel-hair duster with a thick, warm lining. Suzanne helped her into it, then pulled her hair from under the collar. Jennifer felt what might have been the caress of lips at the nape of her neck before her hair settled again over it. Under the coat, parts of her flushed cold and hot all at once.

"Thank you."

"This entire evening has been my pleasure." Suzanne walked her to the elevator.

"It didn't turn out as I expected."

Jennifer ran out of air on the last word. She turned away from the elevator light, hoping the flush she could feel in her cheeks didn't show, let alone the disappointment that Suzanne hadn't kissed her again.

CHAPTER FOUR

Lean slightly right, left shoulder back, arm draped on knee, palm down, chin up. "Now you want my fingers more spread?" She treated the ridiculous photographer to a glare which he completely missed. "Is this natural enough for you?"

"Jenny, Jenny, what are you doing?" Donald kept the camera whirring even as an assistant hurried into the frame to adjust Jennifer's hands again. "You can't cover the product, darling."

His added muttered epithet of *amateurs* didn't help Jennifer's nerves. With a sour back-of-a-taxicab voice, his whining left Jennifer feeling clammy and sticky. Most of the time everyone fell into a productive groove, but new photographers with unknown shooting protocols were always nerve-wracking.

This morning nothing she was doing was right, according to lord-god-king-Donald. His body suit of black spandex with a lavish gold chain was so cliché that she couldn't take him seriously. But her agent said he was the gateway for young models to hundreds of gigs for hand, body and face modeling, the easiest and most lucrative shoots. Make him happy and he'd recommend her onward to the big-ticket advertising agencies. But that wasn't turning out to be easy at all. She wanted in the worst way to pull the not-very-virginal white kimono around her bare legs and cover up the Laverne and Shirley cleavage which always seemed to give people pause.

Kit and Caboodle, Suzanne had called them. What on earth was a "caboodle"?

"Those are *diamonds*, not snakes." Donald's exasperated sigh coincided with setting the camera aside. He stormed onto the dais and glared down at her.

Seated, she had no choice but to look up. If it weren't for her acting lessons she might not have abruptly realized that everything in the layout was designed to make her look small. He'd posed her to be collapsed on herself, hair scraped back into a braid, elbows at her side and leaning forward over her knees. It made her feel shrunken and it was hard to believe the camera wasn't capturing that. He loomed over her, upstaging her so he could have his scripted tantrum for the *amateur* unchallenged.

Surprised by the new thought, she reflected on her acting instructor's attention to blocking and body stance—something a good actor just knows and does without a director telling them. If you have lines, take up more space and move just a little more than a no-lines extra. But don't forget whose scene it is. When it becomes your scene, spread out even more, use wide gestures and body poses to be the center of focus.

Right now it was Donald's scene. Weren't photographers supposed to be invisible—especially for print advertisement images? The shoot was for a local jeweler who wasn't using an ad agency, giving The Donald free rein to nag and upstage both her and the product. It seemed to her that the client would be left wondering why the pretty picture of their goods didn't quite work. Was she supposed to fear getting fired so much that she would put up with anything to please?

Her movements slow and assured, she unkinked herself from the awkward pose and spread one arm along the back of the chaise where for the last ninety minutes she'd been admiring her beautiful diamond bracelet, the perfect wedding gift to June brides six months hence. Her distaste for the way things were going wasn't helped by the fact that Suzanne was expecting her about now.

"No, no, no," Donald whined. "That won't work."

Yes, yes, yes, Jennifer thought. *My stage, not yours, mouthbreather.*
"Shouldn't I look like I love wearing it?"

"I'll decide what you like." He fussed about her hair, readjusted
the kimono neckline to display a generous curve of breast, all the
while leaning over and into her with the violation of private space
that photographers and models took for granted. Except this felt
unlike any other shoot she'd been on before.

When she'd first come to New York she would have wondered if
it was her—too inexperienced to take all the touching and physical
comments impersonally. She might have thought she didn't know
how to act like a model as he fussed for long minutes with the exact
placement of the kimono across her breasts. But designer clients
like Lucius were asking for her by name, and she'd been on dozens
of shoots in the last two months. Maybe The Donald didn't know
that.

How much do I need this job, Jennifer wondered. The Donald's
spandex covered groin bumped her shoulder and she glanced at the
assistants—both female, and both finding someplace else to look.

He picked at her hair. "Maybe we should have you lying back on
the lounge. After all, you'll always look good on your back. As soon
as you marry a rich guy you'll be getting paid for it in diamonds.
They last forever. Looks don't."

It wasn't the first time someone had told her she needed to bag
a wealthy husband and stock up on gifts before her assets sagged.
She hated it even more from this creep than from her family and
so-called friends back home.

He bumped her shoulder again with his crotch and smoothed
the kimono over her breasts one more time. Then he began the
same attention to kimono placement across her thighs, his fingers
more often touching skin than fabric.

She bit her lower lip. Was this why he only worked with "young
and rising" models? Why there was no ad agency involved? The
girls were old enough not to be chaperoned but too young to
protest? Like she'd told Suzanne Mason last night—three months
in Manhattan were like a year in the University of Life. She was
older than her birth certificate said and no frightened little girl.
The Queen of Prussia College for Models had included self-
defense strategies, and what that class might have missed, surviving

as the Hecht's menswear pretty girl bait at the King of Prussia mall had filled in.

The next time his crotch came close enough she met him halfway there with a shoulder check a hockey player would have envied.

The sound of The Donald trying to breathe in was one she was going to replay in her head, it was so satisfying to hear.

"You—you—"

"Bitch? That's me. Yes, I did that on purpose, just like you were fingering me all over on purpose." She rose to her feet and stripped off the kimono in a single motion, proving she had no issue with being mostly naked on her own terms, then headed for the privacy screen where her clothes were piled. "We're done."

She shrugged into a bra, yanked her favorite Kate Spade sweater over her head, pulled on her True Religion jeans and had her elegant but functional Ralph Lauren boots on before Donald had moved from his gasping sprawl across the chaise. One of the assistants was offering water while the other had stayed next to the camera—still whirring on auto-click—to hide a helpless smile.

"Shame on you," Jennifer snapped. "Letting him dickwave in girls' faces."

The laughter instantly disappeared. "Easy to say from your side of the camera," she hissed.

"Some things aren't worth the price of my soul."

"Wait until your first wrinkle."

She let the door slam behind her as she slid into the deep warmth of Suzanne's overcoat. Maybe it was glee at what she'd just done, but the rest of her day was looking glorious.

CHAPTER FIVE

The buzz of the doorman's intercom startled Suzanne out of sleep. She hadn't meant to spend what was left of the night thinking about Jennifer Lamont, and her restlessness had found an outlet in cranking "Rhythm Nation" past eleven and leveling up in *Tomb Raider*. Her thumbs were raw and her eyeballs felt like sandpaper. Not for the first time she reminded herself that she needed to get involved in a project or she'd get lost in late night parties and endless gaming. That might have been her dream life when she was fifteen, but it wasn't sufficiently diverting ten years later, not for more than a night.

Jennifer the Model—now that was a diversion.

"There's a Miss Lamont to see you."

Standing in her bare feet at the intercom she still felt a flash of heat—then panic. It was after ten. If she didn't answer, the bellman would send Jennifer away. If she answered, she had maybe thirty seconds to brush her teeth and hair and look as if she had fallen asleep before sunrise.

She didn't want Jennifer to be sent away. She was a walking dream, like a prom queen, the kind of girl who had never given boy or girl geeks like her a second look in high school. The glamour girls who liked to hang around her since the AOL money came in were witty and flirty, but Jennifer was in another league. Smart-assed and funny, and not afraid of pissing Suzanne off. Even though she looked like the kind of girl who usually made Suzanne feel too small or too big, inept or too smart, and never, ever cool, that wasn't how Jennifer made her feel—at all.

"Send her up."

She dashed from the intercom at the front door for the bathroom. She put way too much paste on her toothbrush and was spitting foam as she dashed for the walk-in closet for her robe to throw over her Mystery Science Theater T-shirt and plain black boxers.

At least she had been asleep for such a short time that her hair was pretty much like it had been last night. She was still deciding if she liked the cut, slightly longer on top than the heartthrob on *ER* it mimicked. Annemarie, one of the Connecks employees she'd kept in touch with after the America Online buyout, had told her to see a personal stylist and so she had. Annemarie knew about that kind of thing.

Running back to the door to answer the chime, she caught sight of her reflection in the window. Even though she sometimes still felt like the girl who had listened to Radiohead's "Creep" a dozen times a day all through college, she no longer looked like it. Her new millions had brought the partygoers and the string of eager paramours. How could she be sure Jennifer, for all her apparent ambitions, wasn't just like them?

So what if she was?

Beautiful was all Suzanne could think when she opened the heavy steel door. *Beautiful.* Unlike last night, her hair was pulled back into a tightly woven braid, putting all the attention on her high cheekbones. The sun pouring in seemed to put a pleased-to-see-you sparkle in the large, dark eyes and Jennifer was all the more feminine and curvaceous under Suzanne's man-cut overcoat. All of that plus an easy smile robbed Suzanne of words.

"I hope you haven't been trapped inside without your coat." Jennifer leaned against the doorjamb with her gaze taking in Suzanne's robe. An eyebrow lifted.

"No, I'm getting a slow start this morning is all." She was abruptly aware of the tatty terrycloth—she'd had the robe for years and it was finally exactly the right feel. She led the way to the kitchen area. "Can I get you something to eat? If you're eating today, that is."

"I ran out this morning without anything. I know that's bad for me, and yes anything in food would be welcome. As usual, the photographer wanted to give me champagne. At eight thirty in the morning." Jennifer's grimace seemed extreme for just dislike of a beverage. "He was a major jerk."

"Did it go badly?"

"He got inappropriate." She slid the coat off and draped it over the back of the nearest chair. "Which I think is his usual deal. I just wasn't going to put up with it."

"Good for you! Does that happen a lot?" Another glance showed a still stormy expression. "Are you okay?"

"He got the worst of it. I just feel slimy. No doubt my agent is leaving me messages even as we speak."

"You don't have a mobile phone?" She gestured Jennifer onto one of the barstools at the counter that framed one end of the kitchen area. "I'll make some coffee."

"I'm kind of Amish about phones and computers." Jennifer laughed. "Not the kind of thing I should admit to someone like you, is it?"

"I think the word you're looking for is *Luddite*." She allowed her gaze to travel across Jennifer's shoulders. The gray and blue striped sweater clung in all the right places and then some.

"What's the difference?"

"To tell you the truth, I'm not sure." She dumped grounds into the fancy little brewer that had been part of the furnishings. There was a chance the results would be drinkable. The fact that it was blocks to the nearest Starbucks was considered a feature, not a bug, of the ritzy location. "Are you averse to technology?"

"Just not exposed to it, and it's expensive. Unlike clothes and pretty things like this purse, nobody gives you a phone or computer for knowing how to walk." Jennifer plopped a red and black shoulder bag on the counter. It was the size of a manhole cover, or nearly, and it appeared to have very little in it. "I never had time, and I'm afraid of buying the wrong thing and regretting it, and when I first got here I was counting pennies pretty closely to make sure I could make it six months at least. Then I could lose it and—"

"How about some expert advice?" Suddenly shy at the happy smile Jennifer gave her, she turned to the enormous refrigerator. "I think I have milk and some leftovers from last night. I sent most of it away with the caterer, but there's lots of cheese. And these puffy things."

Jennifer bobbed happily on her barstool. "Let's try the puffy things."

Suzanne set the plastic-wrapped tray on the counter. "See, you do eat."

"I eat. I work out. Personal trainer, the whole deal."

"Tools of your trade. I can nuke that for you," she added as Jennifer popped one of the cold puff pastries into her mouth whole.

"Next one. I suddenly realized I was starving. If you don't mind, I'd like to wipe off some of this makeup and brush out my hair."

"This isn't your normal morning look?" Her face looked like it had last night.

"Heavens no. There's two layers of foundation and way too much smoky eye for daylight. I'll be right back."

Suzanne busied herself with heating up more of the pastries. Toast would be good. Her mother, who still thought Suzanne needed care packages, had sent some delicious California marmalade.

Jennifer reappeared after a few minutes. Her face was rosier in color and she looked more like a real woman than a sculpture. She'd brushed out the braid and the indigo-highlighted black waves cascaded down her back.

Don't stare, geek weed. "The photographer really offered you champagne in the morning?"

"Sick, huh? Then he started humping my shoulder—it was bizarre and rude."

It sounded to her like the guy needed to be castrated. "Good for you for walking out. Your agent won't back you up?"

"I doubt it. Though I just realized..." Jennifer turned to look over the park. "This will sound conceited."

"Go for it." Good lord, she was beautiful. Sculpted and classic when at rest, graceful and striking in motion.

"I think I don't have to put up with it. Nobody should have to, but some girls would, because making a fuss will be the end of their careers. They're not as...this." She made a vague gesture at her body. "I don't have to put up with that guy harassing me. He has to put up with me."

"So does your agent, for that matter. Who works for who? Your money, you get to say." She knew nothing about the fashion world, but in her opinion Jennifer had a lot going for her.

Jennifer slowly nodded. "It's a new feeling. And all good. I think I'm going to be a success as a model. I already am in the short term. But I really want to be an actress. I'll probably run across people I need and I won't be able to kick them in the gut if they get handsy."

"Last night you said girls like you are a dime a dozen."

Jennifer swiveled back from the window. "That was my mother using my mouth."

"Your mom doesn't want you to be a model?"

"My mom wants me to be her booze and cigarette lackey."

Ouch. Not sure that was a safe topic to continue, Suzanne asked, "Did you really kick him?"

"It wasn't a kick, but he had trouble breathing in for a while."

"Nothing the jackass didn't deserve." She mentally draped Jennifer in the trappings of Xena, breastplate and all. Jennifer wasn't as robust, but the look would suit her lush hair and long, lean curves. The image made the hot dish from the microwave slippery in her hands. "I'd have liked to have seen that."

The stormy expression from earlier was completely gone. "So my answering machine is probably filling up."

"Have some of these." She set the plate down. "And we'll go phone shopping."

"It'll appease my agent some if I get one."

"Why don't you check your messages while I take a shower?" Suzanne pointed at the phone on the counter. "You know how to use one of those, right?"

The knife-edged look Jennifer sent her way was grudgingly amused. "Ha. Ha. Ha."

As Suzanne gathered some jeans and a polo shirt that had some kind of designer label on it to take into the bathroom with her, she could hear Jennifer rapidly tapping out numbers. Her nails were lovely, but not so long she had to have someone dress her. She heard a muttered, "His crotch wasn't in your face, honey," as she closed the bathroom door.

The steam cleared her head of the images of her hands under the warmth of Jennifer's sweater. She didn't want to forget that money was the only difference between now and just a few years ago when women hadn't given her a second look. She thought Jennifer might be different, but for now maybe it was okay if she wasn't. They were still going to have a lot of fun.

CHAPTER SIX

It wasn't even one o'clock when they emerged from the Times Square electronics shop with a sparkly new Nokia banana phone, a warranty and a service plan that would end the need for her answering machine.

Jennifer told Suzanne honestly, "If you hadn't been there I wouldn't have survived."

"Worse than used cars salesmen," Suzanne agreed. "They tried to sell you last year's model at this year's price."

"When you asked about the text-bit-mega-thingy they gave up. Thank you."

Suzanne looked down at her feet. "You're welcome. The next generation, which is going to be out in the spring, will have the kind of calendar function you could probably use. When it comes out I'll let you know. Your warranty includes an upgrade path."

Jennifer nodded like that made sense to her—it did, kind of. "I have an acting lesson at two."

Suzanne glanced at the understated Rolex on her wrist. "Let's grab a dog and I'll walk you to your lesson."

"It's in the Village near NYU."

"A cab then."

Jennifer was unsettled but pleased by the deep, warm glow she felt knowing that Suzanne obviously didn't want to part ways yet. "I prefer walking, if you do. It cuts down on trips to the gym."

Suzanne glanced at the sky and then Jennifer's boots. "You seem weather ready."

"I try. And I have this new toy to pay for now. Walking when I can means I can afford that upgrade path."

Suzanne chuckled. Their steps turned in unison toward Sixth Avenue where hot dog carts were usually plentiful. "You play dumb really well, but I'm not buying it."

"Why, I don't know what you mean." She looked up through her lashes to find Suzanne giving her an indulgent smile. She hoped she sounded casual when she asked, "Would you like to see a movie tonight?"

"Sure."

"It's one that I'm in."

Suzanne's jaw dropped momentarily. "Really? That's great."

She shrugged. "I'm just an extra standing on the steps at Madison Square Garden. I'm clearly in two shots. They wanted pretty girls cheering for Michael Jordan when he walked in. I did it just after I got here."

"That would be really fun. Where is it playing?"

"All over—the nicest theater is the one near Radio City Music Hall."

Suzanne handed over a bill for two hot dogs and bottles of water. Jennifer added relish to her dog while Suzanne squirted on mustard, and they strolled companionably down Sixth Avenue. She gestured at a storefront with her water bottle. "Cheesesteak there is inedible."

Suzanne gave her one of her charming, half-mocking smiles. "You've sampled a lot?"

"Not a lot, but I got homesick."

"You can't take the girl out of Philly?"

"Something like that. I grew up on the plastic version available throughout the King of Prussia mall. My standards are really low." She added quickly, "When it comes to cheesesteak."

Suzanne pointed out a burger joint that Jennifer recognized as new and trendy. "Bacon burger, it's awesome."

"I eat bacon in months that end with Z." If they talked about it more she'd crave it, so Jennifer changed the subject. "Have you been to any of the new plays this season?"

After a noisy swallow, Suzanne answered, "A few. I get invites. Next one I get, would you like...?"

"Sure. If I'm not working."

Jennifer hardly noticed the blocks passing until they reached Bleecker Street and were standing in front of the unassuming door to the studio. Suzanne, she'd learned, had seen more than a few plays. She'd even gotten in to the exclusive opening of *Rent*. So far, she didn't seem all that engaged by a deeper analysis of the actors and stories, and Jennifer would have loved to have talked about that with someone outside her acting class. Well, Suzanne was gorgeous to look at and pretty funny and smart and that was all attractive and unsettling.

And she was a woman. *Surprise, surprise, she's a woman.*

"This is me." She put her hand on the door.

"How long will you be?"

"Ninety minutes. I have to go—the instructor locks the door on time and I still pay if I can't get in."

"I'll be around. Call me."

Jennifer ran up the stairs to the studio, clutching her new phone and for the first time ever wishing her class would go quickly.

CHAPTER SEVEN

This is so weird. I can't do this. I want to blink really badly. His eyes are bloodshot. Does my breath smell like hot dog? Jennifer swallowed and managed not to blink by focusing on the instructor's voice.

"Keep breathing… Don't drop eye contact. It's only been thirty seconds." Constanza's modulated tones were only slightly calming. "A tense body can't fully express itself. Breathe…"

The old building funk of the studio was only partially masked by the sandalwood incense that their teacher lit at the beginning of every class. Of the mix of men and women, nearly all of them were older than Jennifer, and working in technical support jobs with gigs on the side whenever they could find them.

She'd been paired with Franklin again, probably because they were the two tallest people in the room. She personally would have liked working with someone else, but perhaps Constanza had picked up on her mild dislike of him and decided to make her work through it. She probably did smell like hot dogs and Franklin definitely smelled like onions so they were even. They were standing close enough that their noses could have touched if either of them shifted their weight. *Don't blink.*

Constanza shook the bells on her wrist, sparing her arthritic hands from clapping for their attention. "Okay, class, let's all move. Whatever comes naturally to you today."

Jennifer still didn't like motion warm-ups. They seemed lacking in purpose. The people who tried to be raindrops were not successful, that she could tell. She was already comfortable with what her body could do and dance lessons had taught her how important refining small muscles could be. She already knew how to hold a pose without seemingly breathing, and how stride and shoulder position conveyed health and age. Pretending to be a rock just didn't seem useful.

"Not inspired today, Jen? How about an amoeba?"

"Sorry. I was thinking too much." She gave an amoeba a try. Eyes closed, arms swinging wide then close, legs slow-motion pumping, she vocalized a low monotone and waited for a new cue.

"Very good Ethan. Franklin, you're full of energy today. Jenny, does your amoeba have plans to do something?"

"Dancing at Studio 51 later, but right now my amoeba is just hanging around."

She heard Constanza sigh. "Let's try trees that turn into rivers."

Richard struck a rigid pose, arms creating a triangle that peaked over his head, and announced, "The Larch," which made a few people snicker.

She didn't think Constanza would be impressed by her fluid transition from a huddled ball to full height, palms and face basking in an imaginary sun, but her personal trainer would have liked it. She swayed to a rising wind.

"Angelina, that's terrific. Richard, you'd make a great hedge. Franklin, that was a very short-lived tree."

"Tragedy in the Amazon," Franklin said. "Rainforest and all that."

At least Franklin sounded as if he found the exercise somewhat tedious too.

Rivers, then horses, and finally it was time to improvise with a few short instructions as a guide. She liked improv, and the skills it honed—spontaneous emotional reaction, lightning change of demeanor, reading other performer's cues below their character— were ones she could practice and improve. She thought she held her own fairly well throughout the exercises. Sometimes she missed the humor, though, especially when Richard, in one scene, froze into tree pose and said, "The Larch" again. She pretended she got the joke that everyone else clearly did. Maybe Suzanne would know why it was cracking everyone else up.

They took a break and Richard amused them with his decision the previous night to answer all his calls as if he were Elmer Fudd. "I'm sowwy your pwinter dwiver is malfunctioning. That sometimes happens with Wotus One-Two-Twee."

His Fudd laugh was spot-on, like all of his impersonations. "You could be on *Saturday Night Live*," Jennifer told him. "I think your presidents are as good as the people they have."

"But what would they need with someone as good as what they have?" Richard twitched his compact shoulders and peered up at Jennifer, transformed into Columbo. He pointed at her with a mimed cigar. "One more thing. Where were you last night?"

"Playing the part of a model at a party."

"Nice work if you can get it," Angelina said. "I saw the pajamas."

Momentarily puzzled, Jennifer realized what she meant. "That photo made it into the *Times*?"

"Not the *Times*." Angelina gave her the usual hostile eye roll. "Just the gossip page on America Online."

"Oh. She said she worked for the *Times*. It's a good thing she got that picture instead of—" Jennifer was about to explain her near-face plant when Constanza called them back to work.

Angelina gave her a big fat false smile. "You're the star of the tell-all crowd."

It wasn't the first time another woman was bitchy to her for no apparent reason. It wasn't her problem if someone else was threatened by whatever they thought Jennifer had and they didn't. But she wasn't going to be dismissed. "Modeling pays the bills. But I have the same ambition as the rest of you, to work and practice and become an actor."

Laughter could be like a knife, she thought. The teacher didn't laugh, and neither did Richard, but all the others did.

Shoulders back and down, she imagined a thread running straight up from the top of her head that made her even taller. Lauren Bacall had had her share of being dismissed as a pretty face. "I can't have the same ambitions as the rest of you? What am I missing here?"

Nobody said anything, and Jennifer gave Constanza a long look. The classes weren't cheap by any means. She'd settled on this one because the group size was small and the teacher didn't let the students pick at each other—until now.

"Jenny, you're not missing a thing," Constanza said. "We're here to learn and practice and get better." It was said with conviction but contained none of the words that Jennifer would have preferred to have heard. Like *potential* and *talent*.

Shake it off, she told herself. Just like on the runway, whatever is happening backstage can't show. She remembered that Suzanne was waiting for her and then shook that off too.

She had dreams, and nobody was going to stop her.

CHAPTER EIGHT

Suzanne tossed her empty Starbucks cup into the trash and checked her messages again. Hurrying through the clusters of students emerging from NYU buildings she skipped the new, unread ones and reopened the one from "JLMT." Working through the typos that she knew were all too easy to make on the phone keys, she deciphered it to say, "You're my first text. Does this work? Done. Meet me arch in park."

She snagged the attention of a stocky, curly-haired woman in Doc Martens. "Can you tell me where the arch is? In the park? Near here?"

"Washington Square Park? Sure. Hang a right on Waverly and keep going to Fifth Avenue. You can't miss it." She got a lopsided smile. "Hot date?"

"And I don't want to be late."

"Does she have a sister?"

"I don't know," Suzanne admitted, realizing that was the truth.

"Story of my life. Good luck." Waved on her way, Suzanne said a thank you over her shoulder.

The massive nineteenth-century arch was, in fact, impossible to miss. And under it, looking like something that had stepped off the pages of *Vogue*, was Jennifer. She seemed unaware that a couple of tourists were surreptitiously taking her picture. What was that like, Suzanne wondered. She'd had her own fifteen minutes of fame when the AOL buyout had been announced, but never had anyone lurked around her with a camera, just waiting for her to look casually, stunningly gorgeous on a crisp blue and white winter's day. Jennifer was doing just that, and didn't even seem to be trying.

Her breathless "Hi" was not entirely due to having half-run most of the way. "How was it?"

"We were trees and rivers and amoebas, and one of our improvs was hilarious. I actually got a laugh."

"Sounds like fun."

She wrapped her arms around herself. "Tiring, and I have to say, sunshine or not, it's colder than it was this morning."

"How about something more than a hot dog? Or do you want to fetch a coat from home?"

"I'm going to need one. No—" Jennifer waved a hand as Suzanne began to take off her overcoat. "That's very gallant, but I have one at home, and I should get it. If you were serious about going to the movies."

"I totally was." Her phone rang and she gave Jennifer an apologetic look. "Do you mind?"

"Not at all. Let's walk while you talk."

They headed up the Fifth Avenue canyon of posh mansions and condo buildings before turning toward Park, but Suzanne lost track of where they were as she tried to find and keep a connection. "It's a friend from Connecks. Something about a rumor of a merger between two of our former rivals and the new board is looking for someone to run the transition who knows the players and the tech."

Jennifer smiled brightly. "I'm going to pretend I understand what that means the same way I pretended I knew why saying 'The Larch' repeatedly was funny at class."

Suzanne laughed outright. "You're not a Monty Python fan?"

"I've seen *Holy Grail*."

"Your education is not complete—Annemarie?" Suzanne gave Jennifer an apologetic smile as she spoke into her phone. "What's up? How are you?"

Through the crappy call quality she could hear that Annemarie's usually calm voice was laden with urgency. "This merger is going to create a new company bigger than we were, and they're looking for a neutral party to do the transition. You need a team, right?"

"I still don't know what you're talking about. Nobody has called me about anything."

"Your name is being bounced all over the message boards." Annemarie suddenly sounded as if she were speaking from Mars via a long, wet tube. "When it got attached to the project the stock prices of both companies went up."

She glared up at the tall buildings surrounding her. She needed a land line. "I'll call you back from a better connection after I see if I can find out anything. If this is real, yeah, I'm interested and I'd need a team."

Annemarie's happy tone was the only thing the phone really picked up. She flipped it shut and slid it into her jacket's inside pocket, her mind overrun with numbers, possibilities and a list of barriers to be overcome by the two companies. They had complementary assets in networks—

"Ahem."

"I'm so sorry," she said, startled. Glancing around she asked Jennifer, "When did we stop walking? Where are we?"

Jennifer tipped her head to one side and Suzanne could feel the lists and questions she was forming in the back of her mind all start to fuzz. How did a look from those eyes slide right along her spine like that? Leaving her feeling weak and breathless and strong all at once?

"Nice to be forgettable. And if I'm going to my apartment for a jacket, we have to turn here. If you can walk and talk at the same time."

Her brain was turning to soup. Is this what happened when she got to know a Hot Girl? It felt really great to think about kissing Jennifer and all the things they could do when they were alone and it felt totally foreign that she couldn't hold a thought for more than two seconds. "I can't get a solid connection here. I need a land line."

"I have one of those." Jennifer turned her head to seemingly study the side of a passing bus. "But it sounds like whatever it is might be very distracting."

"I'm going to need to use my computer, I think. This would be a great opportunity."

"I understand that. We'll do the movie another day."

"No!" *Think, think, think.* "Sorry. Why don't I meet you outside the theater later?"

"It shows at five thirty and eight." Jennifer coughed slightly. "I might have seen it more than once."

"Five thirty." She glanced at her watch, looked up to see an available cab approaching. "See you five fifteen and popcorn's on me."

The cab had U-turned and crossed the next intersection before Suzanne fully comprehended that Jennifer wasn't in the cab with her. "You stupid nerd!"

The cab driver gave her a startled look.

"Not you, sorry." *Geek with shit-for-brains,* she railed inwardly. Did you even say goodbye?

CHAPTER NINE

If there was one thing Jennifer wasn't used to, it was being left standing on a sidewalk completely forgotten. She had watched in shock as the cab disappeared. Were all computer nerds like that? Dangle a shiny object and you didn't even get a "see you later"?

She sat looking around her tiny studio apartment, glad not to have a roommate even if it meant minimal living space and using the oven made the lights flicker. She'd tacked up her favorite Lauren Bacall poster from *To Have and Have Not*, but otherwise there was nothing here she hadn't purchased in New York. She'd left everything behind because she wasn't that girl anymore. Being left standing on the sidewalk by Suzanne had made her feel like it though. Forgettable. Dime a dozen, as her mother had told her frequently.

At least it wasn't after sex. The only guy she'd hooked up with since moving here had practically fallen out of bed in his haste to get his pants back on. Maybe he'd been married or had a girlfriend. If so, she was glad he'd left without her number. Whatever it was, he'd hardly said goodbye. Part of her had been hurt, but part of her hadn't cared. She'd been lonely. He'd made her laugh once or twice at a party. The sex, like all sex to date, had had moments of pleasure and otherwise been mostly waiting for it to be over. She could manage more and better results all by herself.

Suzanne had treated her differently. Suzanne had also made parts of her body do little quivers and dances. Until now, she had supposed her bits and buttons didn't work with the same enthusiasm *Cosmopolitan* reported they did.

"It would serve her right if I stood her up," Jennifer told her reflection as she updated her street makeup from day to nighttime.

The sweater wouldn't be warm enough. She considered the Yves St. Laurent silk blouse she'd been given after a photo shoot. The peplum style was very feminine and it fit her like a ruby skin. If Suzanne ignored her while she was wearing that… But it would require another layer under the coat to keep her warm in the theater, or she'd have to keep her coat on. Which would ruin the whole point of the blouse.

Anyway, didn't she already know that Suzanne found her physically attractive? Her gaze rested on the utilitarian Brooklyn Bridge sweatshirt she'd bought for emergency warmth a few weeks ago. So be it, she thought. Easing it over her hair, she knew she'd be glad of the warmth. But fashion was never about comfort. She gave herself a disapproving look in the cracked mirror on the back of the door.

She turned profile and pulled the sweatshirt tightly across her chest but the effect was not exactly a showstopper. *It will get her out of my life for good unless she's really paying attention to me.*

CHAPTER TEN

Suzanne arrived in front of the movie theaters near Radio City and Rockefeller Center worried she was keeping Jennifer waiting in the cold. She'd paid the engraver fifty bucks to hurry a ten-dollar project, and was relieved to have a chance to catch her breath when there was no sign of Jennifer.

Annemarie had been the one to suggest a gift. After they'd talked through multiple angles of the merger and why Suzanne's name was being floated as a possible transition leader, Annemarie had asked how life in the Big Apple was treating her. Confessing that she'd abruptly abandoned a very pretty and interesting girl in favor of talking business had left Annemarie aghast.

"You were rude—you need something more than a movie ticket and a large popcorn to make up for it."

"I was going to get large drinks too. That adds up to about sixty bucks in Manhattan."

"You are such a nerd. You are no longer a starving student, if you ever were."

"I know I got reduced tuition at Stanford because of my father—"

"And you lived at home."

"And I lived at home. But my parents are hippies, Greenpeace and Earth Day bona fide hippies. I know it's not quite the same thing as economizing because you have no choice, but if we didn't need it, we didn't have it."

"None of which is going to impress a supermodel."

"She's not dripping in jewels and furs."

"Yet." Annemarie had sighed. "She's interesting, single and she seems to want to hang out with *you* of all people. There's got to be something wrong with her. Meanwhile, apologize for abandoning her in the middle of the street."

She spotted Jennifer in the crowd crossing against the light, ignoring the honking cabs like a seasoned New Yorker. Still in those fabulous jeans and boots, she was also swaddled in a cinnamon-hued shearling coat that reached her hips. Suzanne abruptly felt underdressed. Maybe that just came with the territory of being around someone so casually stylish. Jennifer had seen her—it was too late to pull off the cable-knit beanie that kept her earlobes from turning to ice. This California girl was not getting used to the cold.

After a breathless exchange of greetings, Suzanne handed over the little jewelry box.

"What's this?"

"To make up for dumping you this afternoon. I could have at least had the cab take you to your apartment."

"Oh." Jennifer didn't look very impressed. "It was okay."

"No it wasn't."

After a little silence, Jennifer said, "It was a little abrupt." Her smile was forbearing as she opened the little box. "A bracelet— thank you, I mean, it's very nice but we hardly—"

"It's engraved just for you."

Jennifer tilted the box toward better light. "Does it say 'Suzanne Mason is crazy'?"

"I have those by the dozen in a storage unit in Silicon Valley."

Jennifer's face went still, then a genuine, soft smile lit her up. "Thank you. That's, um, I'll wear it to auditions."

The thin silver band slipped around Jennifer's fine-boned wrist, glinting the words *I am Unforgettable*. Suzanne liked the way it looked before it disappeared under her jacket sleeve.

"So, I can't believe I'm going to the movies with someone in the movie." Suzanne bounced on her toes.

Jennifer pulled her sleeve back to touch the bracelet one more time. "You have to look quick. I'll let you know when the two shots are coming up."

"So you're an actress and model." She took Jennifer's elbow to guide them both into the line for tickets.

"I don't get to claim actress yet. This was totally as a casual extra. It's still a major jazz, though."

She'd barely made a dent in the popcorn when Jennifer nudged her.

"Right here is the first one," Jennifer whispered around a mouthful of popcorn.

And there she was. Wearing the same shearling coat, with her abundant hair glinting for the camera, she cheered as the basketball star of the movie went into Madison Square Garden. Gone in a second and a half.

Jennifer gave a little laugh. "They shot ten minutes of film for that. I'm not visible again for another twenty-one minutes."

She settled in to enjoy the movie, as well as sitting in a dark theater with a beautiful woman next to her. The story was goofy, but it was a movie for kids, and all around her kids were laughing and having fun.

"Next one coming up." Jennifer tapped her arm. "Look in the background right over Bugs Bunny's shoulder."

There she was again and this time in the shot for longer.

"You look stunning," she whispered back.

"Thank you. It was really fun. A total fluke too. We were doing an outerwear shoot in the fashion college down the street and when it was over we saw the film crew. I guess a half dozen pretty girls rushing up to ask if they needed extras caught their eye."

Suzanne started to ask a question, but there was a loud *shush* from behind them. Jennifer giggled and hunkered down in her seat.

"Want to split a twelve-layer cake at Johnny's?" Suzanne asked on the way out of the theater even though she knew the answer.

"Bacon burger recommendations, cake—you're a pusher. The popcorn alone means I have to do an extra hour at the gym tomorrow, and my trainer always seems to know when I've gone face first into sugar."

"So what's your tomorrow like?" Afraid Jennifer would read in a blatant invitation to a night at her place and breakfast, she quickly added, "Or your weekend?"

"I have an audition and I'm also meeting a new teacher—speech and vocal. I need to talk purdy. Moses supposes his toeses are roses, and all that." To Suzanne's puzzled look she asked incredulously, "You've never seen *Singin' in the Rain*?"

"I can't say I'm really into old movies. I like modern stuff. But this one I should see?"

"Well, yes. Duh. It's a classic. What kind of geek are you? You've been hearing lines from old movies all your life and never knew." Jennifer paused to look in the window of the brightly lit Lego store. "Who has the time for these?"

"It's very relaxing. Almost Zen. The rest of the world just goes away." Suzanne pointed out the small details on a *Star Wars* tableau. "The store is closing, but we can get a close look if we're quick."

"You seem to know this place well." Jennifer pivoted to follow her into the store.

"Like I said, it's very Zen." She pulled Jennifer through the doors and over to the Technics displays. "They have the space shuttle. Awesome."

Jennifer's face held a polite look of interest.

"This type you actually build the exterior with bricks and then there are electronics to connect."

"I can see how, if you're you, that's fun."

"Fun for ages fourteen and up. It says so on the box. Wow, they have the complete space and airport set too." Suzanne pulled both boxes off the shelf. Major score. "Could I coax you into helping me with a project then? I make a mean club soda and lime, you know that already. And I have more of those puffy snack things."

"Well…" Clearly it wasn't Jennifer's idea of a way to continue their evening. "How about I help you get started?"

"Terrific. I need a big table for it. Nothing in the loft is big enough to spread out." She dashed to the cash register where the clerks showed every sign of closing down. But as she had suspected, they were happy to pause and sell her the two kits and one of their layout tables.

"They're kind of heavy," the bushy-bearded cashier warned her. "We could deliver it day after tomorrow."

"No, we'll manage."

When they were both standing outside the now locked doors, with a large, heavy box between them that could have held a hundred-pound pizza, Suzanne began to regret her optimism. The table box was awkward, and she and Jennifer could lift it, but just barely. And there were the two kit boxes to somehow carry as well.

"You're stronger than you look," Suzanne managed between grunts.

"You really are crazy." Jennifer was sucking in her breath, but her end of the box was as far off the ground as Suzanne's. "This will never fit in a cab."

"Oh ye of little faith." They made it another dozen feet and set the box down. She glanced around, then called out to two teens about to buy pretzels from a kiosk in the middle of the plaza. "Hey guys, twenty bucks each for some help for a few minutes."

The two boys gave her a skeptical look, but she waved a hand at the box. "We need to get this into a cab. It's heavy. Seriously, twenty bucks each."

She thought they were about to write her off as a crank, but Jennifer added, "You both seem pretty strong."

They looked at Jennifer and Suzanne thought they'd agree to carry the box all the way to the loft for free—they had matching glazed deer-in-headlights expressions. It wasn't as if Jennifer was even trying to get that response, either.

"Sure, uh, sure," they stammered in fits and starts.

Between the four of them, with the two boys intent on demonstrating their muscles, they got the boxes to Fifth Avenue.

"Pay our helpers, Suzanne." Jennifer now seemed well aware that she had two willing supplicants at her disposal. "We'll take it from here."

"Aren't you…?" one of the boys began.

"Yes," Jennifer said. "Whomever you think I am, you're right."

Suzanne handed over the cash and the two boys headed back toward the pretzels, slugging each other in the shoulder as they disappeared.

Jennifer proved her prowess at summoning cabs. The driver muttered nonstop about how the box was going to tip out of the trunk any moment and their lack of foresight to bring bungee cords. The trunk lid bounced as they made their way along Central Park West and every time it smacked the box particularly hard, Jennifer giggled.

"I still think you're crazy."

"You have no idea." They shared a long look that made Suzanne wonder what on earth she was doing proposing a night of Lego building to a beautiful woman who might, just might, be signaling she'd prefer other activities. The sensation of her brain going to soup again was disorienting.

The building elevator was fortunately large enough if the table box was upright, and the doorman helped them get it shifted inside, then put the two other boxes at Suzanne's feet just as the doors closed.

"Do you have any ice cream?" Jennifer's sudden question made Suzanne realize she had worked up a sweat in spite of the nose-reddening chill outside.

"I think I have some It's-Its." To Jennifer's raised eyebrow she added, "It's a Bay Area thing. Oatmeal cookie ice cream sandwich. There's a store on Seventy-Third that carries them."

"I deem that acceptable. If you don't have any—"

"There isn't anything you can't order delivered in Manhattan, 24/7."

Jennifer tapped the box with a slender fingertip. "Except a Lego table."

"You have me there."

They tugged the box out of the elevator and found it easier to drag rather than carry it over the smooth concrete floor of the foyer. Suzanne trashed the furniture *feng shui* by pushing back a couch and coffee table so they could flop the box onto the floor near the east-facing windows.

Jennifer shed her coat and Suzanne tried not to notice how she made an ordinary sweatshirt as suggestive as a negligee.

"We need a box cutter," Jennifer said, eyeing the thick straps wrapped around the box.

"Uh…"

"You have a box cutter, right?"

Suzanne laughed outright. Jennifer didn't look amused. "No, I don't. But I do have a very expensive set of kitchen knives."

"Chefs everywhere are crying out in pain."

Fetching the longest of the knives, Suzanne quoted, "Necessity is the mother of invention."

"Necessity is the mother of emergency room visits. You're on your own, CEO."

Praying she didn't injure herself, she set to sawing the thick plastic straps open, one by one. "Those two kids would have helped with this if you'd asked."

"They didn't look the type to have box cutters."

"No, I meant they'd have happily showed off their muscles for you."

"Jealous?"

Jennifer's curt tone made Suzanne look up. "Of two boys, no. All I meant is that you have considerable power over mere mortals. Like a Jedi. If you knew what that was."

"Sorry. It's just that I got gnawed on in acting class for having just looks."

"Just?"

"You know what I mean."

She started on the last strap. The heavy German blade was getting less effective. She tried not to sound out of breath. "Not sure I do."

"Have you ever had anyone tell you that you were good for only one thing? And you disagreeing made them laugh?"

She stopped sawing. "Yes. I was only good for math. Then only good for computers. Not any good for leadership or management, art design, music, style, parties. Or friendship, or romance."

"I don't think anyone would say that to you now."

"No, not now. It got better when I left behind the idea that how men saw me was the be-all and end-all of my value. In my field that's easier said than done."

Jennifer crossed her arms. "Are you saying that I believe that?"

She'd obviously struck a nerve, reminding her that an AltaVista search had turned up a stunning photo of Jennifer in the borrowed pajamas last night, but hadn't offered any clues about the woman's love life. "No, I was talking about me. I came out and got comfortable in the clothes I liked and then people seemed to see me differently."

"Well, I'd like to be more than a pretty face."

"So you have lessons and you work at it, right?"

Something in Suzanne's expression had made Jennifer relax. She knelt on the floor and pulled at the cut straps. "Let me help."

"Insert *Star Trek* 'City on the Edge of Forever' reference here," Suzanne said.

Jennifer laughed. "Okay, I get *Star Trek* even less than Jedi."

"Well, nobody's perfect."

"Insert *Some Like It Hot* reference here."

"Another movie I should see?" She grinned at Jennifer. "Yeah, I know. Duh. It's a classic."

CHAPTER ELEVEN

As promised, the table was easy to assemble and came with the necessary small tools. Jennifer glanced at her watch—it was nearly ten o'clock and they were only getting started. She glanced out the tall windows to the view of Central Park, glittering with frozen gold and white through dark trees.

Some things were more important than Legos, she decided. "Where's the ice cream?"

Suzanne looked up from a collection of plastic bags and a newly unfolded list of instructions. "I thought I was a food pusher."

"You are. It's your fault." She clambered to her feet. "Keep playing with the pretty plastic. I'm going to forage."

The freezer yielded up a box of ice cream sandwiches. They did look very yummy. So, tomorrow, a trip to the gym even though it wasn't personal trainer day. But it would have to be squeezed in between the audition and getting ready for the Winter Strut for the Cure where she was walking again for Lucius.

"Here's your What's-It." Jennifer handed over one of the frozen goodies, still in its cellophane wrapper.

"It's an It's-It. Thanks." She tore off the wrapper. "Nothing like it," she said around a huge mouthful.

A nibble confirmed that while there was a risk of falling chocolate slivers getting on her sweatshirt, Suzanne was right. Cinnamon oatmeal cookies and vanilla ice cream, plus chocolate, suddenly made playing with Legos exactly the right thing to do.

"I'm going to get ice cream on the pieces." Jennifer licked her thumb. "This is tasty."

"That's…" Suzanne seemed flushed. "That's fine. Part of the whole gestalt."

"If you say so. Where do we start?"

"There's a method to the madness." Suzanne became exceedingly businesslike. "Organize, classify first."

Taking a cross-legged position on the floor she'd last used in a formal Japanese teahouse, she scooted forward until her tummy was against the low table's edge. Carefully listening to Suzanne's instructions, she decided her best contribution was sorting. The white bricks seemed endless so she began with the taupe and black. Suzanne had an explanation for every step, why it was more efficient or logical. Her movements were economical and Jennifer could imagine her building a computer from the inside out, connecting little bits and clips to each other.

She found that brick sorting was, in fact, relaxing, and was inordinately pleased when Suzanne praised how quickly she'd finished, even though she laughed when Jennifer called some of them periwinkle instead of blue. They worked well together on building the shuttle wings as they talked about old movies and new television shows.

At one point their fingertips brushed and Jennifer was momentarily content to enjoy the brilliant thrill that ran up her arms. It was like being in the sun on a cold day, welcome and appreciated for the simplicity.

But it wasn't really that simple, was it? Gay 90s or not, if Jennifer were to believe books and movies, deciding to sleep with a woman came with labels. Chances were high it would put her career on the skids, especially as an unknown. There was a reason why Rock Hudson and Barbara Stanwyck and Raymond Burr had kept their private lives and liaisons as quiet as possible. Ellen DeGeneres had a hit sitcom and the rumors were endless, but she was still holding out from making a declaration, even though everyone knew.

Rumors, slurs, innuendo, whispers. Some people could break out, stand above them. But others were buried forever. She had no idea which fate would await her if she and Suzanne…

She shook off the thought. Or tried to. Her body wanted one thing but her brain was refusing to let go of the worry.

"It's after midnight." Jennifer couldn't really believe the time. She'd gotten all the white sorted, then further into onesies and foursies, and Suzanne was in the middle of setting up the grid for the launch pad foundation.

"Tired?"

"Not really. But I have an audition in the morning. It's near CUNY, ten a.m."

"Time for a cab?"

"I guess." She watched Suzanne's fingertips run over bumps in the bricks as she muttered under her breath. "I'll use my handy new phone to call."

"Mm-hmm."

Well, you knew she was a nerd among other things, Jennifer told herself. You just spent hours playing with Legos. She squelched a laugh—was this what it was like not to be someone's sex object? She managed to get to her feet in spite of her hips feeling as if they would never resume a normal position again.

"Wait." Suzanne had paused in her counting to focus on her. "I'm sorry, you're going?"

"It's late. Audition tomorrow."

"That's right." Suzanne unwound her legs from under the table and got to her feet, not looking the least bit stiff. Her shoes and tie were long gone, shirt untucked and dotted with melted chocolate, and her slacks were rumpled.

They stared at each other across the table and all Jennifer could think was how touchable Suzanne looked. How intimate the last few hours had felt.

"I should go."

"Yeah."

There was another long silence as the room seemed to drain of all air.

"Unless you have another idea." Jennifer was abruptly grateful for her vocal lessons—there wasn't a trace of panting in her voice.

Suzanne frowned. "I'm out of It's-Its."

"Silly." Her legs finally obeyed her and she went around the table. "You think about it."

She gave Suzanne a kiss just like the one that Suzanne had given her to muss her lipstick the night before, then drew back.

Suzanne blinked twice, then grinned, tossing the Legos in her hand onto the table. "That's a much more fun idea. What took you so long?"

Before Jennifer could protest, Suzanne had pulled her close. Their lips brushed, then Suzanne hesitated. "Do you feel that?"

"Yes." Jennifer leaned into Suzanne, closed her eyes and raised her mouth and found herself leaning into air.

Suzanne had plunked down on the floor with a loud curse. She peeled off two Lego bricks that had embedded in the arch of one foot. "They should use these in warfare!"

Laughter and tension burst out of Jennifer in a great whoosh that left her weak-kneed and dabbing tears out of the corners of her eyes.

"Just you wait." Suzanne gave her a baleful look while massaging her instep. "It'll happen to you."

"I can honestly say that this date wins for weird."

"I'll take that as a compliment. And I'm glad you consider this a date."

"I was using the word in its most generous definition." She looked down at Suzanne with indulgence even while part of her was freaking out at the surge of affection that was swamping her common sense. Early appointment, it prodded. She could ruin your career before you have one, it insisted. She touched the bracelet and the babble grew distant.

Suzanne was on her feet again, carefully eyeing the floor as she took a step closer to Jennifer. "Now where were we?"

"Time for me to go."

"You asked if I had another idea."

"I think—maybe we should wait on other ideas."

She watched Suzanne's expression go carefully neutral and had a sudden vision of her at a boardroom table using that expression to hide her thoughts as she negotiated over millions of dollars. The thought left Jennifer disquieted, almost chilled. Suzanne could add up a situation with the blink of an eye and decide which assets she needed and which she didn't, and then she would take action. Cool, dispassionate—skills she used even when making toy spaceships.

All Suzanne said was, "When can I see you again?"

"I have another Lucius event tomorrow night. It's important. The Winter Fashion Strut for the Cure."

"I'll see you there." A muscle under one eye twitched in what might have been a wink.

Jennifer opened her mouth to ask how Suzanne thought she could manage tickets to an event sold-out for months and then simply smiled. "See you there."

She didn't risk another kiss.

CHAPTER TWELVE

Suzanne hobbled to the nearest sofa and pulled off her sock. No, she was not bleeding, though her instep held the purpling imprint of a corner-thick brick. A two-thin had also caught her right in the soft spot past the ball of her foot. Both bruises were worse for the fact that she hadn't felt either at first and she'd had her whole weight on them, anticipating a long, slow, exploratory kiss.

A kiss with a gorgeous woman who had sorted Legos like one of the nerds.

The first time she'd offered a glamour girl a hot dog for lunch, she'd been given a look of such horror they'd taken a cab to an exclusive Asian fusion place in Chelsea instead. Jennifer had gobbled up a hot dog and made an appreciative noise or two. The image of Jennifer licking food off her fingers was a favorite replay on Suzanne's mental VCR.

Yet Jennifer's clothes dripped with designer labels. When she wasn't engaged with someone she had a face of carved ivory with that cut-you-dead stare of "I am not for you" Suzanne knew so well from high school and college.

She had wanted to persuade Jennifer to stay the night, but a pulse of panic made her feel that she might just lose all her cool by devolving into the stammering teen who hadn't been able to get out a coherent word at her first science fair.

Plus there had been the throbbing in her foot which felt like torn skin, gushing blood and shattered bones even though the skin wasn't even broken.

The Legos giveth, the Legos taketh away. Someone should invent protective footwear.

It had seemed so easy last night to pursue Jennifer. Gorgeous girl, wooing, then bed. A simple and straightforward series of events. Again she wondered if Jennifer had ever been with a woman. It wouldn't be the first time Suzanne had attracted a lesbian virgin. A couple of times it had been just curiosity and Suzanne didn't mind obliging. The other women had been quite honest about it and she herself had been trying to live the life of the carefree New York millionaire. It had seemed an attractive choice at the time. So many museums, so many plays, so many people who wanted to party with her.

Magical times for the too-tall geek from Cupertino, California, who still couldn't believe she lived in a place that only had walls around the bathroom. Sure it was chic—until you wanted to tack up a to-do list. She missed her Grace Hopper poster too, but that was back in a storage locker in California.

She massaged her bruises and thought about losing herself in another raid on ancient tombs, or wiping out a stronghold of orcs, but she felt too keyed up. Even the Legos held no appeal for the moment. Instead, now that her brain seemed to be clearing from the Jennifer Lamont-induced fog, the checklist to review with Annemarie tomorrow was clamoring for more attention.

She got comfy at her desk and started digging into public listings for the companies involved in the merger rumors. No one had approached her to run it. Maybe no one would. But if they did, work would begin immediately, and all the players were in California. It was entirely possible that her space shuttle project wouldn't be taking flight anytime soon.

CHAPTER THIRTEEN

"That's attached to me!" Jennifer glared into the mirror at the hairdresser. "There's no weave to take out."

"Sorry darling." The vapor-thin stylist ran his fingertips along her scalp as if checking to see if what she'd said was true. "My card says you're supposed to be in a French braid."

"Lucius has never had me braided." His comb jerked her head back before she could get a good look at the note card on his desk. "I'm Lamont, Jennifer."

He paused in his torture. "No you're not."

She gave him the look he deserved.

"Don't go all diva on me." He turned to the controlled chaos of the rest of the room to shout, "Who's supposed to be doing Lucius's girl?"

"I wouldn't mind," the Goth stylist at the next table said. "Mm-mm-mm."

Jennifer's angry retort was cut off by her sudden sneeze. The air was thick with sprays and oil turned to vapor by flat irons. She blinked rapidly to keep her base eye makeup from running. At this point in the prep she was not supposed to have tear ducts.

The audition had gone badly. She didn't look or sound like a Jersey girl, a verdict delivered after four lines. Plus one of the producers had slipped her a card for a "special project" and just smiled at her when she'd said he had to call her agent. Another casting couch invitation. She'd three times as many of those as she'd had actual auditions.

What irked most was that they had wanted working-class Jersey and that was what she believed she'd given them. If any of those producers had ever lived there, they'd know there wasn't a lot of difference between West Jersey and eastern Pennsylvania, even less so for anyone grinding out a living in a steel mill. She'd grown up with Jersey girls and Jersey girls made pilgrimages to the King of Prussia mega mall. She knew the tone, the accent, the poses.

She could hear that someone else was better for a part, but to be told she didn't have the first clue about a role had been a blow to her ego that couldn't be made better by walking up and down a runway. Yes, the meeting with the woman who would be her vocal coach had gone well, but that was someone being paid and she would of course say nice things about her potential.

Why wasn't she content with what she could so easily do? *You never want what you have*, her mother's voice hissed in her ear. *You're not good for anything else.*

"Honey, you're in the wrong seat." The stylist shooed her to her feet.

"I went where I was told."

He pointed and she spied another equally ethereal young man frantically waving at her. When she was close enough he fussed, "I've been looking all over for you."

The hotel meeting room turned dressing area was a mass of voices and confusion, and not helped by the bass-fueled electro-swing pulsing from the adjacent banquet hall. The two dozen or so temporary makeup stations had two or three people at each, and racks of garments were lined up the middle, guarded by seamstresses and tailors waiting for their turn at the models. Sure, it was all for charity. But the designers were still nervous wrecks about every last detail, including where in the show the organizers had ranked them. Lucius was peevish about not being later in the program, but Michael Kors had four models and two competing lines. Of course his work was going last and a Big Name Model was doing the final walk, in, what else, a wedding gown.

Like their designers, the models were aware that there was nothing else going on in the fashion world this week and so everything they did would be under a microscope. Jennifer wasn't immune to the pressure, and it was heightened by the charity folks having their own backstage photographer taking pictures of the prep, so they were all supposed to look gorgeous throughout the makeup and hair process. That picture of her in Suzanne's pajamas had moved from the gossip page to AOL Style and would be run in the *Daily News*. Lucius had crossly told her he'd wasted too much time that day explaining that he had absolutely nothing to do with some off-the-rack garments. And that it was all her fault.

Her little phone was chirping and buzzing in her handbag. She resisted the urge to check if it was Suzanne. More likely it was her agent wanting an update about the audition and to chide her again for walking out of the photo shoot yesterday morning.

It hadn't escaped Jennifer's notice that while her agent was yelling at her for what she'd done, she hadn't threatened to dump her. Hadn't even come close.

"Jennifer, there you are, darling girl."

She hadn't seen the *Glamour* reporter with the unmistakable retro black beehive sneaking up on her. Talking to Monique DuMar was always a gamble. It was either sugar sweetness or bitter acid. It was tempting to gossip, but she understood Ingrid Bergman's warning about the perils of the two-sided press game. Once you played, you were in for life.

"Tell me about those pajamas! You looked edible."

"I tripped and ruined Lucius's gorgeous dress and someone found them for me. Necessity and all that." She closed her eyes as the stylist dusted her roots with dry shampoo to keep her hair from sagging under the heat.

"You started a new rage."

Jennifer opened one eye. Monique was serious. "Silk jammies—I slept in them last night too."

Monique grinned and wrote something down in a notebook that bulged with scraps of paper and photos. "Thanks, darling. Is this you at Washington Square?"

Jennifer gaped at a snapshot from yesterday afternoon. She'd known people were taking her picture, but how had Monique ended up with it?

"Sure, that's me. I was just out for a walk." Thank goodness her makeup was okay and it was before she'd changed into the sweatshirt. She realized that it was Suzanne walking toward her in the background, but not really recognizable to anyone who didn't expect to see her in the photo.

"You're wearing Kate Spade."

"I know. I like her work." It was the truth. It was also the only right thing to say.

The stylist none-too-gently forced Jennifer to face the mirror.

Monique had again scribbled something down. "You should be walking for her. You go well together."

"How did you get that picture?"

"Sweetie, you're the feature on AboutTown.com."

"I am?"

"You need a new publicist if you're just hearing it from me."

"I don't have one yet."

Monique cocked her head. "The Luciuses of the world are fine for some of these girls, but he's holding you back."

"He's a great and well-paying client."

"Then sweetie, you need a new agent." She scrawled something on the last page in her notebook and tore it out. After folding the sheet over, she held it almost within Jennifer's reach. "Promise to always return my calls."

"I will try," Jennifer said. Heedless of the stylist's displeased hiss, she relaxed fully into her chair as she met Monique's gaze full-on. Like yesterday morning she was abruptly aware that she wasn't the extra in the scene being played out. She was, for a few lines anyway, the featured player. She didn't reach for the paper.

After a moment, Monique leaned forward to put the note easily within reach. "When you speak of me, darling, be kind."

Jennifer tucked the folded paper into her handbag and then acquiesced to the position the stylist was prodding her into. As the words "Thank you" left her mouth she became aware of the photographer snapping a dozen quick photos of her with Monique and the stylist as reflected in the mirror.

A flicker of her concern for how the photo might look must have shown, with her hair half done and an unplanned expression on her face, because Monique leaned forward to whisper in her ear, "I'll make sure they pick a good one. Who wants to share a bad photo with La Lamont?"

Hair finally done, she moved on to makeup and then she was standing still for the seamstress who was sewing her into her garment. Once that was complete she had no choice but to go on standing. There could be no wrinkles in the sleek layers of blue silk and charmeuse that created Lucius's empire silhouette negligee. If she stood still she looked almost demure. The Louboutin pumps with their sammy-red bottoms sent a different message when she walked.

It was a lovely enough gown, clever even in what it did and didn't expose when still or in motion, but she eyed the show-closing Michael Kors' winter lace and Basque-waist wedding dress and knew there was a difference Lucius would probably never achieve.

She wished she'd taken the time to look at Monique's note, but it had seemed important to let Monique know she would take care of it in due course. That this girl did not answer "how high" to anyone's "jump." High school already felt like a decade ago, but the lesson of never letting a cat-calling, harassing masher see her flinch had been a good one. Working in the menswear department at the mall had underscored the need to seem above all the crude remarks about her figure, the invitations to tour the dressing rooms and the outright groin rubs by guys who wanted to be sure she saw them touching themselves. She channeled her inner Lauren Bacall and they became invisible.

Monique DuMar's note seemed to glow inside her handbag. Was it a personal referral to the kind of agent who hadn't even responded to the delivery of her portfolio a few months ago? And a publicist? Was she ready for that?

She was about to risk moving from her assigned place to dig into her handbag when a harried intern thrust a padded envelope at her.

"Someone dropped off something for you. Said it was part of your outfit."

Lucius looked up from fussing around another girl's winter-in-the-park ensemble. Was she becoming a horrible egotist that she thought the outfit looked pedestrian on someone else? Hadn't Lauren Bacall said that looking in a mirror was a poor reflection of life?

"You're complete," he snapped. "I don't know what that is, but you're not wearing it."

She bit one finger of her three-quarter length glove and pulled it off in spite of Lucius's despairing groan. Careful of her nails, she pried up the envelope corner and out tumbled a small green Lego brick.

Her laugh of delight turned heads.

"Get that glove back on!"

"Yes master," Jennifer said.

The envelope had nothing written on it so she let it float to the floor along with the rest of the dressing room detritus. The tiny Lego piece she tucked in between Laverne and Shirley.

CHAPTER FOURTEEN

I'm a stranger in a strange land, Suzanne had to admit. Normally, her interest in attending a fashion show would take an electron microscope to detect. The difference between teal and cerulean wasn't a battle she wanted to pitch. Preferring masculine cuts and leaving the decision of just how narrow her ties should be to a tailor had simplified her life to no end, that much was clear.

There had been a point in her past when being surrounded by this many gorgeous women giving her a second glance would have caused a euphoric asthma attack. Frothy bits of lace and sleek jackets that wouldn't keep anyone warm were walked up and down the elevated runway that split the long, narrow banquet hall. She pretended interest for the sake of her host, a friend of a friend of the Wealth Management Specialist from her investment brokerage, who had been regularly offering her gratis tickets to plays and charity events for the past few months. When you had money lots of things were free. She could easily imagine her parents shaking their heads over the unfair irony.

She glanced at the catalog she'd been presented with at the door. Around her, some people were following along eagerly while others were chatting and sipping champagne. At the back of the room was an amazing display of cut fruit and canapés arranged like a fashion runway with a winter bride as the centerpiece ice sculpture. No one was eating any of it that she could tell. Her stomach rumbled.

She'd spent half the day on the phone with Annemarie discussing the right people to handle finance and legal. Those specialties were outside her expertise and trust was important. She'd followed that by reading the most recent prospectuses for both companies. Her missed dinner was talking loud in her empty stomach. Would it start a scandal if she touched the food? It was after nine—just entering dinner hour for some Manhattanites.

Fanning forward a few pages she could tell that Jennifer's designer was coming up. She would wait and take Jennifer out somewhere quiet. She hoped.

"Were they Armani or Brooks Brothers?"

It took Suzanne a moment to realize the petite woman was talking to her. Her black hair was outrageously coiffed into a rolled shape on top of her head that "bun" didn't even begin to describe. She could have been any age between thirty-five and fifty. The only inelegant touch was a notebook stuffed to breaking with photos and loose papers.

"I'm sorry?"

"La Lamont's pajamas the other night. I understand you were her…" Keen dark eyes appraised her from head to toe. "Her knight in shining armor."

"A guest fell and I had an unopened package. It was those or one of my suits."

The woman's pen danced across a notebook page. "The mind reels at the image. Jennifer Lamont as the new Dietrich." She tucked the notebook under one arm long enough to proffer a pale hand. "Monique DuMar, features at *Glamour*. It's a pleasure to meet you Ms. Mason."

The brief, limp handshake was preferable to the air kisses everyone else was sharing.

"I have bad news for you," she went on. "If you're here to reclaim your pajamas, La Lamont told me she's been sleeping in them."

Suzanne's hackles rose. DuMar had obviously sought her out looking for some kind of salacious tidbit, like a circling shark looking for chum in the water. "They were of course a gift."

"And your presence here tonight is just coincidence?"

Yes was a lie and *no* was blood in the water that would involve Jennifer. Jennifer, who was managing her name, exposure and career so carefully. Jennifer, who wasn't out, and for all the signals she was sending might consider herself straight. Suzanne hoped her slight hesitation was unnoticed as she decided to mix truth and lies to avoid the topic of Jennifer altogether. "It was on my to-do list, to attend a fashion show in New York. I might have new business to tend to in California soon."

Her feeling that DuMar was only interested in gossip about Jennifer was confirmed when the reporter didn't follow up with the obvious question. She'd given an opening a financial journalist would have jumped all over.

Instead, DuMar asked, "What made you choose blue pajamas?"

"It's the only color I had."

"Happy circumstance? Creating the kind of unforgettable photograph of your gorgeous loft and the most beautiful young woman of the year lounging gracefully in front of a view of Central Park?"

"Can fashion be accidental?"

"Not fashion," DuMar said. She glanced at the runway and said, more to herself than Suzanne, "Style."

Her brain finally offered up a way to get rid of the woman. "Can I get you something to eat?"

A flash of horror preceded a wry smile. "Aren't you gallant?" She patted Suzanne's tie and again gave her a visual once-over. "I can't think of a single way to improve you."

"That's a compliment?" She let her puzzlement show.

"Imogene!" DuMar waved a frantic hand at someone behind Suzanne. With a parting glance she said, "Yes darling. Ask anyone."

Feeling as if she'd crossed the Gorge of Eternal Peril, Suzanne retreated toward the buffet table. There were very few people near it, so it seemed safe. The music changed from an electronic beat blended with swing to something that sounded like blocks of cement grinding on asphalt. She'd been wrong that the music was as loud as it could get. The only word she understood in the emcee's announcement was "Lucius."

After two models displayed day wear more practical for winter on Venice Beach than Central Park, the next two were lingerie.

Scanty scraps of snowflake-imprinted gravity-defying fabric clung to hips and breasts, drawing scattered applause. But neither of the models was Jennifer, which seemed odd given her flawless, generous curves.

An outpouring from the fog machine billowed across the stage. The mist swirled and retreated to reveal Jennifer in a long, deep blue gown that at first glance seemed so demure it was out of place.

Jennifer seemed to falter, her gaze downcast. Then a unique twist of shoulders, lift of chin and slow blink of her lush lashes promised there was much more than a proper lady under the dress. Her first steps, revealing floor-to-hip bone slits, confirmed it.

Never in her life had Suzanne ever felt as if she were drowning in desire. She remembered to close her mouth, tried to swallow. There was spontaneous applause as Jennifer reached the end of the runway. She paused long enough to slowly strip off her gloves, then spun on her toes to look over her shoulder toward the bank of photographers. The panels of the dress parted again to reveal a tantalizing glimpse of thigh-high stocking. Camera flashes dazzled Suzanne's eyes. There was a roaring in her ears so loud she thought the music had stopped.

She wiped her palms on her pants. She would never again joke that tongue-tied, sweating arousal was exclusive to teenage boys.

Jennifer had disappeared into the mist and been replaced by a new designer's models before Suzanne could make herself move. Even then she didn't know what to do with a body that didn't feel like it belonged to her anymore. Her clothes were too tight, her fingertips were tingling. A deep breath didn't help.

She gave it a college try by reminding herself that Jennifer, like all women, was not her sex object to drool on. But innate business sense reminded her that Jennifer's career, at least for now, was marketing her looks. The woman walked like sex. Exactly what was the right reaction to have?

She's not her career. She's more than that. You don't want to be like some guy grabbing for what's not on sale.

Sure, thinking about it more was going to help.

What's wrong with me?

Or maybe it was that there was something right with her.

She felt her phone buzz in her suit pocket. Flipped it open, then closed. JLMNT would be in front of the hotel in thirty minutes.

CHAPTER FIFTEEN

Jennifer's first thought on leaving the hotel was how glad she was she'd stuffed a scarf and gloves into her coat pockets. The night had turned bitterly cold.

Her second thought was how happy her eyes were to spot Suzanne, huddled deep inside her overcoat, standing just past the bellman's desk. It hadn't even been twenty-four hours and she had news to tell, though her thighs' appreciation for the pressure of Suzanne's, after a warm hug of greeting threatened to drive everything else out of her head.

Suzanne was the one who pushed away, saying, "Holy tennis balls, it's cold."

"Did you enjoy yourself?" She double-looped the scarf around her neck and zipped the ends under her jacket. She'd decided on the peplum blouse over Imperioli boyfriend jeans. At least the UGG boots were keeping her toes warm.

"I was just there for the one thing. And that I enjoyed very much."

She thought that Suzanne looked a little pale. "Fun dress to wear. For what it was. Are you hungry?"

"I was thinking you'd never ask. One block over there's a new place in the basement of the Marquis. Big central fireplace. I have no idea about the food."

"A fireplace sounds great." Her toes felt warmer just thinking about it.

They turned toward Lexington and Jennifer shared with her the best part of the evening. "I have big news! Sorry it took me a little longer to get out."

Suzanne steered her out of the path of a winding box office queue. "It's okay. What's up?"

"A reporter gave me the name of one of the two top agents for models, but even better, both of those agents left their cards for me. But the best part is that the second one is also a theatrical agency for models who do both. Who knows, another month and I could be a dead body on *Law and Order*."

"You're so, so, so much better as a live body."

Jennifer linked her arm with Suzanne's, their steps in rhythm. "Thank you for thinking so."

They had crossed the street and dodged around people making a beeline for the subway entrance before Suzanne said, "I'm afraid of sounding like everyone else. You looked incredible. I mean, I've seen photographs of you, obviously, but you were all that and live. Bet you hear that all the time."

A quick glance revealed that Suzanne's expression was unusually guarded. "I know I'm just starting out, but I think I can tell the difference between idle flattery and a compliment from someone who's really looking."

At the top of the stairs leading to the promise of warmth and food, Suzanne turned her to face the glow from the streetlight.

Jennifer looked up at her inquiringly but Suzanne said nothing.

The silence became charged, growing hot against Jennifer's cheeks and throat. Then she realized it was a deep flush and she knew it had to show. Suzanne's lips parted—they might have trembled, Jennifer wasn't sure.

What am I supposed to do? Boyfriends had never been shy about what they wanted, but Suzanne was just looking at her, waiting. Waiting for what?

A couple coming up the stairs from the restaurant jostled past them, snapping the taut, expectant silence. Jennifer turned to descend, pulling Suzanne after her.

The restaurant lobby, lined with highly polished oak paneling, was beautifully, deliciously warm. A table near the fire opened up and Jennifer shrugged out of her jacket. The heat immediately warmed the silk.

She glanced at Suzanne and was pleased at the look in Suzanne's eyes. Score one for Yves St. Laurent, she thought. A fast-beating flutter of tension settled deep in her stomach.

"Bruschetta perhaps? Or are you hungrier than that?" Suzanne's voice was tight and low.

She stopped herself from saying, "I'm hungrier than that," because it was going to sound like she meant sex, which of course she did. She studied the menu for a moment so she could confirm exactly what bruschetta was. "Little toasts. Sure. Maybe the bison sliders—split an order?"

"That sounds fantastic. I worked through dinner as it turned out."

"More about the merger deal?"

"Yes, though I'm waiting to be approached. It's all gossip right now."

Another silence fell, broken by the trim, pale waitress who cheerily encouraged them to have a frothy coffee drink or hot buttered toddy, the house specialty, and launched into a description of the chef's special for the evening.

Suzanne interrupted the description of something that sounded like "charred cuticle" with a request for the sliders. Jennifer ordered the coffee because she didn't want to risk being carded.

"So if no one has called you about the merger thing, why are you working on it?"

Suzanne was gazing into the dancing yellow flames. "Something to do. If they do call, I want to make an impressive, full throttle start. Everybody knows I know the technology. I want to build confidence in my competence for the rest of the business. Leadership, organization. I guess—most people think I just got lucky. I'd like to change their minds."

"I can understand that."

"Plus being gay, a lot of people are eager to discount the value of anything I do."

"That's the same almost everywhere, isn't it?"

"There's been a lot of progress this decade. A president who can say *lesbian* without choking." Suzanne looked as if she was going to say more, then she sipped from her water and returned her gaze to the fire.

I want to spread her out on the table and run my hands over every inch of her. It was a terrifying, thrilling image that played out over and over on Jennifer's mental movie screen, right up there with Deborah Kerr and Burt Lancaster rolling around on the sand.

Their desultory conversation was filled in with long silences—some velvet, others pins and needles. Jennifer couldn't remember what any of the food tasted like even though the plates were now empty.

"You don't seem to like the coffee."

She shrugged. "Not my favorite thing. I needed the water more than anything."

Suzanne suddenly smiled. "I like that you like food."

"Duh. I just can't eat that much of it."

"You were one of the few women I saw on the runway tonight that I didn't think was maybe too skinny."

"So you did like the dress?"

"Of course." She shook her head slightly. "Of course. I thought it was a mistake not to use you for the lingerie but then I saw the dress. Not the dress. You in the dress," she added quickly.

"It's what Bette Davis meant about flannel nightgowns." Suzanne looked confused so Jennifer continued, "About a bare shoulder in a flannel nightie being sexier than a naked body."

"Good lord, that's the truth. I didn't even look at the other models once I knew they weren't you."

Jennifer exhaled hard.

Suzanne blushed to the roots of her hair. "I said that out loud, didn't I?"

She nodded.

"Do you want to—"

"Yes." Jennifer reached for her jacket.

As they neared the restaurant exit, Jennifer gestured toward the posh powder rooms. "I'll just be a moment."

Suzanne continued toward the stairs.

"Earth to Suzanne. Yoo-hoo."

Suzanne startled. "Sorry. You're… Sure."

"What's wrong? The merger thing?"

"God no."

"You're shivering."

Suzanne just looked at her.

I want to give her what she needs. It was a blazing hot thought, weakening her knees.

A glance showed a green "vacant" indicator on the nearest bathroom door. The hallway was deserted for now but that could change at any moment. Jennifer seized Suzanne's arm and propelled them both through the door.

Turned the lock.

Pushed Suzanne against the back of the door so hard the louvers creaked.

"Shh." She kissed Suzanne in a rush of breathless abandon, holding her face with trembling fingers.

Suzanne came alive under her hands. They were panting together, struggling to get Jennifer's coat off, then the heat from Suzanne's hands through the silk covering her back threatened what control Jennifer had left over her knees.

Suzanne pushed her fingertips under the snug waistband of Jennifer's jeans. "Have you ever?"

"No." It was a tight, high inadequate admission. "I mean—I've been—I've had boyfriends."

"It's not going to be like that."

"I know."

Boys back home had used words like *beautiful* and *hot*, but never so that the words were breathed into her ear like prayers. None of them had feathered their lips along her jaw. Their worship had lasted minutes, done before she had scarcely felt what *Cosmo* so faithfully assured her was normal.

But how could this be normal, this blinding ache to be touched? Her breasts felt swollen and the silk was burning hot across her chest. Another hint of teeth at her earlobe pushed all the air out of her lungs. She didn't know what to ask for. The academic part of her mind had figured out how women could be together, but all of her sources about sex and her own experience—none of it said she would want her skin to melt, that she would be holding back hoarse, needy pleas, that the dignity she'd been trying desperately to cobble into her portfolio to build a career wouldn't matter when another woman's breasts moved against her own.

"Show me," Suzanne whispered. "Show me how strong you are."

"I don't feel strong, I want..."

"Taking is strong." After a ragged breath, Suzanne added, "Please let me."

She cupped Suzanne's face and kissed a fierce *yes*, felt Suzanne's hands slide along her hips. Two backward steps and Suzanne lifted her onto the counter.

Her wild hair was abruptly a nuisance, falling into her face when she wanted to see Suzanne. She shook it back over her shoulders as Suzanne unbuttoned her blouse.

Jennifer helped part the ruby fabric and without hesitation unhooked her bra.

A small green object tumbled out.

Suzanne laughed with a touch of wonder. Then, "How can you possibly be real?"

"Don't step on it," Jennifer said against Suzanne's mouth and for a long minute lost herself in the pleasure of Suzanne's delicate touch on her breasts.

Suzanne shrugged out of her overcoat and Jennifer ran her hands down the front of the simple Oxford cotton shirt. Without consciously choosing to, her fingertips teased at the hard nipples she could feel under the cloth. Suzanne's responsive shiver made her light-headed. A woman, she reveled. A mystery and known all at the same time.

The zipper on her jeans caught on her panties. Their fingers tangled and Jennifer was thrown by the fact that the thin fabric was soaked. What would Suzanne think of her eagerness?

The zipper finally gave and Suzanne's hand cupped and played between Jennifer's legs and then it all made sense. The heat in her shoulders, the clenched muscles in her back, the trembling along her thighs and calves all made sense. The sensation that she was turning to liquid no longer scared her.

"Is this okay?"

"Do what you want."

"I want to make you dissolve."

She gripped Suzanne's forearm. "Go ahead and try."

Suzanne let out something between a gasp and growl as she eased her slick fingers inside Jennifer.

Desperate for balance and some kind of control, Jennifer managed to get one hand braced behind her on the counter as she clutched Suzanne's shoulder with the other.

"Show me." Suzanne's jaw was clenched. "Stay with me."

She let out a trembling *yes* and lifted her hips and Suzanne yanked her clothes further down even as she pushed her fingers deeper. Though she tried to hold it back, Jennifer's moan echoed in the small space. Suzanne kissed her to silence even as she stroked against nerves that made Jennifer want to cry out.

"Quiet," Suzanne warned.

"I can't." Through gritted teeth she admitted, "I don't know what to do."

"Enjoy it. Can you?"

"Yes."

"Look at me."

Suzanne's eyes were shimmering and Jennifer kept her gaze locked on them as she seized a handful of Suzanne's upswept hair. Almost too short to grip, Jennifer still managed to yank Suzanne's head back, earning a fierce groan. Her gasps for air matched the rhythm of Suzanne's hand.

She saw Suzanne's eyes widen as a jolt ran through Jennifer's body. "Right there."

At the last moment Jennifer closed her eyes, it was too much, too intimate. The strain in Suzanne's face, her plea for something Jennifer didn't know how to do. She let go of Suzanne to clamp a hand over her own mouth and stifled the hard, sharp cries as she lost control. It felt as if she'd left her body and it would have been frightening except for the strong arm around her.

Suzanne was repeating in her ear, "I knew, I knew."

The little room had gotten very warm. "Knew what?"

"That you were strong."

"I feel a mess." Her arms and legs were quivering. She was dizzy.

"Beautiful. Jennifer, look at me."

She exhaled at the naked desire in Suzanne's face, igniting a throb of *more* inside her. She knew it showed and she washed over with awkwardness.

"Don't do that," Suzanne said. "It's late to be shy."

"I just—I didn't know I could be that way."

Suzanne kissed her softly. "I knew. Let's talk about this somewhere else."

"Somewhere horizontal."

Suzanne let out a low chuckle as Jennifer slid down from the counter.

"I said that out loud, didn't I?"

"Do you want to—?"

"Yes."

CHAPTER SIXTEEN

Suzanne stretched her legs, sleepily realizing that she was taller than the bed was designed to accommodate. She wiggled her uncovered toes. Cold feet were going to make more sleep impossible unless she could change position.

She pried open one eye. Jennifer's bed was narrow but she'd hardly noticed the surroundings. An Uptown traffic jam had made turning the cab south a good idea. Where hadn't mattered. Last night there had been only Jennifer.

She was sleeping on her side, face half buried in the unanchored blankets, hair tumbled across the pillow in deep blue and black waves. Sometime in the night they'd taken a shower and the faint, clean smell of vanilla and cherry soap made Suzanne drowsy and hungry for food and sex both.

A faint rustle from somewhere in the pile of her discarded clothes repeated. That's what had woken her—her mobile phone. The tiny, streaked window over the bed let in little light but given how late they'd been up and how reasonably rested she felt, it was probably late morning.

With a slow, careful twist she managed to get her feet under the edge of a blanket. Jennifer didn't budge. Craning to see if

Jennifer had a clock near the bed, she spotted the bracelet she'd given her draped over the lampshade so that *I am Unforgettable* was visible. From there her gaze was drawn to a large poster of Lauren Bacall—at least that's who Suzanne thought it was. The luminous eyes promised that she could handle whatever the world put in her way, and she would not lose her cool.

Below the poster was a bookcase that appeared to be upright only because there were so many books wedged into it. Biographies and memoirs of actors seemed to be a favorite choice, along with acting guides and movie buff compendiums. To one side of the bookcase a box overflowed with magazines, the uppermost featuring Jennifer on the cover. The door to the other room was partially blocked by a clothes rack tightly packed with garments in dry cleaning bags. Underneath, in a long, neat trail leading to a clearly inadequate closet, were pairs of shoes and boots.

Suzanne figured if she were to count up every pair of shoes she'd ever owned from birth onward, she wouldn't have half of what she could see just from the bed. Tools of the trade and Jennifer knew how to use them well. In spite of the overcrowded conditions, there was a sense of order. The shoes appeared to be roughly organized by color. One pair of high heels with some kind of grime on the toes sat atop the trash can. Everything on the clothing rack looked like it was black, with dresses on the left, blouses in the middle, pants on the right.

Her phone rustled again and she decided that she probably ought to check it. She didn't want to wake Jennifer, though. She had nothing but her shirt to use as a robe, and it helped fight down the shivers as she stealthily made her way to the bathroom. The old basket weave tile was covered by a thick, warm, foot-soothing mat that made her not quite as sorry she hadn't grabbed her socks.

Stranger in a strange land, she thought again. A behind-the-door rack was crowded with little pots and bottles of makeup, nail polish and palettes of eye shadow, a dozen tubes of mascara at least, pencils, lipsticks, gloss and an entire shelf of implements that might have been right out of the Inquisition. The sheer variety was mesmerizing. Yet again there was a clear organization by color and function.

She caught sight of her awed and dumbfounded expression in the mirror and clapped a hand over her mouth to stifle a giggle at her own befuddlement. Around the mirror, held in place by a clever use of cup hooks, were two different sets of lights sharing an electrical power strip with items she was willing to bet had to do with hair but wouldn't have looked out of place in an auto shop. She wondered how often Jennifer blew a fuse.

The door wouldn't close all the way so she made her use of the facilities quick. The calls to her phone were mostly from Annemarie but there were a half-dozen numbers she didn't recognize. She pulled on her pants and overcoat and stepped into the hall, using a can of soup from a cupboard to prop the door open.

"Where have you been?" Annemarie's impatience was loud and clear.

"Having a life. Is this important?"

"Cute, young supermodel—that's living all right."

"What?" She hadn't meant to bark. "How the hell did you know?"

"*Men's Pajamas and a Millionaire's Loft Prove that a Woman's Style is No Accident*, by Monique DuMar. Here's how it starts: 'It is a photograph worthy of Marlene Dietrich, but most noteworthy for being completely unstaged—'"

"Where the hell did that come from?"

"*Around Town Style*. I was searching to see if there were any mentions of you and the merger and your name came up. This article is also linked to from *AOL Business*."

"I told that woman I was just being a good host."

"The model sleeps in them, did you know? Says so right here."

Not last night, she didn't. Suzanne was devoutly grateful that Annemarie couldn't see her face. "That's what passes for business news these days? I give a guest something to put on after she ruined her dress?"

"It's a great picture. Whoever wrote the article is right. Casual, classic, stylish because all the parts are all those things, even if no one ever set out to deliberately combine them. So anyway, surprised you haven't been getting calls."

"Maybe I have. I slept in."

"Up all night shooting bad guys?"

"Legos," she lied.

"That's your contribution to the gay agenda for the week? You are *so* scary."

"Go away." Suzanne disconnected, then queued up her voice mails. Reporter. Reporter. Reporter.

Not a reporter. She listened with a leap of exhilaration. Her folks would be thrilled. She immediately called Annemarie back.

"Guess who's coming to California?"

Annemarie's whoop made her pull the phone away from her ear.

"I haven't called back. Yes, yes, I'm doing it. Go away again."

She was grinning at her phone when she realized that Jennifer was now standing in the doorway of her apartment.

Damn, a bare shoulder from a terrycloth robe… She got palm sweats. It took her a moment to find words. "I just got great news."

"You're going home."

"Yeah—"

"Now that you've done everything you wanted to do here?"

"Not by a long shot." She realized that Jennifer's smile was forced. "This is bad timing, I guess."

"Is it?"

"Of course."

"I thought you'd left and there was no note." Jennifer turned her face away. "I'm glad you're not like that—but you're leaving anyway."

"Maybe. It's looking like, yeah, maybe." She glanced at the phone. She should call them back. She should talk to Jennifer. Be with Jennifer—last night had been—her phone was buzzing again, nobody she knew. Yet.

She caught herself before she flipped it open. Instead, she dropped it into her coat pocket where its zzz-zzz was muffled by her gloves.

Jennifer picked up the can of soup and let Suzanne back into the apartment. "I understand. It's not like we're actually dating."

"Legos until midnight? That's a class A date."

Jennifer gave her a sideways smile. "Coffee?"

"Sure. First, though…"

She pulled Jennifer to her and buried her face in the curve of Jennifer's neck. "You are amazing," she breathed out and was rewarded by Jennifer's shiver. "Only an idiot would leave without waking you."

"There are plenty of idiots in the world."

She studied the dark eyes, seeing a ring of bronze and gold for the first time. "Most people agree that I'm a smart girl."

Jennifer laughed. "Smart girls are apparently incredibly sexy."

"Let's skip the coffee. Go out for lunch. In a little while."

"You have business. And I have an event tonight. Lucius's ever-present arm candy. It's possible I could run into those agents."

Glad that the decision to part ways for a few hours wasn't entirely on her, Suzanne untied Jennifer's robe. "Then something to tide us over."

CHAPTER SEVENTEEN

It took every ounce of effort Jennifer had to make small talk about Lucius's dress. Another high-profile holiday party, this time in a SoHo brownstone with a frigid interior in shades of white and ecru. Every lull in conversation immediately filled with images of Suzanne. They hadn't even made it back to the bed. She could still feel Suzanne's soft cheeks against the insides of her thighs. Goosebumps erupted down her arms as she relived the chill of the floor under her while heat had flooded her body.

But Suzanne was leaving New York—this is just a fling, she told herself. Some great sex, some laughs, it's nothing more than that. She wasn't even going to ask herself if she wanted it to be more. It couldn't be, and that was Suzanne's choice.

"Miss Lamont?" A trim older man, so well-groomed the effect was almost fussy, held out his hand. She wouldn't have been surprised to learn that a ruler had been used to fold his pocket square. "I had hoped we'd meet last night, but this will do just as well. Tomas Tilden."

"A pleasure." She returned his firm, brief handshake and hoped her inner squirm of delight didn't show. Of the two agents showing interest, T&T was the one that could also act as theatrical representatives. "I was going to call you first thing Monday morning."

"Let's seize the moment, shall we? I believe that Tilden and Tilden can launch you into super stardom in the fashion world. For one thing, your present representation doesn't have the kind of reach into international work that we do. We can triple your income in a few months."

As he spoke, Jennifer allowed him to steer her toward a quiet corner behind an opulent, flocked Christmas tree decorated completely in white ribbons, ornaments and lights. "Can I be equally blunt, since our time is probably brief?"

"Absolutely."

She'd been rehearsing her speech for that Monday phone call. "I want to be clear that… What I'm looking for is representation as a model and as an actor. I'm in performance, improv, voice and diction classes and I believe I can succeed in the field well enough to make your efforts worthwhile."

The smile under his gray Napoleon mustache was smooth and practiced. "My colleagues and I have already discussed this as a possible path for you." This time a little noise of excitement did escape her and his smile broadened. "I think we might come to terms fairly easily. Would you have time free on Monday for a sit-down?"

"Absolutely," she assured him. "I'm committed to something in the late afternoon."

"Let's say eleven then." He tipped his head as if studying the brilliant smile she could no longer hold back. "Yes, we can do well for you."

After that the party seemed not nearly so dull. The thought that she might be earning a living without arm candy gigs and local photo shoots was incredibly appealing. More money, travel—*could it be real?* Don't jump to conclusions, Jennifer warned herself. Every gift has a price. This is what you wanted—*why are you afraid?*

The feeling lasted until she was changed back into street clothes befitting nine p.m. on a crackling cold night. Thick snow-laden clouds hid the stars, but the glittering skyline made up for it. Swedish base layer tights under her jeans plus silk and wool ankle socks under her boots made walking the few blocks to the subway bearable. The subway crowd and clatter was oddly charming and she kept hearing snatches of Sinatra in her head. She had made it here, she could make it anywhere—right?

At the top of the steps at Madison Square Garden station she paused to get her bearings. A quiet little sushi bar, Suzanne had sent in a text. Skirting media vans and cameras reporting on some event at the Gardens, she spied Suzanne across the street, looking anxiously through the crowd.

"Jennifer Lamont, right? Are you attending tonight's event?"

She blinked into the glare of the light atop a camera and had the sense to put her hand in front of her face. Though she recognized the bright-faced reporter as one she'd seen covering red carpet events on the local news, she didn't appreciate being sandbagged. This was not a red carpet. "I don't know what's going on there. Just leaving the subway. Excuse me."

The reporter seemed desperate for any kind of comment. "What did you think about your feature from *Glamour* this morning? Do you like living in New York? What's your next photo shoot?"

"I'm sorry, I have a date—an appointment." Suzanne had seen her and was jaywalking with the crowd to join her. "I'll be late."

"What are you doing for nightlife this holiday season?" The camera followed her as she moved in Suzanne's direction. And then it hit her. Any moment they would catch her in the frame with Suzanne. Suzanne was likely going to kiss her hello. It was possible, with her hair in a beanie and long men's overcoat Suzanne might be taken for a man at first glance, but not for long. What if the reporter followed her to find out who the mystery date was? What if the blasted woman recognized Suzanne Mason and cared about names in the business news as well as entertainment celebrities?

She'd saved money from her crappy mall job to pay for modeling school while other kids were joyriding in cars or taking the SATs. She'd struggled and finally closed her ears to her mother's negativity and spite. Even though it meant closing some doors, she'd remained aloof and suspicious when people tried to give her things, especially the free drugs. She'd put herself out there, stared down rejection, accepted the small successes.

She could lose it all over a second of film, over a headline. For Suzanne, who was going back to California.

She would get applause and "good for you being true to who you are" from people who had no jobs to give her. Meanwhile, the people with work would decide she was never right for the part.

She didn't want to have to deny anything. She didn't want to lie. But she wasn't going to set herself back over sex—it was *just sex*, she told herself in panic.

Mind-blowing, fire-hot sex. With another woman.

Her future was suddenly on a razor's edge and she wasn't ready to dance in Suzanne's world, had no preparation, no protection and no way to know what to balance. Or if there was anything she could trust.

Veering into an opening in the crowd she hoped Suzanne could navigate too, she put a block between her and the Gardens before a skid across sidewalk ice made her pause.

Suzanne caught up with her, breath steaming before the bitter wind snatched it away. "You're going the wrong direction."

"I was getting away from a reporter."

"The price of fame already?" Suzanne's hands were in her pockets. She looked tired yet satisfied, as if she'd had a long but successful day.

"I made the mistake of saying I was late for a date."

Her expression freezing, Suzanne slowly said, "And you couldn't have her figuring out it was me."

"Do you want publicity about your sex life right now?"

"I'd survive it."

Jennifer didn't actually say, "I don't think I would," but the words dropped into the space between them anyway. A rock of something acid and cold settled into her stomach.

Suzanne finally said, "Plan B then? Greek diner?" She shrugged toward the door only a few feet away.

Jennifer managed to get, "Yes. I'm starving," past her icy lips.

The bitter coffee failed to warm her. The only heat she felt was in her fingertips. They itched to stroke the back of Suzanne's hand. Just to touch her skin for a moment. But it felt like a lie instead of a promise.

"There's no closet for me to go back to," Suzanne said quietly over her cup. She abruptly frowned.

Jennifer followed her gaze and spotted a man eyeing her, likely trying to figure out where he knew her from. "I was apparently in some big article today on the Internet. There's no place for me to hide my face right now, I suppose."

The silences were long as they waited for their order and continued after it was delivered. Finally Suzanne looked up from toying with her feta and spinach omelet. "The article was on the web today, an advance of one that will be in a future magazine. You haven't seen it yet?"

"No—not a peep from my agent about it. I need... The agency I hoped would be interested? I'm meeting with them Monday. They'll have a publicist and..." She managed to swallow a half bite of toast. "They have stuff I need."

The man who'd been staring at her left, but only after walking very slowly past their table. With mock cheer she asked, "So how was your day?"

Suzanne's little laugh didn't hold much humor. "Busy. My lawyer has sent a contract to review. My business associate is pulling in people and we've got an org chart for a transition team taking shape. If you'd bought stock earlier this week you'd have already made a killing."

"Wish I'd thought of it. I could have gambled my rent money."

"Time will tell if the price will go up or crash and burn once we're through the merger. The market seems to think I can add value. I have to prove it now. If I do, then I extend potential future partnerships. Maybe even outside tech, but who knows?"

She made herself eat a few pieces of her skewered chicken and tomatoes. Her stomach stopped grinding and grumbling. She had hoped it would clear her mind, but she couldn't stop looking at Suzanne's hands and remembering them on her breasts, between her legs.

As they left the diner the wind buffeted all the way down her back and Suzanne clutched her beanie. There was finally enough privacy to talk openly but Jennifer figured they'd both freeze to death in minutes.

"Could we—" Jennifer shook her head as the wind snatched her words.

Suzanne leaned close.

It was too much and too powerful and her brain gave up trying to sort out her entire life in an hour. "This," she said into Suzanne's ear before nuzzling her lips against the soft lobe. "Can't we just do this?"

Suzanne's gloved hands were in her hair, tipping her head back. "Do you think it'll help?"

Suzanne kissed her before she could answer, "I think it's going to hurt." Even with the layers of their coats separating them, Jennifer thought she could feel the pounding of Suzanne's heart.

They parted when a cab disgorged passengers into the warmth of the diner, and Suzanne held the door for Jennifer. The heater was barely holding its own and she huddled in her coat, unable to think of a word to say. When Suzanne pulled off one glove and slid her cool fingers inside Jennifer's sleeve, fingertips stroking along the soft skin of Jennifer's forearm, Jennifer lost herself in the sensation. Delicate, gentle, and sending her pulse higher and hotter with every touch. And driving away the vision she had of a future in flames.

CHAPTER EIGHTEEN

Jennifer was all abandon, wild with desire. Her lips were red with kisses and the slow strip of their clothes as they made their way across the loft to the bed had created an urgency inside Suzanne that she didn't recognize. She didn't think anyone else had ever seen Jennifer like this either.

This one's gonna burn, Suzanne thought. She's deep under my skin but I'm just scratching an itch for her.

She couldn't stop herself—didn't even try. Jennifer's tiny whimpers of need fanned a fire that danced over all of Suzanne's body.

"Is this what you want?" She skimmed Jennifer's thighs with her lips.

"You know I do. You make me feel—real. Like this is how I'm supposed to feel."

The rush of tenderness Suzanne felt surprised her. She gently kissed Jennifer's thighs and closed her eyes. In spite of Jennifer's hand on the back of her head there was no hurry. The taste of sex and Jennifer was more intimate than anything she'd experienced. The sharp cries and long, rising moans filled Suzanne again with the awe and power that loving women fueled inside her.

This was how they were both supposed to feel.

"Let me," Jennifer whispered. "Tell me if I'm not doing this right."

She let her forehead rest on Jennifer's shoulder and considered shushing Jennifer with a kiss. She ached for Jennifer's touch but her fears were suddenly in her throat. It could be too good. She could never recover. Then she pushed away the foolish thought. She had never needed anyone that way. A hiss of pleasure escaped her as Jennifer's touch became more confident, moved more quickly, then deeper.

"Is this okay?"

She raised her head enough to meet Jennifer's gaze. There was no uncertainty in it. Jennifer knew…

"I just want to hear you say it." Jennifer's other hand trailed lazily over Suzanne's back, nails raising goose bumps.

"Yes. That's…okay."

A low, sexy laugh accompanied the feel of Jennifer's fingertips on her nipple. Suzanne found herself straddling Jennifer's thigh, grinding on her palm, and it was too late to hold anything back.

"Say it again."

"Yes."

"Again."

"Yes."

Gasping for air, she said it again, in Jennifer's ear, and again when Jennifer was behind her, tongue tracing Suzanne's shoulder blades and still deep inside her. And again when Jennifer rolled her over and their slick bodies merged in breathless need.

She wanted to join Jennifer in welcome, exhausted sleep but the impulse fled and her mind turned to solutions. They could still see each other. Planes went from New York to California multiple times a day and she'd happily buy Jennifer as many tickets as she wanted. Jennifer could even end up in Los Angeles if her acting career took off.

She wasn't sure why it had seemed impossible earlier. She relaxed and gathered Jennifer close. The scent of her hair and skin rolled down Suzanne's body in a warm tide of satisfaction.

Sunlight in her face woke her. Jennifer was gone.

ACT II

CHAPTER NINETEEN

Present Day

Jennifer had scarcely grasped the fact that she was once again in Suzanne Mason's arms before Suzanne swirled her upright.

They might have been dancing. Except she was only wearing one shoe and her dress was halfway to her waist. But those unforgettable strong arms were wrapped around her, allowing no light between their bodies, and she was being guided toward the nearest doorway. A hubbub had broken out and Jennifer could see her ex, Selena Ryan, on her way toward them, with the young, talented, *nice* Gail Welles in her wake. Gail would be genuinely sorry for Jennifer's plight. Lena would not be able to hide her *schadenfreude*.

Suzanne didn't ease her grip until they were in the cabana, where the servers were stacking dirty dishes. She arched an eyebrow at Suzanne.

Suzanne let her go.

Clutching at her dress before her navel joined the strip show, she gathered it up until Laverne and Shirley were at least covered. The molded breast cups were tangled in the dress and the body glue had left a tacky residue on her nipples as usual. Not that she wanted to explain that to anyone at the moment. She kept one hand splayed across her chest, holding the silk in place. As if it weren't already hard enough to feel dignified, the loss of one of her shoes put her off balance by four inches.

"Is it torn?" Suzanne was sliding out of her sleek white linen jacket.

"I don't think so." *Don't mention the past.* "Thank you. I thought I was going to crack my head open."

"This will get you back to the main house." Suzanne slid the jacket over Jennifer's bare shoulders.

"I couldn't—" Suddenly she could. Whether it was the warmth from the silk lining or the accidental brush of Suzanne's fingertips at the nape of her neck, Jennifer found herself pulling the jacket close around her. "Thank you. I've lost my shoe."

"Your Choo's dead." Selena, sleek in her habitual understated elegance of a masterfully tailored dark charcoal suit, appeared from behind Suzanne, holding up the stiletto. The heel was almost completely detached from the rest of the shoe. Jennifer knew better than most that Lena was a master at hiding her thoughts. Right now she wasn't bothering to mask her merriment. "Not that anyone will care."

Jennifer took the shoe, saying, "You're right. I don't think it can be repaired."

"Sure. *That's* the headline, Jennifer." Lena gave a meaningful glance at the closed front of the suit jacket.

Gail Welles, true to her Iowa nature, looked concerned and kind and helpful all at once. "It's not as if other people haven't tripped and fallen, Lena. I did a face plant the first time I met you, remember?"

Lena made what was for her an absolutely *gooey* face in answer, leaving Jennifer to point out the obvious. "I'm half naked and in one shoe. Can you two do the sweet nothing remembrances later?"

Gail's face was a lightning fast succession of emotions that left Jennifer in no doubt that the two of them would have a romantic discussion later and that she didn't want to know another thing about it.

Damn Gail and her handsome, tall, thin, talented, unpretentiousness. She was like a baby bird that Jennifer wanted to step on sometimes, mostly because Gail had ended up happy with Lena after Jennifer had salted and scorched their relationship until not even weeds would grow. It would be a colder day than this before Jennifer would admit to anyone that she had been stood up by a producer tonight while her ex was here with the love of her life.

Suzanne gestured discreetly at the catering staff, some of whom were lingering close by. "Should we go back to the house?"

"Good idea." Lena turned toward the door. "Jen's already provided one news cycle. Sorry, make that *two* news cycles. Two *ample* news cycles."

Not for the first time Jennifer wished her eyes had real daggers.

"Follow me and we'll be mostly out of sight of the party." Suzanne ushered them along a side path that wasn't as brightly lit as the main walkway.

"I'm really sorry about all this." Jennifer bobbed up and down with every step. She swore she heard Lena snicker.

"It's no trouble." Suzanne glanced back and yes, she was laughing at Jennifer as well.

Oh *goodie.*

"No, I mean about what's going to happen tomorrow. Someone got a picture, if not a dozen, you know they did. I understand the tabloid mill. A picture that used to take a week to circulate is now around the world in an hour. You're going to get calls."

"They can talk to my P.R. people." Suzanne led the way through a side entry into the enormous great room that took up half of the mansion's ground floor. Jennifer had only glimpsed it upon her arrival. The dark beams against the white ceiling underscored a simple, elegant Spanish influence interior. Modern art paintings Jennifer knew were not reproductions added color. The dark woods and terra-cotta tiles were warm, as were the soft and appealing pale green cushions covering open, wooden-frame couches and chairs.

On the far side of the room floor-to-ceiling sliding glass doors were pushed open to let in the night air, which carried the hint of offshore fog and promise of sunshine tomorrow that was typical of La Jolla and San Diego beaches in the early spring.

It was a far cry from the chilly steel and concrete of the New York loft where they'd met.

They continued past the spacious kitchen and dining area at the rear of the great room and were into the powder room before Jennifer even realized it was one. She'd been on television sets that weren't as large. Once the door was closed behind them, she sat down on the chair at the vanity and slid off her other shoe. Both of her stockings were ruined.

"Have you ever dealt with the parasitic paparazzi?" Lena was giving Suzanne her no-nonsense face.

Suzanne was equally reserved. "I know something about it."

"I know you've dealt with the press. Actual, real journalists." Lena looked sympathetic and Jennifer wondered what she'd missed. "That's not who'll be calling. It'll be the type of people that if you say nothing, they just make something up."

Jennifer went on removing her thigh-highs. It was so much fun, listening to her exes talk to each other.

"You're in a photograph with Laverne and Shirley," Lena went on. "You have no idea the scope of the feeding frenzy that is about to happen."

Gail burst out laughing. "Now I understand your reaction whenever you see an ad for a rerun of that show."

Yeah, this was just *peachy*, Jennifer thought. "Gee thanks."

Gail gestured at her own chest. "Hey, I've got nothing but envy here."

"Thanks to the cloud and wireless and those bloodsucking scandal sites, I'm going to spend the next year talking about my boobs." She glared at Suzanne as if she'd invented all of it, which in part she had.

"Get out in front of it. Err, them." Lena blinked rapidly, but failed to look the least bit innocent. "Both of you need to get out in front of the story. Tweet about it, and then move on."

Suzanne spread her hands helplessly. "All I did was catch her."

Lena repeated, "You're in a picture with Laverne and Shirley."

"Stop calling them that!"

"You're the one who calls them that." Lena ran a hand through her short brown hair, which, as a result, was never completely tidy.

"In private! I don't want the whole world to know." Jennifer was not going to think about the nights when she'd enjoyed the feeling of that hair against her mouth or her thighs.

"I won't say a word either," Gail offered. "Even though I could totally get on *Late Night* with that tidbit."

"It never crossed my mind that you would do such a thing." Jennifer gave Lena an evil look before turning a more benign one on Gail.

"I think that's the nicest thing you've ever said to me." Gail looked at Jennifer's bare feet. "What are you going to do for shoes?"

Jennifer glanced at Suzanne's elegant Marc Jacobs loafers. No help there. "I can't get the dress and accoutrements back together." She shrugged off the jacket and immediately missed the way it felt on her shoulders. The dress slipped and Shirley saw the light of day for a moment. "I'm a mess!"

Suzanne let out a chuckle, then seemed to quail at Jennifer's glare. "I'm not laughing at your condition. I'm laughing that you think it's unattractive."

Jennifer glanced in the mirror. Her hair was tousled out of place, her dress crumpled and barely covered her assets—she looked as if she'd just gotten out of bed. The thought sent a flush across her chest and down her arms. She was very much aware that while memories of Lena were potent, it was Suzanne's open appreciation that was leaving her just a little bit breathless.

This entire situation was completely and utterly unacceptable. "Bette Davis—"

"Flannel nightgowns," Lena and Suzanne said simultaneously.

Lena cocked her head, then tipped it the other way to give Jennifer a long, speculative look. Her smile faded.

Not again, she quailed. *We can't do any of this again.* No one should ever have to be in the same room with more than one ex at a time even if she deserved it, which Jennifer knew she did—but still! *So unfair.*

Lena had turned a forced smile on Suzanne. "I had no idea you two knew each other."

"We met in New York. Initially," Suzanne said.

Lena had transformed from relaxed party guest to the buttoned-up CEO of an independent, award-winning film production company, a woman who didn't tolerate liars and opportunists, who forgave but never forgot. "So. Jen. This is the captain of industry? The venture capitalist millionaire? A woman?"

With all of her lies and fear echoing around the room, Jennifer really had nothing to say. She'd dumped Suzanne because she couldn't come out. She'd dumped Lena to chase what had turned out to be her first box office blockbuster and lied, lied hard that it had been over between them anyway. That was only the beginning of her sins.

"You never said he was a she. You said I was the first woman in your life."

Jennifer was dead certain that telling the truth now wasn't going to work out either but she gave it a try. "I lied."

"Did you ever tell me anything that was true?"

Before the more than seven happy years Lena had had with Gail the question might have been as sharp as a razor blade, but there was only a trace of the old anger in it. Gail still heard it and averted her eyes.

Suzanne heard it too and the faces of both women held the same expression of long-banked bitterness. Clearly, Suzanne was wandering through their shared past and adding up Jennifer's long list of failures.

"Google *bitch* and there's my picture, right? Are we revisiting my failures as a person or fixing my dress?" She'd told Lena a lot of lies. The only true things she'd told her were not going to be discussed now—even if Jennifer itched sometimes to set the record straight on a few accounts, Lena no longer cared. She had loved Lena, at least what love she was capable of. Which wasn't much, given her dismal track record.

Gail broke the heavy silence by gesturing at the poor Jimmy Choo. "You could get it fixed, maybe?"

The sad, dangling broken heel was only the start of the damage. She brushed a fingertip over a gouge in the crimson toe before dropping it into the wastebasket. "It's a goner."

"Jennifer prefers to discard what she can't use." Suzanne snatched open the door. "Be right back."

Into the heavy stillness Lena said, "She knows you well, doesn't she?"

Jennifer nearly agreed. Yeah, that's what this situation needed, more truth. That would make everyone feel just dandy. Instead she said, "My date stood me up."

"You're here for the sculpture auction." Lena was as dry as the desert.

"Maybe," she evaded. "They're not starting the auction soon, are they?"

"They won't start it without their host. And there are other items on the agenda."

"Good thought. Fine, I'm here for the Beck piece."

Gail, always helpful and kind and simply too darned nice, offered, "Leah Beck is actually here. I met her."

Wailing inwardly at the difference between the party experience she might have had mingling with the sculptor and other interesting women, and the stuck-in-the-bathroom Bad Jennifer time-out she was instead enduring, she decided there was nothing useful to say.

Suzanne reappeared holding a crinkly cellophane-wrapped package.

"No way," Jennifer said. All of a sudden she was in that Manhattan loft again. The tingles were there, as was her awareness of desire that had never abated. But there was also a sense of dread, as if the anguish of the past was just waiting to happen all over again.

CHAPTER TWENTY

Any other night, a picture of La Lamont in deep blue Brooks Brothers pajamas at a party would have set the Internet ablaze. The almost twenty-year-old photo of her in a New York loft, that accidental picture that had put her on the fashion map, would have surfaced for a side-by-side look. Jennifer knew that Internet commenters would gleefully announce she hadn't aged well, that her practically forty-year-old boobs weren't as perky, perhaps even that she was now fat, though her weight hadn't moved an ounce. Which was damned hard work that no one ever wanted to hear about unless you were agreeing to sign your name to their unproven fad workout or diet plan. Thank goodness she'd never sold her soul down that poisoned river—she did have some scruples.

There was little hope anyone would care about anything except the various shots of her boobs unleashed. No doubt by midnight someone would claim they could spot scars from never-happened plastic surgery. The more serious viral news media would pixelate Laverne and Shirley into modesty, while pointing links at a web destination where they could be seen in all their naked wonder. By morning *#jenniferlamontboobs* or something equally click-bait would be trending.

She'd managed to restick the breast shields back over the girls. At least she didn't appear bra-less underneath the silk pajama top. Score a point for the staying power of roll-on butt glue. Being barefoot wasn't a hardship on the pristine tile, still warm from the summer afternoon. She was presentable, and everyone at this type of gathering would be sympathetic. But this was not the real world.

The real world, or what passed for it in her profession, was the text from her agent: *This is GOLD!* And there'd be plenty of Blogasses and anonymous Tweetfeebs who'd claim it was all a stunt designed to prop up her sagging career with her sagging boobs.

All the while the part of her brain she no longer allowed to decide anything was babbling about Suzanne's eyes and arms, how wonderful she smelled and hadn't all the times they'd been together been the best ever? Except when they weren't.

Except when Jennifer walked out.

Lena, with a roll of her eyes that summed up her relegation of Jennifer to the list "Huge Mistakes I Have Made," had returned to the party with Gail. Jennifer hovered at the edge of the open patio, gathering her poise. Most of the women were wearing suits not unlike Lena's, but enough were clad in haute couture caftans and flowing silks that her pajamas might be taken as an avant-garde choice. Though, if the pajamas had been a choice, she'd have had a pair of FM pumps to sell the outfit, instead of being barefoot. Without shoes there was no getting over the fact that she felt tiny and vulnerable. It was not a feeling she liked.

Head up, she told herself. Aplomb was a skill she had long refined. The earliest lesson of modeling? No matter what happens, just keep walking. Her stint in a soap opera had taught her to shake off a flub because the camera didn't stop rolling.

Suzanne left her conversation to join Jennifer at the patio's edge. "Any lasting damage?"

"I think I'll have a sore shoulder tomorrow, but it'll pass. I'm as ready as I'll ever be."

"You look...repaired."

Unable to clearly see Suzanne's face, Jennifer was left to decipher the meaning of the hesitation and word choice. Something a little more effusive would have been good for her bruised ego, but that was, she supposed, a lot to ask given the circumstances.

Alternatively, it was possible that *repaired* was a compliment of the highest order from Suzanne's techy side.

Maybe. But right about then she would have given something for a date who could at least come up with, "You look *hawt.*"

They did not make any kind of entrance, and for that Jennifer was grateful. Instead, they simply joined a cluster of women already chatting. She didn't immediately recognize any of them, though everybody at the event was—like her—a Somebody in their own field. Ostensibly for breast cancer research, the evening also featured political speakers and an auction of a few collectibles and one art piece to benefit Planned Parenthood and a political action committee that backed women's health advocacy.

The ticket had been very expensive, and Lena had been quite right. It was the sculpture auction that Jennifer really had her eye on. Politics didn't up her heart rate—Leah Beck's art did. She had long been hoping to acquire a piece. She had also hoped for a somewhat relaxing private evening away from Hollywood. That hope had died along with her Jimmy Choos.

A server paused with a tray of hors d'oeuvres that Jennifer waved away. Moments later another offered glasses of wine just like the one Jennifer had lost and she gratefully lifted one from the tray.

"That was a nasty fall," observed a slender brunette in a fabulously fitted Donna Karan suit.

"I broke my heel and bruised my dignity." Jennifer sipped the wine and truthfully said, "This is delightful. Does anyone know what we're drinking?"

The brunette immediately said, "A two-year pinot grigio reserve, courtesy of Ardani Vineyards. You'll notice the full citrus undertone with notes of apricot."

A lush, dark-eyed woman turned toward them with a laugh, putting her elegant hand on the brunette's arm. "Toni, you sound as if you bottled it yourself."

"It's a family affair, isn't it?" Toni made a gesture of introduction. "This is my wife, Syrah Ardani, and I'm Toni Blanchard."

"Jennifer Lamont." She lifted her glass to both of them. "A pleasure twice over—to meet you and to drink your wine." The invitation to the event had promised a Who's Who of Women movers and shakers and Jennifer had certainly heard of Toni Blanchard's high-profile corporate rescues. It made perfect sense that Suzanne the venture capitalist would know someone like Blanchard.

There was an awkward pause that ought to have been filled with Jennifer introducing her nonexistent date. She heaped mental curses on the producer whose name would be expunged forever from her contact list.

Suzanne was suddenly there offering a puff of pastry from her small plate. It was golden brown with a twist of filling and curls of red and purple somethings atop it—gleaming and seductive from top to bottom. It looked to be all the calories Jennifer would have had for a normal lunch. "I don't know what this is but you should have one. I asked the caterer for a whole tray for just myself and she laughed at me. Quite disrespectfully, I might add."

Blanchard and her wife had turned slightly away to talk to the couple on their other side.

"Sounds like she knows you." Jennifer quickly added, "I'm making a feeble joke."

Suzanne let it go. "You should eat something or you'll get the shakes. Adrenaline drain after a scare." She turned the plate to offer a more prosaic carrot stick.

"I don't really experience that. Practice."

"You fall down a lot?"

She narrowed her gaze. "Only around you. I should perhaps take notice of that fact?"

"Coincidence is not causation."

"Flirting with math again?"

There was no amusement in Suzanne's face. "That was your thing."

Jennifer studied her wine. "I'm in a profession where things go wrong all the time and you're expected to reset your emotions and move on." She took some of the edge off her tone. "Thank you for the thought. The food looks delicious."

She didn't know why Suzanne was being thoughtful. Nothing good came of it. It required that she be nice back. She was bad at that—and Suzanne knew that just as well as anyone did.

Her thoughts must have shown in her face, damn it all, because Suzanne said, "I'm being a good host. I don't remember seeing your name on the guest list, however."

"The ticket was bought by someone else. But I have my eyes on something in the auction and didn't realize... Didn't know this was your address of course. You've moved since Santa Cruz."

Suzanne gave her a tight-lipped smile. "My date likewise failed to appreciate that this evening is going to be talked about for months. Which was going to be true before your kit and caboodle..." She vaguely gestured toward Jennifer's silk-covered girls.

After a long silence, Jennifer said, "Go on."

Suzanne cleared her throat. "So I took the liberty of moving your name card in place of my date's. It spares us both comment."

A cold flush swept across her chest, followed by a sensation of vulnerability that was frightening and appealing and very unwelcome all at once. "Maybe here, but not in the blogosphere! People will think there's something between us. You're in a photo with Laverne and Shirley and now we're going to be described as dating. Are you *nuts*?"

"I have never cared what that kind of media says."

"That's not quite true." Jennifer kept a bright smile on her face though her tone was low and quiet. "You just care less than I do."

CHAPTER TWENTY-ONE

"That's not quite true. You just care less than I do."

Suzanne left the remark alone. Now was not the time to argue. What would they argue about that would make a damn bit of difference, anyway? Jennifer was unaware of just how angry Suzanne had been to spot her oh-so-casually sauntering her sexy way into Suzanne's life all over again.

One thing she knew after all these years—she couldn't care less about Jennifer's image anymore. Front page and trending topics always featured pictures of La Lamont on the arms of men. She'd had one notorious affair with a woman in her public past, and whatever identity label Jennifer was using was Jennifer's problem to manage with the press. The media didn't know about the two of them and it would stay that way. Not to protect Jennifer but to spare herself being on a public short list of people Jennifer Lamont had eviscerated. Only Annemarie and her parents knew she'd ever been that stupid.

Her villa-sized patio and surrounding Spanish-inspired gardens had been transformed into an elegant, very California event. It had taken a crew a day and a half to hang all the fairy lights and set up the white-linen draped tables. Translucent lumières drifted across the darkened swimming pool, spilling flickering candlelight across its still surface.

A decorator had temporarily stripped the great room of evidence that Suzanne actually lived there, and the faint aroma of her father's pipe smoke that lingered after his visits had been driven out by vases of hydrangeas and lilies. The couches had been rearranged so the room served as the greeting area and, at the end of the evening, would be where people could wait for their car or for the coach that would ferry them to the helipad at the nearby University of California. An advance team from their surprise guest of honor had approved the layout in terms of security.

A thousand details had gone into this night. She had a caterer hovering, a party planner tapping at an agenda on her tablet and a patio filled with some of the most fascinating women she was ever going to meet. She was not going to be distracted. Not this time.

"Excuse me. Hosting duties call." She said it to Jennifer but with a glance that included anyone else nearby who might care.

She turned to the caterer first. When Suzanne had been approached to host the party she'd immediately suggested the Los Angeles office of *The Food's the Thing* to do the catering. Her friend, Laura Izmani, had come out from New York to supervise the night personally, and even roped in her more famous wife.

"Quantities are all fine and we're on time for dinner. I did run out of morels for the risotto, and there are probably a few palates out there tonight that will notice. I didn't want you to think I was trying to pass off portobellos in their place. Half will be morel, half portobello."

"I wouldn't know the difference myself," Suzanne assured her. "I hope at least after dinner you'll be able to join the party."

"The pastry chef is excellent, so that's my plan." She smoothed the front of her black chef's jacket. "What kind of wife would I be if I missed Helen's speech? And did I hear correctly that the Speaker of the House will be here?"

Suzanne knew her smile was too gleeful to be mysterious. "Surprise guest of honor."

Laura tipped her head ever so slightly in a nod of respect. "How did you pull that off? Seriously, you already had Reyna Putnam and then Sydney Van Allen said she'd show up?"

"It's my charming personality."

Laura gave her the look of someone who had heard plenty of B.S. in her time. "We did not just meet, you know."

"Then you know I was actually hoping to meet Putnam's partner."

"The mathematician? Okay, geek crush makes way more sense than your charming personality."

She ignored Laura's one-finger salute disguised as a nose itch. "Other people think I'm charming, you know."

"They don't know your shrunken capitalist Grinchy heart like I do."

The remark stung, even though Laura didn't mean it. Laura didn't know she was still getting hate mail over the Earth Tides project gone sour, tainting the entire solar industry. To some people, she was still the poster child for all that was wrong with high tech and billion-dollar global business put together. "It could grow three times larger today. Especially with your good cooking. My ass will grow, that's a guarantee."

"I'm going to smear extra butter all over your salmon just for that."

The party planner cleared her throat and Laura gave her a guilty look. "Enough comedy. Anyway, I'll prepare some extras for take-away style. Politicos never get to eat, and their security details live on nutrition bars. But I can't have anyone start on that because I've been down this road. At least one security person will want to see that the food is coming directly from what's being served to everyone else."

"I hadn't even thought of that. Please don't poison the elected official."

"Why do I even like you?"

"Charming personality, remember?"

Suzanne next gave her attention to the party planner with her ever-blinking timeline. Out of the corner of her eye she could see that Jennifer was chatting with the sculptor now. The pajamas were too long without heels. All those years folded in the package hadn't helped the creases much either. Not that she'd admit that she'd kept the second pair from all those years ago, just because.

She should have gotten rid of them after she moved out of the house in Santa Cruz.

There was no time to dwell on the past, but dwell she did over another glass of wine, through the few teaser auctions of interesting—and expensive—collectibles the women from Sotheby's had brought, and through the appetizer course. Jennifer seemed in high spirits, though she was lamenting that she already had pings from social media featuring her wardrobe malfunction.

"Thank you, everyone, for that. Lord knows I needed two more ways to be notorious."

Helen Baynor, the Broadway maven who'd been lucky enough to marry Laura Izmani, was just as warm and funny and dynamic in person as the Broadway scuttlebutt said she was. She lifted her glass to Jennifer. "In our profession I've long learned to believe ten percent of what I read about anyone. I hope for that same mercy from others."

Jennifer gave a chagrined shrug. "Ten percent is probably low in my case. There are people here who would go state's evidence in a heartbeat."

Suzanne managed not to snort. After Santa Cruz she'd deleted all the search bots that had brought her updates about Jennifer and her career. The breakup with Selena Ryan had spilled over into the LGBT news, and that was how she'd heard about any of it. She had been nowhere near happy that Jennifer had been caught having an affair with another woman. It hadn't been her, so screw Jennifer and the high heels she'd walked in on. Whenever Jennifer's name had come up in a headline or movie teaser, Suzanne had deleted, blocked and moved on.

It had been in no way amusing to see the same twist of bitterness in another woman's eyes and realize they could form a Jennifer Lamont Blue Screen of Death club. How many others were there? Or were she and Selena Ryan the lucky ones?

She lost the sense of the conversations around her, but everyone seemed to be having a good time. She knew she shouldn't let her mind wander, but the shock of seeing Jennifer tonight had been as profound as the shock of literally bumping into her in the restroom of a San Francisco theater almost a decade ago. Memories she'd tried so hard to archive forever came back to her in full digital resolution.

CHAPTER TWENTY-TWO

Nine Years Earlier

It had been a long line, as usual, to get to a stall in the ladies' room. Suzanne pushed the door open and realized too late that it wasn't empty. The next moment she stood rooted, blinking into Jennifer Lamont's eyes. Startled recognition made both women catch their breath.

After all this time Suzanne had not expected their paths to cross. And certainly not in a restroom. Don't look at the counter, she warned herself, but the memory of that first time, in the Manhattan restroom, turned molten in her brain.

"How are you?" It was a stupid question but at least she'd found the strength to speak. Was Jennifer as flushed as Suzanne felt?

"Fine." Jennifer was wearing one of those form-fitting dresses with one shoulder bare that looked as if a puff of air would melt it.

"What's it been, ten years? Since New York?" She was ridiculously glad she was wearing a new suit and had had her hair cut recently, even if it had been at her stylist's insistence.

"Eleven years at Christmas." Jennifer looked as if she regretted admitting she knew. "Look, you wanted to use—"

"Yes, there's a line." Suzanne paused half-in, half-out of the stall.

"There always is for the ladies' room."

Jennifer was going to walk away. Suzanne found herself asking, "Buy you a drink at intermission?"

The sweep of Jennifer's gaze said that she was aware that people were listening. "I'd like that."

The snaking bathroom line cleared out of the path of Jennifer's high heels. Some things never changed, Suzanne thought.

As sponsors of the venue, CommonTech Inc. had a block of seats for the premiere of the play *The Color Purple*. Suzanne bought a round of drinks for the employees who'd donated Bayshore cleanup time and earned the night out, but as they reached their seats Annemarie gave her a quizzical look.

"What's got you all wound up?"

Suzanne considered not telling her. Annemarie had already heard the entire *Jennifer left, Jennifer doesn't return my calls, Jennifer sent back my gift* whining that had gone on longer after New York than Suzanne was willing to remember. She was pretty sure if the word *Jennifer* came out of her mouth Annemarie would rip the arm off her theater seat and beat Suzanne to death with it. So she just pointed.

"What?" Annemarie peered through her cat's eye glasses. "Who is…" Her voice faded away to a hiss.

There was a pregnant silence as Suzanne ignored Annemarie's scrutiny.

"We can leave from the other side when it's over." Annemarie's fingers tightened on the small leather messenger bag she used as her fancy-going-out purse. She usually kept a notebook, wallet, snacks and a small bottle of water in it, so if deployed as a weapon it would likely hurt quite a lot. "We already peed so we can just stay in our seats during intermission."

"I'm supposed to buy her a drink then."

"The cat! Did she just, like, demand a drink for old times' sake?"

"I offered. It's been ten years. We've both moved on."

"You are such a moron." Annemarie wagged a finger in Suzanne's face. "Love is not supposed to hurt."

"Unless you're into that."

"Which you aren't. And you know what I mean. Walking around like a shadow for a year over someone you'd only known for a few days?" Annemarie lowered her voice. "If you like that kind of hurting you need to see a shrink."

The lights were lowering and the crowd grew expectantly quiet. Just as the curtain bobbed in preparation for rising, Annemarie whispered, "If you go out with that woman again don't even talk to me."

The first act was brilliant, Suzanne could tell. But her mind still wandered and she hated the feeling. Jennifer meant distraction and incoherence. Inability to focus, loss of priorities. Pain. She meant pain.

And pleasure. Suzanne's skin tightened at the thought of winding fingers into Jennifer's hair while her other hand explored and played until Jennifer trembled with release. Had anyone else seen her like that? Suzanne hadn't even realized until right then how much it mattered to her to at least be—if nothing else—the best thing Jennifer had ever felt. To have left a mark.

It was fortunate Annemarie couldn't hear her thoughts. A successful out lesbian tech geek moneymaker in the roller coaster of the last couple of years, and she was pining over some model? Who'd been in a couple of not-very-good movies? Moronic.

Annemarie was right. She was always right. Just ask her.

Applause woke Suzanne to the fact that she hadn't heard a word of the last scene. She spared herself asking Annemarie to move her knees by waiting for the aisle to clear in the other direction. Annemarie mouthed *loser* at her and added a finger-and-thumb "L" to her forehead in case there was any chance Suzanne misunderstood.

She mostly expected Jennifer not to appear. She'd probably said yes to get out of the situation. Nevertheless, Suzanne secured two drinks from the bar and removed herself from the crush. Jennifer was more likely to see her if she waited near the picture window that framed a view of the streetcars on Market Street. At least she made herself turn away from the crowd. She wasn't going to linger hopefully.

It didn't matter that her back was to the room—she could hear Jennifer's approach. Within the hubbub of conversations there was a rising note of surprise and interest. A face most people recognized from a satiric Super Bowl ad and countless cosmetics and clothing commercials was catching their attention. Then hushed whispers rippled through the crowd, getting closer and closer. She ought to think of it as the approach of danger, not the precursor to the sound of sheets rustling and cries in the night.

"Suzanne?"

She turned, remembered all over again how much she liked how tall Jennifer was, and knew nothing had changed. While she herself was sweating under her jacket Jennifer walked like it was sex. "I wasn't sure you were serious."

"I wasn't sure you were either. Thank you." Jennifer took the cocktail glass and sipped. Then her full, deep red lips curved in what seemed like a genuine smile. "Club soda and lime. You remembered."

I want to hate her, Suzanne thought. I'd be better off. "For old times' sake."

"Is that what this is?"

"We're just old acquaintances catching up."

She stirred her drink with a tiny plastic stick shaped like a sword. "What shall we talk about?"

"Politics."

Jennifer gave her a look worthy of Annemarie at her most scathing. "Seriously?"

"Then you pick."

"The rise of Firewire and peer-to-peer networking?"

Suzanne couldn't help a bark of laughter. "Do you even know what that means?"

"Of course I don't, but I said it in a movie. It's the smartest line I've ever had and I got to wear a lab coat. It didn't close over my cleavage but it wasn't a bikini."

"I must have missed that one."

"You'll see a movie I'm in?"

"If my date picks it." Suzanne instantly regretted the words, but maybe it was good for Jennifer to know she hadn't been pining.

"Ouch." Jennifer didn't show a reaction beyond the tightening of her fingers around the glass. "So you're seeing someone? The woman you're with?"

"That's Annemarie."

"Ah, I don't believe I've ever seen a picture of the power behind the throne."

She searched Jennifer's expression for sarcasm, but there was only studied, polite interest. Jennifer flicked her gaze toward the room and Suzanne did likewise. Two women had the new iPhone toy pointed their direction.

Her lips hardly moving, Jennifer asked, "Can those things record what we're saying?"

"At this distance they're taking pictures."

Jennifer's expression became fixed in a highly photogenic smile. "I really don't want to have this conversation with an audience."

"Are we having *this* conversation?"

"Would you like to? Be old acquaintances catching up?"

"That's not what I want at all." The admission escaped her with too much force.

Jennifer's drink trembled just enough for the ice cubes to clink against the glass. "We can't just pick up where we left off."

The two women were now consulting their phone displays, no doubt picking a picture to upload. She hoped the sunlight from the window made it murky. "Whatever we do, we need more privacy than this. I don't know how you stand it. The staring. I get my share, but it's a chosen audience. This is different."

"Means to an end. I am all about means to an end."

"And I'm not particularly useful."

"I wouldn't say that."

They shared a long look that began as wariness and ended with Suzanne holding her breath.

Jennifer was the first to look away, making a show of putting down the cocktail glass. "I'm only in town for a media blitz on this movie I'm in. My roles are tiny but they like to get the supermodel in front of the photographers. What else is new?" She rolled her eyes. "I'm leaving for LA tomorrow afternoon for an audition in an indie film. It's a small but highly respected production company. A leading dramatic role, so it would be a definite pace changer."

"Sounds promising."

"It could be. My agent sees it as a stepping stone. There's also far-off rumors of a damsel-in-distress love interest part in an action film—big budget, mainstream."

"It sounds like things are moving along for you then." Too slowly, Suzanne thought. It wasn't the way the old Jennifer had seemed to have it planned. Ten years just to get a hint of a sidekick girl role? Her face was known all over the world, but as a model and not an actor. How long would she keep trying with so little to show for it?

Flickers in the lights signaled the impending end of intermission.

Jennifer's facade cracked slightly around her eyes. "You remembered my drink. Do you remem—"

"I haven't forgotten anything. Are you seeing anyone?"

"I'm seen with people, but not seeing anyone."

"Tonight?"

"The production company's media tour assistant found these tickets. Part of being visible while they're paying the expenses. At least it's a very good play."

"I'm sure it is. I've been distracted." The lights flickered again but Suzanne was certain Jennifer had shivered. "Come for a drive with me."

Jennifer gave her a glance that held a simmer of panic. "Is that a euphemism?"

"Do you want it to be?"

"No." She swallowed. "Yes. You are so unfair."

"What did I do?"

"You—" Jennifer turned a finger stab at Suzanne's necktie into smoothing a nonexistent wrinkle. "You. Looking so... You."

Take it and run, a little voice inside said. She hasn't forgotten you at all and that was what you said would make you happy, right? You know other women will treat you better. "We could leave now or after the play."

"Now." Jennifer muttered a low curse. "Now. I shouldn't." She fumbled a newish Blackberry out of her small turquoise purse that was a shock of color in contrast to the vivid red dress. "Let me just tell the assistant she's on her own."

"She won't worry?" The crowd had thinned out and they were almost alone, except for the curious bartender and a few stragglers looking over their shoulders.

"No, it'll give her a chance to relax."

Suzanne likewise tapped out a message, sent it, and had an immediate answer back: *You stupid shit. I knew it.*

"You have the strangest look on your face," Jennifer observed.

She looked up from Annemarie's message. "I owe someone her favorite barbecued Shirayaki roll." She looked down at the black stilettos that no amount of money would ever induce her to wear. "Can you walk in those or should I fetch the car and pick you up in front of the building?"

Jennifer took a half step back, dripping with attitude. "Did you seriously just ask me if I know how to walk in my Louboutins?"

"I know you can work your shoes. Do you want those red soles to touch pavement for more than a few steps? I suspect not."

The attitude made a lightning change into a smile of concession. "You're right."

"I'll be downstairs at the main doors in about five minutes."

The wait for the valet was spent mentally agreeing with Annemarie and calling herself names. She half-hoped Jennifer didn't show. This was madness.

Jennifer was waiting at the curb as Suzanne brought the car around to the front of the theater. A security guard almost hurt himself getting to the passenger door before Jennifer touched it and Jennifer repaid him with a smile more easy and genuine than any Suzanne had received so far.

"I knew it would be a BMW," Jennifer said.

"It's small and easy to park."

"Why did you drive at all? They don't have cabs in San Francisco? Or do all those hills make it impossible to walk anywhere?"

"I live in Santa Cruz, south of San Jose, but not as far as Monterey. The office is what's here in the city. I'd take you to visit the office, but it's profoundly boring to look at. It does have a spectacular view and that's about it."

"Let's not then."

"If it was midsummer we could see the sunset from Twin Peaks, but it's just about done at this time of year." She turned in the direction of the southbound freeway.

"It's already chilly in New York at night. Why Santa Cruz?"

"The quiet. A long beach to walk on. Near enough to my family. The escape from some of the light pollution. When I'm lazy there's a helicopter service from the closest airport."

"Wow. Living large."

"Just a way to get from point A to point B sometimes. Where shall we go?"

"Show me the beach."

"The beach it is."

Jennifer added quietly, "This is a bad idea."

"I know."

CHAPTER TWENTY-THREE

The cool autumn night air was everything Suzanne loved about San Francisco. Breathing it in was cleansing and relaxing. Or would have been if Jennifer hadn't been seated next to her. She wound through the streets in the direction of Highway 1 because it was a stunning drive even at night. It gave her time to think better of what might happen later. Was she really going to take Jennifer to her home?

At the main stoplight in Half Moon Bay she triggered the convertible top. "I think we're far enough away from the bright lights that no one will recognize you. Traffic will be very light from here on out."

Jennifer had found a scarf in her handbag and was wrapping it over her hair. "Am I smelling the ocean?"

"You are. I pull off south of here sometimes to think."

"I can picture you doing that."

Suzanne pointed upward.

Jennifer let out a little gasp. "Look at those stars! I see what you mean. The moon is beautiful tonight too. Nearly full."

Don't look at her, Suzanne thought. *You really don't need to remember her face bathed in moonlight.*

With the heat set to high and blasting onto their feet, it wasn't too cold in the car, especially at the slower speeds that the twisting, winding highway demanded. Raising her voice to be heard she said, "I should have offered to stop for something hot before we left Half Moon Bay. There's nothing out here but beaches and nurseries. In the spring the orchards and flowers are stunning."

"I had no idea anyplace in California was this deserted. I thought there was a Starbucks on every corner. Except in Yosemite and Death Valley. I've done photo shoots in both and believe me, there's no Starbucks. Which is as it should be, I suppose." Jennifer had adopted a light, mocking tone that Suzanne decided was probably for the best.

"Most of this shoreline is protected from development. I wanted a house on the ocean and finally found one in Santa Cruz. It's very small and built before restrictions went in but each new owner has tried to make the most of the space available. You could buy ten houses in most of the rest of the country for the price I paid."

"It feels like we're driving out to the Hamptons, though the constellations aren't as easy to see. Not like this."

Suzanne resisted the urge to look upward. The highway was mostly deserted, but night creatures like possums occasionally wandered across the road. She'd even seen a coyote once, much later at night, near where the highway left the shore and dipped close to the wooded foothills. "It would have been faster to stay inland. But it's about as generic as it gets. Office complexes, fast food."

They continued talking about nothing that mattered until Suzanne coasted to a stop on an overlook. The engine's hum faded and was replaced by the rumble of waves crashing on rocks. The faint aroma of salt and kelp hung in the night air. "I love to stop here. I don't often get the chance."

Jennifer had closed her eyes. "This is pure therapy. Last year in a movie I did all of my lines in a wet swimsuit splashing around in a shallow pool in front of a green screen as eventual shark bait. It looked like I was frolicking at Coney Island but it was a backlot in Culver City. I still feel like I haven't gotten the sour salty chlorine smell out of my nose."

Terrific. Now she was picturing Jennifer in a swimsuit. "That doesn't sound like much fun."

"It wasn't, but the movie was a hit. A critic even declared me 'surprisingly competent.'"

"What an asshole thing to say."

"That's one of my kindest reviews so far."

Given how Jennifer had tossed her aside without a word, Suzanne supposed she should feel vindicated somehow, but Jennifer's simmering bitterness was disheartening to hear. Somewhere during the past ten years her own rancor had eased. When she had thought of their past and the possibilities that had died before they'd even been given a chance to grow, she had at least hoped Jennifer was making her own dreams come true.

An inner voice whispered that maybe Jennifer was ready to choose something else. She tried to ignore it. Tried to tell herself that she didn't want to be Jennifer's fallback. She wanted to be a beautiful, accomplished woman's first choice. Or at least tied for first.

"I understand why you stopped seeing me." *Way to avoid a sensitive topic.*

Jennifer gestured toward the ocean with her chin without taking her gaze away from the deep, dark expanse. "Is the next stop Asia?"

"From here? Yes. You heard me, right?"

"I heard you. I am sorry for—cold turkey was easier."

"For you."

"Yes, for me. I pretended you were a novel I'd read and lost so I couldn't go back. I know that sounds mean. Maybe it is. I was twenty and I needed for it not to be real. What did I know?"

"You're older now."

"I am decades older—on the inside."

"I remember Manhattan word problem math. You're like sixty now, right?"

At last she got a sidelong glance. "You're richer of course. No surprise there. More handsome than ever."

It rang a chill bell of warning inside her. She was never going to be able to stop at this spot again if... If what, she could hear Annemarie demanding. *She breaks your heart again, which you know she's going to do?*

She flopped about for a change of subject. "Do you ever have fun?"

"Yes." Jennifer seemed to relax. "Yes, some things are really fun. I learned how to play baccarat in Monaco. Spain is so beautiful.

Let's see..." She tipped her face up to the stars again. "When they were filming that really bad King Arthur movie I used my breaks in Sherwood Forest to read the script of *The Adventures of Robin Hood* and I read lots of Shakespeare. Major highlight—a bit part on a sitcom let me help Anne Bancroft into her coat." Her voice trailed away for a moment. "All my good and bad stories revolve around work."

"Tell me about Spain. Somehow I've never been."

"So colorful and warm. The people are lovely. I was there for two weeks. It was supposed to be three days, but there was a strike and the set was closed. So I went to the coast. Everything was oranges and olives and sunshine. It's a place where you ask yourself why you let stress into your life. Why, when you can eat a peach and look at the stars? I could model one month a year and spend the rest of it on the beach in Spain."

"But you don't."

"Well, you could not work for the rest of your life and come here every single day, right?"

"But I don't."

"Right. Instead... Another audition." The bitterness was back.

"Another investment to make." Unlike Jennifer, however, the prospect of work for Suzanne meant risk, failure, and success all wrapped together. They'd been fortunate backing more winners than losers, especially in the turbulent market.

"What are you doing these days?" Jennifer finally faced her, face mostly in shadows, but her eyes were luminous in the moonlight.

How to explain how big CommonTech had become? The brainchild she and Annemarie had birthed after the successful management of their first merger was growing in ways they hadn't expected. "Our latest investment is in solar grid management software for residential purposes. Another is three different clients all pursuing digital health record management, which is both lucrative and in high demand. One of the things I'm really proud of is our investment in connecting small digital memory with the emerging cloud storage services—"

Jennifer's lips were warm and impossibly softer than Suzanne remembered. Her hands were caught between Jennifer and the console or she would have done damage to Jennifer's dress.

"Was it something I said?" she asked as their lips parted.

"You and your vocabulary." Jennifer brushed her lips against the corner of Suzanne's mouth. "It's extremely sexy."

"Arithmetic overflow? Locality of reference? Virtual memory paging?"

Jennifer laughed against her mouth and they kissed again. Heat coursed through Suzanne's arms and chest. She untangled one arm so she could pull Jennifer more tightly against her and let the scent of Jennifer's perfume fill her head.

Jennifer wound an arm around Suzanne's neck and let out a gasp as Suzanne wrapped Jennifer's hair around her hand and tipped her head back. Images of the last time they had been together, wild and desperate, played vividly across her mind.

They could be that way again, couldn't they?

Headlights swept over the car as a truck rumbled along the highway. Suzanne hadn't even heard it coming. Her ears had been full of Jennifer's ragged breath and her own pounding heart.

It was no use trying to get her other arm free, however. Between the low-slung seats and the high dividing console there was no room. Jennifer let out a surprised *ouch* when Suzanne's shoulder caught her on the chin.

"As you can see, I didn't buy this car for making out." She caressed Jennifer's arm and realized her skin was cold. "I'll put the roof up. You're chilled."

"I was, a little. But not now. How much further to your house?"

She started the car and raised her voice above the hydraulics as the ragtop lifted, stretched and locked into place. "About fifteen minutes with no traffic."

Earlier they hadn't been able to talk about anything beyond the sights out the window, and now there was only silence heavy with pent-up desire. The highway widened as they reached the long, curving Santa Cruz Beach and Boardwalk. The amusement park still showed some lights. The beach was illuminated by the full moon and the white crest of surf was visible against the pale sand.

"How lovely."

"Do you want to walk on the beach? It'll be very chilly tonight."

"No. That's not what I'm in the mood for." She lifted the back of Suzanne's hand to her lips. "I'd forgotten how strong your hands are."

"Are you trying to dissolve me into the seat?" She braked slowly to a stop at the last light before she would turn off the highway toward the water.

"Do you want me to?"

She extracted her hand before making the final turn. "Yes. But I'd also like to open the gate. It's just along here." The narrow street turned to parallel the beach and Suzanne tapped the remote to open the security gate across the tiny driveway. The garage door slid up. "Is this what you expected?"

"When I got up this morning none of this was in my plans."

With the garage door closed behind them, Suzanne realized it was too late to find answers to the questions that had hammered in her brain the last few miles. If they had just wanted to have sex, why hadn't she picked a hotel and ordered room service as she did for her infrequent encounters with other women? It kept things casual and fun. Why bring Jennifer here, her personal, intimate hideaway? She felt exposed.

Jennifer opened her door first. Her candy apple-red dress was pure crimson in the overhead light. Suzanne found her wits, marveled at her racing heart and sweaty palms. This again? Would Jennifer always make her feel like it was the first time?

They met in front of the car, the steps to the house just beyond. "You look intoxicating," Suzanne murmured.

Jennifer slipped a hand inside Suzanne's jacket and leaned close. "Do you want me to leave the shoes on?"

Suzanne felt a primal growl begin deep in her chest. She jerked Jennifer into her arms for a bruising kiss and Jennifer responded by raking her nails down Suzanne's back. "Let's start right here then."

Jennifer's dress had no obvious zipper, so Suzanne pushed it up to run her fingertips across the tops of Jennifer's stockings. Jennifer's hands were suddenly on hers and Suzanne paused. "I'm sorry. I was rough."

"I want your hands here." Jennifer's voice was taut with desire. She leaned back on the hood of the car and pulled Suzanne's palm between her legs.

The heat and wet she could feel through Jennifer's panties knocked the breath out of her. The garage was cold from the sea-chilled wind, but Jennifer was a radiant fire. She pushed the fabric aside, tried to tease. Jennifer's gasp sent her vision into silver and black. Her fingers were slick in a matter of moments, and she slid inside Jennifer, remembering how much they had both liked this.

Her arms braced behind her, Jennifer locked gazes with Suzanne, her hips lifting in response. "Please."

"Are you strong enough?"

"You know I am."

"Show me." Suzanne leaned into Jennifer to share a panting kiss. She groaned as Jennifer hooked one leg around her hips. "This is just the beginning."

"Prove it—don't you dare stop."

"Your dress is going to get ruined."

"I'm stronger than it is." Jennifer yanked her other shoulder bare and Suzanne leaned into her, burying her face in the soft, inviting neck.

Jennifer's perfume was like a drug she couldn't get enough of. Without conscious thought she pushed a little deeper and Jennifer's supporting arm gave out. Suzanne covered her body with her own and reveled in the surrender in Jennifer's eyes, her limp arms and the eager rise of her hips. They shared a surge of energy that sent sparkling pulses behind Suzanne's eyes.

Jennifer panted against her mouth in desperate, challenging pleas. "You make me like this."

"You let yourself be like this with me. There? Is that what you need? For me to touch you right there?"

She brought one knee up on the car to help keep her balance as she held Jennifer down. Jennifer's hair had tumbled across her face and shoulders. Suzanne closed her eyes to focus on the slick, wet flesh and muscle pulsing against her fingertips.

"Yes, Suzanne, yes. There..." Jennifer gasped in a voice thick with tears.

Alarmed, Suzanne managed to get a glimpse of Jennifer's face but saw only passionate disbelief in a rising storm of release. One of Jennifer's heels was grazing her thigh, but she ignored it. Her reward was a long cry of ecstatic pleasure that rose and fell as Jennifer shuddered underneath her.

Only when Jennifer had begun to quiet did Suzanne realize she had matched Jennifer's cry with an elated one of her own. There was not one thing, not one single thing in the last ten years that had been as satisfying.

The garage was suddenly very quiet.

A low laugh escaped Jennifer. "Your suit isn't going to survive this either."

"I have another one."

She brushed her hair out of her eyes. "I bet you—oh, do that…"

Suzanne let out a low laugh as she brushed her palm between Jennifer's legs again. "I will. Let's go get comfortable."

They were both unsteady as they stood. Suzanne shook a disbelieving head at the BMW—who knew? She pushed away the thought that if Jennifer left again she would hate this car.

Jennifer was clutching her dress to her breasts. "I can't seem to keep my clothes on around you."

"Am I supposed to complain about that?"

"Could I perhaps take a shower? I have sticky stuff on to keep the dress in place."

"It didn't work."

"It's not designed to resist hot, handsome women."

"That makes me happy." Suzanne led the way through the laundry and into the living room. "The loft in New York was larger than this house, but location, location, location. There's two bedrooms, a den and a backyard with a view. All the essentials."

She turned up the heat and conquered one last hesitation. If she looked at Jennifer, did all the things she knew they would both enjoy, would she ever find this house relaxing again? Finding peace had been a long, hard haul.

But there was no stopping now. Even if this was the same path they'd walked before, there was no way off of it that she could make herself think about, not with the scent of Jennifer on her hands and body, and washing through her brain.

"Which way is the shower?"

"Over here—but there's something I'd like to do first." She sank to her knees in front of Jennifer, reveling in the faint salt now on Jennifer's skin.

Jennifer gasped and the dress fell around Suzanne in a pool of scarlet and silk.

CHAPTER TWENTY-FOUR

Jennifer stirred in the night, aware of Suzanne's arm around her. Unlike that last night in New York, her first thought wasn't how to escape from safety and warmth and run headlong toward the cold and lonely world that held all her dreams. She snuggled back and felt something inside her uncoil.

Suzanne's quiet breathing in her ear was accompanied by the subtle thunder of rising and falling waves. Being in Suzanne's arms was impossibly like being on a beach in Spain—no stress, no worries, just air and warmth. No passport or long travel hours. All she needed was…this.

Moonlight poured through the open curtains in a luminous silver glow. She knew the ocean must be gorgeous under the moon, but didn't want to leave the peace and warmth to see.

A soft kiss on the back of her neck gave her other ideas.

"You awake?" Suzanne very gently cupped one hand around the curve of Jennifer's hip.

"Yes, just barely. Enjoying the moonlight."

"A couple times a year the angle is like this. Like a silver shower."

"It's magical. Directors and lighting gurus spend hours trying to fake that."

Suzanne's lips nuzzled at the nape of her neck. "You love making movies, don't you?"

"When I'm working I'm happy. I just don't work enough. I mean acting, not modeling. I'm in plenty of demand for that." She arched her neck against Suzanne's touch. "My new agent says I should stop modeling and focus just on acting so people take me seriously. He has lots of other ideas…"

"But?"

The wheels in her brain were waking up. "I'm trying not to be desperate. I don't know if I can do them. Visibility stunts and that new Tweeter thing—"

She felt Suzanne smile against her neck. "Twitter."

"That. If you put provocative things online you get buzz and then you get parts. Supposedly. I can hire someone to do it for me but it's a rabbit hole. Once you cooperate with the blogging media machine…"

"It's a rabbit hole you don't get to climb back out of."

"Yeah." She rolled over to face her. "If I have to go to those lengths then I'm really not who I thought I'd be. Who wants to be famous through tricks, not talent?"

The moonlight softened all the angles of Suzanne's face. "Lots of people, from the looks of it."

"I don't think I want to be that person."

"Are any of us who we ever thought we'd be?"

Jennifer had planned on being Lauren Bacall by now. "Back in King of Prussia I made big dreams."

"Cupertino, just over the hills from here, I did too. But dreams aren't always rooted in reality."

"Where would you be if you let a little thing like what people thought was real get in your way?"

"I think there's a difference between dreaming up something new out of what is already there to work with versus creating outlandish fantasies about the future and being perpetually disappointed when it doesn't happen."

"I'm being outlandish?"

Suzanne's tone sharpened slightly. "I didn't say that. I was talking about me. Like how I built a dream about being known for my tech savvy and ability to make ideas real, doing what I'm doing right now. I am living that dream. But that dream also had a moment when I'm in a fancy car and pull up to a red carpet and it's a party for me and my high school science teacher is in the crowd literally green with envy. He was a sexist ass. In that dream I either make sure he can't come inside or I'm gracious and let him come in. I haven't decided that bit. But either way I get to say, 'You said I should leave the hard stuff to the boys, remember?'"

Jennifer kissed the side of Suzanne's mouth. "Sounds like a pretty good dream."

"But it's not realistic. It's giving that guy more than he's owed, for starters. And that kind of thing really does only happen in movies and the fact that I can't make my pretty damned good life into a movie starring me shouldn't make me disappointed with myself."

"When did you become a philosopher?" She nuzzled Suzanne's shoulder.

"When the woman I was crazy about dumped me."

Jennifer sighed. "I wondered when that would come up."

"I'm sorry. I didn't mean to say that."

"If not now, you would have eventually. I was mean. And scared. Quitting you seemed easier than weaning."

"I get that now."

"I shouldn't be here either."

Suzanne brushed her lips over Jennifer's. "Are you sure about that?"

Jennifer wanted to fall hard into Suzanne's mouth again. She pulled away slightly, trying at least to put her fears into words. "Nothing has changed. I'm closer than ever to what I want from life and further away too. Every year is a setback, time is an enemy. Every last little thing is about how you look. If you look right, then they'll decide if you have talent. I'm still waiting for the right people, anyone with some parts to cast, to think I have talent. It's worse than modeling, where at least a sense of style and confidence are valued too."

"Everybody is judged by how they look in acting. It's a brutal profession."

Jennifer sat up with a sigh, pulling the sheet around her. "Yes, it's just that *most* men aren't put through the same rigid standards that nearly *all* women are put through. Men with beer guts and blotchy skin get plenty of parts, big and small. They get work and opportunities. Women with muffin tops or wrinkles don't even get cast for store clerks or friend of a friend unless being supposedly unattractive is the point. Then she's the girl who gets killed that nobody misses or the female friend who can't possibly be a distracting love interest for the male lead. A director can decide that a guy who rolled out of bed and put on a hat is just the right look for the sidekick with a heart of gold. For romantic leads a man is getting past it when he's pushing sixty. For a woman it's thirty. Which is right where I am."

Suzanne's hand was warm on her hip, like sunshine. It would be so easy to push away reality and melt into her embrace again.

"I'm sorry," Jennifer went on. "I'm not very good company when I'm like this. I get like this before big auditions. I imagined we would meet again and you'd have invented some new way to put the world's knowledge on a potato chip and I'd have an Oscar in each hand."

"Silicon, not potato." She laughed at Jennifer's swat in the shoulder.

"Irony, okay? My dreams about you are coming true for you. Meanwhile—"

"Did you really dream about me?" She gathered Jennifer to her, one hand slipping around to stroke her backside.

"Why does it feel so good when you do that?"

"I'm magic."

"I knew that." The chiming bell of her own desire rang sharply through her mind. Like a warm sun, she wanted to feel the magic as deep as her bones.

For the first time it didn't feel as if she were losing herself in Suzanne's touch. She didn't feel swept away by their overwhelming desire. It wasn't like the few times when loneliness had made her choose brief hours of intimacy with a guy she was fairly sure she'd never see again. It was easy to reach a very quick we-both-get-what-we-want situation with men.

She was finding something else as she yielded to Suzanne's kisses. Pleasure mixed with laughter, surrender melded with intimacy, even roughness softened by a tenderness that quelled any sense of fear. Except for the fear that was in a place Suzanne couldn't touch, the fear that it was temporary. Like a beach in Spain, only for a while.

Suzanne drew Jennifer's arms over her head. "Let me."

"Yes." She loved the feeling of Suzanne's lips on her breasts. The light trail of her tongue followed by the brush of teeth against her nipple sent a shiver through her.

Suzanne's laugh was full of easy pleasure. "You do like that."

"I think we're clear on that, aren't we?"

"Abundantly."

"You don't want me to act all virginal and uncertain?"

Suzanne raised her head and met Jennifer's gaze. "I don't want you to act with me at all."

She swallowed. "I know. It's just—you feel so good."

"We're not supposed to enjoy sex. Women aren't, I mean." Suzanne shook her head and leaned up to kiss Jennifer softly. "The fact that you do, and that you're not afraid to show me what you need is what I want from you. That makes it very, very, very powerful for me." She punctuated each *very* with a kiss.

There were no words for a long time after that. Jennifer thought the moonlight was fading and she might have heard the cry of an early rising sea bird as she slipped back into sleep.

CHAPTER TWENTY-FIVE

Suzanne found English muffins in the freezer and some cheddar that was edible once she chopped off the blue edges. Jennifer had scampered to the shower after a shy hello from the kitchen doorway.

The large bay windows were showing off a stunning morning on her little piece of the coast. The fog was still far offshore and a brisk wind was whipping the waves into frothy white lines. Sea foam blew across the pale sand below the cliff. Her small backyard ended in an abrupt drop of about twenty feet to the beach below and from several angles there was nothing but surf and sky. Not even the low, wrought-iron fence got in the way of a beautiful day.

Jennifer reappeared in the clothes Suzanne had put out for her. Her shabby sweatpants and a worn Stanford tee had never looked so stunningly awesome. "Thanks for these. Your socks are just a little big, but they're warm."

She grinned as Jennifer wiggled one foot, the toe of the wool sock flopping with a couple of inches to spare. "Coffee?"

"God yes."

She gestured with her chin. "Mugs are up there."

Jennifer helped herself to coffee and added a healthy slug of milk. "I wonder why I feel so hungry and shaky this morning?"

"I haven't the faintest clue. Were you up late? Sleep poorly?"

"I slept really well, as a matter of fact. When I slept. I love your bathroom. The shower was a religious experience."

"Remodeling to make use of every inch."

"You're right, this place is half the size of that loft you were in. How did you squeeze into it?"

"I lived in San Francisco, up on Russian Hill, for a couple of years. It was pretty chaotic. Deals were flying so fast it was numbing." The sliced muffin halves popped up but they were too light so she set them through another cycle in the toaster. "Life became more predictable but the workload was intense. I wasn't home for weeks at a time and I decided I wanted home to be as alluring as it could be so I would make being home a priority. Because you have to go barefoot to stay grounded, as my mom always said." She swallowed hard, finding it as difficult as usual to mention her mother.

"I'm sorry," Jennifer said. "About your mother. I hadn't realized—I saw the black ribbon on the photograph."

"This place came on the market while she was sick. She loved the beach. I cleared every afternoon I could to bring her here for the evening. My dad would drive down after his classes to pick her up. Until she couldn't manage the drive. Cancer sucks."

Jennifer's head rested on Suzanne's shoulder for a moment in wordless comfort.

She cleared her throat. "Anyway, when my priority became to get a place near the ocean where my mom could spend peaceful time, I realized that I had a lot of stuff I really didn't need. Collectibles are in storage, though I keep a few favorites here."

"So this is ideal."

"Close. Lately I've been hamstrung by the poor connectivity. This whole pocket of houses has serious construction restrictions because it's so close to the water, so they haven't laid fiber optics yet, and satellite dishes are forbidden." She slid the toasted muffin slices onto a plate. "I can practically tell when a neighbor boots up."

"One of the hazards of getting away from it all is, well, getting away from it all, I guess." Jennifer had gone to the windows that framed the far end of the living room to look out over the ocean. "So connectivity is the big thing in tech these days?"

"It'll always be a big thing. There's no end to the money to be made when you can offer someone an improvement in speed. But the most secure thing to have, I've found, is partnerships. You can invent something new, but you can't get it out to the world on your own. You need to know people with money *and* with experience. But you also have to avoid the assholes. Like gropey photographers."

Jennifer's smile was rueful. "And producers with parts you can only audition for in their bedroom. Creeps and liars are everywhere."

"Exactly. I think who you work with matters as much as why you're working together. Everybody has to agree on mutual goals or somebody ends up feeling taken advantage of. Some people see it as a battle and live to go to war. I'm focused on the outcome."

She added the tub of whipped butter and a jar of her favorite marmalade to her plate. She nodded at the other plate with a knife and cubes of the cheese. "Could you grab that one? Let's enjoy the sunshine."

Jennifer fumbled with the sliding glass door lock, then slid it open. "Whoa!"

A gust of wind threatened to whisk the plate out of Suzanne's hand and scatter the contents across the living room, but she'd been ready for it. "Go to the right. I'll get the door."

"This is gorgeous." Jennifer had quickly scooted behind the plexiglass windbreak that sheltered a redwood table and chairs. She was darned adorable in floppy socks, Suzanne decided.

"I could lie and say every morning is like this, but only a few of them are. You brought sunshine with you." She retrieved beach towels from the tightly sealed plastic tub under the table and quickly dried the chairs and table top of the salty morning dew. She selected another towel and draped it around Jennifer's shoulders as she kissed her on the tip of her ear.

"Thank you. What a fab idea—the barriers. It feels like I can see all the way to China."

"It's great for brunch with my dad, though he's been known to cancel if the weather isn't sunny. I come out here even when it's misty and damp. It's very quiet."

Jennifer reached across the table to lightly touch her hand. "Your dad is doing okay?"

It had been two years now, but when her mother was alive she'd stopped at their house at least once a month for a home-cooked meal and just to talk. Now she found her dad only at the university, as if the house where she'd grown up was no longer home for him. "He's doing okay, though he seems a little lost to me sometimes. How is your family?"

"Well enough to ask for money a couple times a year. I send checks instead of visiting and everyone is happy."

Even though she'd known that Jennifer had been more or less on her own in the world since her teens, it was a situation Suzanne didn't really understand. Between her older brothers' toughen-up-the-girl ethos and her parents' happy scholar-cum-hippie lifestyle, she'd had a supportive and generous safety net all of her life.

After a lengthy swallow of coffee Jennifer sighed happily. "Can we get down to the beach?"

"Sure. Do you have time this morning to take a walk?"

"If you can get me back to San Francisco by noon or so."

She didn't mention the string of profanity-laden texts she'd gotten from Annemarie for postponing this morning's teleconferences. "No problem. When do you leave for Los Angeles?"

"Two thirty. Going into Pasadena, not LAX. The audition is at five thirty near UCLA, if that helps."

"I've done a guest lecture there. And after the audition?"

"An investors' party for the production company of the film I'm promoting. Tomorrow starts the media cattle call for that market. I answer the same questions for different reporters. Over and over."

"Really?"

"I know, who does that on Saturday? Apparently they all do these days. But LA is the last place I have to do press days. I wrap that up on Sunday afternoon."

Suzanne looked her next question, but didn't put it into words.

Jennifer licked a dab of marmalade off her fingertip. "I start a photo shoot on Wednesday evening in Vancouver."

Suzanne smiled. "That means you have Monday and Tuesday to find something to do with yourself."

Jennifer blinked at her very slowly. "I can't think of a thing, can you?"

CHAPTER TWENTY-SIX

The audition had been simply wonderful, and Jennifer's elation buoyed her through the queue of entertainment reporters who asked the same questions nonstop for four hours on Saturday and another five on Sunday.

What was it like to be in a scene with the dreamy leading man?

How did you take time out from modeling to be in a movie?

Who is your favorite designer right now?

Who are you wearing today?

Over and over and over.

None of that bothered her after the assistant at Ryan Productions had called to ask her back for another audition, and had eagerly agreed when Jennifer had suggested first thing Monday morning. It meant staying over in LA another night, but Suzanne had understood.

"Just come to the office when you get in," she'd said when Jennifer had called. "I have two important meetings I can't change first thing, but by lunchtime I'm free."

The movie studio's assistant had happily gone back to New York immediately after the final press interview, leaving Jennifer with no one to explain her schedule to. The private car service she'd ordered before leaving LA was waiting at the security egress at San Francisco, and now the driver was trundling her luggage to the parking garage. A quick call to her agent and no one would wonder where she was until Wednesday morning.

"It went great," she told Phillip. He'd only been her agent for a scant six months, but he had gotten her more auditions than her old ones. T&T still handled her modeling assignments, but if she took Phillip's advice and stopped modeling, it would sever all ties with their agency. It would be hard to bid them goodbye—they'd been very good to her. But the clock was ticking. She had plenty of savings to live on. "They're looking for someone who can be underestimated by the audience."

"A card that can be played only once in an actor's career. It's flattering," he assured her. "That means they know your work and are looking to build the picture around a surprise performance."

"It's not exactly making me happy that they see me as a somewhat unknown."

"You live in New York which means you don't exist. The whole concept for the part plays in with our plans for your brand."

She still didn't care for how smug-sticky his voice sounded, but work was work. The part had real meat to it, a chance to show more than tears or boobs, and he'd persuaded someone to give her the chance. "I promise to look at that packet you sent."

"Ticktock, Jenny dear. You need a social media presence and package. Let's get people talking about you, and looking to you to tell them what to think about movies and music and fashion."

"I thought we were going to play down modeling."

"We are. But you can't let go of the fact that you've seen more fashion and fashion-makers than nearly any woman your age. You're gorgeous, let's make an entire generation think they just *have* to be like you."

Phillip's advice was echoing in her ears as the car left the airport. Was that what it would take to become a name that was always brought up in a casting discussion? If she gave up her hard-won place in the modeling world she'd lose the steady good press in those circles. La Lamont walked last in fashion shows now, and she knew that at least in part she had the Monique DuMars of the fashion world to thank for it. Who did she know in entertainment journalism? Nobody. A situation the Phillip Questor Agency was supposed to fix.

The sky directly overhead was bright with the sun of early afternoon, but ahead of them it looked like the fog bank towering over the hills was going to engulf the area within a few hours. She hoped she didn't regret her choice of clothes. The short, form-fitting skirt and jacket in vivid lemon drop yellow had been perfect for LA's eighty degrees. The cotton-satin blend, however, was not up to San Francisco's damp autumn chill. The Victoria's Secret underneath was of no help either.

Suzanne would find a way to keep her warm, of that she had no doubt. Even when she'd been doing all those interviews she'd been reliving the night with Suzanne, a distraction that had never happened before. She couldn't believe she wanted more of the passion, and even more of the tender morning that had followed. What could be wrong with wanting to start more days in a cozy hideaway, just being...people?

Unsure what Suzanne's plans were, she paid the driver to park in the lot below the skyscraper and to keep her luggage with him until she called. She didn't want to stroll through Suzanne's office with suitcases. The honk and roar of the busy street was muffled as she crossed the glossy, pristine lobby. The path to the elevators was blocked by the reception desk staffed by polite but no-nonsense guards.

As she allowed a search of her handbag, the guard broke protocol to whisper that she loved Jennifer's shoes. "I wouldn't last five minutes in a pair like that but they are really beautiful."

"Thank you. You're right, they're not comfortable." She'd changed out of the lower heeled pumps she'd worn to the audition to the Manolo stilettos because, well, Suzanne seemed to like them on her.

When the elevator opened on the thirty-third floor she stepped out into a nondescript space flanked by closed doors with security keypads. Its beige chill was at odds with the hint of pizza and popcorn in the air.

A buzzer sounded and the double doors to her left swung open. Glossy black tile led to a walnut and glass reception area where a waiflike, dark-skinned young man in an exquisitely paired Jos A Banks sweater and tie rose to greet her. His puppy-brown eyes gobbled her up from shoes to suit to indigo-black princess braids that swept her hair back from her temples. She got the impression that if asked he'd promptly reply, "Chanel, Milan Summer, 2006."

"Ms. Lamont, uh…How can I help you?"

She slid her white-framed sunglasses off her nose and tucked them in her handbag. "Ms. Mason is expecting me."

"Of course. One moment." He tapped rapidly at his desk phone and said into his headset, "Jennifer Lamont is here to see Ms. Mason." After listening briefly he said to her, "Someone will be right out," and limited himself to quick glances in her direction.

Behind him was a translucent wall of architect's glass blocks, inset with COMMONTECH and the corporate logo. Through the blocks she could see glass-framed offices lining the walls with a large array of cubicles in groups of four and six. A moving form solidified as it came closer and then Jennifer could tell it was the formidable Annemarie.

They'd never spoken, but she knew that Suzanne and Annemarie were close. Therefore, she assumed that Annemarie knew all about Jennifer's disappearing act in New York a decade ago. Her breaking things off had left Suzanne and Annemarie to run that merger that Suzanne had been so excited about, and had no doubt added to their fortunes. So really, Annemarie should be grateful, shouldn't she?

It took one stiff, fiercely forced smile to assure Jennifer that Annemarie didn't see it that way.

"Suzanne is on a call, but she asked that someone take you to the conference room."

"How nice of you to volunteer."

"This way." Annemarie turned on her booted heel, leaving Jennifer to follow at a quick pace.

When the first head popped up behind one of the frosted glass and dark wood partition walls Jennifer gave the sandy-haired man a wave. More heads, three-quarters of them male, suddenly appeared. Annemarie looked over her shoulder and caught Jennifer winking.

"Don't make me turn a hose on all of you," Annemarie muttered just loudly enough to make those nearest disappear again.

The premises were considerably more corporate than Jennifer had expected. She'd been envisioning pizza boxes and empty cans of Red Bull. The general attire was California casual but not too casual. There were no suits at all, and jackets seemed optional. Polo shirts instead of T-shirts, khakis instead of jeans. There was no heavy metal blasting or trails of popcorn across the lavishly thick gray carpet. The steady babble of voices reminded her of a busy bank.

One of the office doors opened and a brush-cut Asian man in chinos backed out saying, "I'm not kidding. Your office is mine in two months. We're trading places!" He said it with humor and after a moment ducked a beanbag aimed at his head.

Annemarie made a reflexive attempt to bat it down but it sailed past her. Jennifer caught it single-handed before it could nail her right in the throat. Self-defense training had its uses.

She held out the velvet covered square. "I believe this was for you?"

The young man looked pale around the eyes as he approached Jennifer. He could have been any age between twelve and forty, but she was betting it was closer to twenty-five. She dropped the bag into the outstretched hand. "Good luck getting that office."

His mouth opened and closed and Jennifer was pretty sure he thought he'd spoken. Annemarie was shaking her head as she resumed her rapid pace toward the far corner of the floor.

Suzanne's expansive, glass-walled office was in the corner and Jennifer could see that she was on the phone, but she was following Jennifer's progress toward her with one hand smothering laughter. She must have seen the beanbag interplay. Annemarie opened the door next to Suzanne's office and lights automatically came on.

"Please make yourself comfortable. I'm sure Suzanne will be with you as soon as she can." Jennifer heard the double entendre in Annemarie's voice, but her back was turned as she snapped the blinds closed between the conference room and the rest of the floor. She let the door swing quietly shut, but instead of being on the other side she turned to face Jennifer, her back now to Suzanne who was staring at her desk as if trying to focus on her call.

Annemarie had style. Jennifer was impressed. Her short-cropped white hair was fringed with orange-tipped bangs. Her Dockers had razor creases in the front and she was firm-bodied with muscles that showed below her short-sleeve Alligator polo shirt. Jennifer was pretty sure that if Annemarie wanted to, she could bench press Jennifer quite easily.

Annemarie fixed her with an unflinching look that wasn't the least bit mitigated by the cat's-eye glasses she wore. "We have about sixty seconds, I'm guessing, so I'll make this brief. Break her heart again and I'll find you."

"I wasn't aware that I'd broken it before."

"How convenient."

Knowing that Suzanne could look up at any moment, Jennifer kept her expression as charming and open as possible. "Do you threaten all of Suzanne's friends?"

"You're special."

"Thank you, then."

"The pleasure is all mine." Annemarie made a graceful exit, the door snapping closed behind her.

Jennifer glanced at Suzanne who was now staring at her. She answered the inquiring look with a reassuring smile. Fashion was a sea of bitchery and it would take better than that to disturb her.

She leaned back in the chair like an art patron studying a favorite work. Suzanne looked like the boss in her black chinos, white shirt and, if she wasn't mistaken, light blue Bonobos sport coat. The look suited her, but was definitely conservative for the woman who'd given a bunch of high rollers kazoos to play with at a swanky party.

She blew her a kiss. Suzanne flushed and gave her a warning look.

She checked the buttons on her jacket and, oops, the top one came undone. It wasn't a suit that required a blouse, and the next stop was the Victoria's Secret. Suzanne closed her eyes, said something into the phone, then looked again. Jennifer made a show of checking her stocking. When she glanced at Suzanne she discovered her standing at the separating wall of glass, a note pressed to it.

She left her seat to read the tidy words: *Ms. Lamont are you trying to seduce me?*

Her laughter turned into an open-mouthed smile. After a long look that ran the length of Suzanne's body, Jennifer mouthed a slow *yes*.

Suzanne's gaze was caressing her through the glass. She thought about unbuttoning her jacket all the way, but no doubt if she did someone would walk in.

Suzanne crumpled the note and thrust it into her pocket. She turned away, but not before she'd focused for a long moment on Jennifer's lips.

The conference room felt stifling and small. Jennifer imagined a hundred different ways she and Suzanne could break the table.

CHAPTER TWENTY-SEVEN

Only the reminder to herself that she was the boss and had to set an example of decorum prevented Suzanne from kissing Jennifer the moment she was within reach. Of course, Jennifer was delightfully emitting every bit of sex appeal she had, and the looks they shared through the glass ought to have melted it. After asking about her flight, she said, "I want to show you something. It'll make you laugh."

"Lead on, Macduff."

Suzanne was amused as a few people had leaned out of their cubicles as she escorted Jennifer out of the conference room. "I'm sure it's the glow of your outfit."

"You have something against Chanel?"

Suzanne said under her breath, "I like Chanel against me just fine," and was gratified at the little noise Jennifer made.

It was her turn to whimper when Jennifer said, hardly moving her lips, "It won't be Chanel against you for long."

"Now that we have that settled, I'm feeling much better." When Jennifer didn't answer she glanced back and shook her head. Jennifer appeared to be in her element, returning the prairie dogging gawks with a wink or a finger wave. Suzanne was willing to bet that later there would be a discussion as to which of them had been on the receiving end of a *real* connection with the fashion goddess.

Deep down there was a squeaky little voice telling the high school version of herself that life certainly got better. That it was okay to vigorously parade her brains and challenge the boys-only science club. That college would be great, and she'd be able to fly all her flags. And maybe, just maybe, later on, she'd get the girl who wanted her, and only her, just the way she was.

She paused to give Jennifer a sidelong glance. "I'm not sure you should feed the wildlife. They'll lose all appetite for what's in their normal habitat."

"I've tried playing it as if I didn't notice when people look, but it's more fun to notice. And admiration from a safe distance is a kind of gift. I might as well say thank you."

"Also from a safe distance."

"Exactly."

She pushed open the door to the playroom. Jennifer laughed, just as Suzanne had known she would.

"Is that the same table we hauled across Manhattan?"

"No, it's bigger." She walked around the half-finished tableau of the Battle of Minas Tirith. She waved a hand at the diagrams pinned haphazardly to the wall. "I have no room for this at home, obviously. Anyone who wants to can take a break and add some pieces too."

"All the sorting is done." Jennifer tapped a bin full of tan corner thicks. "I won't be of any use."

"I have a better date planned, I hope." Suzanne tried not to mentally replay all the various ways she'd found Jennifer more than merely useful. Time for that later.

"That was a Class A date. Or so I was told." Jennifer broke off with a glance behind Suzanne.

Jacques was leaning in. "The valet is downstairs."

"Thanks. Good luck tomorrow night."

"The Good Lord knows I need it." He made a rapid departure back to reception.

To Jennifer's inquiring look, Suzanne said, "He's dancing in a fundraiser tomorrow. First time in full drag and he's nervous."

"I remember all too well my first runway. I felt as if the clothes were going to swallow me whole."

Suzanne picked up a freeform sculpture that might have been an Ent with death ray eyes and roots on fire. Someone had finished the largest of the Black Ships and it looked awesome. "I don't have the time for this, not like I used to."

Jennifer's voice was low and even. "Let's make the most of what time we can steal, then."

Suzanne heard the familiar warning bell. *This is just for now, geek girl.* One part of her told herself not to want what she was never going to have, but the rest of her brain wasn't listening.

On their way to the elevator they rounded a cubicle corner and Jennifer bumped into one of the brokers. His face immediately flamed and the man Suzanne knew as competent and articulate dissolved into a stammering adolescent right before her eyes.

Jennifer apologized. When he seemed unable to move out of her way Jennifer pinched the front of his corporate wear CommonTech polo shirt and pulled him gently aside. She stopped his spluttered apology by pressing a fingertip to his lips. "We'll always have Paris."

He laughed and said, "Sure," against her fingertip.

"*Casablanca,*" Suzanne murmured. Jennifer gave her a pleased nod, but Suzanne was left wondering if that was how she was around Jennifer too. She didn't want to be led around like a bemused rabbit and Jennifer looked very comfortable doing the leading. Annemarie thought that was already the truth.

But holy tennis balls, that jacket fit her like skin, and the long, long legs didn't stop all the way down to the floor. Jennifer's sex appeal was not something most mere mortals could ignore.

Suzanne keyed open the exit door and found Jennifer had diverted to Jacques' desk.

"For what it's worth," she was saying, "remember you're using the costume, it's not using you. It's not a mask, it's a tool."

"That's terrific advice," Jacques said. He waved and cupped his hands in a way that encompassed Jennifer. "If I can get a fraction of all that on stage, I will be very happy."

"I have faith in you." The elevator pinged and Jennifer left him with a smile over her shoulder as she hurried to rejoin Suzanne.

They were halfway to the ground when Jennifer said, "There are security cameras in the elevator, aren't there?"

"Yes."

"Damn."

"You're just going to have to wait."

She fixed Suzanne with the same look that had made it hard for Suzanne to keep track of the conversation on the phone, like she wasn't just imagining Suzanne naked, she was picturing her in a tangle of arms and legs and sweat and desire, complete with a soundtrack heavy on the bass. "So are you."

The elevator bristled with electricity that tightened all the places where she wanted Jennifer's touch. She was almost glad when the doors opened.

As Jacques had said, her BMW was waiting in the parking garage's loading zone, guarded by Suzanne's favorite valet. The bright-faced older woman, who chattered mostly in a language Suzanne had decided was Tagalog, masterminded the Tetris project of transferring Jennifer's luggage into the trunk. The space problem was solved when Suzanne moved her overnight bag to the small area behind the driver's seat. The compact two-seater was not ideal for escorting a clothes diva. Not that she thought two large suitcases and a carry-on bag were excessive, not in Jennifer's line of work.

Jennifer sent her driver on his way. "So where are we going? You packed a bag—not back to Santa Cruz?"

"A beautiful retreat in Napa. They are booked solid for weekends, but this early in the week we'll have a cabin all to ourselves. Near the vineyards. There's a hot tub. Have you ever been to Napa?"

"No."

"I think you'll love it."

They were at the front edge of the afternoon commute and whisked quickly across the Golden Gate Bridge and onto the foggy twists and climbs of the Marin highway. The scent of redwood and eucalyptus was not as strong in fall as it was at the height of spring, but it still had the effect of clearing Suzanne's head. When they emerged from under the fog at Petaluma, the early evening was sparkling blue and gold.

The rumblings all through the financial markets had made for a very stressful year. A few days' escape from the world in the company of someone who made her nerves sing for sex—a prescription for renewal if there ever was one, she thought. Wanting more the first time around had been why it had hurt so much after, and she had decided she wasn't going to make that mistake again.

CHAPTER TWENTY-EIGHT

Even though she wished they had gone back to the lovely little house in Santa Cruz, Jennifer was charmed by Suzanne's choice. The cabin set apart in its own secluded grove of oaks and pines, was very private and peaceful in the orange glow of the setting sun. She didn't know why she felt unsettled as they rolled in the suitcases.

A picnic basket greeted them on the scrubbed oak dining room table, bulging with cheese, olives and wine. Underneath those goodies was a container of cut carrots, a loaf of focaccia that was still slightly warm, and chilled roasted chicken. The scent of rosemary and cheddar set Jennifer's stomach to growling.

"Oh good." Suzanne's head was stuck inside the refrigerator. "There's diet Mountain Dew and Coke as requested. Limes and club soda too, just for you. I think they were able to get everything."

Jennifer debated opening the cheddar or pouncing on Suzanne. Her hungers were in conflict. "Any of those ice cream sandwiches?"

"Alas, no It's-Its," Suzanne confirmed after a look. "We'll have to go on a hunt for them. There's a great brew pub in town. Or the vineyards would be beautiful for a picnic tomorrow. The weather is supposed to be warm."

"There's enough cheese for two picnics with a heart attack to spare."

Suzanne slipped an arm around Jennifer's waist. "I think we'll find ways to work it off."

The shocking pleasure of Suzanne's nearness made Jennifer close her eyes for a moment. But when Suzanne would have lifted her onto the counter she playfully pushed her away. "Let's explore."

"There's plenty of time." Suzanne made a grab for her hand.

Jennifer ran toward the back of the cabin, counting on finding one of the bedrooms. Her gleeful squeal turned into alarm as Suzanne easily caught her.

"You can't escape me, wench."

"No fair, I'm in wenchy heels."

Suzanne hoisted Jennifer onto one shoulder, took a staggering step and let her slide back to the ground. Jennifer was laughing in earnest as she balanced against Suzanne's chest.

"How do the guys make it look so easy in the movies?"

"The woman helps, silly."

"So, like real life."

Jennifer kissed her and let Suzanne walk her backward into a spacious bedroom complete with paneled walls of unfinished wood and a solid four-poster bed.

Suzanne threw back the covers as Jennifer unbuttoned her suit jacket. Catching sight of the black lace covering her breasts, Suzanne said, "Does it sound super creepy if I admit that I love all the stuff you wear under your clothes?"

"If I wake up in the middle of the night and you're wearing it and there's a sheep in the room—that's creepy."

Suzanne's warm hand slipped beneath the hem of Jennifer's short skirt and a lazy finger traced around the top of her thigh-high stockings. "I'm never sure how to compliment you. You're beautiful, but I'm sure you hear it all the time."

Jennifer let out a shaky breath. "Context is everything."

"Is this an okay context to remind you that you're beautiful? Like this?" A fingertip slid over the front of Jennifer's panties.

The hungry look in Suzanne's eyes sent flames across Jennifer's body. She was swollen with heat all in an instant.

Suzanne settled back on the bed, pulling Jennifer on top of her. As her skirt rode up to her waist and legs spread over Suzanne's hips, Jennifer looked down into Suzanne's face. "I think you know the answer."

"I do. But I love hearing you say yes."

Jennifer said yes, then yes again. Suzanne found the way inside her with her voice, her knowing eyes, with her sensitive fingers.

The amber glow of sunset had deepened to an inky topaz when Suzanne asked, "Why do you still have your shoes on?"

"I think you like it."

"I do. But only if you do too." Suzanne nuzzled the inside of one breast.

"I like that you like it. You changed your hair." Jennifer had admired the old Clooney bad boy cut, but the faux hawk was equally handsome. Now it was mussed and even spikier from Jennifer's fingers.

"Annemarie is my fashion consultant."

"She has a lot of style. She also doesn't like me much."

"She's not overly fond of people in general."

Jennifer resisted the urge to fall asleep. Their time was too short for naps. It was clear to her now that there would be no repeat at Suzanne's house. This place was lovely but there were no framed snapshots of family on the table. No faded, battered cushions on the sofa. The house in Santa Cruz had been Jennifer's first real glimpse behind the super smart business woman. She'd been charmed by the wind-scrubbed table and open jar of jam, with the English muffins going stale in the cold breeze. The crumbs swept into the grass, then a long, deep breath to capture the morning air. All of it was a Suzanne Jennifer had only glimpsed during their night of Legos.

Like the loft had been in New York, this cabin was almost like a movie set, designed to create a mood, but not meant for breathing or living. A space for temporary moments and feelings. The mood was certainly fun, but she had wanted...expected something different. A something she would not name, certainly when it seemed unlikely to happen.

Her stomach growled in Suzanne's ear. Laughing, Suzanne pulled her up. "Off with the shoes. Do you need a pair of my socks for slippers?"

"I have some." Jennifer kicked off the Manolos and got to her feet. The thick carpet felt wonderful. "And pajamas. It'll be warmer."

"I'll light the fire. Unless you'd like to take a shower to warm up?"

"Later." Jennifer said it as a promise. "After hot tub and…more exercise."

She found her hotel nighttime survival gear—lightweight pajama pants and a super soft cotton T-shirt. A long chenille cardigan served as a robe, and she truly never did leave for a trip without her shearling slippers. Being warm enough was always her challenge in any hotel as she often finished a day's work half-frozen.

The gas-powered fire logs were doing their best to crackle merrily, and the living room was warming up. Suzanne greeted her with an appreciative kiss and then popped a cube of delectably soft, aromatic cheese into her mouth. "Can't have you fainting."

"Thank you." She melted into a hug, liking the careless rumple in Suzanne's soft Batwoman T-shirt and brushed cotton drawstring pants. They, at least, seemed like a genuine piece of Suzanne.

"You look comfortable."

"I am, at last. A girl can't do designer 24/7. At some point, you have to go with some relaxed cotton. You may find this disappointing, but I only wear a negligee if someone is paying me and it's for a camera. I guess I'll always be a little bit of the girl from King of Prussia—I can't sleep in something that costs hundreds of dollars. It's nerve-wracking enough walking around in it."

They created a nest in front of the fire using oversized cushions from the couch braced against the solid oak coffee table. Jennifer set her slippers aside and wiggled her toes as close to the heat as she could bear. Warm at last.

In answer to Suzanne's question, she said, "I hadn't really understood why it was called prairie dogging until everyone's heads started popping up and down over the partitions."

"Not to burst your bubble, but they do that for anyone delivering food." Suzanne spread the soft cheese on a cracker and passed it to Jennifer.

Jennifer thought the cheese was just about the most delicious thing ever. She handed over the container of carrot sticks. "Next time I'll bring pizza."

"You'll start a riot. When will you hear about the part?"

"Soon, I hope. The production company specializes in short filming schedules. They're the same group that produced *Royal Candide*. The busy big names can fit a five-week art-film type project in between their six-month blockbuster shoots."

"Any big names in this one?"

"They wouldn't say, though someone made an offhand reference to 'the superhero guy' which means somebody with a high profile. I hope so. But it's a good part, finally. Not just a one-note bubblehead princess to be rescued like in the one I'm doing all the media interviews for."

"I saw it over the weekend," Suzanne admitted.

Jennifer swatted her. "Get out. You did not go see it."

"I did. I figured I should know. It was entertaining. You were, of course, excellent. And you got to do more than be a model on film. And then last night I saw you in an ad clip—coming up at eleven, an exclusive interview with Princess Neowa—whatever it is."

She popped an olive into her mouth and took a moment to savor the salty bitterness. "You can spell it any way you like, but it's always pronounced Helpless-with-Boobs. Not even the love interest, just the dead woman who makes the hero all manly."

"I'm glad there's something different on the horizon for you."

Jennifer found only sincerity in Suzanne's eyes. "Unless I get the Ryan Productions part it'll be more of the same. I'm working on my fencing again. Basil Rathbone went far just being good with a blade."

"Are you good?"

Jennifer lifted an eyebrow. "Not good enough for competition, but if I were Zorro they wouldn't need a prop guy to carve the Z." She demonstrated an economical flick of the wrist.

"What about archery? Very popular for the ladies these days." Suzanne tore off another piece of the herb-scented chicken and offered it to Jennifer.

She finished that piece and started another before answering. "I tried archery, but I have two, ahem, big impediments. Costume designers won't want to include the kind of chest protector I need. The first time the bowstring hit Shirley I decided it was not worth it."

"Shirley?"

"Laverne on the left, Shirley on the right." Jennifer pointed. "You called them kit and caboodle, remember?"

"I remember." Suzanne snorted into her wine. "I didn't think you would. By any other name—"

"They'd be in the way. I have a love-hate relationship with them. They open doors, but not always the right kinds of doors."

"What do you do when that happens?" Suzanne was regarding her thoughtfully.

"I try not to enter. But then again any door is better than no doors. I do not plan to end up selling real estate or hawking clothes on some shopping network."

"I really don't think you have to worry about that."

"I wish I was as certain as you are." She let Suzanne pull her closer. "I feel sinful, just doing nothing. I have a condo now, in SoHo, and I don't spend much time in it. This feels wonderful."

"Are you traveling a lot?"

"A model's life is about being seen and not just at paying gigs. Do you get as much time on the beach as you want?" She tried not to sound as if she wished that's where they were. Why couldn't she be happy with what Suzanne had planned?

"Never enough. I don't travel, I'm sure, the way you do. But I head for places sometimes for a couple of weeks because it takes time to get to know people and places and be sure they're the right kind of partnership. I like Tokyo a lot."

"So do I. *Auber-Marche* did a full shoot last year at the Kanda Myojin Shrine. I got my latest Blackberry blessed. So far so good."

Suzanne laughed. "I went there too. I still couldn't get reception for my iPhone, but I'm not sure that's something they could fix."

Jennifer rubbed her cheek on Suzanne's shoulder before resting her head in the crook of her neck. "What's exciting you right now?"

"Seriously? You have to ask?"

She drew Suzanne's arm around her waist. "In business I mean. We'll get to the other thing later."

"Let's see. I spent a chunk of last month meeting on and off with the guy who is changing the way everyone uses power. Inside small relays, city-wide power grids, everything to do with energy. We want to pull in some of the gurus of renewables, offer funding and see what happens. It'll be exciting."

The rumble of Suzanne's voice through her chest was soothing. "This is going to seem like a stupid question."

She felt Suzanne kiss the top of her head. "Ask away."

"So you're working on some kind of invention? I'm not sure exactly what you do. What CommonTech does."

"Some of what I do is hands-on. For example, I and six other people have a joint patent on a type of jump drive."

"I don't know what that is."

"You will. Anyway, most of my time isn't doing that, though I love when something comes along and I can use that part of my brain. Mostly someone comes to us with their idea and we find the capital and partners."

"Oh." Jennifer stretched back to give Suzanne a look a comprehension. "You're a venture capitalist."

Suzanne nodded. "Specializing purely in technical innovation."

"Every time I saw your name it was related to something about a new gadget or something like that."

"That's pretty much the only time the media cares."

She settled back into Suzanne's embrace. "Now I understand why the office seemed sort of formal. But not quite."

"You only saw one of four floors. Lawyers, HR people, fund managers, the works. We pick more winners than losers, and even the losing propositions have elements of success in terms of what everyone learns along the way. Like a new methodology for digital rights management that didn't work from almost the beginning. The woman behind it came back six months later with a completely different paradigm. It takes failure to succeed."

Jennifer wiggled around to kiss Suzanne's neck. "Is this the right context to tell you I think you're really smart?"

"Sure."

"How about now?" She brushed a fingertip over the nipple outlined under Suzanne's T-shirt.

"You're going to give me crazy ideas."

"Seems like we have a paradigm to explore." The nipple grew more noticeable.

"You and your sexy talk."

Jennifer smiled into a long kiss.

CHAPTER TWENTY-NINE

The cool morning air, infused with a tang of pine, awakened Jennifer with a hunger that seemed quite mutual—first for each other, then for the rest of the contents of the picnic basket. Sated, they opted for a peaceful walk on the tree-lined trail behind the cabin and discovered a vista overlooking rolling hills with row after row of grapevines. To Jennifer they were a little bit sad, stripped of fruit and leaves going brown. A winding road in the distance was deserted but for a pickup headed toward the outlying buildings of Napa's small town center.

"We're going to have to go in search of lunch, I'm afraid." Jennifer looked up from shaking a dirt clod out of her running shoes. Suzanne had seemed surprised that she owned practical footwear. It wasn't as if she wore Manolo Blahniks to the gym.

"I'm not the celebrity you are, but I've been told that celebrities are left alone up here. I could loan you a hoodie that's got Kermit on it."

"It's not that. I like being alone with you. It's very restful and pleasurable." She leaned into Suzanne's arm. They could have had the same experience at Suzanne's little house on the ocean, but there seemed no point in saying so. In the cooler light of morning, it seemed clear that this was a tryst, nothing more. All Suzanne wanted from her was the thing they seemed to be best at together. "Thank you."

"Like I said, there's a great brew pub."

"Do you come up this way often?"

"Not often. Business retreats. The occasional date, to be perfectly honest."

"You haven't lived a monk's life. Why would you?" She gave Suzanne an appreciative glance. The years had deepened the lines of humor around her eyes and mouth. Standing braced against the occasional puff of wind, she seemed equally rooted and yet coiled to leap into whatever a situation might require. Jennifer could feel the pull of that energy in her skin's yearning to be closer.

"I assume you haven't either." Suzanne's gaze was fixed on the horizon.

"A solitary monk? No. I go to a lot of parties, true. Things have changed since we met." She wasn't sure how much Suzanne really wanted to know. "Instead of wearing something a designer picked out that I have to return, I get a lot of free clothes and accessories and contract offers to reward me if I wear them. That means being seen and photographed in very public spaces. Fashion Week, Cannes, Newport Jazz. That's in addition to runways and photo shoots. I'm paid to be seen instead of hoping that being seen will turn into work. It's *all* work. I'm rarely completely off someone's clock, so thank you for this."

She slipped her hand into Suzanne's. "When I do get free time I'm home reading entertainment scuttlebutt, watching a movie, at the gym or lessons, or practicing the beauty regimen called sleep."

It occurred to her that her new agent was right. The rhythm of the modeling life and the connections she made didn't readily overlap with her acting ambitions. Even at someplace like Cannes, she was greeted as a model who made the scene fashionable and photogenic, not as an actress who belonged there. "When the parties start to wane—midnight or so—I'm usually tired. I keep a strict schedule for the gym in the mornings, most photo shoots start around ten if they're local, and I will literally go to any audition at any time. I still do dance and diction lessons. Parties are a kind of dead end. I mean, so I spend time chatting with some group of people. If we click, I'm eligible to go their next party."

"Sounds like high school."

"It's a *lot* like that. There's the sophisticates who get all life and death over the wine and quail eggs. Seriously, what's more pretentious? Insisting on quail eggs or thinking quail eggs are passé?"

Suzanne laughed. "That's a tough call."

"Anyway, people with regular jobs head for home and the later it gets the more the parties are about drinking and drugs and casual sex. That's the happy place for a lot of people who get the gossip headlines, and it's all they want from life. I tried it exactly twice."

"And?" Suzanne didn't seem shocked.

"It was *exhausting*." She laughed in recollection. "The second time I realized that everyone was high because if they weren't they'd realize they were surrounded by a bunch of drunk, stoned people. Then I remembered all the times my dad got home from work already blitzed. Had a long talk with Lauren Bacall when I got home and it's not something I need or have to do."

Suzanne gave her a sideways look and pretended to sidle away. "Lauren Bacall talks to you?"

"The poster, remember? I still have it. We talk. All my favorite quotes are written on the back where my mom couldn't find them and make fun of me."

Suzanne squeezed her hand. "I confess—I talk to Nikola Tesla." Jennifer's blink must have given her away because Suzanne continued, "An inventor, visionary. Came up with more breakthroughs than Edison, but lost the marketing campaign until recently."

"Oh, the guy that car company is named after?"

"You win Double Jeopardy."

She bumped Suzanne's shoulder. "But I forgot to phrase it in the form of a question."

Suzanne laughed and passed her the bottle of water she'd carried.

As she took a refreshing swallow, Jennifer thought of several of the young models who had just gotten to the popular stage only to disappear into the entourage of some hard-living rock group. "People get lost in the party life. Women especially get chewed up by it. It shows—there are girls my age who party hard and look like leather put through the rinse cycle and dried in a microwave. I don't like being just another body for whomever is dispensing the night's treats. I don't like being just another body regardless."

"It's not why you're there."

"No." But it was looking more and more like that's why she was here. This was just another tryst for Suzanne. Meanwhile, Jennifer found the bare vines vaguely depressing. But they would bloom again. Enough water and sun and every year, the grapes would turn into something beautiful.

Whenever she was between parts she felt just like the vines, she realized. Fallow, and for her, without a guarantee of another turn in the sun. All the party lights and camera flashes didn't warm her. Most of the time she felt alone in crowds. But when she was on a set, creating something out of a team of other talented people, producing something they made together—that exquisite energy was what made her own lights shine.

Actresses can do modeling on the side, Jennifer thought. But models aren't hired to act, they're hired to be a voiceless body. The two nights with Suzanne had been the first in ages where she hadn't fallen asleep picking at the problem of how to finally transform herself from one to the other. "I am still hoping I don't have to do the party life, and trade my health to get acting jobs."

Suzanne touched her shoulder. "You never have to do what you don't want to do."

Surprising tears stung at her eyes. "I know I'm lucky. But I'm trying not to be desperate. Trying not to remember that Marilyn Monroe dated almost every producer she ever worked with. So far the only thing anyone seems to want me for is the part of the Doable Girl, and any cookie cutter can play that one. Lots of times by proving in private she's a doable girl. When there are women willing to pay that price for the part, why do I think I'm worth more? Worth better? Nobody seems to believe me."

"Maybe the Ryan Productions movie will change all that."

"It could." Jennifer swallowed hard. She tried not to attach much importance to the fact that Suzanne hadn't said that she, at least, believed Jennifer was worth more. "I'm sorry, that was intense. I—my agent doesn't want to hear it. I don't meet a lot of people who think more than a few weeks ahead. Or believe any doubts and worries I have about my future are justified. They all say the same thing—why can't I just settle for what I know I can have?"

Suzanne took her hand to pull her back toward the trail. "Let's get some food. When is your flight to Vancouver, by the way?"

"I should be at SFO by one tomorrow."

"Not too early a start then."

"No." Jennifer followed Suzanne down the trail, wondering about the sudden change of topic. If Suzanne was already tired of the subject of Jennifer's career, then she was just like everyone else. The moment she tried to share her worries, most people offered trite, half-assed solutions that would not work for her. And then they stopped listening.

This fire and attraction between the two of them was temporary, and fleeting pleasures didn't begin to measure up to how devoted she was to her work. It was a simple fact. Suzanne's face in the throes of triumphant climax, the tousle of her hair in Jennifer's fingers, the urgency of her voice begging Jennifer to show her how strong she was—they were moments to put on a mental shelf and that was all.

The peace of waking up in Suzanne's arms in the cozy house in Santa Cruz washed across her senses. That feeling had just been the light of the ocean and the aftermath of good sex. That she'd only ever felt that with Suzanne was just lack of trying with other people.

Sure, Jennifer, there's a good lesson—make something wonderful into something casual and forgettable. Suzanne was a woman, and there was nothing casual or forgettable about how that made her feel.

And.

And Suzanne was a woman, and that complicated all her worries and fears even more. For all that had changed in society, some things were very much the same.

Would Suzanne ask when they'd see each other again? She wasn't sure—Suzanne seemed unreadable, except when they were in bed.

She knew how she ought to answer if Suzanne asked. All at once she was back in the loft, easing herself out from under Suzanne's arm. She'd known then that being outed in a relationship with a woman would end all her dreams. Nothing had changed. Her head knew it and her heart had no business thinking otherwise.

CHAPTER THIRTY

"So when did you watch *Casablanca* and *The Graduate*? If I remember the old Suzanne, she didn't like classic movies."

Suzanne delayed her answer until after the waiter delivered their orders, accepted their thanks and beat a discreet retreat. "A couple years ago. I like that channel that does Oscar movies all of March."

"Do you have a favorite?" Jennifer separated the halves of her grilled cheese.

Suzanne was distracted from digging into her bison burger by Jennifer licking melted cheese off her fingertip. She does that on purpose, Suzanne thought. "*Return of the King* and *The Sting*. Even I thought the suits in *The Sting* were the bomb."

"You'd look great in the Redford suits. That classic Forties look, you'd rock that hard."

"I didn't think I'd like *On the Waterfront* but I did." She studied a spot just past Jennifer's shoulder. When Jennifer turned to follow her gaze, Suzanne went for the nearest beer-battered onion ring on Jennifer's plate.

A fork in the back of her hand brought her up an inch shy of her goal. "You could just ask."

"You'll say no because those look delicious. And so, so fattening."

"Oh, that's cold." The pressure on the fork increased. "Are you saying I haven't gotten enough exercise to have earned onion rings?"

"I would never imply such a thing." She moved her hand out from under the pointy tines.

Jennifer studied the rings, then held out the largest and most deeply golden of the lot. "This is for the shower. Can I have some fries?"

Suzanne made a show of thinking about it, then passed over a handful. "Yeah, the shower was worth it."

Jennifer mimicked a mechanical voice. "Your feedback is welcome and valued."

On the surface they both seemed relaxed, but Suzanne couldn't forget what Jennifer had said during their walk. Did she represent "settling" to Jennifer? She rubbed the fork dents in the back of her hand. Take them as a metaphor for what this weekend is going to do to your heart, she told herself. The shower had been every type of awesome, with Jennifer aggressive and playful until Suzanne had finally admitted that she was losing her ability to remain standing. She would never forget the feel of soft sheets against her back and Jennifer's wet hair on her thighs.

When they finally wandered out of the pub and into the early afternoon sunshine Suzanne no longer felt like limp lettuce. The streets were reasonably quiet as the afternoon warmed. She'd been in Napa on a holiday weekend for a music festival and it had been wall-to-wall people. This sleepy autumn day was completely different. A couple was emerging from the Welcome Center and a woman was reading a book under a massive oak tree just starting to drop its leaves. The only crowd was on the patio of a celebrity chef's branded restaurant, and a light breeze carried the scent of fresh bread and barbecue. "That almost makes me hungry again."

Jennifer groaned. "I don't think I could eat for a week. And I'm hoping the clothes fit tomorrow. They measure down to the quarter-inch."

"I have one solution." Suzanne turned Jennifer to face her and leaned in for a nuzzling kiss.

After a split second Jennifer pushed her away, glancing nervously left and right.

Suzanne was so startled all she said was, "Oh."

"I just—"

"Nobody cares." Suzanne turned her gaze to the woman reading her book.

"It's not that, I—"

"Seriously? Still?"

Now several steps away and looking at her boots, Jennifer started to answer but something in her handbag began chirping. Jennifer grabbed her cell phone as if it were a life preserver. "It's my agent."

So nothing's changed, Suzanne thought. Jennifer liked a woman in bed but that was as far as it was going to go. Ten years ago, when Jennifer had apparently deleted Suzanne's contact info and sent back the card and necklace, she'd tried to comfort herself with the excuse that Jennifer had been very young and passionate and scared. She hadn't known Suzanne would protect her.

The woman who had this morning covered Suzanne's body with her own, who had whispered, "I love the way your breasts feel against mine," was not confused about anything. She had a very successful modeling career, money and fame. Suzanne could give her all the security in the world. There wasn't anything Jennifer could want that Suzanne couldn't give her.

It was impossible to go back into a closet she'd never been in to begin with. Her place in an *Advocate* feature of queer business leaders, significant donations to marriage and employment equality, they were all part of her public wiki. Depending on the press outlet, the label *lesbian* often came before *entrepreneur*. Being with her meant being out. Jennifer would have to choose.

For a brief moment, not even as long as the space between two beats of her heart, she believed Jennifer would pick her. The thought was incandescent, lighting up a well of pleasure that flooded her skin.

A look of disbelieving relief swept over Jennifer's face. Her voice stayed calm even as she spun around on her cute little ankle boots in a mad dance of frenzied joy.

Suzanne knew what the news was before Jennifer ended the call. The glow inside her faded.

"I got it. *I got it.*" And then Jennifer buried her face in her hands and began crying in loud, shuddering gulps.

"What's wrong?"

"N-Nothing. I'm happy!" She let Suzanne pull her into a hug and cried against her chest. "I didn't let myself think it could happen. A big part, even if it is in an art film. I'm finally getting a chance to show I can *do* something."

A vast door had opened for Jennifer and Suzanne knew what that meant for her. The choice had been made, and life with the too-tall geeky girl had lost.

A bottle of wine, the dregs of the picnic basket, and the discovery of *To Have and Have Not* on the cabin's cable feed was enough to fill the evening. Suzanne didn't bring up the aborted public kiss while Jennifer talked about Lauren Bacall as if her life depended on it.

We'll just let go, Suzanne kept telling herself. It won't be hard, but I have a life, so does she. We'll just let go.

CHAPTER THIRTY-ONE

"Somebody believes in me." The little voice whispering in Jennifer's ear didn't stop. She wanted the filming to start tomorrow. She tried to tell herself that one part wouldn't guarantee people took her seriously afterward, but maybe it could. This role had range and subtlety. A pampered, kept woman who carries money across the border for a small-time casino boss appears to be the victim of circumstance when a huge sum goes missing.

Up to that point it wasn't much to write home about for range. Emphasis on makeup and cleavage, bosom to heave on cue. In this movie, however, she'd be revealed as the master manipulator of cops and robbers alike with a core dramatic shift required in the final scenes to turn the story on its head for the audience. Somebody thought she could pull it off.

Phillip had had to repeat the news twice. Then she'd been overwhelmed with a giddy loss of reality, unanchored from the ground with her stomach swooping like a roller-coaster ride. She wasn't even sure why she'd cried and remembered only the firm security of Suzanne's embrace.

Except this morning, with the mist rising from the oak grove and their suitcases back in the car, Suzanne was aloof, almost taciturn. Her mind perhaps already back on business?

"This was lovely, thank you." Jennifer settled into the passenger seat and glanced at Suzanne.

"You're welcome. I'm glad you liked the place." She started the car.

In the long silence that fell, while Jennifer pretended to listen to the CD Suzanne had pushed into the player, it dawned on her that Suzanne wasn't going to ask if they could see each other again. That would make it easier, she thought.

Except it hurt. It wasn't supposed to, but it did.

There were too many good things within her reach but she couldn't have all of them. She accepted that, or at least she thought she had. She had thought that whatever this thing with Suzanne was, it wouldn't be any harder to give it up than it had been in New York. Tilden and Tilden, as promised, had tripled her work in just weeks, then doubled it again. Her image was *everywhere*. And there had been a couple of small parts in movies with lines and a stint in a short-lived off-Broadway play. Holidays and birthdays came and went in the continual blur of work.

Now she wasn't as young, already past thirty, and staring the same choices in the face all over again. She knew Suzanne didn't think she had anything to be afraid of if she announced she was with a woman. Suzanne had never had her hand out, her dreams nearly in her grasp, all the while knowing a puff of gossip could blow it all away.

Suzanne didn't have a terror of ending up with a frustrating life of pats on the head, gropes from photographers, being called *honey* and *baby* and *Jenny* for a few more years before the ticking clock ended even that. She didn't want to be sixty and thinking that thwarted life had been the "good ol' days."

Nothing had changed, not even the fact that she loved being in Suzanne's arms.

Except this time Suzanne didn't seem to care what Jennifer did. It had been fun. Now it was over. And it hurt.

They emerged from the tunnel north of San Francisco into a drifting mist that was too much like Jennifer's mood. As traffic slowed for the Golden Gate Bridge approach the fog closed in on the car. Then to Jennifer's amazement the thick white drapes parted. In what seemed like only moments the sun was shining down on them, the ocean spread blue and clear on one side with green and rocky islands dotting the bay on the other. The orange towers of the bridge and spires of the city sparkled in the clear, bright sunlight.

She found her breath. "That was incredible."

"The fog is often worst just before it lifts." Suzanne glanced at her watch. "It's rolling out at eleven, probably back in around three."

"I'll be sorry to miss it."

"Will you?"

"Yes."

"I'm glad you'll miss something then."

Jennifer cocked her head to look at Suzanne. "What's that supposed to mean?"

"I didn't mean to say that aloud." She swerved to avoid a minivan whose driver didn't seem to understand the meaning of the lines on the roadway.

"But you did."

"Look, we've had a great time. Let's just leave it at that. It's what you want."

"How do you know what I want?"

"It's pretty plain. You can't be with me and not get outed. I'm not going to hide. Your career matters to you."

"Yours matters to you." Suzanne clearly thought there was a difference.

"It does. But I'm not hiding who I am."

"You don't have to in your field. Science rules."

"You've never heard of Alan Turing, have you?"

"You've never heard of Lizabeth Scott. Name one out gay actress who has even been nominated for an Oscar."

Suzanne laughed and to Jennifer's ears it dripped with patronizing disbelief. "You're like a prima ballerina who wants to win a gold medal in ice dancing too."

"*E tu, Brute*? With all this—" She gestured at herself. "Why can't I just be happy?"

"With all that—" Suzanne waved a hand at Jennifer and then at the vista outside. "And all of that already at your feet." She put her hand on her chest. "And all of this, yes, I guess I don't know why you're deciding it's not enough."

"You haven't even asked me if I want more of you. Of us."

"I know the answer, Jennifer. And why are you waiting on me to do the asking? Are you thinking I'm the man in this relationship?"

"You're the one with all the success and nothing to lose. In your profession you have all you need to be safe and going on climbing. I'm not safe where I am, and it's really easy to head down instead of up."

"There are people I want to work with. And yes, money to make."

"And nobody will care that a lesbian is doing it. That's your world."

"There are people who want to chew me up because I'm a woman who dares to be smart and doesn't have her wagon hitched to any man besides Nikola Tesla."

"Your money protects you. It makes those people irrelevant. They hide their bigotry because you have something unique they want." She'd been at this ten years, and knew the score. "People think I'm unique and that's why I get paid really well. But if I died tomorrow they'd hire a replacement for every modeling job I have within twenty-four hours, and the only thing they'd change is the length of a hem. Maybe."

"Then why do you do it?"

"It pays my bills, and rather well, thank you."

"A big bank account isn't the only way to measure success. I used to think it was and then I grew up."

"That's incredibly easy for someone with millions in ready cash to say. I do the job that pays me but I want a better one, one that I love doing. Isn't that what we're all supposed to want? Live our passion? But for some reason when I put that first, I'm chasing childish dreams, and you think I'm old enough now to know better."

"That's not what I meant. We are talking about me right now."

The sparkling day outside seemed suddenly a lie to Jennifer. She didn't know why she hurt so much, like a chisel cracking at her chest from the inside. The city of dreams and love, rainbow flags snapping in the wind, and no part of her felt welcome. She'd been at home in Suzanne's house, in her bed, in her arms, but now that all seemed like a something from a romantic movie. A beautiful lie. Love, happening to someone else.

Love. She didn't know what it was supposed to feel like, but surely not this. Not this confusion and fear and pain.

Suzanne muttered a curse at a driver who turned left in front of them. "I think this is a bad time to talk about any of this."

"There's a better time?"

"When I'm not driving in sucky traffic—damn it, here. Fine." Suzanne dug one hand into the middle console and dropped a small jeweler's box into Jennifer's lap.

She knew a light blue, white ribboned Tiffany's box when she saw one. This size and shape would hold a bracelet or pendant. "What's this?"

"A gift."

"From Tiffany's." She thought of the engraved bracelet Suzanne had given her standing in Times Square. It had felt liberating and encouraging, an honest expression of support. Completely different from New York and how the Tiffany's diamond necklace and a card asking to resume contact had felt. Now it was more jewelry, after a fancy setting for sex. "Is this something I put on as proof that you've added me to your collection?"

"What the hell?" Suzanne's anger was loud and clear. "What are you talking about?"

There was a last moment when Jennifer thought of their first night, then the morning in Santa Cruz. The powerful exchange of passion. All the easy moments. The deep and happy thrill that ran through her at the sight of Suzanne.

I can't love her, she thought.

"I'm a stamp you'll have collected, a fancy piece of jewelry to show off, one more way to let the world know that you're the successful lesbian they can't touch."

Suzanne colored and Jennifer wondered if she'd hit the mark in some deep way. "That's not what the box is about. But I'm not an idiot or a liar. Of course I'd love showing the world you're with me. The problem is you don't want the world to know. You want to have the sex and not be one of us. You don't want any of the work or worry or fear."

"You're on the lists of wealthy Americans, maybe one of the richest lesbians in the country. What do you have to be afraid of?"

"Just because I can't lose my job and have money to back up my rights, doesn't mean I'm comfortably numb to the rest of the world.

A woman in Florida died while the hospital barred her partner from the hospital room, in spite of having all the right paperwork. Do you think that just because that probably wouldn't happen to me that I'm not angry and afraid?"

"Well, at least you admit that money doesn't fix everything."

"I'm just an inconvenient bit of muck stuck to the bottom of your bloody red shoes."

"What are *you* talking about?"

"Something you don't even bother to wipe off. You just throw away the shoes so there's no proof your life was ever complicated. You're afraid being with me will cost you your career. That's why you dumped me in New York."

"I'm not making it up! Ask any casting agent. Ask directors. *Pretty face. Pretty voice. Great figure. Can act a little,*" she mimicked. "I've been knocking on doors for ten years and the part I just got is the first one where I raise my voice for a reason other than calling for help." She tried to take a calming breath but the words tumbled out. "I've made up my mind. I'm going to move to LA. Stop modeling, it just gets in the way. Hollywood is getting my full attention."

"That means you can't have a private life?"

"There's no such thing as privacy for performers." She fought back tears. "I don't want to be a footnote and forgotten. You have no idea, no idea at all how many actors are closeted because they know what coming out will do to their careers."

"The world is changing, Jennifer. Gay marriage is going to happen, and soon."

"Marriage is not the be all and end all of being treated fairly. Money can't buy equality. None of it will be fast enough for me. My clock is ticking. I have maybe five more years. Tops. Then I'm too old to play across from leading men twice my age. Let alone headline my own movie."

"You're selling yourself short."

"Give me credit for knowing my industry the way you know yours, even if it's not the all-powerful and important world of computers and games and gadgets."

Suzanne's jaw flexed. "So now I'm being a chauvinist?"

"Tell me how all the sacrifices to make this work won't be at my expense? You give up nothing to be with me."

A flush of color ran up Suzanne's neck. "And I'm a sacrifice? I think what you're saying is that I'm not worth the sacrifice."

"I end up the little missus while you have a job. Maybe you can buy Warner Brothers for me, that would solve everything. Except I'd be Pia Zadora all over again, an actress everyone agrees wouldn't have a part to her name if it weren't for her spouse's money. I'll resent it and resent you and that means we're doomed. So I will have given up my career for nothing in the end."

"Wow. So I can't possibly give you anything worth having?"

"Money. Everyone will say I stay for your money. You'll start to wonder if it's true. If that's the only mutual advantage we share— your money."

"You could go on modeling. You can be out and still model. If you earn less I can make it up to you."

"I can't believe you just said that." Jennifer actually looked down, expecting to see a knife in her chest.

Suzanne let out a sharp, flat breath. "I think you're a coward and all you want is the pretty, bright lights, that's what I think."

Maybe I am, Jennifer thought, but if she was taking the easy way out why did it hurt so damn much? "That's what you wanted for yourself, isn't it? The whole setup in New York was about being rich and famous. Except your pretty lights have *substance*, have meaning and value, while I just want to be a vapid actress."

"I have never implied—"

"But it's okay with you if I'm a vapid model instead. As long as I'm pretty. I feel like some prize in the game show of your magic life."

"Of course you can—"

"I will be a royal bitch if that's what it takes," Jennifer announced viciously. "Watch out Hollywood! I'm not going to marry well and settle down to be someone's trophy wife."

"Well. You've already achieved one goal." Suzanne veered into a hotel entrance. "Can you take a cab to the airport from here?"

"Yes." There was nothing more to say. She'd said far too much. She got out of the car and dropped the unopened Tiffany's box onto the seat. Closed the door.

"I smashed it," she repeated to herself, over and over. "I smashed it to pieces." There was no going back, only forward. She'd made sure of that. The knives they'd just thrown could not be removed.

I *did that on purpose, but it was all Suzanne's fault for not understanding*. It had to be Suzanne's fault. It just had to be or she was going to fall to pieces.

The cab's path to the airport went directly past the building that housed Suzanne's company. She closed her eyes to the past and thought about the new part and wondered if she could wrap up the Vancouver photo shoot more quickly. She needed to make a decision, needed to make sense, needed to do something with the screaming voices that pleaded with her to go back, to apologize.

To do the asking.

This is just a place I'm leaving, she told herself. She was so intent on not crying that she didn't hear her phone ringing at first.

It wasn't Suzanne. Not that she had any hope of it ever being Suzanne again. "Phillip, what's the good news?"

He summed up the contract he was putting together for the production company. "I think I've got all the bases covered, Jenny, and I'll FedEx it to your hotel in Canada."

"Phillip? Can you do me a favor?" Her razor-edged voice sounded like a stranger's. "Call me Jennifer. If you call me *Jenny* again you're history."

He didn't miss a beat. "Absolutely. In fact, I'll put that in the contract so there's no way it shows up on the set. It's *Jennifer*, all the time."

Damn right, she thought. She would not have regrets, and she was not going to be stupid about her feelings ever again.

ACT III

CHAPTER THIRTY-TWO

Present Day

Suzanne snapped back to the party with a jolt that nearly toppled her wineglass. But the echo of Annemarie's "I told you so" was reverberating in her ears along with the memory of impotent fury that had sent her into months of all work and all bitch.

She'd moved out of the house in Santa Cruz, went for an anonymous condo south of Market, traded her BMW for an Audi, and never drove Highway 1 south of Half Moon Bay. Jennifer couldn't just leave for her audition in LA all those years ago, she'd had to torch the landscape on the way out of Suzanne's life. Then she'd unleashed a wave of ruin on Selena Ryan and marched her stilettos up the Hollywood ladder, never looking back.

And now she was walking around in places that had been free of her shadow. Not just disturbing Suzanne's composure, but tearing her in two. She was furious at Jennifer's presumption and yet unable to let the woman out of her sight. The places where her body had been pressed against Jennifer's bare skin still felt like they were on fire.

The stir that had brought her out of her reverie was a procession of two women and two men in blue suits, all with faces of concrete.

Damn it all, she had not meant to be caught off guard by the arrival of their high-ranking, last-minute guest. Sydney Van Allen was on a tight schedule and here she was mooning about La Lamont all over again. Santa Cruz had been such a mistake. They had devoured each other, and then Jennifer had spit out her bones.

She reached Van Allen before any kind of pause could leave the impression that the Speaker of the House had just walked into a room and didn't know what to do next. Optics, optics, optics the party planner had insisted.

"Madam Speaker, it's an honor to meet you. Thank you for taking the time out of your schedule to be here." They shook hands. A wave of charisma and charm just from the handshake left Suzanne feeling that their meeting was the most important thing Van Allen had done all day. *I could be her willing slave.*

Van Allen introduced her to her wife, Faith Fitzgerald. Suzanne tried not to gush about Fitzgerald's histories of world-changing women, but managed to convey she was a fan.

"In a gorgeous setting like this I'd rather talk about Faith's books too," Van Allen admitted. Her eyes seemed to miss nothing.

"Do you have time to dine with us?"

"I'm afraid not. They just did a fruit-basket upset on my itinerary, and we're heading back to DC tonight."

"Truly, I wish we could stay." Fitzgerald's handshake was quick but firm. "I have great sentimental fondness for San Francisco, but it was ice cold there. You have all this warmth. And something smells delectable."

"We suspected that you wouldn't have time, so the caterer will put together plates to take with you." She nodded at the party planner who did a head count with her eyes and departed in the direction of the kitchen followed by a Secret Service agent.

"Thank you, that's very kind. We'll picnic in the backseat," Fitzgerald added.

Van Allen's cool, pale skin took on the slightest edge of pink.

"That sounded rather racier than I meant it to be," Fitzgerald muttered. "All these years and I still forget to use my *inside* inside voice."

One eyebrow lifted so subtly that Suzanne thought it might not have meant anything, but it made Fitzgerald blush while Van Allen went back to serenity personified. A pinched-faced woman with a notebook meaningfully cleared her throat and Van Allen glanced at her watch.

Suzanne addressed the room as Van Allen touched shoulders and shook hands with nearly everyone on her way to the podium. "I don't need to make an introduction. You all know who she is, what she stands for, and it is an amazing surprise that her schedule allowed her to join us in celebration of women's health initiatives." She caught Jennifer's gaze for a moment and nearly forgot what she was going to say next. She should have seated the woman behind a tree. "From the great state of Illinois, Congresswoman and Speaker of the House Sydney Van Allen!"

Van Allen had already reached the podium as Suzanne finished, and she shushed the applause and urged everyone to enjoy their dinners. "I don't know what it is, but it smells delicious, and I'm not getting written up on the Curmudgeon Report as having ruined the meal."

Laughter settled everyone as Suzanne returned to her seat. Jennifer looked starstruck—a feeling she undoubtedly didn't experience very often. That's right, Suzanne thought, I know famous people who aren't you. She didn't need Jennifer to complete her life. She wasn't getting on that road again.

Her own dinner had grown slightly cool, but she made a point of resuming eating so that others would. There was no reason the delicate poached salmon and Laura's mushroom risotto should go completely cold.

Jennifer laughed at something Van Allen said. The low vibration of it continued to stir images of the hours she'd spent holding Jennifer close. Honestly Suzanne, what sick masochistic impulse led you to think Jennifer seated right next to you was a great idea? You've been waiting six months to meet some of these women and you might be eating tortilla chips with squirt cheese for all you care.

The memory of other tastes and pleasures were throbbing under her skin. Not this abyss again—she knew where it led. It was a good thing Annemarie wasn't here or she'd be on fire from the laser eyes.

Two tables over she caught sight of Carina. She could have asked Carina to be her spur-of-the-moment seat filler, but she was sure Carina's new wife wouldn't have appreciated it. It would have stirred up old gossip. Like a few other intriguing women Suzanne had gone out with, Carina had become a friend. They took each other's calls on the assumption that the need was genuine and not out of proportion to the fun and affection they had shared.

In other words, they had boundaries. Trust. Qualities that simply didn't apply to the woman she had crazily decided was okay to be seated next to her. The woman with the perfume that always burned and the charm that hid a knife.

CHAPTER THIRTY-THREE

"No one should have to worry about losing everything they've worked for because their child is born prematurely, or they break an ankle, or suffer a cataclysmic health event." Sydney Van Allen's laser gaze swept over the assembled guests so powerfully that Jennifer almost ducked.

"Amen," someone from the crowd called out and Van Allen didn't miss a beat when she answered, "Amen, sisters, amen."

Sydney Van Allen was a gifted speaker—there was no doubt in Jennifer's mind about that. Judging by the standards of her acting craft, she thought it was the pitch of her voice and the fiercely rigid posture blended with a sense of absolute conviction. "Even worse, what help and coverage we can receive shouldn't blow with whatever political winds are popular or what our employers decide is moral."

Jennifer could sense the speech was coming to its climax and she tried to pay attention, but her body felt Suzanne's nearness and the resulting flush was aggravating. Suzanne was proving some kind of point, maybe? That they could be near each other and keep their clothes on? Now that they were nine-plus years older they weren't the rabid bed bunnies they had once been?

She hardly expected Suzanne to have forgiven her for the way they'd last parted. Santa Cruz had been the do-over, the chance to get it right. It hadn't worked out and she'd made sure the door was slammed shut. There was no place in her life for the memories of Suzanne's hands and mouth or for that morning she had felt— so briefly—that everything she could want to be happy could be found in Suzanne's arms. She didn't want to remember the way Suzanne used to look at her or compare it to the way Suzanne had looked at her tonight—the same look of wariness, distrust and remembered pain Lena sometimes wore.

All of it more or less deserved. She'd earned it all. How could she ever tell Suzanne that as badly as she'd behaved on the drive back from Napa, it paled next to the destruction she'd loosed into Lena's life? Even if Lena had gotten past it professionally and personally in her usual overachieving, ethical fashion, it didn't change anything. Maybe Suzanne already knew the gist of it— it had been online tabloid fodder for a couple of weeks. *Jennifer Lamont hooks up with female producer, then dates male director after dismissing Sapphic fling as "one of those things."*

Then, of course, there had been the subsequent trip to rehab for a fabricated substance abuse problem. Suzanne wasn't crazy about stupid people, and Jennifer had been spectacularly, publicly stupid.

She belatedly realized the speech had ended. She scrambled to her feet and applauded madly as Van Allen took her leave. The Secret Service agents didn't exactly back out of the room, but within moments it was as if Van Allen and her entourage had never been there.

Suzanne was leaning into the microphone at the podium. "The rest of the evening's events will begin after we've all enjoyed our dessert."

She settled into the seat next to Jennifer with a sigh. "Wow, that was all kinds of breathtaking."

"It was, wasn't it?" Jennifer had a sudden thought. "Where's Annemarie? Have I just not picked her out in the crowd?" There had to be at least a hundred people there, perhaps more.

"No, she has the flu. This afternoon she swore she'd be here if it killed her, but the hundred and three temperature won."

"I'm so sorry."

"It'll somehow be my fault. Everything usually is."

It was probably for the best, Jennifer thought. She felt awkward enough without avoiding any not-so-veiled barbs Annemarie might still want to send her way. Suzanne, who looked distracted again, didn't need yet more drama tonight. Even if she hadn't fallen literally into Suzanne's arms, just running into each other so unexpectedly would have probably thrown them both for a loop. As it was, Jennifer had already provided enough upheaval to a tightly planned schedule.

Suzanne was making a point of chatting with the woman on her other side. A mathematician, someone had said, and here with the other big speaker who was a political analyst of some kind and the daughter of a former Vice President. The woman next to Jennifer was having a lively conversation with the women on her other side in what sounded like Italian. Jennifer grasped a word here and there. Something about love. Or a donkey. Those who understood were wiping away tears of laughter.

She and Helen Baynor shared a mutual nod of appreciation for the plum-cherry velvet of the pinot noir that had been poured with the entree. It had taken Jennifer a number of years to like the taste of wine but now reds were her favorites and this Ardani vintage was very tasty. The chair next to Baynor was empty, and Jennifer had noted the name on the place card was Helen's partner, Chef Laura Izmani. No doubt attention to the kitchen had kept her from joining them.

Jennifer wondered if someone like Baynor had anything like Marley's chains to carry around. Closing in on sixty, she surely didn't look it. Baynor's blue-gray eyes were bright and expressive, and the wave in her salt-and-pepper hair highlighted the cheekbones that made her instantly recognizable. She continued to hold court on Broadway past the years when women were only cast as moms, shrews and crazies. Jennifer was trying not to blow what cool she had left by admitting to the star that she'd seen *Auntie Mame* three times during its first run.

The worst ear worm ever, she decided, was "Here Comes the Bride." But the version in her head went, "You're wearing pajamas, you're wearing pajamas. You're wearing paJAMas, and everyone saw your boobs."

If she'd been properly attired, she probably wouldn't feel as awkward as she did. But she'd still be out of place. Politics weren't her thing, so while she recognized many of the other women, she couldn't reel off that many names. Toni Blanchard and her winemaking wife were chatting across the next table with Leah Beck and her partner, both of whom Jennifer had met at a gallery opening in San Francisco. Jennifer would have rather been seated near them. She didn't want to be catching hints of Suzanne's cologne and watching her fingers tap idly on the table.

It wasn't fair, Suzanne and her hands. Nothing about Suzanne was fair. Not the brain wattage and confident ambition. Not the shape of her head or the angle of her jaw, not the soft lips Jennifer knew could reduce her to a whimper. From that creepy photographer onward, far too many people thought buying her time meant they'd also bought her body. The only thing she looked forward to as she got older was an end to the relentless propositions. She said *no* constantly.

It wasn't fair that Suzanne was automatically *yes*. Not that she would ever ask again.

Suzanne was chuckling at the story Helen Baynor was telling about meeting her wife. Something about an amusement park and fear of heights. Jennifer's attention wandered and she added more faces to her growing list of "I should probably know who that is."

Gail Welles' unmistakable laugh from somewhere behind her was full of good humor. Unlike her response to any news she encountered about Suzanne's dating life, Jennifer ultimately had been pleased to see Lena happy. Even if it was with someone who acted circles around, well, everyone. At least Lena's heart was no longer on her conscience.

That she had a conscience would surprise a lot of people.

Tonight, however, their marital bliss stung. Lena had been the only woman to come close to Suzanne in allure. That they had met just a few weeks after the last time she'd been with Suzanne might have had something to do with how easily she'd succumbed to Lena's attraction, not that Jennifer would ever admit it out loud. She certainly hadn't told Lena she was on the rebound from a relationship that had never gotten beyond the flare of hot sex.

She closed her eyes for a moment, picturing Lena in the rainstorm that had driven them, laughing, into Lena's car for shelter. Lena's reluctance to get involved with one of her hired players might have been part of the attraction. When she'd been seen with the private but definitely lesbian Selena Ryan even after production had ended, the bottom-feeding, blood-leeching gossip bloggers had made their usual sly insinuations.

Almost simultaneously she'd landed her star-making break, a leading role in an action blockbuster. Its director had thought dating her would cover his own huge personal issues. She knew Lena thought events had happened the other way around, but it made little difference. She'd pretended poor Corey was her new beau and tossed Lena aside, as Suzanne had said, like a broken pair of shoes. Corey had also been discarded. Every year since anything like a personal life had been discarded. There was work. There was resting from work. There was room for nothing else.

She decided to stop drinking the wine. It would only make her morose. The lies piled on by gossip sites about her seducing and abandoning someone on every project she'd ever worked on didn't usually bother her. The truth produced enough angst to keep her from worrying about lies. She stared into the red depths and knew if she finished it she'd be seeing the faces of all the people she'd wounded floating up at her.

That her publicist and social media contractors loved to splash around photos of Jennifer accompanied by Hollywood's most eligible bachelors was, she supposed, a continuation of the same career-salvaging lies. People didn't question what they expected to see. The formal comment was always that while La Lamont enjoyed the nightlife, she was married to her career, and you only had to look at her IMDb filmography to see the truth of the statement.

She surreptitiously checked the trending feed again. *Buzztastic* was tweeting a stream of comments, including an extreme blowup with arrows.

Hey @realJenniferLamont Are those tuck and lift scars we see? #Boobarella

Bombshell @realJenniferLamont Trying out for aging Playboy bunny biopic? #Boobarella

Look @realJenniferLamont Thanks! Love watching you flaunt it for the ladies! #Boobarella

Wow @realJenniferLamont Is it time to check in for a rehab refresh—

She blocked the site again. It had been a mistake to even look. She would just leave it to the publicist and crew to deal with online issues. Her agent would come up with a way to exploit it because BeBe LaTour was very good at what she did.

She'd survived her actual mistakes and she would survive whatever viral storm the boob accident stirred up. She'd sit here in pajamas and pretend everything was just peachy.

You, she reminded herself, are the woman who acted opposite Hyde Butler in the against-type performance that had won the action movie star an Academy Award. While sex appeal was arguably still her strongest selling point, her consistent ability to provide strong, crafted performances that elevated the profile of productions kept her agent hopping with offers.

Helping a man win an Oscar was a weird kind of job security. *Viva Hollywood.*

She knew it could all go away in a heartbeat. The remake of Hitchcock's *Rope* releasing this summer might flop, and she'd take the blame for botching a role originally written for a man.

An attractive black woman in a classic forest green Dolce & Gabbana suit dropped a kiss on Helen Baynor's cheek and slid into the chair next to her. Chef Izmani had freed herself from her duties. To Jennifer's eye, she looked only a little frazzled.

"Did you get to hear any of the speech?" Helen casually tweaked the other woman's collar flat. "She was earlier than expected."

"I caught the last half." To Jennifer she said, "I am such a huge fan. I don't miss an episode of *American Zombie Hunters*."

"Thank you," Jennifer said. "It's the first time I've done a show like that and I simply can't believe the fan base. It's intense and really vocal."

"Laura's not exaggerating," Helen said. "When the DVR gets full my shows mysteriously are the ones that get deleted."

Laura shrugged. "I don't know what she's talking about."

Suzanne left off her conversation with the mathematician to say to Laura, "Dinner was fantastic. You are a magician."

Jennifer raised her glass. "Absolutely delicious." She saw a flicker of speculation cross Laura's face as her gaze went from Jennifer to Suzanne. Jennifer quickly added, "My date stood me up."

"What an idiot."

"I know, right?"

"I don't suppose you'll tell me if your character dies at the end of the season?"

She grinned at Laura. "I can't breathe a word."

"Well, can't blame me for asking." Laura glanced toward the house and got to her feet. "Sorry, dessert should have been on its way out by now."

"I knew she wouldn't make it for five minutes." Helen followed Laura's departure with an open, intimate gaze.

More marital bliss. Jennifer felt like an outsider with her nose pressed up against the glass of a world she couldn't believe existed. When she'd been on *Ellen* to promote the first of the Bot franchise movies, she had tried to like the woman, but the echo of Suzanne's "I think you're a coward" had left her choking with bitterness. Ellen had made the leap, but she'd landed in a place that wasn't open to Jennifer. Nobody, but nobody, believed Jennifer Lamont was *nice*.

When the truth was ugly, the blogosphere increased the font size. When lies were juicier than truth, they put the headlines in red. Once upon a time she'd fed them anything they wanted to hear. A lesbian dalliance in the past was tolerated as long as she was actually straight and only flirted with women where men could watch. Ironically, it had been another project with Selena, one she'd forced her way into, that had made her take stock of the deals she'd made with too many devils. Hyde Butler had tried to tell her she had a choice, that she could change. As if reinventing herself would be *easy*.

Chef Izmani had lit a fire under someone because waiters bearing dessert plates were making their way to the tables. This excruciating evening would soon be over. You're just here for the sculpture, Jennifer reminded herself. Thinking about the past isn't going to get you anywhere. You burn it, then it doesn't exist and there's nothing but blue skies in your life.

Fiddle-dee-dee. Right.

"I can't believe our luck," Helen Baynor was saying. "I thought about moving to Illinois just to vote for Van Allen."

"I've never met her. Kind of glad I didn't tonight." Jennifer couldn't help a mournful look down at her pajamas.

"You look delectable. Very Dietrich."

Good gracious on steroids, she'd just pity pumped Helen Baynor for a compliment. *Pathetic, just pathetic.*

CHAPTER THIRTY-FOUR

"Life is a banquet!" Helen Baynor's empty cigarette holder traced an extravagant circle in the air. "Let the auction begin!"

Suzanne was positively tingling with anticipation as the two women from Sotheby's whisked the drape off the woman-sized sculpture. An initial shared gasp of pleasure deepened to match her own murmur of awe. She had seen it while it was being set up this afternoon, but the bay of filtered lights deepened the natural shadows of the work, showing off new angles of color and depth. A broken cocoon of highly polished chrome revealed an inner figure of light and dark blues, shot through with yellow and a pale green. The spotlight behind the piece amped up the color spectrum while showing off curves and fluted waves of crystal clarity. It might have been a woman's hair, or her shoulders, or the sea, or all three at once.

After Leah Beck had taken a bow and the applause died down, the auctioneer read the catalog listing, a copy of which had been placed at every seat. "On offer tonight to the highest bidder is a six-foot mixed media sculpture in chrome, silver, air, glass and acrylic. The piece is not part of a series. It is uniquely cast, carved, molded and worked by artist Leah Beck and completed within the last three months. This is the first time 'Jackie Sunday Morning' has been offered for acquisition."

"I think this is going to be too rich for my blood." Helen Baynor put down the numbered paddle that had been next to her plate with a resigned air.

"It's stunning." Suzanne risked a glance at Jennifer, who had a white-knuckle grip on her paddle.

"I'll have to be content with the vintage Wonder Woman print from earlier. Laura will love it." Baynor shrugged. "For some reason I thought the Beck piece would be small. That beauty will start high and go up from there."

"Twenty," a voice said from the back of the room.

"Twenty plus one," Suzanne said with a wave of her paddle.

Jennifer lifted her paddle and called out, "Thirty."

"Thirty plus one." Suzanne's prompt response created a ripple of laughter.

The voice from the back said, "Thirty-two."

Jennifer twirled her paddle in her fingertips. "Forty."

"Forty plus one."

"Forty-two." Helen Baynor suddenly waved her paddle with a grin. "I can put it on loan to MOMA and visit it whenever I want."

Suzanne suspected that Helen was helping drive up the price. It was for a good cause, after all.

Jennifer turned her head to dare Suzanne with a look. "Fifty."

"Fifty. Plus. One."

"Isn't it bad form for the host to be bidding?"

"I'm making sure it's a fair price for something that will still be here long after we've reverted to star dust."

Jennifer gave her a narrow look. "Sixty."

Suzanne dipped her paddle and the auctioneer promptly said, "I have sixty plus one. That's sixty-one thousand. Do I hear sixty-five?"

"Seventy."

"Seventy plus one."

Jennifer snapped, "I can do this all night."

Suzanne's smile was sunny and innocent. "If you can, I can."

A blush began in Jennifer's cheeks while her eyes tried to carve open Suzanne's skull. "Don't go there."

After the amused burst of laughter died down, the voice from the back upped the price again and Jennifer set her paddle down with a regretful shrug of surrender and a very fake smile of acceptance.

Suzanne and the other bidder got to their feet, each calmly counting upward in increments of five. She knew the other bidder was an art dealer that Leah Beck's wife had pointed out early in the evening as someone who'd only be here if she had a serious, committed client backing her. The client was probably an Orange County mega-church pastor with backward views on equality for anyone who wasn't a member of his flock. He collected art and had lately been picking up anything by artists over the age of fifty—speculating on their eventual demise and the rise in the price of their work. Jackie Frakes had called him a vulture, but seemed resigned to the prospect that the piece would end up in those hands. It would be a lot of money to a good cause, which was why her wife had donated the work to begin with.

One of two things are going to happen, Suzanne thought as she raised to one-fifteen. She would either win and be extremely pleased to place the sculpture at the Getty alongside their small collection of Beck paintings, or the collector would win and the new owner's conservative-values name would be listed as a prominent donor to Planned Parenthood of Southern California. Even if she lost it would feel like winning.

There was a collective gasp when she took the bidding over two hundred thousand, then a spontaneous burst of applause when she yielded to the other bidder at two-sixty. Champagne began to circulate on trays and Suzanne sat down, very relieved. A speech from Reyna Putnam would cap off the evening and she could look back on the months of planning as a job well done.

Jennifer gave her a cross look. "You needn't look so pleased with yourself."

"But I am pleased."

"I didn't stand a chance, and I sacrificed my poor Jimmy Choo's."

"I hope the evening wasn't a total waste." Suzanne belatedly realized how that sounded. "I honestly did not mean anything else by that."

Jennifer gave her a tight nod but said nothing as Suzanne rose in response to the auctioneer's wave. She shared a congenial handshake with the winner, took note of the name the auctioneer inked onto the work's title of ownership and hid her inner mirth. It was indeed the conservative thrice-married family values pastor whose use of the church's revenues to build an automobile and art collection he personally owned scandalized everyone but his own parishioners. Maybe he had no idea where his money was going. More likely he didn't care. Integrity was not a value he embodied.

She reminded herself to tell Carina about the scathingly brilliant idea she'd just had. Carina would laugh, quite a lot. So would Annemarie. Goodness, she really liked pushy women.

The sculpture remained beautifully lit as she introduced their featured speaker. Reyna Putnam wasn't the charismatic powerhouse that seemed the hallmark of politicians like Van Allen, but she had an intensity of focus and careful attention to the power of her words that showed in her investigative exposés. Yet as interested as she was in Putnam's speech, she was once again distracted by the memory of catching Jennifer in her arms and the brush of Jennifer's hair at her throat. Get a grip, she warned herself.

She couldn't stop herself from stealing a quick glance at Jennifer. She was studying her phone and put it back out of sight with a pained expression. Clearly, the auction over, she wanted to be elsewhere.

She drew on all her cynicism as Jennifer ran her hands through her hair, apparently listening attentively to Putnam's findings about the link between race, income and access to health care. She needed to stop watching her. She was going to get caught.

CHAPTER THIRTY-FIVE

Black SUVs arrived to whisk guests to the exclusive hotels in La Jolla's downtown, only minutes away. Others were being ferried to the helipad at the nearby university, where Suzanne had arranged quick transfers to the San Diego airport before the final flights out for the evening. Laura Izmani and Helen Baynor had been among the first to depart, hoping to make a connection that would get them back to New York by morning.

Jennifer kept checking the texts from her agent. BeBe was calling talk show producers to shop an interview while the picture was the talk of the web. As Lena had said, she should try to get ahead of it.

She needed to get back to Los Angeles. The alarm clock would go off at five a.m., and they were in green screen for a couple of hours first thing after makeup. At least the traffic would be better than it had been driving down in the late afternoon.

She surreptitiously hiked the pajama bottoms up one more time and did her best not to step on the hems as she circulated among the remaining guests. She thanked the lovely winemaker with the Sophia Loren eyes for the very much enjoyed vintages, and paused to shake hands with anyone who expressed interest in her work—it salved her bruised dignity to gather a few compliments.

"I read that it's really you with the sword." A mid-forties woman in an intricately beaded dashiki was finishing a mini tart with minced fruit and chocolate. Jennifer had managed to stop herself at two. "Not a stunt double?"

"Really me. The producers thought they'd have to hire me a coach for the sword play, but I was already proficient with several types of blades. Once they found me one with the right balance the zombie heads started to roll." I should know who this is, Jennifer told herself. She didn't think they'd met before, but they had been in the same places at the same time. Black women in the industry stood out in the sea of white at almost any gathering. Her mind refused to dredge up the setting that might have helped her remember the woman's name. "Aren't those tasty? I could have snarfed an entire tray."

"They truly are a wonder. I'm curious—will you be doing more television than movies in the future?"

"I'll consider any role that pays." It was her stock answer. "Signing on to do a limited role in a series often dovetails perfectly with filming schedules too. *American Zombie Hunters* wraps up about the time I'll be starting promotion tours for *Rope*."

"I'm looking forward to that. Did they have to make many changes because you're not Jimmy Stewart?"

Jennifer desperately wished she could remember the woman's name. "Most of the changes were due to updating for a contemporary time setting. I loved doing a one-set movie. Not like hunting zombies, which is exhausting." She quickly added, "Not that I'm complaining. It's great fun. It has been a good change for the industry, letting go of the idea that performers are locked into one medium or the other."

"And it's also good that production companies can create projects without a mandate to reach the eighteen-to-twenty-year-old male demographic." Lena had joined them. "How have you been, Clementine? Your mother is recovering well?"

"Mad as a hornet that she waited to get a new knee. Claims I never told her it would improve her life. Listen, Lena, can put a word in your ear about something?"

"Sure." Lena turned away as Jennifer realized she'd been chatting with Clementine Molokomme. She hoped no one had taken a picture or BeBe would demand an explanation as to why her client was talking to a rival agency. No amount of saying it was just at a party would make a difference and she'd be sending muffin baskets for a week.

"You're heading back tonight?" Gail, being Gail, looked genuinely interested in Jennifer's answer.

"Yes, early call. It's the final weeks of the shoot for the season."

Gail leaned closer. "You can tell me—who's going to die?"

"I would never say. You know they make you sign the confidentiality agreement in your own blood."

"Spoilsport." Gail was about to add something when Lena gestured and she immediately joined her.

Jennifer tried to summon up the ill will to think of Gail as Lena's lapdog, but she was suddenly just too tired. Her brain was spinning in too many directions. It didn't help that Suzanne was in her line of sight and something she'd just said made the woman she was talking to laugh with delight.

Duh, she thought. Of course Carina Estevez would be here. *Perfect.* The living proof that Suzanne had moved on. She knew Carina's serene face from too many Google searches for updates when a random headline had made it clear the two were dating. Jennifer felt like a painted doll next to all that fresh, unblemished, naturally tawny skin.

Well this night just got better and better. She was surrounded by lesbians who thrived, two exes and she was wearing pajamas. It was like an anxiety nightmare. She was in the wrong place. Hadn't studied for this test. She was the thing that wasn't like all the others and everyone would notice.

They had all figured out something she hadn't and taken chances she didn't have the guts to take. It wasn't a nightmare, this was the life she'd earned. Suzanne had had it right all along: she was a coward.

She knew Carina and Suzanne had stopped dating after a year or so. Like everyone else, she had no idea why. They had clearly remained friends. What did it matter? Jennifer was no Carina Estevez. In this little triangle there was the smart one, the good one and the bitch, and Jennifer had no illusions about which role was hers.

It's nothing to you, she told herself. Nevertheless she took a deep breath and went to make her thanks for the evening. Life just wasn't complete until you'd met your ex's ex.

Carina was still laughing as she said, "It's a pleasure to meet you, Ms. Lamont. I am a big fan."

"Jennifer, please. And likewise." There was nothing to indicate Carina was being ironic or even knew that she and Suzanne had a history. "Did I miss a joke?"

Suzanne assumed a too-innocent expression as Carina explained. "The person who bought the sculpture is that so-called family values preacher. The one with the three-thousand seat church up in Orange and a dozen Rolls Royces."

"Oh no! What a waste." Jennifer glared at Suzanne. "Why did you stop bidding?"

"I think I got twenty thousand more out of him than he wanted to pay, which feels good."

"And—" Carina pinched Suzanne's arm playfully. "She just sent texts to take out full page ads in the *Los Angeles Times* and the *Orange County Register* thanking him."

Jennifer shook her head. "I'm missing something."

Suzanne's expression was smugly pleased. "One of the major beneficiaries of his largess is Planned Parenthood. I think people should know what a swell guy he is."

Jennifer's hoot of amusement turned heads. "You're going to post copies on the net, right? I'll retweet that image." She thumbed her phone back to life. "Twitter, follow… @MasonGeekGirl… Got it." She caught Suzanne giving a little nostalgic shake of the head and for a moment Jennifer was back in that tiny electronics shop in Times Square, getting her first lesson in mobile messaging. "You're right. He needs to be thanked. Loudly."

Carina turned to wind her arm around another woman's waist. After a smooch on Suzanne's cheek, the couple made their way toward the front door. A glance at Suzanne's face didn't reveal any particular reaction. Jennifer didn't know why she was even checking.

"I really must be going. I have an early wake-up." She gestured at her clothes. "Thank you for the pajamas."

"You're wel—" Suzanne broke off to exchange a hug with someone Jennifer recognized as a local luxury car dealer. It was rare, a woman with an auto empire. "Thanks, Anna. Regards to your better half. She's stuck at home with the offspring?"

Suzanne wandered away and Jennifer felt dismissed. What else had she expected? All that was left was fetching her dress from the low bookshelf where Suzanne had tucked it. Unlike the Choos, the dress could be repaired.

Her phone pinged again. Another direct tag to a clever little GIF someone had created putting the pictures of her falling in order. Nearly as good as video. Thankfully it ended while Suzanne was still blurry.

Dress over one arm, she hiked up her pajama pants hopefully for the last time, and joined the queue for the valet. Suzanne towered over everyone the way she did in any crowd. Jennifer mused on that first party at the loft when Suzanne had been eager to fill her world with a crowd. In Santa Cruz it had definitely felt as if she needed space and distance from people. That phase was obviously over—this house was large enough to hold a battalion. It was also a long way from CommonTech's offices, but with the latest in modern technology Suzanne was certain to possess, distance meant nothing, she supposed.

She discussed the state of her cocktail gown with several other women as they stood in the rapidly shortening queue. "I'm lucky only the shoes got hurt. When I turf out, I turf out *hard*."

As everyone nearby laughed she noticed that Suzanne had withdrawn to one side. She'd gone very still while staring at her phone. What had popped up on the web now?

She excused herself and as she neared Suzanne her curiosity turned to dismay. Suzanne's skin had gone translucent around her eyes—she was clearly shaken.

"What is it?" She glanced at Suzanne's phone display but saw only the usual text messaging screen.

"Annemarie. She's in the hospital. She stopped breathing."

"Oh no!"

"The text is from an EMT using the ICE list on her phone. She's breathing again. I've got to get myself to San Francisco. I'm family. I have—all her papers." Suzanne's voice was tight with worry.

"The helicopter to the airport?"

"It did its last run twenty minutes ago, and the last flight to the Bay Area leaves in twenty anyway. Believe me, I know them all."

"I am literally driving right past LAX to get home. If the traffic is good and the cops are sleeping, I could drop you off in ninety-five minutes. If they have flights. Or a charter." She clicked through the freeway map in her mind. "Even better, John Wayne Airport is maybe an hour from here right now."

"Checking." Suzanne rapidly tapped at her phone. She was so pale her lips were tinged with blue.

"Sit down," Jennifer ordered. "Before you fall over."

Suzanne didn't check for a chair, just began sitting. Jennifer kicked an ottoman under her in the nick of time. "John Wayne will be just about done for the day. I sometimes fly out of there too. At LAX I see a cluster of flights leaving for San Francisco or Oakland. One will have an empty seat. It's too close to departure to use online booking. I'll try calling or just chance it at the airport."

"I'll drive."

Suzanne looked up from the phone as she had only just realized who she was talking to. "I can drive myself."

"You won't need to waste time parking. Plus you can call the airlines and the hospital while I drive."

The woman who had been Suzanne's shadow most of the evening suddenly appeared, tablet cradled in one arm. "Is there something I can help with?"

Suzanne got to her feet, the color coming back into her face. "I have an emergency and need to leave."

"Don't worry about a thing." Fingers flew over the surface of the tablet. "I've got the caterers to oversee and the cleaning crew in the morning. I'll have all those delicious leftovers to myself."

She seemed efficient, but kind of fidgety, Jennifer thought. Did she live here? Amanuensis? Girlfriend? Not your business, she reminded herself, even as Suzanne ruled out that last possibility by rapidly going over several points of security and assuring the planner it was fine if she held on to the card key until Suzanne claimed it.

Jennifer's hybrid Lexus was promptly retrieved by the valet. They were settling into the car when Jennifer said, "What about luggage?"

Suzanne held up her wallet and cell phone. "My place in San Francisco has anything else I might need. If I have no luggage to check, they'll let me on with only thirty minutes ticketing."

"Seat belt."

Suzanne buckled up and muttered to herself, not appearing to notice that Jennifer was well over the speed limit as they left the cliffside community, then whipped past the gates to the university. The medical center flashed by, then they were northbound on the freeway.

Suzanne was prodding her phone. "Tell me which flight has a seat... Come on," she urged. "That is so my password, what the hell?"

Jennifer kept her eyes on the road. Password rage was not something she wanted to interfere with.

"Finally. Who designs these protocols? One but not all capital letters, no special characters and no repeating numbers or letters. This is why twenty percent of email generated by business is password resets."

"Perhaps that's something your think tank could work on."

It was as if she hadn't spoken. There was more muttering, then a small noise of success. "There are three that say they have seats."

"Good. Hopefully there won't be construction to slow us down." She often took off her shoes to drive, so being barefoot didn't bother her. One eye checked continually for CHP in the rearview mirror while she stuck with the strategy of being the second fastest car on the road.

Suzanne finally looked up from her phone. "You're going very fast."

Jennifer eased over a lane, let a black Bugatti go by and then moved over to the fast lane again. "That guy is volunteering to take the ticket, so it's all relative. Until you invent a transporter, this is how I roll. Literally."

Suzanne called first one and then a second airline and ended up with an unticketed booking. "Into Oakland, but same difference at this hour."

"The GPS says we'll have about ten minutes to spare." Jennifer tapped the display on the dash. "It factors in my, uh, average speeds."

"Your feet are so dainty. Who knew they were made of lead?" Suzanne screwed her earpiece more firmly in place. "Trying the hospital now."

She listened as Suzanne convinced someone she was Annemarie's next of kin.

"An infection? She had the flu—it's not the flu? I know. I know." She clenched her hands into fists, then visibly relaxed them as she took a deep breath. "I know. Is she in any danger? Well, what can you do to bring down her temperature?"

Camp Pendleton was behind them when Suzanne dropped the phone into her lap. She'd left messages for several staffers and called the hospital again for another update.

"Does Annemarie live in San Francisco? Where did they take her?"

"She's near the Presidio, so they took her to Cal Pacific."

"An infection?"

"She thought she had the flu, but they think it's bacterial pneumonia."

"Then antibiotics will help right away. It'll be okay." She tried to lighten Suzanne's tension. "I'm not a doctor, but I have played one in the movies. More than once."

Suzanne seemed to relax slightly. "I think she'll be okay. She called 911 herself. Which is contrary to her whole superwoman ethos."

"Hang on." She eased off the gas and changed lanes, slowing until she could slip in between two trucks. A black-and-white zoomed past them, lights flashing. She gave it a moment, letting by several cars all using the high-speed corridor the CHP car had created, then moved back into the fast lane. "I never heard how you two met."

"I hired Annemarie at Connecks, way back when. I wasn't so evolved and she called me out for the lack of women in management. She suggested I could right many of my wrongs by hiring her. We've been friends ever since."

Talking seemed to slow the nervous jiggling of Suzanne's legs. Jennifer picked up more speed as the freeway finally opened out to five lanes. Road work near Disneyland didn't even slow them down.

Suzanne finished another update call to the hospital. "Still running tests which means they're waiting for results." Pointing at the sign listing upcoming exits, she asked, "Wait, we're nearly there? We want Century, right? Did we fly? Is this *Chitty Chitty Bang Bang.*"

"Fun movie."

"The book is better."

"It always is. And no, we didn't fly. I have mad skills at speeding. You live in LA for long and it's what you do. Plus it might not be fair, but I have good success at talking my way out of tickets."

"I don't doubt that."

It sounded like a compliment, or at least Jennifer was pleased to take it that way. She made all the lights on West Century Boulevard, more cautious now that she was nearing the well-patrolled airport zone. Suzanne pointed out the airline and Jennifer looped to the correct approach lane.

"I appreciate this."

"You'd have found a way, but I was going right past," Jennifer repeated. She didn't want Suzanne to think this created an obligation. A perfect stranger could have made the same offer. "I really hope Annemarie is okay."

"Me too. She's very fit, but heart issues run in the family and she's already got a stent. So any infection is risky. She has this really obnoxious brother who thinks he should run her life, and even though she's signed a ream of papers stating he is not to ever have a say in her care or funeral or anything, the last time she ended up in the hospital he showed up and tried to get me thrown out of her room. I'm the bad influence, you know."

"I bet that confrontation was epic."

"It was. I'm not ashamed to say I used influence, bribery and threats to get him removed. He's picked up where her father left off harassing her. Religious bigot wingjob."

"And that explains why you're so pleased to get those full page ads."

"Who knew money could buy irony? Irony is funny when it happens to other people." Suzanne grinned suddenly. "Annemarie will choke up a lung laughing."

"I rather hope not." She evaded a security patrol to pull up behind the only other car, a slowly departing taxi. "Have a safe flight. Give her my best."

"Maybe not. She'll choke up the other lung."

"True."

Suzanne opened the door, then turned back. To Jennifer's surprise, she cupped her face and kissed her, slowly, softly, and lingering long enough to brush her nose to Jennifer's. "We might never meet again. That's a better memory."

Jennifer couldn't catch her breath as she watched Suzanne lope through the doors and hurry up to the lone ticket agent. Free to stare for the first time all evening, there was no denying that Suzanne was devastating in Armani. Something she said brought a smile to the young man's face. He handed her a boarding folio and she dashed away. Jennifer eased the car forward along the curb, able to keep her in sight until she turned into the security corridor.

Would it be the last time they saw each other? She hadn't intended to see Suzanne again, ever. Now—now the idea that she'd just watched her walk away for good was twisting her heart in two.

What a fool she was. Suzanne hadn't looked back and there was no point in telling herself that the kiss had been anything but goodbye. For good.

CHAPTER THIRTY-SIX

Annemarie pushed away her hospital tray, croaking, "I'm not eating that."

It was a welcome sign of life. Though dinner was long past, the nurse had decided to leave the tray in the hope that Suzanne would be able to coax Annemarie into eating something. Intravenous feeding could only do so much. It was nearing the twenty-four hour mark since admission and, even though Suzanne had told them that a healthy Annemarie was still a picky eater, the lack of interest in food was causing concern.

Her back creaked alarmingly as she rose from the stiff hospital chair. She hadn't moved since she'd gotten back from her quick trip to the cafeteria. She was regretting the burrito, but it had been the most appealing item on offer.

"I know your throat is sore from the tube, but look." Suzanne dipped a spoon into what appeared to be applesauce. "Slightly yellow ground up food matter, and it's all yours. Not like pizza at the office, I didn't lick it or anything. My cooties have been nowhere near it."

"I do not want that, and you can take that chocolate-flavored chalk away too."

"If you eat they'll stop waking you up every two hours to ask you to eat. Plus, if you think I'm smuggling in your favorite sushi, you haven't gotten a good look at the nurses. But I'll make you a deal."

Annemarie's bloodshot eyes momentarily blazed with laser death rays.

"If you eat some applesauce I'll read you some of today's mail." She had expected to spend the day after the party overseeing the cleanup and Annemarie likewise had not planned to be in the office. There had been no missed meetings, but email had arrived all day as it usually did. "I didn't think to bring you some of Laura Izmani's leftovers. She had these crispy strings that turned out to be red and yellow beets and the goat cheese pesto was so good with those on top."

"You creep. Stop talking about what I missed." Annemarie dipped her spoon in the applesauce and put the barely coated utensil in her mouth. "Ooo. Yummy."

"Stop spitting at me like a wet cat. I spent the day watching you breathe." She gestured at the tall narrow window. "I missed out on San Francisco sunshine because you wouldn't get with the program and bring down your temperature."

"Yeah, my day has been one grand adventure too. A real barrel of fun." Annemarie put the spoon in her mouth again and this time it had actual applesauce on it.

Suzanne flicked up her messages and read off the subject lines and senders she thought might interest Annemarie, and let her choose if she wanted to hear the actual contents. The high temperature was stubborn, but after an anxious morning it had finally come down several degrees. Somewhere around noon Suzanne had fallen asleep for an hour, and as the clock ticked toward midnight she felt increasingly gritty. "Rosie reports that the EU estimates are under, but they know why. They feel our stake is as secure as it can be."

Annemarie grunted which was exactly how Suzanne felt about it.

"This is more interesting. Rosie and Farouk want to pursue the reverse converter stake."

Annemarie's eyelids drooped. "I'd be fine if I weren't so dizzy."

"And still running a fever. And sleeping an hour for every five minutes awake. And setting new personal records for white blood cell count."

"If I'm that sick I deserve better food. This doesn't even taste like apple." The dish was nearly empty, though, which would please the nurses.

"It's what you get, and you have to eat. Now if you finish the broth I'll let you have your phone for fifteen minutes."

"I'm not drinking cold chicken broth."

"Silly rabbit. What makes you think it's going to taste like chicken? Drink-ee and you get-ee, there's a good little girl." She dangled Annemarie's iPhone just out of reach. She was pretty sure Annemarie would find it difficult to focus on the small screen, but after several gulps from the small bowl accompanied by Annemarie's colorful descriptions, she handed over the phone.

Annemarie sighed almost happily as the device powered up. She cooed to it, "We've been parted too long, my dear friend."

Suzanne didn't comment that some color was coming back into Annemarie's lips and cheeks. "You like your iPhone more than you like me."

"I like it more than I like all people. Siri and I were meant to be together." She adjusted the hospital bed and propped the phone against her empty bowl. "It's awfully heavy though."

"Right. You're just a little dizzy, sure. Not running on half voltage."

"Delete, delete, delete, forward to calendar, delete." She laughed, which turned into a half-wheeze. "You took out full page ads thanking that woman-hating cretin for donating to Planned Parenthood?"

"I kind of did, yeah." It had created a great deal of amusement in some quarters of the web.

"You are so good when you're evil and that's right up—" Annemarie gaped at her phone. "What the hell, Suzanne? What. The. Hell! Are you nuts?"

"What did I do?" Oh crap. She'd forgotten why she'd been happily supporting the doctor's no phones edict. "I had no idea she'd even be there."

"Yeah, and when I woke up this afternoon and you went on and on telling me about the greatest party of the century that I missed out on, you never even mentioned her name."

There was a chance that Annemarie would get faint or dizzier and not see the red burning heat Suzanne could feel in her cheeks. "I didn't want to upset you."

"She's waving her boobs at you!"

"It was an accident."

"Hashtag *Boobarella*." Annemarie snorted. "Okay, that's pretty funny. At least tell me you didn't talk to her."

She could sit calmly at a table and discuss millions of dollars and billions of data points, tell guys who thought they'd invented numbers that they'd made a mistake, but Annemarie could still make her feel like a blithering fool. "Well, we had to speak. I had to be a good host."

"Hello, goodbye and don't let the door hit you in the ass. That was all you needed to say, right?"

Suzanne had never been so happy to see a nurse in her life. It was even the petite one who was so far Suzanne's favorite.

Nurse Jackson's dark brown eyes didn't miss a thing. "You're eating, that's good. But you shouldn't be using your—"

"It was how I got her to eat." Suzanne was happy to change the subject. "She has seven more minutes, then I'm powering it down."

"Yes, and then I'm going to spend an hour reminding my friend here that she is an idiot."

A professional flick of the hand changed the readout on the bedside monitor, displaying a barrage of numbers that the nurse scanned without a change in expression. "If you think that's why you were put on this earth, go for it."

"Hey!" Suzanne protested. "She already believes that, no need to further empower her."

"Hospital beds are boring. She might as well do something she enjoys." She fixed Annemarie momentarily with a side-eye that would freeze most mortals. "Within reason."

"You are my favorite caregiver," Annemarie volunteered.

Nurse Jackson tweaked the bed covers and checked the water level in the pitcher next to the bed. "By the way, if I'm not mistaken, your friend is going to be on TV later."

It took Suzanne a moment to realize the nurse was speaking to her. "What?"

"Jennifer Lamont. I saw the picture of you two on Facebook during my break. She's on one of the late night shows." She gave Suzanne a wink on her way out the door.

"She's not my friend," Suzanne corrected, but the door was already closed.

"That took you a little too long to deny. You're still a moron. And you didn't answer my question." Annemarie pushed her phone away with a weak cough. "You probably sat next to her and drooled."

"I did not drool."

"You shit. What are you thinking? More abuse? Don't give me garbage about how she's changed."

"I don't think she has." Throughout the boring, anxious day she'd recalled the kiss in the car. "She's more beautiful than ever. Success suits her. Since we're being honest."

"Honest would be me finding out she was there from you, not Twitter."

"Your weak heart…"

"Con artist. I know all your moves."

"Fine. She drove me to the airport."

Annemarie put up a hand. "Okay, I can't take anymore. Just tell me that you have no plans to see her again."

"I don't. We said goodbye and that was it. Finis." She was never, ever going to mention the kiss.

"I'll believe you for now." She closed her eyes and pulled the hospital blanket a little higher. "Wake me up in time to watch the show she's on."

"Why?"

"So I can throw a brick at the stupid TV, stoopid. So stooo…"

Annemarie would be out for a few hours at least, and there was no way Suzanne was going to wake her. In fact, she was going to go right to her condo, take a shower and get some real sleep herself. She was not going to sit here and wait for Jennifer's face to show up on the television set.

She could always catch it online later. If she decided she cared.

CHAPTER THIRTY-SEVEN

It was an entrance like any other, Jennifer told herself. Her exhaustion was hidden under a thick layer of makeup. She'd dressed the part and had a story to tell. The curtain swept back and she stepped into the bright stage lights—and paused. The laughter washed over her in a roar of natural joy that soaked into every part of her. At some level, any applause was good applause.

The affable host of *Live from Late Night* joined the gleeful howls, applauding as she went from runway model attitude pose to slinky walk. He rose to usher her into her seat next to the interview desk, saying as the laughter died down, "Way to rock that cardigan!"

"It's Ralph Lauren—and you must be crazy if you think after what happened last night I would dress any other way!" She brushed fingertips over the buttons that ran from neck to lap. The sweater was a distinctive men's golf plaid with sleeves almost to her knees. "If only I'd been wearing this."

As they chatted about the hazards of high heels, the studio monitors displayed the least unfortunate shot, adding pixelation over The Girls. At least in that one she wasn't gaping like a beached fish.

"Of course I caught my heel," she answered. "And there I was, a-splay."

"A-splay? Is that a word?"

"It is now. Trending hashtag by tomorrow. It's truly galling as a former model to appear so clumsy. Butt glue doesn't hold up when you floor dive facefirst."

He lit up with his signature boyish grin. "Butt glue! You're kidding. That's a real thing?"

"It certainly is for models. Clearly not you."

"I don't have what it takes to be a model?" He feigned dismay.

"Let's find out, shall we?" Jennifer treated him and the audience to the smile she used just before her zombie hunting character cleanly sliced off a zombie's head. He faked a nervous swallow while the audience let out a low "oh" of warning and anticipation.

As the stagehands rolled a table out to center stage, Jennifer shucked off her cardigan to reveal her sleeveless little black dress. She showed the audience the product, which would make the manufacturer very happy, demonstrated how the ever-so-useful roll-on latex glue was easy to apply and then would anchor one of the pre-cut squares of silk from the table into place on her forearm. "Pageant contestants hold their bikini tops and bottoms in place with this stuff. I was covering my assets…" She paused to allow the audience to laugh. "Covering them with typical shields I didn't want to slip. You know, when a regular bra won't work."

"Yeah, I know all about that," he deadpanned.

She pulled the square of silk from her forearm, showing the sticky residue and patch of annoyed skin. "Butt glue is no fun to yank off all at once. Your turn."

He protested but yielded to the egging-on from the audience, and feigned euphoria as Jennifer unbuttoned his shirt. She got cuddle-close to him and did her best femme fatale blink. "Ready?"

"Sure." He fed the audience laughter by adding with a start, "Oh you mean for the butt glue."

She coated the middle of his unshaved chest with the roll-on. "I haven't used that much. And I avoided your nipples." She smoothed on a square of silk.

"This is a family show after all."

"I can't say nipples?"

"You can say nipples, you just can't play with them. So how do you get the stuff off?"

"With a little rubbing alcohol in the shower." Making the most of the moment, she mugged another mischievous look at the audience. "If you're lucky. But it's not your lucky day."

She yanked. He yelped and patted mournfully at his now patchy and mottled chest. The audience roared with delight and she could see the producer laughing appreciatively just offstage.

Make the most of the story, her agent had said. This was going to make the highlight reel.

"Ya big baby—that's nothing compared to a real bikini wax." She menaced him with the roll-on again and he waved her away.

The rest of the interview passed quickly with a few questions about *American Zombie Hunters*. At the break she retired to the green room, found it empty, and slumped gratefully into a chair. Her phone was buzzing from inside the leather bag she'd left on the table.

A text from BeBe. "Great bit! Worth it."

Goodie. Her agent was pleased.

After begging forgiveness from the director for leaving the day's shoot three hours early, a production assistant had driven her and luggage to LAX to catch a nonstop to JFK. A helicopter to the Metroport and a cab to 30 Rock had delivered her just in time to plan the gag with the staff and then grab chair time with a makeup artist who had managed to hide the circles under Jennifer's watery, sleep-deprived eyes. Her adrenaline was now depleted.

She hoped it was worth it. The *Buzztastic* filth was in full swing: *Is Junkie Jen back?* It wasn't even out of line, given her supposed history with rehab. She sent unkind thoughts in the direction of Phillip Questor and his brand of publicity. When poor Corey had been busted with cocaine, Phillip had advised her to play his tragic, misled girlfriend, and go to rehab with him. "Everybody's doing it," the idiot had gushed. He hadn't meant just rehab, he'd also meant using the director to squelch the sly insinuations from bloggers surrounding how much off-screen time she and Lena had been spending together.

The damn of it all was that it had worked. Talk shows suddenly wanted to book her, and while most asked about her struggle with substances, some also asked if she was gay. She told them all what they wanted to hear, which was coy lies sold with cheesecake smiles. Phillip was sending her audition requests and scripts by the dozen.

She was considered *serious* for stupid reasons, and she'd paid for her sudden visibility with the last glimmer of respect Selena Ryan had ever had for her.

Just playing the Hollywood Game. Exploiting the real misery of substance abuse for personal publicity and winning. Sure.

She didn't like the tiny voice that reminded her that all of it had been her decision. It had paid off. Those early years of success as an actress had included reviews where her abilities were equally discussed with her looks. She was living the big dream she'd cherished from childhood. It was nearly everything she had thought it would be.

Nearly.

God, she was tired. She was not going to think about Suzanne.

A production assistant knocked on the door, his young face a picture of serious attentiveness. "Would you like me to get you a cab?"

"Yes thank you. My luggage already went?"

"I personally took it over and gave it directly to the front desk."

Being tired made her feel old, but his earnestness was heartening coming from someone who probably worked twenty-hour days for pizza money. "Thank you so much, that was really very sweet of you. Do you have a book?"

He glanced over his shoulder.

"You didn't ask me, I asked you. I'm happy to. You were a doll earlier."

"You were tired after a long flight and late for makeup. I was glad to help." He surreptitiously withdrew a small autograph book from his pocket.

Jennifer signed the next blank page with a flourish. "Selfie?"

"My boyfriend will *die*. He loves, loves, loves you in *American Zombie Hunter* this season. Do you get killed or live in the season finale?"

She leaned into the frame of his camera. Just as he pressed the shutter she planted a smooch on his smooth, brown cheek. "He'll have to wait like everyone else to find out."

She wanted to say that of course she got killed, it was going to be a typically bloody season finale. Her contract was for the season and she had other projects on her schedule after that. Practicality alone meant she was going to lose her head in the end. But who knew for sure? She could be resurrected and do another season later on if the show continued to thrive.

She had washed the airplane out of her hair, peeled the stage eyelashes off and scrubbed her face down to real skin before she felt her brain finally stop spinning in circles. There was a good chance she'd sleep well, but she had a very early call to make a morning interview on a talk show. She'd be back on a plane to LA by noon and in her own bed by nine p.m.

In her own bed, by herself.

She couldn't shake off the feeling of Suzanne's mouth on hers. She'd expected anger and recriminations. The kiss and its tenderness had been the biggest surprise of the night.

CHAPTER THIRTY-EIGHT

Ignore him, Suzanne told herself. Just get your coffee and go.

Everyone waiting for their order in the tiny Java Stop was catching up on their morning feeds. She'd found in large cities the world over, that coffee pit stops were about as anticelebrity as it got. Everyone's eyes were on their devices, the flow of people in and out was brisk. She was willing to bet that Jennifer Lamont herself could walk in the front door and no one would notice. Suzanne liked knowing she could come and go and nobody took notice of the fact that the CEO of CommonTech liked espresso tall, room for milk.

The suit-and-loafers man next to her was studying a still of Jennifer from last night's late show. The sweater pic was positioned right next to the now infamous *#Boobarella* shot. The headline read "She Takes Off Her Sweater and You Won't Believe What Happens Next."

Gak. At least there wasn't a picture of her, and so far the comment from her P.R. firm of "Ms. Mason is grateful that only her guest's shoes were harmed" seemed to have kept her off the media radar. She inwardly groaned when she realized the guy was clicking down the link chain to find the undoctored pics of Jennifer's chesticles. His quick scroll got to the photo of Suzanne down on one knee, with a topless, swooning Jennifer in her arms. At least *her* gaze was on Jennifer's face.

Gross, he was zooming in.

She turned her back and glanced at her own phone. Annemarie hadn't answered her text from earlier saying she would be at the hospital after she sat in for Annemarie at two meetings. It was to be hoped that the patient was sleeping. She'd gotten update from the efficiently sassy Nurse Jackson just as she went off shift and knew that all vitals were improving. Sleep while the heavy-duty antibiotics did their work was the best thing.

Her coffee name "Geeky" was called by the barista and when she turned with her cup Mr. Loafers was giving her the "do I know you" look. She stared back. *All short-haired lesbians look alike, dude, but if you click her boobs again you're going to be wearing my espresso.* Fortunately he found something else to occupy his eyes.

When she was in San Francisco she liked to get her own coffee on the way to the office. The ritual allowed her to do her daily attempt at cooking, and few places were as anonymous. She was stirring in just the right amounts of cocoa and cinnamon when she heard Jennifer's voice.

See what happens when you think about her? Poof! She materializes.

Jennifer's face filled the flat-screen TV mounted to the far wall. The camera made the most of her expressive eyebrows and dark eyes, simple pearl earrings in delicate earlobes, red-tinted full lips and a classic cameo choker around her smooth throat before zooming out again. One of the show's hosts, all blond and giggles, asked, "How did you know you were a star? What was that like?"

"I still don't feel like one." Jennifer's modest shrug appeared genuine.

"You've been acting for twenty years."

"Mumble when you say that!" Jennifer rolled her eyes at the small studio audience, drawing laughs. "It still feels unreal sometimes. I'm working more than ever. I really can't say when I knew I'd leveled up, so to speak. Except maybe the time they removed the 'don't make eye contact' rule from my contracts. I mean, I no longer had to avoid making eye contact with the stars. And I realized that meant I was one of the names in other people's contracts, telling them they weren't supposed to make eye contact with me."

"What did that feel like?"

"It seemed so weird at first. You see people duck out of your line of sight, or they realize they caught your eye and look like you're about to get them fired. But then I was lucky enough to be on a huge, huge film with Hyde Butler—the second one we did together. There were sometimes fifty, sixty extras in a single scene. For all of them, that's a moment. I was thrilled to be on the same set with him, anyone would be. Who wouldn't want a selfie or an autograph or just to say a few words? But that would totally ruin the shoot schedule if thirty-forty people did that every day."

"Is it true that you two were an item at one time?"

"No truth to it whatsoever." Jennifer smoothed the front of what looked like a velvet dress in a stunning shade of violet. There was lace all around the neckline, like something out of Jane Austen. Her thick, blue-black hair was pulled back from her face with glittery clips. To Suzanne, she was the picture of relaxation and poise, even though just doing the time math, Suzanne could imagine how grueling it had been to get to New York for the appearance last night, then up again for another one.

The bubbly blonde was saying, "So come back after the break. Jennifer Lamont is going to give me a lesson on how to defend myself in the zombie apocalypse." A commercial for tooth whiteners began to play.

Her phone buzzed. Annemarie texted, *"The beeyotch was on my TV while I was eating. Bet you watched."*

She sighed. *"It was on at Java Stop. Not like I could turn it off. I needed coffee."*

The reply was quick. *"We need to talk."*

Terrific. It was a mild spring morning in San Francisco, with no sign of fog. The kind of day where she'd order in sandwiches and those who wanted to would camp out on the steps near U.N. Plaza to bask in the sunshine as they ate. Instead, she was going to get a lecture from Annemarie that she'd heard before.

She didn't need to hear it again. The airport had been goodbye, even if Jennifer was all over the TV and web. That would stop. Meanwhile, she should leave with her coffee and not stand around watching.

Too late—the commercials ended and the cheerful blonde was back. The cameras were trained on the space where musical acts sometimes performed, but instead of a band set up there was a fencing practice dummy to one side. Jennifer and the host were both holding long, slightly curved weapons. The host was in a thin little short-skirted dress and wearing spindly heels. Jennifer's dress, on the other hand, sleekly fell to midcalf where it brushed the tops of modestly-heeled leather boots. She looked even taller, and, well, *damn*. The outfit was demure and dangerous all at once. Was this what she wore on the TV show?

"I'm not a real zombie killer," Jennifer was saying. "I just play one on TV."

"How do you make it look so easy?"

Jennifer sighted down the length of the blade, then casually swung it in a tight figure eight. "It's a lot like playing tennis. You have to pay attention to blade position and angle, extend your arm while keeping in balance, and always follow through." As she spoke, Jennifer slow-motioned her way through each action. "Put it all together and you get this."

She was a sudden blur, a whirl of rippling skirts and supple knees, light flashing on her blade. Suzanne knew better than anybody that Jennifer was as strong as she was graceful. She shouldn't have been amazed to watch her spin and lunge, twirl again and then freeze, her blade a quivering inch from the practice dummy's neck.

It was a move Legolas would envy. Suzanne was not just amazed, she was awed.

Her phone buzzed.

Annemarie again. *"That's YOUR neck, dude."*

Suzanne headed for the street, not sure why what she'd seen left her so unsettled. It wasn't Annemarie's suggestion that Jennifer would figuratively decapitate her again. They had no plans to see each other and that was that. It was just that Jennifer had been, for those two seconds of dervish energy, not a Jennifer that Suzanne recognized. At all.

ACT IV

CHAPTER THIRTY-NINE

"Arguments against?" Suzanne glanced at the legal team's side of the conference table. "Kay? Vara?"

Kay made a concessionary gesture. "I've already said my piece. I'm not happy about the renewal clauses."

Vara seemed equally resigned. "You've heard our input. The device itself is promising but we are not in a strong enough position to reap the benefits if it becomes highly profitable."

Annemarie looked up from her doodling across the top of the presentation deck. "If it makes it past trial they've already said they'll consider going open source. Share the patent."

"That may be," Kay answered. "But those good intentions are not in this agreement. We want the world to share in this battery—"

"Energy storage medium," several voices from around the table corrected.

"Energy storage medium," Kay amended. "It's not a battery, I really do get that. Regardless, given the level of our participation I don't believe we're offering enough to bring them back to the table later to honor that ideal."

"I tend to agree with you," Suzanne said. "I'm afraid if we go back to them with revisions now, they'll head to another source of capital, one that won't even care about a more altruistic outcome down the road. At least we'll try."

Manuel clicked his pen open and closed before tossing it on the table. "Let's not act as if our own financial interests are completely secondary. I don't think we should miss out on the profits and exposure. Period. End of story. It could be hugely good for our bottom line and it's a great product to add to our history of picking winners."

Bickering broke out as it usually did. Their investment review meetings practiced creative dissent with a passion. Suzanne didn't know if it was the baking hot weather lately or something else that had left her feeling cranky and tired for the past few weeks. This kind of deal was what CommonTech did best, but she wanted to be anywhere but here. Maybe she ought to have teleconferenced and stayed home. A dip in the pool would be heavenly.

Annemarie wasn't chiming in, which wasn't like her. Then again, she'd been trying to be less alpha female since the health scare in the spring. She detested delegating, but was practicing it more.

Suzanne waved a hand and all the side conversations wound down. "We should go ahead. I'm going to kick this back to your team, Rosie. You've done a great job. I don't see why you shouldn't take it the rest of the way. Report back only if a magnitude of something changes. And that, my friends, is the last item on the agenda. See you all next week. Same bat time, same bat channel."

The room slowly cleared, but she stayed where she was because Annemarie didn't get up either. When the door closed she asked, "What?"

"Are you tired?"

"I'm something. Not tired. But something."

"I'm wondering why we're doing so many things the hard way."

Suzanne was surprised. "What do you mean?"

"Trying to do good and run a smart, profitable business at the same time. I don't mean we shouldn't try. Every business should try." Annemarie chewed on her little fingernail. "After Earth Tides failed so spectacularly, you know, we have to try harder."

That bruise didn't need anyone poking it to feel sore. "And?"

"Almost half the initiatives we back fail—because we take risks, and we should. But wrapped up in every failure is something good we hoped would come of it. So that dies too. And you know, lately, that's been depressing the hell out of me."

"I think you're on to something," Suzanne admitted. "CommonTech is humming along the way we built it to. We now ask ourselves where the good of all humankind is for everything we do, or we try to. But it feels...unsatisfactory, I guess."

"When I was in the hospital, the longest three days of my life, I thought about what would be left if I'd died."

"You've contributed to a lot of change," Suzanne protested.

"I know." Annemarie waved one hand dismissively. "But it's nowhere near what I feel I could do."

Suzanne paced in front of the conference room windows as they talked. She knew exactly what Annemarie meant. They both worked long hours and had massive resources at their disposal. CommonTech Foundry, the company's foundation arm, was making improvements to resources in schools. Many of the clients they'd invested in donated significant proceeds or product to underserved communities. But it still didn't feel like enough.

"Like Rosie's project today," Annemarie went on. "The urban upscale market will eat up that sleek little unit. It solves the electrical deprecation for new solar storage, increasing efficiency even in old installations. Companies like us will want the cleaner power supply and we'll pay for it. But if our clients don't decide to share the patent, where does that leave developing countries? They could build their own if they had the design, but they can't afford to buy it. So they won't. The global digital divide gets worse."

"Same for rural communities here at home. We've been after the stable power supply issue for years." She gazed out at the South of Market skyline. The sky was low and silvery with heat. It was still ten degrees cooler here than at home in La Jolla, and it was only just past Memorial Day.

Annemarie sighed. "Trying to do it through new innovations isn't fast enough. Clearly, not fast enough, because here we sit, still not sure the next breakthrough will make any difference to people who couldn't afford the last big breakthrough."

Suzanne went still. "What if..."

"What?"

"What if they *could* afford that last big breakthrough?"

"I don't follow."

"We buy the patents for single dwelling power storage, the ones that have the sweet spot of being both reliable and affordable, but they're no longer sexy. Two or three generations in technology back. Then we open source them."

"That's not what CommonTech does. I mean, how do we justify doing that to all of our employee owners? Spending their money for literally nothing? The stock will take a dip, which is going to wig out the analysts about our dividend projections. A lot of people count on the checks."

"Easy. We don't use their money."

"The Foundry could do it, I suppose."

"No, I don't want to deviate the foundation from its focus on education."

Annemarie's eyes widened and she slowly grinned. "You mean use *our* money. Because we're Two Not Broke Girls."

Suzanne laughed. "That's what I'm thinking."

"Our own foundation." Annemarie went silent for a long minute, and Suzanne knew to keep quiet. Finally she said, "We can back whatever the hell we want. Tech. Not tech. We're free from our corporate mission."

"We can do big and little things. There are people I think I'd love to work with, but they're not in tech, and I've let that stop me."

"Why can't you and I give out some genius grants?" Annemarie was grinning as she gathered her papers. "I have tingles. I haven't felt like this in years. Honest, Suze, I was thinking about quitting. It's not like either of us is here for the money."

"It was never just about money." With a rueful laugh she added, "But money is nice."

"When we were picketed after the Earth Tides investment went belly up with those huge losses, I almost got out." Annemarie had never admitted that before. "But I thought if I took my pile of money and ran, it made what they were saying about us true."

"Just in it for the money. Couldn't care less about anyone but ourselves. Yeah, I remember. Good times." Suzanne grimaced. "Well," she went on, "Rosie and Manuel are both ready to take on more. You take the driver's seat of our new adventure."

"You really are serious, aren't you?"

"The idea of working on something, being hands-on? I am dead serious. I guess—lately everything feels like a game I've mastered and I'm still playing it over and over. No exploits left, no new high score that means anything. A grind."

"Are we nuts, though? This is pretty profitable grind and sometimes it *is* fun."

"No, you were right. It's been a long time since either of us has done anything just for the money." She broke off. "Huh."

"What?"

"Just taking in how incredibly elitist and privileged that sounded." Suzanne turned away from the windows. "Wow. My father's voice just came out of my mouth. But I can hear him going all Yoda on me."

"There is no try," Annemarie intoned. "Yoda is right. Let's stop trying and do."

CHAPTER FORTY

Jennifer tucked her car under the awning behind her trailer and reluctantly turned off the air-conditioning. The set of *American Zombie Hunters* was baking hot, and the sun over the LA basin meant it was going to be a brutal day, and it wasn't even summer yet. Shimmers of pent-up heat poured out of her trailer door even though it was just past six a.m.

She tossed her bag inside, waved at the security guard, and turned gratefully toward the cooler confines of the aircraft-sized hangar where all the interior production took place. The large main doors stood open, allowing forklifts to come and go. It looked like another exterior set model was being shoehorned in with the others.

The hangar's interior was a maze of modular buildings ranged around the central, larger sets. Her destination was makeup and costume—a mix of trailers and portable buildings. The arrangement was like a Tetris game. Wherever it fit was the best place for it. It had taken her a week to learn her way around. She'd be saying goodbye to all of it soon with only four more days of production left on the season.

By seven a.m. she was ready for the first series of Unit B's takes for the day. The frequently used small interior sets, some enclosed in modulars, while others too big for that ranged almost the length of the hangar's back wall, with hallway sets on the right to create long, moving shots.

Every set, big and small, was easily accessible to the central wheel of camera and electrical, all of which were surprisingly mobile and temporary. It was very different from her experience with movie sets, where once an electrical supply was taped down it stayed there forever.

On the far side of the hanger, with a completely different light setup and platform, the green screen loomed. Zombies and those who hunted them could fly—who knew? There was no flying today, at least not for her. *AZH* was her first long-term practice at wire work, and she'd never been more grateful for dance practice and strength training at the gym.

Today's schedule was taxing with numerous scene changes to piece together her squad's assault on a stronghold inside an abandoned school. The three main stationary sets were all bristling with the usual pretake activity of light checks and *mise-en-scène* placement.

She'd learned to stay out of the way of the technicians. Her input was not needed, and it was part of the magic of any set that all these working parts were brimming with experienced, talented people in their own specialties.

Her arch-enemy on the show had a script in one hand and was running through his blocking. A set carpenter was tacking down a piece of flooring over a drain. The zombie horde, about a dozen extras, was a small hum of chatter that quieted as she approached, then resumed. She gave a friendly wave in their direction.

"Jennifer, looking ready to work and yet impossibly beautiful at this hour. As always." Gary Dobliczek joined her at the catering table. He had a bear claw in one hand and a huge mug of coffee in the other. As usual he urged her to have a doughnut and as usual she refused. Egg whites, scrambled, with avocado and chopped tomatoes, was her working breakfast. This morning she'd had time to toast a half an English muffin. "Final countdown. How does it feel?"

"I can't believe how time flew. That the season is nearly over." He was an affable Pooh Bear, and a gem of a set manager, only raising his voice if he was forced to ask for something a second time. This was her third TV series, including a soap opera, and she had definitely noticed the intangible value of working with people who were enjoying themselves. That hadn't been the case on the soap, and it had brought out everyone's bad side.

"Sorry about cutting your head off." Director Melanie Rodriguez's sleeves were already rolled up. "Unit A had to stay one more night in Joshua Tree, so we moved a few things around. Did you get the notes?"

Jennifer nodded. "I've got my waterproof undies on."

Gary and Mel laughed, and Mel snapped her fingers, signaling that she was ready to start the Unit B schedule for the day. Jennifer was increasingly impressed with Mel's cool command. Mel had initially been a little wary around her, but Jennifer put that down to her either having heard the rumors about how Jennifer had a habit of seduce-and-abandon to get ahead, or she wasn't sure Jennifer would adapt to the hectic demands and bare-bones pampering that TV gigs offered. Whatever it had been, Melanie and she understood each other now, and everyone was pleased with the result. If she and Lena were on better terms, she'd tell Lena to get Mel into a film production. Latina directors were rare.

The next two hours included a lot of crouching, running through sets and hopping over obstacles while managing dialogue that didn't sound out of breath. Jennifer's body roll over a desk took four takes, but she nailed the last one, landing on both feet with her sword drawn. After a close-up shot of her boots on the floor, she got to swap them out for platform sneakers. They looked weird, but maintained her height and were much more comfortable to wear for the rest of the takes, none of which would include her feet.

By the time they broke for lunch most of Jennifer's day was done. She limped her way back to her trailer, nursing a bruise in one thigh from a choreography gaffe by one of the extras. He'd gone left instead of right and they'd collided. For an emaciated zombie, he'd outweighed her by at least forty pounds and his knee in her thigh felt like it. Several hands had helped break the fall and the floor had only knocked the breath out of her.

She was nearly at her trailer when the extra caught up to her. Peering through his zombie makeup and mask he said, "I know

I'm not supposed to talk to you, but I am so, so sorry. That's all I wanted to say."

"It's okay. It happens. Don't worry about it."

His gaze went to someone behind her.

Rushing toward them was BeBe LaTour, her vivid red hair gleaming in the hot sun. "*Precious!* You're hurt!"

"It's just my agent." She lowered her voice. "Speaking of the zombie apocalypse."

He laughed and scampered away, which made Jennifer smile, because zombies weren't known for their scampering.

"BeBe!" Air kisses completed, she said, "I wasn't expecting you."

"Just checking on my favorite client! I am still getting calls about how good you were in all those New York talk show appearances, precious. Perfect in every way. Best of all, I know what you're going to be doing at the end of next year."

It was how BeBe began all of her pitches. Jennifer waved off the offer of help up the trailer stairs. Her leg hurt, but not that badly. After letting some of the heat out, she went inside. "Come on in."

BeBe's air of making a grand announcement was, as always, undercut by her clarinet-with-a-head-cold voice. "In a world of ancient gods and sorcerers you will be the Namibian Queen with empires at stake, and—"

"Wait a minute. Let me get settled." Jennifer triggered the air conditioner. As with the past several years, there had been no spring season in Los Angeles. They'd gone from a dry winter to summer in two weeks. The little unit was surprisingly effective, making a midday rest feasible in the otherwise oven-like trailer. One of the reasons she specified a small trailer was that they were quicker to heat and cool. That meant a short break would be comfortable. It also meant there was no real place for anyone else to make themselves at home. Hospitality had never been her strong suit.

She peeled off her outer garment, glad she wouldn't need it again today, and put it on the rack just inside the door for the wardrobe assistant. "I thought I was going to melt."

BeBe's shoulder-length page boy swung madly as she shook her head in disgust. "They should have someone to fan you, precious. How can they let you be so hot? And was that an extra talking to you? Have they no respect? It's in your contract."

Jennifer eased down into the wide chair that had seen plenty of catnaps. "He knocked me down in a big fight scene and was really sorry—not the last time that will happen. I'm fine. I just need some Advil."

"I've got Oxy if you'd like some." BeBe was already reaching into her shoulder bag.

"That'll put me in a coma. Seriously, no thanks. You could get me a bottle of water from the fridge, though." Hyde Butler had warned her about the walking pharmacy that BeBe considered part of the good service she provided her clients.

She accepted the water with thanks and asked, "So what about the Namibian Queen?"

"You'll be Queen Nefertiti."

"She was Egyptian, not Namibian." She uncapped the bottle and took several long swallows. "But if she's Namibian, then she's black. Which I'm not."

"She's not black in this story. She's got dark beautiful eyes and long, thick hair, like you. You can tan—"

"I'm not tanning myself into a part for a black actor." She tossed back two of the painkillers and half-drained the rest of the water. She'd been happy to sign up with Hyde Butler's agent, hoping it was the last change she'd need to make. Eight years and so far so good on the work front. The woman brought her roles, wheeled and dealed some of the highest salaries for a woman in the business, and had been instrumental in making Jennifer the voice of commercials for everything from makeup to health insurance. The moment rumors had surfaced that the casting for a remake of Hitchcock's *Rope* would be a woman instead of a man in the lead BeBe had been relentless. The bulk of Jennifer's summer would be spent promoting the film's release.

Yet, for all that she understood about the business, BeBe had blinders stapled to her forehead sometimes.

"Has anyone actually looked at a map of Africa? Who wrote this thing?"

BeBe named two men Jennifer didn't recognize. "It's a fantasy *epic* based on some real people and places. It's got a *huge* budget. They're shooting on location, authentic to the last detail, near Bangalore. And a 3-D version is guaranteed."

"You do know that Bangalore is in India, don't you? Which is not a part of Africa. Not that I'm a geography buff, but I have been there." BeBe usually didn't get on her nerves this much. "I'm not Ann Baxter and living in a time where nobody thought it was wrong to set a story entirely in the part of the world where everyone has brown skin and cast it almost completely with white people who look like they'll burst into flames in direct sunlight."

"You're perfect for it." BeBe waved a dismissive hand. "And the salary will be enormous."

"I'm not spending six months explaining my reasons to the media." After all that it took to build a reputation in this business, she'd watched performers lose all their ground as they squirmed through interviews trying to answer questions about the equity of casting them to specifically play a race they so obviously weren't without any necessity to the story. If the producers and writers were as stupid as BeBe was making them out to be, it was going to flop, and they'd all wonder why after spending fifty million of other people's dollars.

When high-budget pictures didn't meet revenue expectations, performers got the biggest share of blame, she thought bitterly. The producers would get bankrolled for another picture while the cast went begging for another chance. The actors were always the ones tasked with, "You should have known."

There was no piece of that scenario that worked out for her except a paycheck. One thing she didn't need more of was money, and lucky her.

"It'll all be on the writers. Nothing to do with you," BeBe was saying.

"They're not going to ask the writers, or the casting agent or you what you were all thinking. They're going to ask *me*. No matter what I say it's hashtag *LamontSoWhite*, and I'd deserve it. There are far too many wonderfully competent and beautiful actresses with the appropriate skin color to play a black African queen no matter how long ago in the past it was or how many sorcerers and what-have-you they throw in to bleach the world white." A new thought struck her. "If someone in my position can't turn down that kind of part, nobody can. But I can, so I am."

"Well." BeBe slid into the only other chair and gave her a sunny smile. "They can't say I didn't try though I *told* them that's how you would feel."

Jennifer sincerely doubted it. "Anything else?"

"Actually, darling, the much better offer is a thriller with *enormous* box office potential. I'm sure I can talk them into a justified base for you. You are so easy to work with and everybody knows it."

BeBe mimed taking Jennifer's picture. "The most beautiful girl in the world, and she's not complicated, doesn't want a larger trailer for a nanny or a kid. Your extras are so reasonable, why shouldn't you get the little you ask for?"

Jennifer sighed. "It just means I have no life."

"You're one of the hardest working women in the business and Hollywood's most eligible bachelorette. It's part of your appeal, darling. That you're not asking for breastfeeding time or Fridays always off makes you much more valuable. They can put more into the paycheck."

That was one of the standard operating explanations, that it cost more to accommodate women than men on the set, so they paid women less. "If I don't have more extras than men want, they should be offering me something in the ballpark of what the men are getting, right?"

"I will certainly take that position with them. You know I always do."

Jennifer wondered if Suzanne ever had to put up with this kind of nonsense in the financial or tech worlds she straddled. The pay and opportunity inequities in Hollywood were woven through every aspect of production. BeBe didn't question them at all, but today the realities were working her last nerve. Like she was some kind of Carina Estevez or Sydney Van Allen, which she wasn't. "The part—I presume I'm the wife of the detective or something?"

"You're the victim, but you're onscreen the whole movie. Nearly. You're just…You know. Dead."

"Sounds like it might be worth pursuing." Jennifer finished the water and hoped BeBe was done.

"Good luck with shooting the end of this season here. You'll knock 'em dead! I wish I could be there." BeBe gave a wiggle of anticipation that a passerby might have mistaken for a seizure. "Is there anything you can't do? You are just the best client in the world, precious. The best. I have to run."

BeBe flung open the trailer door and nearly knocked over the wardrobe assistant. Jennifer saw her veer in the direction of the production offices and didn't give it another thought. Forty minutes later, the veggie and hummus plate from the caterer completely consumed, Jennifer could manage a limp-free walk across the asphalt to the very welcome shade of the hangar.

Sets had been redressed or changed out. She was in the first two scenes and then done for the day. A long soak in a hot bath was high on her list.

Mel waved her over as everyone else assembled on the set. It was unusually quiet, and Mel lowered her voice. "I just wanted to let you know that he'll be gone at the end of the day. I can't replace him now, there's nobody made up."

"What are you talking about?"

Mel tipped her head. "I—nothing."

Jennifer wasn't sure what to make of the look Mel was giving her. Disappointment? Wariness? "I really don't know what you mean."

"The extra, the one who took you out."

"Yes?"

"Your agent was all up in my face in front of everybody about getting rid of him. She said you were upset. Very upset."

"No." Jennifer shook her head. Now she knew why it was so quiet. A quick glance showed that she was getting the evil eye from all directions. Damn BeBe, damn her to hell. These people had actually *liked* her, or at least working with her. Now they thought Jennifer the Royal Bitch was the real her. "No, I absolutely did not tell her to do that. He apologized, I said it was okay and I meant it. He didn't do it on purpose."

"I thought she was giving you deniability." It was almost a question.

"Have I ever needed a proxy to express my unhappiness about something?"

Mel's expression was carefully neutral and Jennifer wasn't sure Mel believed her. "Then it was just a misunderstanding?"

Jennifer wanted to find a bus, throw BeBe under it and then drive it back and forth over her. What would Lauren Bacall do, she asked herself. Not air private business with sixty people listening, that's for sure. "I guess… She misunderstood me. I did say I was hurt, but it's better now. She's very protective."

Mel's lips twitched. "*Zealous* is the word that comes to mind."

"You're not wrong." Jennifer followed Mel toward the cluster of assembled cast. "What can I do to reassure him and everybody else?"

Mel pitched her voice to carry. "Everyone, just FYI. Jennifer's agent took something she said the wrong way. Nobody's getting sent home."

"Accidents happen," Jennifer interjected. "That I nearly finished out the season before I got even mildly hurt just shows how good you all are at this."

"So let's forget all about it and move on, no more drama, nothing to see here, get to your places." Mel snapped her fingers and everybody moved quickly.

With the zombies all back in full makeup, Jennifer had no idea who was who, so she mouthed a huge, "I'm so sorry," at all of them and hoped it was convincing. She was inwardly seething and wanted to vent, but nobody needed to see that side of her, not right now. She'd been nothing but tired and out of sorts since that miserable party. Weeks later and she was still picking at it.

Decapitating waves of zombies with efficient glee and the occasional pithy remark got rid of some of her anger. The cast was laughing with her at the end of takes, treating her like one of them again.

Making her weary way to the trailer to get into street clothes and head for home, she couldn't shake the not very pleasant feeling she'd had at the party of being the self-absorbed lightweight in the room. Meanwhile, the people she'd been working with for a couple of months now had easily believed that every evil thing they'd ever heard about Jennifer was true.

These were the choices you made, remember? Fear is better than apathy.

She knew BeBe would claim she'd thought that's what Jennifer wanted, just like BeBe was probably going to tell the Namibian Queen people Jennifer might be more interested if there was more money. It's my *job*, she'd say.

With the A/C and Taylor Swift cranked up in the car, she felt better by the time she turned off Santa Monica toward Sunset. She loved where she lived, right at the western edge of the Sunset Strip with a penthouse view in all directions. The heat today made pedestrians far and few between, otherwise the Strip was known for its foot traffic.

Dinner. Shower. Maybe yoga. Definitely sleep. In that order, though she desperately wanted to sleep first.

After parking her car in the secure garage below the building, she keyed open the elevator and entered the code for her floor. From the table next to her door she scooped up a package— probably a script—and a pouch with the few pieces of mail the publicist had cleared for her to see. There was also a thick envelope from her business manager. Probably quarterly updates. The little table where they were left for her was the only furnishing in the tiny lobby of the thirty-first floor.

She waved a salute toward the security camera and punched in her security code to open the only door. The moment it latched behind her she relaxed, letting her handbag and the packages slide to the floor.

A light touch on the remote control triggered a whoosh of moving curtains as they rolled back, panel after panel, to reveal the floor-to-ceiling, south-facing windows that stretched the length of the floor. Right now, in mid-afternoon, the sky was a muddy orange of heat and smog dotted with airplanes and innumerable helicopters. The ground below was thick with the straightline streets and pulsing freeway mazes of Los Angeles. Later, when the sun went down, she would see nothing but twinkling lights and red stripes of taillights on Sunset Boulevard as it bordered her corner of the grid. If it was still too warm, she could walk around the balcony to the north side, where cooler breezes drifted down from the Hollywood Hills. The shorter, cozier balcony off the master bedroom on the western side would frame a stunning sunset that she'd watch as she got ready for bed.

The intercom buzzer sounded before she had a chance to change out of her crumpled clothes. Her dinner, probably, ordered by app from a local restaurant. She liked the food, but even more liked that she could buy with a nickname that the guard downstairs would know meant her. The address alone told the restaurant it was a celebrity, but they didn't have to know which one. She had always thought Lena was super paranoid about security, but some precautions were easy to take.

"Would you like me to bring it up?" It sounded like Billy was on duty.

"Please. I really appreciate it."

"I'll leave it on the table. Have a good evening."

"Thanks." She went to shower. The housekeeper, who came and went with quiet efficiency several times a week, had taken care of last week's laundry, and several new dry cleaning bags were hanging in the closet. What had been two two-bedroom condos had been converted by a pop diva into a four-bedroom penthouse. Jennifer had had the smallest bedroom outfitted as a walk-in closet. Finally, one that was big enough.

Refreshed and only limping a little, she fetched her dinner from the lobby table. The view from the bar that separated the kitchen and dining area framed the mountains to the east. The sun had shifted low enough that the distant horizon almost looked like blue sky. She'd turn on music later, but right now, after extroverting all day, she wanted quiet.

Her dinner of shrimp and vegetables smelled wonderfully of five-spice and garlic. She took the time to plate it and eat at the table like a real person would, then cleaned up and brewed a cup of tea. The #Boobarella affair had been a disruption to her life, but now everything was back to normal.

Except she didn't feel normal, not at all.

Pacing across the pale carpets to gaze down at the busy corner where trendy nightspots were just now opening their doors, she tried to shake off her malaise. This was happiness, or it had been until Suzanne's party.

Suzanne. Had she ever truly gotten Suzanne out from under her skin? She liked to tell herself yes.

Laughing aloud in the quiet space, Jennifer made her way to the bedroom she used as an office. The space was split between her utilitarian desk and file cabinets, and a large table with a comfortable chair that faced the southeastern view of city and hills. Her old Lauren Bacall poster, matted and reframed, was on the wall opposite the window. Lauren deserved a good view.

She sat down, telling herself she ought to do yoga instead. Once she started it would probably keep her up too late. She queued up Adele's latest album and foraged through the tan bricks of the Lego set for an eight-thick—and all the worrisome voices went away. It was the best meditation she'd tried. Another thing Suzanne had been right about. A couple of hours and she'd have all four walls of the Ghostbusters headquarters completed. Legos rocked.

CHAPTER FORTY-ONE

"I'm glad you could come down. What do you have to do with your summer, anyway, retired old man?" Suzanne led the way to the great room where her father took his regular seat in the wide leather armchair while Suzanne sprawled out as usual on the couch opposite him. Her stomach was stuffed with grilled tilapia and corn on the cob. Her father's visits always meant home-cooked food. "You still know your way around a grill."

William Mason heaved a pleased sigh. "I couldn't burn a thing with that fancy setup you have. I'm used to briquettes and open flame. That was tasty if I say so myself."

She punched down a cushion a little bit. "It feels great to relax. Annemarie and I are working on a new idea and I've been spending more time in San Francisco than usual. Tell me all about Denmark. How long were you in Jelling?"

Her father's lifelong passion for Nordic and Germanic culture was evident as he whisked her through pictures of cool, blue and green landscapes and close-ups of runic antiquities. His idea of retirement was to winnow down to just one graduate seminar at Stanford for his beloved comparative Nordic literature, and take on guest lecturing appearances at universities from Antwerp to

Oslo. She intended to be every bit as active and resilient when she was seventy.

"That's probably more than you wanted to know," he concluded a while later. "I'm planning to go back next summer. I don't think my bones would adapt to winter. June was brisk enough for me."

"I thought you were a big believer in experiencing the full range of nature. You know, remaining connected to the planet and all that? That's why we had windows open year round and no air-conditioning?" She got up to refill her iced tea. "Want more?"

He nodded. "I am, especially for the young. It didn't hurt you or your brothers, did it?"

"No, it works in the Bay Area, mostly," she called from the kitchen. "Not above the fiftieth parallel."

When she returned with their fresh drinks she queued up an episode of *Jeopardy!* on the DVR, because that's what one did after dinner with her father. It wasn't often that she knew something he didn't, but every once in a while a category was in her favor. She was in luck tonight. After he ran the *Composers by Country* category the contestants started on *Oscar Shutouts*.

"Who is Susan Sarandon."

"You have the advantage over me."

"I know, you don't go to the talkies."

"Disrespectful child." He dipped a fingertip into his glass and flicked droplets at her. "I remember actors by their roles, is all. I don't know the difference between Ethan Hawke and Elijah Wood unless you say Frodo."

"And... Who is Glenn Close." She flicked him back. "Evacuate the Death Star because it is *on* like Alderaan."

Her trash talk was premature. She got to enjoy her iced tea while her father and a contestant ran the *World Rivers* category. Answering a half-second too late was the same as wrong.

"You were saying?" he asked, after answering ahead of the contestant with, "What is the Paraná?"

The category switched back to *Oscar Shutouts*. "I was saying 'who is Sigourney Weaver,' that's what I was saying."

The last clue on the board was revealed as *Hyde Butler walked away with the trophy, but his leading lady is still waiting for hers.*

"Who is Jennifer Lamont," Suzanne said slowly. Part of her thought someone she'd been with being an answer on *Jeopardy!* was extremely cool. The voice of reason bemoaned that there was no escaping the woman. She paused the program. "Remember when I told you about getting dumped by a model years ago?" She'd told her parents about the first time the woman had dumped her, but not the second. She hadn't wanted to parade her stupidity.

"Vaguely. When you were in New York?"

"Yes. So that's who it was."

"I'd forgotten her name, if you ever told us."

Suzanne shrugged. "I ran into her recently."

"Isn't she starring in a Hitchcock remake? She always seems very competent. I was intrigued at the idea of a woman playing a part written for someone as iconic as Jimmy Stewart."

"She's as attractive as ever."

He gave her a sideways look. "This sounds perilously close to a discussion of your love life. Where's your mother when we need her?"

"Valhalla." They lifted their glasses in a shared gesture of remembrance.

"Your mother has Valhalla eating vegan and using renewable energy by now," her father pronounced after a fleeting expression of still hurtful grief had passed.

"Why would they need renewable energy? They have Thor. He can store lightning any time he wants with the right collection and storage design."

"Not everybody has access to the hammer."

"Not everybody is worthy."

He laughed and said, "So are you dating Ms. Lamont?"

"No, it's not like that. We met up again once before, about ten years ago, and it still didn't go well. She believed that coming out would end her career."

He looked up from packing his pipe with the cherry-smoke tobacco, the aroma from which she found deeply comforting. "And you didn't believe that?"

"No, I did. It's just…"

"You wanted it not to matter to her."

"Not so much that we—we didn't get as far as seriously dating or declarations or anything. She just walked away after some good times. I didn't have anything to offer her that she wanted."

"She doesn't seem like the kind of woman who could be won with mere baubles."

"Yeah, I definitely found out those don't work."

"I see. Well, like anything worth having in life, if you want it, earn it."

"I don't want it." She sounded like a huge liar, even to herself. "I can't change the fact that I am too risky for her."

"A situation with no happy resolutions."

"She could have done other things for a living."

"Why should she? She's pretty good at acting, isn't she? Where's the 'you go girl' for a woman who's put her career first and achieved great results?"

She should have never brought it up. There were things he didn't understand. "She's treated a lot of people badly, and pretty much, after a fling with a woman was discovered, she said it was just an experiment. We know how much guys love that whole scenario. Boom, suddenly she's a big star."

"Then she sounds like a not very nice person you should steer clear of."

She felt like a teenager, not a forty-five-year-old who ran a multimillion dollar venture capital fund. "That's what Mom told me after Ricki Laguna said she'd go to prom with me and went with that awful Kirsten Hughes instead."

"I always thought you and Annemarie might settle down."

"Gross! She's like my sister. Don't ship us."

He puffed lightly on his pipe until the tobacco caught. The nightly ritual was one of her earliest memories of childhood. "Ship?"

"Relation*ship*. It's when you take any two people and propose a relationship between them, usually in disregard for their actual reality, or in the case of fictional characters, their established canon. Somewhere out there someone is writing love stories about Frodo and Loki."

He looked pained. "I see. It doesn't explain why, if you don't want to be single, you still are."

"I like single. All the best superheroes are single, after all. I don't feel incomplete. It's just that I know my life would be different, possibly better, if She-Boob Sword Mistress hadn't been afraid of being outed."

"Suzanne Marie," he said sadly.

Both names. She was in trouble.

"You know you'd call out a man who talked about any woman that way. By her anatomy."

Holy crap, her father was a better feminist than she was. "It's not the body, it's that she doesn't use her powers for good."

"Therefore, she sounds like a not very nice person you—"

"—Should steer clear of," they finished together.

"Maybe instead of your love life we should talk about work. Or better yet, are you going to do any more lecturing at the university? You enjoyed it didn't you?"

"I loved the place so much I moved here, and I really think the students liked the seminar." She hadn't fully understood the attraction of her father's academic life until she'd prepared and delivered a ten-week lecture series and worked with students. "I was going to put a feeler out to the provost about this fall, but starting a personal foundation with Annemarie is more of a priority."

"I thought you already ran a foundation."

"The company does. We're not the company, not completely. She needs some fresh horizons, and I have some interesting ideas about applying what CommonTech Foundry has done to make girls ubiquitous at science fairs and math competitions to other fields, like the arts."

"You always were more like your mother."

"I prefer to think I'm a blend of both of you. Your big brain and her activist heart. Shall we finish up the rest of *Jeopardy!* or do you want to watch a movie?"

He drew on his pipe while scratching under his trim gray beard. "*Jeopardy!*, then movie."

"Hang on, text from Annemarie." She frowned at her display. "She wants to call our new foundation *Annemarie and Suzanne Save the World Together.*"

Her father let out a bark of laughter. "That's probably not a good idea."

"It's very descriptive."

"A.S.S.T.W.T. Think it through, oh my daughter."

She'd been had. Grateful that he'd seen the joke, she sent back, "I know you are but what am I?" before hitting play.

CHAPTER FORTY-TWO

"You know why men don't take us seriously? Why none of us ever gets a seat on any of the news that airs after three p.m.?" Jennifer gestured at the semicircle of bare legs as she rose to her feet. "Because serious people don't have magnifying glasses in front of their crotches. They have desks!"

She planted one stiletto against the shin-high clear glass coffee table and shoved. Shoved again. The fine fishing lines that were supposed to help topple the table in the right direction quivered as set techs pulled. The damn thing didn't budge.

Her four scene mates broke into giggles.

Jennifer dropped character. "Did someone nail this thing down?"

"Cut!" The director's harsh voice was loaded with annoyance.

Filming this episode of *Baghdad by the Bay* had been a nightmare, Jennifer gathered, the least of which had been finding a last-minute replacement for their originally planned guest star, one who could get to San Francisco on a few days notice. Another score for BeBe, who had found her two days of highly lucrative and visible work while touting it as Jennifer saving the day.

Jennifer had given up major R&R at home with two scripts, a novel and binge watching the last season of *Fargo*. It hadn't been hard to do—her brain was so preoccupied with this Friday's release of *Rope* and the upcoming media blitz it was hard to relax. It had been hard for weeks, ever since her work on *American Zombie Hunters* had wrapped up. If anything else was making her restless she didn't want to think about it. She'd get home tomorrow night, put last minute things in her already packed bags for the trip back east, and make her flight to New York by three.

Technicians swarmed the elevated set for the show's newsroom, one sheepishly muttering, "We forgot to undo the safety hooks."

"Ms. Lamont?"

Jennifer turned to one of the co-stars. Amy Lebeaux was a disarming bundle of button-cute blondness with a southern drawl. "Call me Jennifer. I mean it."

"Jennifer." The last syllable came out as a soft "fuh" that Jennifer quite liked. "I've been telling myself not to go all fan girl on you, but I can't help it. It's been one of my dreams to work with you. The whole time I was in acting school I told myself I wanted to be just like you."

Caught off guard, Jennifer said, "Is that wise? I've terrified a few people from time to time, but only when I meant to."

"Who'd want to scare people on accident? You stand up for yourself and that makes it easy for me to do. I ask mahself, 'What would Jennifer Lamont do?'"

Even though she sincerely hoped there were things she'd done that Amy Lebeaux would never, ever do, Jennifer was won over. "I'll take that all as a compliment."

"It is." Amy's cute little nose twitched, an irresistible attribute that had won the public heart. "You've never been anybody but you."

"You have to be yourself. Everyone else is taken."

"I love that quote! Isn't that Oscar Wilde? Y'all crack me up."

"Places!"

Jennifer reacted to the director's command by returning to her seat on the stage. She was surprised she needed to blink back a threat of tears. "Thank you, Amy. You made my day."

She honestly did not know what to make of what the young actress had said. On the one hand, she had never shied away from admitting she was ambitious. She understood her own worth. She didn't need anyone to like her, only to respect her. But her lies were like chains around her neck, and lately they had been threatening to choke her. Had adorable Amy not read the gossip pages? Some of it was true, at least about Selena Ryan.

Like a ticker at Times Square, the thought marched across her mind: *I'd rather be the person she thinks I am.*

What would Amy say if she knew Jennifer had walked away from all personal entanglements so she could ignore the emptiness of life in a closet? It was a very nice closet, complete with professional and material success, but still a closet. Her real need for quiet after a day of work was the excuse she used to keep her personal life empty. While her agent and publicist and fans could be put off with workaholic explanations, she couldn't afford friends—friends asked questions she no longer wanted to answer with lies. Better to simply avoid them altogether.

The next take worked beautifully with the table imploding and shattered safety glass harmlessly spilling across the stage. On-air personnel headed for dressing rooms while the technical crew began the job of cleanup and resetting for the busy schedule tomorrow. Jennifer headed for the dressing room designated for her, shooing away an eager intern who asked if she needed a cab or a restaurant recommendation. She had been in and out of San Francisco many times, though this was the first time since Suzanne's party.

Amy Lebeaux's comments were still ringing in her ears as she left the studio clad in walking shoes and wicking workout clothes she'd brought with her in the morning. The small studio district connected to the pavilions near the ballpark, and she could walk miles along the waterfront on sidewalks shaded by skyscrapers. It was still unusually hot for San Francisco summer, but nothing like the temps in LA.

The walk would do her good. Any day now the first critic reviews of *Rope* would hit the trades. It could be okay. But the reviews could also start with "Who does Jennifer Lamont think she is, taking on a Jimmy Stewart role?"

Her tote with her street clothes and the day's essentials slung across her back, she pinned back her hair and pulled a *Project Runway* ball cap down to shade her eyes. Dark glasses in place, and she was just another woman enjoying the warm afternoon.

She set a brisk pace, but there was no outrunning her churning thoughts. The media blitz promoting *Rope* began the day after tomorrow and it wouldn't be like any movie she had done before. She'd taken on what was regarded as a man's role, and she knew there would be plenty of pushback. The classic film purists didn't think anything modern could compare to the Golden Years, and that Hitchcock was sacred and nobody should ever touch it.

Then there were the outright creeps who were already lined up to decry the woeful state of political correctness that said the wimmins had to have all the big parts these days and woe, oh woe, the poor mens who couldn't get work anymore. They would be loud and persistent.

The marketing people for the production company were anticipating the hand-wringing, happily intending to use any chauvinist outrage to promote the film. Jennifer was ready to stare them down because she was proud of her work. She was proud of the two young male co-stars who had never once questioned the gender dynamic. When someone had told them there would be people who'd think they weren't manly because a woman ultimately outsmarted them, both Cliff and Sibo had been dumbfounded. The memory of Sibo saying, "Women are smart. What's their problem?" deeply pleased her.

She navigated around a young woman out for a jog in a "Gay by the Bay" T-shirt and found herself falling into a sad funk. There was no sign of any kind of endorphins as her mood continued to sink into worry—and something else she didn't want to name.

It's just nerves, she told herself.

The crowds of tourists clogging Pier 39 sent her back the way she had come. She knew she should eat something. The fragrant streets of Chinatown lay between her and her hotel and dim sum was a fine idea. But when she reached the little hole-in-the-wall she'd found on an earlier visit her feet didn't stop. She walked on, head down, fighting off a growing sense of fear and anxiety. Doubt. And regret.

Footsore and completely run out of steam, she took stock of her reflection in the black glass windows of an office building. Her hair had escaped from under the ball cap in a crushed, lopsided mass. The sun and heat had flushed her face, which she hadn't bothered to touch up after washing off the heavy stage makeup. Her sleeveless yoga top was damp at the collar and armpits.

It was a long way from Chanel.

She went inside anyway. This had been her destination all along, she knew that now. She lied to the guards about having an appointment, and told herself that she had no reason to expect Suzanne to even be in her office. Captains of industry were busy. Suzanne could be in La Jolla. Or Tokyo. Or Timbuktu.

This was absolute madness.

And ten years too late.

Contrary to her fears, the receptionist must have judged her harmless because the double doors immediately opened. The adorable Jacques wasn't there. Of course he would have moved on, Jennifer thought. A tidy young woman in a CommonTech polo shirt greeted her with only a hint of raised eyebrow under her kinky black bangs. "How can I help you?"

"Is Ms. Mason in?"

"Are you expected?" The receptionist was far too poised to let on whether Suzanne was even in the building.

"No, actually. But if you tell her it's Jennifer Lamont she might be able to find a few minutes. I'm in town unexpectedly."

The young woman cocked her head as if she was considering calling security.

Jennifer belatedly shucked off her sunglasses and smiled. "It really is me."

The brown eyes widened. "If you'll give me a moment to check."

Jennifer stepped away so as not to eavesdrop. She had no idea what the young woman was conveying, or to whom, and it was a long minute before she hung up and said, "Ms. Mason will be out in just a moment. If you'll have a seat…"

"Thank you."

The layout behind the wall of translucent glass looked much the same, though the carpet had been changed from gray to blue. She tried to hide that she was looking toward Suzanne's office, and simultaneously resisted the urge to run for the stairs.

"Jennifer?"

She scrambled to her feet, heart pounding in her throat. Suzanne had come from the other direction. "Hi."

"This is a surprise." Suzanne glanced at the receptionist who was busily tapping at her keyboard.

Jennifer gazed up at her, words coming in fits and starts. "I'm doing a sitcom shoot, out of the blue. I was out trying to get some exercise, you know how that is, done for the day. Trying not to eat my way across the city. Suddenly I was in front of your building and took a wild, crazy chance that you'd be in."

Suzanne stepped in the direction of the elevators and Jennifer followed, all the while telling herself to stop babbling like a fool.

"I thought maybe we could have dinner. Just, you know, a sandwich. Or coffee. If you have a few minutes." She ran out of words. Her heart felt outside of her chest, in plain sight, dangling like a piñata.

She couldn't interpret the emotion the passed over Suzanne's face and rippled through her shoulders.

After an odd gasp for air, her voice clear and even, Suzanne said, "I don't think there's any point."

The polite smile was what pierced Jennifer to her core.

It was years of training, hours and hours of vocal lessons that let her form a smile, quell the response of her tear ducts, and answer easily, "I understand."

She rang for the elevator, which immediately opened, said a cheerful "Thank you" to the helpful receptionist and pushed the button for the ground floor.

There are security cameras, she reminded herself. Perhaps not clear enough to tell that she was taking in little gasps of air and whimpering slightly on the exhale. Keep it together, she told herself. Hold on.

Hold on, she repeated, as she walked the blocks to her hotel, crossed the frigid lobby and kept smiling all the way into her room. Only when the door had closed did the wave of grief engulf her. She groped her way to the bathroom and cried over the sink, splashing water on her face, telling herself she couldn't do this, it would show in the makeup chair in the morning. There wasn't enough air to breathe. Eventually she fumbled through a scalding shower that didn't ease her shivering.

What had she been thinking? Ten years too late.

Ten years too late.

CHAPTER FORTY-THREE

"This brings back old times." Jennifer slid into the booth across from Selena, setting her handbag and sunglasses on the seat beside her.

"This was never our place." Lena put down the Betty's Diner menu she no doubt had memorized. As tailored as always, the only thing that wasn't crisp and tidy was Lena's short brown hair, which looked as if Lena still had the habit of running one hand through it while talking on the phone.

"This is where you met Gail. I didn't know that at the time."

"You were busy trying to get us photographed together again, for whatever reasons made you happy at the time."

Okay, they were going to pick at old wounds. Not that Jennifer had expected otherwise when she'd asked Lena if there was any possible way they could talk privately for ten minutes before she left on her ten-day press tour. "As soon as I heard Hyde Butler was in it, I was determined to get that part in *Barcelona* in spite of our history. It worked out." The awards, the publicity and breathtaking box office for a "little" indie film—it had most certainly worked out for all concerned.

"You have always been a better actress than a person."

"Ouch. Well, at least you think I can act."

"I've always known that."

Jennifer glanced at the menu then quickly at the tables nearest them. It was on the early side for lunch and they almost had the place to themselves. Even full to the brim, Betty's couldn't hold more than a hundred people—hardly a rave spot even though it had retro black, red and chrome diner chic. Their table was out of the sight of nearly all the others and was undesirably right outside the kitchen door where most people wouldn't appreciate the noise. But, Jennifer realized, that meant food arrived unseen by other people, and she'd seen so many fat-shaming pictures in the tabloids of actresses near a pile of fries not to appreciate the location.

Clever Lena, as usual thinking of all the angles. Given Lena's extreme aversion to publicity, Betty's was a great choice. And she'd met the love of her life here. Gail's hilarious reenactment on *Between Two Ferns* of her face plant in Lena's lap with a plate of chicken and vegetables had been viewed hundreds of thousands of times.

Their waiter, who looked as if she had worked the breakfast shift and then some, took the order for Lena's "usual" and then suddenly seemed to recognize Jennifer.

"So that was an iced coffee with vanilla?"

"Sugar free. Girlish figure and all that."

"I wouldn't have thought you had to worry about such things."

Jennifer's laugh was sincere. "I doubt there will be a single day of my life where I don't. And yes, that's kind of sad."

"I met somebody famous. You made my day. Thanks."

"You made my day too." She shot a glance at Lena, clever Lena, who ran a powerful, successful production company and would never be a household face, which was exactly what Lena wanted.

Lena appeared to be deeply amused. "I'd forgotten how easily you gather willing slaves."

"It wears off."

"True, that. You know, I have to ask. Could that purse be any larger?"

"You mean this pretty thing?" Her Cole Haan handbag was a favorite because it was functional enough to make a great "personal bag" as specified by the airlines. It held everything she would need during the long flight to New York. "I carry it around to repair bridges, fix manhole covers, that sort of thing."

Lena's laugh was welcome. "I can actually picture that. Femme fatale superhero saves runaway bus by patching roadway with her handbag."

"Believe me, I've pitched the idea. Why not make them killer shoes for real? *Pew-pew-pew* from the heels."

"Not a film Ryan Productions would be interested in."

"Not even if you got the right script?"

"Do you have the right script?"

"No."

Lena sighed. "I see. So, to what do I owe this honor?"

Banter time was over. "I need advice. About something personal."

"Gail would be better than me."

"She has a heart I haven't stomped on, is that what you mean?"

Lena gave a slight nod.

"Yes, let's agree to agree on that and move on. Besides, she's so nice and it comes so easily to her." Jennifer didn't mean to sound so vexed about that. Lena was not the one she wanted, but there had been a time when she had angled to get Gail out of Lena's life. Her own fault, all of that.

Lena's eyebrow arched as far as it would go. "I don't find that a flaw."

"I'm aware of that. It's just that what would work coming from her isn't going to fly from me."

"Nobody really thinks that what they see is what they get with you—this is true."

"Actually, what people see is what they think they're getting. They're just not looking above my shoulders."

"Perhaps you should wear a tiara to divert the eyes of the easily bemused."

Jennifer gave a beauty pageant wave of the hand. "I'm always wearing a tiara. Only the best people can see it."

"And we're still not to the point of this conversation." Lena broke off to smile at the approaching server.

Jennifer gathered her thoughts as her iced coffee and Lena's hot tea were delivered. After assuring the waiter she had everything she needed, she gave Lena her full attention. "They say that one of the hardest things in life is knowing when to try harder or walk away."

Lena's hooded, dark eyes took on a scalpel-like quality. "You have perfected the art of walking away."

Don't argue about it, Jennifer told herself. "Again, agree to agree. I never looked back. Always forward to when I would be accepted as a real actor who is taken seriously."

Without hesitation Lena said, "And now that you are?"

One of Lena's irritating qualities was her relentless honesty, but it wasn't until that moment that Jennifer appreciated knowing she could believe Lena meant what she said. "Thank you, that's nice of you to say. *Rope* comes out day after tomorrow. Reviews will start appearing today but I haven't seen any yet."

Lena gave her a quizzical look. "You're nervous?"

"That's putting it mildly."

After a sip of tea, Lena observed, "I'm fascinated by the idea of you in a psychological thriller, for one thing. Plus a small cast, one set. It'll earn back costs, and easily."

Jennifer stared.

Lena cocked her head, as if puzzled by Jennifer's reaction. "I'm not being nice. I knew right away you were perfect for it. I wish we were producing it. "

Jennifer drank some coffee to hide that she still had no words.

Lena's eyes held a mix of mockery and surprise. "It's ironic that you of all people don't know how to accept a compliment."

"Not about acting, I guess." Lena was right, which was disconcerting.

"So is this about self-doubt?"

Jennifer let her tone grow rueful. "The long version is, I suppose."

"This is about Suzanne Mason." Lena's smile as she sipped her tea was aggravatingly all-knowing.

"Fine. Yes. Suzanne." Suzanne who had kissed her and then sent her away.

"I gather I'm not the only lesbian heart you've shattered."

"I know you don't care. But the truth is I broke yours because I broke hers."

"That doesn't really make much sense."

Keeping her voice low, Jennifer said, "I had to prove she didn't mean anything. That how I felt could be turned on and off, like a switch. I practiced on you and it worked."

"Jen—for heaven's sake. Are you *still* debating about whether women matter to you? Or was Cabo just an incredible act? You lied about it being the first time, after all."

"I lied about it being the first time, but how I felt wasn't an act. Part of it was real. I've always wanted you to know that, though it doesn't matter to you, I don't think. You have Gail. Gail is obviously perfect for you."

"How do you make that sound like a bad thing?"

"Hello? It's me, remember? Look up *bitch* in the dictionary." Don't pick a fight, she told herself.

Lena had her most impassive face on. "Why are you telling me all this?"

"I bought into the idea that anything I did for my career, including how I treated people, was okay. Men don't apologize for using people."

"Those men are jerks. And we both know men who aren't like that either."

"It was not my finest hour, deciding to conquer the worlds I wanted by being a user."

"Hallelujah for you." Lena gave the waiter a pleased smile when her Cobb salad arrived. When they were alone again she said, "Would you like some of this? I don't just come here out of nostalgia. The food is good."

"There'll be plenty to eat on the plane. And I think you do come here for the nostalgia. Where's Gail today?"

"In Ottawa."

"You sent her a selfie with the menu, didn't you?"

"Maybe." Lena was making an ooey-gooey-I-remember face, and probably didn't even realize it. Those two were going to be married forever, like Joanne Woodward and Paul Newman.

"Anyway," Jennifer continued, "I realize everything I've burned in my past is creating a smoking ruin in my future. Like you told me it would. It took me way too long to realize that if you're rewarded for behaving badly, you end up surrounded by people who only like you when you behave badly. And they're not people you can like back."

Lena leaned away from her, mug in one hand. "I'm asking myself how I can believe a word you say. Then I remember that it doesn't matter. I don't need to believe you. You're not a part of my life except professionally."

And with reluctance, Jennifer knew that, and accepted it. "I've earned that from you. I get it. Lena…" Jennifer blew out a short breath because she didn't want to cry. "I really am sorry. You mattered enough to scare me. How do I stop letting fear run my life?"

Lena had another bite of her salad before answering. "Are you better with her or without her? That's really all that matters."

She didn't think Lena needed to know that Suzanne had, quite literally, shown her the door. "What about whether she's better without me than with me? You know I'm not exactly a relationship prize."

"Is that your call to make?"

"I've made it twice before."

"And how did that work out for her? Or do you even know?"

Jennifer picked up her coffee, then put it down, not sure she could swallow. "I'm a mess. She doesn't deserve me, she's way better than I am."

"Are you expecting me to argue with you about that?"

She spread her hands on the table. "I don't even know why I'm here."

A long silence followed as Lena ate and Jennifer didn't drink any coffee.

Finally, Jennifer shook herself out of her funk and asked, "You're better with Gail?"

"God yes. I try to make her life better for having me in it too. We are certainly better together. That makes all the time we have to be apart bearable." After a sip of tea she asked, "Are you better people together?"

Jennifer didn't see how Suzanne could possibly be better off with her. "I've never even given us a chance to find that out. I don't think she wants to find out anymore, but I can't let go. I've played the part of Jennifer Lamont, independent woman, so well that I bought my own act."

"As I said earlier, you are an excellent actor." Lena put down her fork and sighed. "That first movie, after… You told the tabloids that I had your part cut to get even for you dumping me."

There was no escaping it, though it was the last thing Jennifer wanted to be reminded about. "I know what I did."

"Do you think that's why some of your scenes didn't make it to the final?"

"No, of course not. You have too much integrity. I knew it at the time and accused you of being petty anyway. There, full allocution."

"The director and film editor felt you were overpowering the star. You were riveting. Unconsciously outclassing him. We thought we'd cast a solid talent who could rise to more than that in a key scene." She frowned as she ran a hand through her hair. "You were more than that in all of them. We probably shouldn't have cast you at all, but who knew that the world wouldn't be able to take its collective eyes off you?"

Jennifer struggled to breathe in. Lena was not a panderer like BeBe. She had no motive to lie and no incentive to tell the truth. It was too much to believe. "I don't know what to say."

"Have you considered giving your internal lack of confidence some thought?"

Pushing away the deep down suggestion that she had somehow slipped into an alternative universe, Jennifer could only say, "I've never thought I lacked for confidence. But I guess I do. You ask excellent questions."

Lena's expression changed to one of sly calculation. "I have another for you."

Jennifer didn't hide her wariness. "Go ahead."

"A cameo, half day's work. For scale. Interested?"

She cocked her head, considering. "Who and why?"

"A film student. She has an incredible director's eye and is aiming at a scholarship for the UCLA masters program. Talent will only take her so far. My name only takes her so far."

"You believe in her?"

"Yes. And we need more women with connections behind the camera. You know that."

Jennifer nodded. "I'll do it, provided scheduling and the usual backend conditions." She made a show of waking up her phone and sending a text to BeBe to take a scale job from Ryan Productions when they asked. "There. Done."

"Thanks." Lena smiled, just a little.

"That's why you even agreed to see me, isn't it?"

"Maybe."

"Fair enough. I do have to go, but thank you."

"One last question. Was it easy to walk away from me?"

"Yes," Jennifer said honestly. She wasn't proud of it and she wasn't going to lie. "Yes it was."

"I always suspected that it was." Lena shrugged. "I could have done without the drama and—"

"Those were not my finest hours. I was lying my ass off about needing rehab which tops the list of my public stupidity. I figured if I torched everything the smoke would keep me from seeing my reflection in the mirror."

"Can you walk away from Suzanne?"

A glib comeback was on the tip of her tongue but a sudden pain, like a long needle through her stomach, brought a shock of tears to Jennifer's eyes. The truth was Suzanne was walking away from her and she didn't know what she could do to change a thing.

"Well," Lena said. "I never thought I'd live to see that."

After a too-large swallow of coffee, Jennifer managed a weak, "I'll have to use that in my acting."

Lena laughed. "Sure, those feelings are an academic exercise."

"I really don't know how to do this."

"Trust your feelings?"

"Love somebody more than myself." She spread her hands on the table. "I've completely lost my center of gravity. How could this happen to me, of all people? Why can't I just walk away this time?"

Lena's chuckle was slightly sympathetic yet shaded with a dash of cynicism. "I can't decide if you deserve it or are just getting what you deserve."

Hours later, Lena's words came back as turbulence kept Jennifer from dozing on the plane. It didn't matter how comfortable first class was, jolting in midair was not something she could sleep through. Her book didn't hold her interest and she left her phone off—she had long treasured flights as an excuse to disconnect from the web.

She didn't know what she'd expected to learn from talking to Lena or why it had seemed so urgent. She felt as if the world was on a tilt and if she didn't fix it now it would be broken forever. It was highly likely that it was already too late.

The next week and a half was going to be hideously hectic. At least she would be talking about a movie, about her craft. Immersing herself in her work was a cure for everything that bothered her.

At least it used to be.

CHAPTER FORTY-FOUR

Manuel leaned in Suzanne's office door, phone lifted in camera mode. "Smile!"

"What's this for?" She had two teleconferences to juggle and a closed-door meeting with Annemarie in five minutes.

"You are going on Twitter with the hashtag *What smart looks like*."

"Thank you, I'm honored, but why?"

"I am putting up a picture of every not-male identified person on this floor with that hashtag." He rocked on his feet, looking very pleased with himself. "Chris and Nik and Rosie are already up."

"Still confused."

"You haven't seen it? Some asshole movie critic said women aren't convincing as smart people in movies. A friend of mine at Viral Media sent it over, saying he was pretty sure I worked with people who'd disagree."

"For real?"

"For real. In the *Times*, no less."

"Hashtag away. Wait. Let's do mine again." Suzanne quickly scrawled on two sheets of paper with a black Sharpie.

Manuel laughed. "Add arrows."

She did as he suggested then held the pages up. Pointing at her, one read "IS SMART" and the other "AND GETS PAID FOR IT."

He snapped the new picture and thumbed his phone. "I figure men need to take offense at this crap. The Dudebro Commentariat will swarm. And—posted. Take that, assholes."

"Nice idea. The review was in the *Times*? I'll Google it. What was the movie?"

"That Hitchcock remake. I mean, I haven't seen it and I don't know if Lamont is smart or not. That's not the point. You'll see—a total misogynistic prick review."

Suzanne ordinarily would have paused to think how much she loved working with men who used *misogynistic* in sentences. Instead she was realizing she'd been sucked into something involving Jennifer. Again. As if the universe simply would not leave her alone. Seriously though, the critic had said *what*?

She kept Annemarie waiting long enough to scan the review. Right there, in black and white: 'Suspension of disbelief is strained to breaking when tweedy academic Cadell transforms into a sleuth. The audience has no reason to accept that the woman has the deductive reasoning she needs for the task. The trendy overturning of gender norms continues Hollywood's pandering to optics over substance. Lamont is lucky to have Stewart's coattails to ride.'

The quote had been picked up along with an assertion from the film company that the script of the Hitchcock film and the new version were nearly identical. To top it off, someone had dredged up the reviewer's blissful high marks given to the original years ago.

This critic wasn't even saying that Jennifer's performance didn't match Jimmy Stewart's, he was saying that a woman in the role was automatically, unquestionably unbelievable. Optics over substance—what an asshat.

The image of her high school science teacher came to mind. She could still see the condescending smile on his face as he told her that girls' brains weren't wired for science.

Taps to her Instagram and Twitter feeds showed that Manuel's hashtag was catching on. Her display was awash with his pictures of women associated with tech. Other people were adding pictures of fictional female detectives—she paused to admire Helen Mirren for a moment, because Helen Mirren... Then photos of real female detectives and police officers in uniform flowed into the mix. She tended to agree that hashtag activism was not a way to create permanent change, but today it was glorious.

She opened her personal Twitter account, thought for a moment, then tapped out, "*An actress pioneered frequency modulation = wifi, bluetooth. Hedy Lamarr & @realJenniferLamont #whatsmartlookslike.*"

She looked up from her phone to find Annemarie tapping the toe of one boot. "Meeting?"

"Sorry. Someone said something stupid on the Internet and it needed fixing. I upvoted your picture."

"I saw. You know what this means, don't you?"

"No."

Annemarie spread her arms in a mixture of acceptance and despair. "That woman is going to be on all the late night talk shows again."

"You'll survive."

"Will you?"

She hadn't told Annemarie that she'd sent Jennifer away earlier in the week. "Of course."

Annemarie was scowling. "You know I do get it. I was alone with her for thirty seconds and I wanted to jump her bones, and I really, really don't go for femmes. She's got that...that sex appeal thing on steroids, or at least she did. Anyway, we're now running late."

For the entire duration of the meeting, and through the teleconferences that followed, Suzanne was plagued by visions of Jennifer playing over and over again in the YouTube of her mind. Not in bed. Not licking jam off her fingers. Not even as Suzanne had seen her in movies. Instead, on a repeating loop she saw Jennifer whirling across a live stage with such confidence and poise that Suzanne had forgotten it was Jennifer at all. She'd been trying to put her conversation with her father out of her head, but it kept coming back: If you want her you can't buy her, you have to earn her.

She and Annemarie decided to have a working dinner that turned into an extended planning session complete with flow charts written on drink napkins. On the way home she had the sudden inspiration to check, and found that *Rope* was showing at the Metreon at midnight as an early premiere event. She only had an hour to kill.

The theater was about half full—not bad for a midnight show on a Thursday night. She crunched her popcorn and mused that going on twenty years ago she'd been sharing popcorn with Jennifer to glimpse her as an extra in a kids' movie. Now that woman was on the screen and the focus of almost every scene in the movie.

Then she forgot it was the same woman. Swept into the taut story of two murderers who dare their former mentor to find them out, she was absorbed into the movie. Only when the screen went black and the credits began to roll did she startle out of the film's grip.

Jennifer's name was first. Suzanne wanted to applaud. At times she hadn't even looked anything like the woman Suzanne had thought she'd known. Expressions she'd never seen on Jennifer's face—distaste, horror, panic—had seemed completely natural to a tweedy academic thinking her way through the unthinkable.

This was what Jennifer had dreamed of becoming. What likely would never have happened if she'd made different choices.

What if, just a little, Jennifer had been right? That Suzanne had only been interested in Jennifer as the ultimate collectible? Had she really thought Jennifer wouldn't be giving up all that much?

Something shifted down deep, as if true north had moved and it was going to take some time to reset her sense of direction.

CHAPTER FORTY-FIVE

Jennifer was among the first people up the Jetway at JFK airport. The moment she'd powered up her phone again it had begun shaking, chirping and whistling with notifications for texts, messages and missed phone calls. She saw the words "jerk" and decided a minute or two in the ladies' room would give her the privacy to catch up. Once she'd latched the door to the ladies' room stall she queued up the most recent voice mail from BeBe.

"Don't you worry about a thing, precious, the whole *world* is coming to your defense. It won't hurt a thing—in fact, this will sell tons of tickets!"

There were six other voice mails from BeBe and maybe one of them explained what had happened, but she moved on to a message from the production assistant assigned to her while in New York. Even while she listened to a stammered suggestion that they meet when Jennifer reached her hotel to "go over things" she watched the counters on her email and messaging apps continue to tick upward.

Suzanne's name flashed by and she scrolled back, trying to find it. Had someone found out about their past and waited for the release of *Rope* for maximum gossip impact? She tapped the wrong thing, had to close an ad, then a video that began playing automatically. She resisted the urge to throw the phone against the nearest wall.

Her hands were shaking as she fought back panic. What had happened while she'd been on the plane?

Finally, among the earliest messages, were links to a review. She took a deep breath, pushed away a number of unwelcome and distracting realizations, and read the thing, not at all sure what to expect.

A woman needs different or more lines than a man to be perceived as smart? She was riding a man's *coattails*? Her hearty laugh echoed off the tile. She hoped it hadn't startled anyone, but relief and a steely kind of glee combined to fill her with delight.

"The Internet—so helpful," she muttered as she clicked open her Twitter feed to quickly scan over the posts from the accounts she kept on her A-list. Viral media reported *#whatsmartlookslike* as a national trending topic. The marketing people for *Rope* must be euphoric, she thought. Her TV appearances and media interviews had just become a whole lot more interesting and newsworthy. Yes, she thought, let's talk about why leading roles requiring determination and intelligence were so rarely played by women.

A text from BeBe forewarned her that media had called to locate her and she'd given them Jennifer's rough time of arrival. *Thanks for offering me up like meat on a tray.* But she didn't mind too much—not for something like this.

By the time she reached the narrow security exit she was prepared for the sight of several reporters at the end of the hallway brandishing microrecorders and press credentials. Newbies or freelancers, she surmised, as she already had emails asking for comment from the entertainment journalists with names she recognized. She'd give them something to work with for the trouble they'd taken to come to the airport.

She was able to intersect with the driver holding the production company's placard before the journalists reached her. She gave him her luggage claim slips. "Two large bags, both bright yellow. They're hard to miss."

"They warned me to expect press and said I should extract you as soon as possible." His gaze swept over the little gathering and his dark features showed concern.

The media gurus probably thought Jennifer needed help with messaging. "This is not my first time at this rodeo."

"I'll take your bags to the car, and then be at the curb outside the doors." He headed for baggage claim as she turned to face the hubbub.

"Do you have a comment?"

"What would you say to the *Times*?"

"Can women play smart people?"

Even though she had refreshed her makeup in the bathroom, she was glad there were no cameras. Her lack of sleep the last few nights would be apparent in the unforgiving industrial lighting. "Can women play smart people? What a ridiculous question to have to ask."

The pallid young man with a man bun who'd asked the question visibly bristled. "I don't like having to ask it."

She moved slowly toward the exit doors where the driver would appear and the little cluster kept up with her. "I understand. I'm glad we can have a meaningful discussion about how failing for decades to cast women in challenging, intellectual roles means *some* people still think there are parts women can't play. There's no reason every Hitchcock movie there is couldn't be recast with a woman in the lead. With a person of color in the lead for that matter." It was a discussion she'd had with the director and screenwriter, and she knew that they hoped to cast a black couple as leads in a remake of *The Man Who Knew Too Much*. "It's the same kind of thinking, and it limits opportunities for movies to look like the real world."

She gave quotable comments to each of the others as well before saying, "It's late and you all want to get to your beds more than I do. I'm still on West Coast time."

As she walked toward the driver, the young man followed her to ask, "Are you looking forward to the premiere of the movie?"

She nearly answered sarcastically, caught herself and said instead, "Very much so. I know that my two co-stars were bone-chilling good, and I can't wait to see what the editing and post-production team has done to make our work look even better. There will be layers of excellence in every frame."

The driver moved in between her and the reporter in a subtle way that indicated the interview was over. Jennifer thanked him as he saw her into the back of the dark-windowed town car. "That was fun."

"If you say so, ma'am."

"I do," Jennifer said. "How's traffic?"

"The tunnel is moving fine. It'll be about forty-five minutes to your hotel."

She thanked him and turned her attention back to her phone. She quickly sent a text to her assigned production assistant, an easily worried young woman named Kelsey, to decline meeting tonight. "Used to rising early. Meet for breakfast at hotel 6 a.m.? Studio by 7:30."

She got a prompt text agreeing to the arrangement. It would feel earlier than usual due to the time change, but she intended to take a sleeping pill and crash as soon as they got to the hotel. She didn't want to take the chance that a business strategy session an hour from now would have her mind spinning for the rest of the night.

It would be a good idea to get some kind of response from her on the web. That was easy. She had to reword a couple of times to get under the character limit and finally posted, *"A shame when one of the great newspapers props up caveman thinking. @Times tell me you didn't mean it. Love, Jennifer #masculinitysofragile."*

Finally, she scrolled her way down in her notifications to the direct tag on a posting from Suzanne. "So I'm what smart looks like?" She wondered why Suzanne had taken the trouble. Don't read more into it than what it says, she told herself. Suzanne knows how women are discounted in her world. She's just being supportive.

The rest of the drive she spent tweeting thanks and sharing some of the postings to her personal accounts. She was touched to see one from Helen Baynor. Only when they were within a few blocks of the hotel did she answer Suzanne.

"Thanks for the props from the smartest woman I know @MasonGeekGirl. Math word problems are sexy." She left it at that. Nothing anyone could read anything into, except maybe Suzanne.

CHAPTER FORTY-SIX

At just after eight the next morning she was live on the first morning show, with another to quickly follow after a sprint from 30 Rock to studios at Times Square. After that the conversations blended together. Because of the "controversial review" as the media had taken to calling it, new interviews were added to the schedule right up until the premiere the following evening.

Just when she thought she had a grip on the rest of her day, the whole schedule blew apart at two p.m. when the production company's personal assistant pulled her out of a cast meet-and-greet to grab a taxi to NBC for a cameo in a music video that would air late night Saturday. The female cast members sang a parody dressed as Barbie dolls. At the chorus they spliced in a clip of Jennifer in a borrowed leather jacket, coiling her hair around her finger. In her best Jersey Girl voice she delivered the punch line: "My vagina can't do math."

She took a selfie on the legendary sound stage, thinking about Robin Williams and Gilda Radner. There were some things that fame and travel didn't prepare you for, she thought. She looked down at a stage mark and heard Lauren Bacall saying in her head, "Acting is a profession. Stardom is an accident."

Rope began early public showings at midnight. By the time Jennifer finished a special guest appearance on NPR's daily entertainment review, film tracking sites were showing a steady positive buzz. She and her co-stars crossed paths several times during the day, appearing together or in sequence on the same programs. It was a crazy whirl culminating in not enough time with two stylists in her hotel room working on her hair and makeup before helping her into the Michael Kors little black-and-white dress she'd brought with her.

She was exhausted. Her feet were not loving her Manolos today. Her public persona had never felt more like a needed mask. She loved it, every bit of it, and yet under it all she continued to replay the moment she'd realized that all the furor was about a review and not her sexuality.

There had been relief that the movie and everyone who had worked on it weren't having their contribution overshadowed by Jennifer's private life. But that paled next to the relief she'd felt that the decision had been taken out of her hands. For just those few moments she'd thought she would be free of choosing career over life, over love.

Some role model she was. She didn't want to be the one who pulled the trigger on her own fate. A pathetic coward. Suzanne had been right.

The crowd gathered at the barriers screamed continuously. She didn't remember walking the red carpet on the arm of the director. She paused for selfies with fans, spoke into microphones, smiled at cameras, let herself be led to her reserved seat in the theater.

She'd learned from premieres in the past that it took a certain kind of disassociation to watch herself in a role. Objectivity over her own work was impossible. If she focused on herself all she would see was the flaws. Instead she kept her gaze on the other actors and her ear tuned to the score. Its minimalist tension was perfect for a psychological thriller and the film editor's respect for the long, continuous takes was obvious in that none of the editor's work showed. It just made everyone in front of the camera look better.

Air kisses and handshakes, another walk on the red carpet to cross the street to the hotel ballroom where a fundraising gala was scheduled—it was all a blur.

The evening didn't become something like reality to her until she finished an impromptu interview with Monique DuMar, who wanted to write a feature on movies, fashion and leading ladies. She owed Monique a lot for positive press over the years and was happy to give her the time.

The moment Monique moved away, a husky masculine voice drawled in her ear, "You are still the most beautiful woman in the room."

She spun around and threw herself into Hyde Butler's arms for a hug. They were both too schooled to get any of her makeup on his pristine shirt front but the contact was more than just show.

"I didn't even know you were here," Jennifer said. She re-straightened his tasteful black silk tie. "No matter what you wear you look like James Bond."

His chiseled, all-American face was sincere when he said, "You were a smash in that movie, Jennifer. That moment when you realized where the body had to be blew me away."

"Thank you for saying so." She beamed at him, grateful for his praise. The two movies they'd made since that first one with Ryan Productions had been highlights for her, and his generosity was a big reason. If only some of it had rubbed off on her.

"I am not just blowing smoke, Jenny dear." He stopped in mock horror. "Jennifer, sorry."

"Okay, I'll call your bluff. What did you see in that moment?"

A couple of media people who had drifted toward them looked eager to hear the answer to her question too.

"First there was this excitement and exultation about having solved the puzzle. Then self-disgust for being excited about something so horrible. Then everything in your eyes changed and there was that little queasy swallow. Right at the end of the shot, the eruption of anger. I want to watch that fifty more times."

Touched, Jennifer blinked back tears. "That's what I was trying to do."

Hyde turned to the listening crowd and pulled her close. Camera flashes escalated into a wall of popping white. "This is what talent *and* smart looks like."

The producer was hustling two backers in their direction.

"I'm not going to crash your moment," Hyde murmured, but Jennifer latched onto his forearm with a steely grip.

"Please stay. If you can."

He might have felt her hand shaking because he covered it with his own. A receiving line was all but forming. Handshakes and air kisses were shared all around, and it was another hour before she got the chance to ask him if Emma and the kids were with him.

"Emma's home, cussing me out."

"What did you do?"

"Well, my part in it was brief."

"She's pregnant?" He winked. "Number three?"

"Third and last she says."

They had paused near the buffet table. Hyde piled a little plate high with cheddar cheese cubes and tiny meatballs. He caught Jennifer rolling her eyes. "What? I missed dinner."

"You're eight inches taller than I am, and have a man's metabolism. I should hate you for that alone." In heels the top of her head met his jaw, which had always made them a photogenic pairing.

He skewered a meatball with a toothpick and offered it to her. "You look peaked, darlin'."

She glared at the meatball until he popped it into his own mouth. "I won't see the gym for nearly a week, so stop tempting me." She remembered, suddenly, Suzanne and It's-Its and English muffins stale in the morning winds off the ocean. How could something so simple be out of her reach? "I'm just really tired. I tell myself to take breaks in between projects, but BeBe finds me work, and I like work. This is brilliant fun and it's only the beginning of ten days of nonstop talking. You know how it is."

"That wasn't just a tired look. You looked very broken up about having to say no to a meatball."

So her makeup wasn't concealing her mood. "I was remembering ice cream."

"No." His drawl was out. "That wasn't an ice cream look either. I know exactly when Emma would rather be looking at a bowl of vanilla ice cream instead of my vanilla face."

"It *has* been a year since you were the Sexiest Man Alive. It's a mystery how she can stand to look at you. Why does she even keep you around?"

"I beg her every day not to leave me. It seems to help."

She knew they ought to be circulating, but his presence felt like a lifeline though she didn't know why. "How did you know it would work out? When you proposed?"

He swallowed another meatball while shaking his head at her. "I didn't know. Who knows about these things? I got down on one knee in an airport because waiting to know would have taken too long."

She remembered the blurry pictures that had immediately made it to the gossip sphere. Romantic mushball. "Did BeBe try to talk you out of it? She was still your agent then, right?"

"Yes, my bachelorhood was a good commodity. She was sure getting married, and to a dentist, would cost me fans."

"Was she right?"

"Not so anyone would notice. So, *precious*. Are you considering changing your status from Hollywood's most eligible bachelorette? Love you, mean it!"

His impression of BeBe was so spot-on that she laughed in spite of feeling as if she were slowly sinking into a whirlpool. "I haven't been asked. And likely won't be."

"Then he's a fool."

"It's not a him." Her heart stopped. *I said that out loud.*

Hyde immediately amended himself. "Then she's a fool."

Jennifer stared at him. *I can't cry in public.*

He turned her away from the dwindling crowd and began pointing as if asking her if she'd like something to eat. "It can't be that bad," he murmured.

Rhythmic sips of air distracted her tear response, but her sinuses filled. Finally she was able to say, "You knew."

"Actually I didn't. I mean I knew you and Selena had been an item but I thought that was an exception."

"It's what I wanted everyone to think."

"I think the world has underrated you as an actor all along."

A strangled laugh escaped her. "Well, technically we do lie for a living. Did you know that Lauren Bacall said her career suffered for putting it second during her marriages? She said you can't have it all."

He touched her arm. "But if you're lucky, if you're with the right person, maybe you can have most of it."

"My heart's not big enough."

"Well, if you believe that, it never will be."

"I know I'm a coward."

"You know nothing, Jennifer Lamont."

Damn the man, he was making her laugh. The tears already pooled in her eyes threatened to spill over. "I know I've wrecked the chances I had with her and I don't think she'll even have me now." She added sarcastically, "But the good news is that if she did, I'd have no trouble juggling time for her and my work, because I wouldn't have work."

"I can't speak for the rest of the world, but I can promise you that if I have a say, you'll have work."

"You're sweet." Some of her poise returned and she was able to lean away from his sheltering bulk. "Every woman should be lucky to have a champion like you."

"You make my heart go pitty-pat when you talk like that."

"Of course it would be better if women didn't need champions to begin with. If the world were fair and equal and equitable and all those other impossible things."

"That's the world I want my girls to grow up in." He pulled out his phone with a genuine Proud Papa grin. "I have pictures."

Hours later, utterly exhausted, she stood at the window of her hotel room looking down at the pulsing neon of Times Square. Even from the fortieth floor at two a.m. she could tell the streets weren't empty. The city never did sleep. She'd be lucky if she managed any herself. She tried closing her eyes to the memories, but then she would smell Suzanne's cologne. Her sarcastic side had presented an ear worm of the chorus from "Send in the Clowns."

She'd have loved to have found an old movie on TV, but choices were slim. She resorted to mindlessly thumbing through her newsfeed and messages. There were congratulations from fans about *Rope*, photos from the reception including one with Hyde that was blowing the roof off the Twitter count, emails from media wanting more quotes, continuing *#whatsmartlookslike* posts directed at her, and even links to reviews that looked positive, judging by the headlines.

None of it held any interest for her. She had hoped there might be a math word problem. Something. Anything from @ MasonGeekGirl.

In a petulant fit she emptied most of her makeup on the bathroom counter to get to the bottom of the kit. She found what she was looking for, an engraved silver bracelet. The least expensive and most precious piece of jewelry she owned.

Turning it to the light she read *I am Unforgettable*.

Apparently not.

CHAPTER FORTY-SEVEN

From New York to Chicago for the local morning shows, then on to Atlanta and Dallas, Denver and Seattle. Most of the time Jennifer was with her two young co-stars in a too cold or too stuffy hotel meeting room turned studio, seated in front of a backdrop emblazoned with *Rope*'s film logo. Every five minutes a new reporter came in, asked the same questions and left. Some represented newspapers, other entertainment recap shows, some were podcasters and still others represented online outlets, news aggregators and highly ranked social media feed sites. It didn't matter where they were from, they asked the same questions, over and over.

Even before she and her co-stars left New York, all of them had run out of new ways to answer.

Yes, it had been so fun to work with each other.

No, they hadn't been worried about tackling a Hitchcock film.

Yes, they were excited about the reviews and box office.

No, they hadn't struggled to do the long takes, they all had stage experience.

It had been truly fun to take questions from a Boys and Girls Club drama program in Denver. That half hour had been a highlight of the trip. Every once in a while an interviewer would ask a question about the furor around *#whatsmartlookslike* and Jennifer let the guys answer most of the time. The men who didn't think she had any business tackling a man's role wouldn't listen to her justifications, but they might listen to the charming Cliff Raines and Sibo Bonali. Cliff, the avid outdoorsman, was especially fervent, and told the story several times of being lost on a long distance hike as a boy and a woman in the group had figured out where they were using two pencils and line of sight to the horizon.

Finally, late on day ten, they landed in Los Angeles. The boys were escorted to the Four Seasons while Jennifer collapsed into her own bed and rose too few hours later for the last of the press days.

Los Angeles was home, and it was a major market full of casting directors who might someday hire her, so Jennifer took extra care with her outfit. It was a relief to have her full closet to roam. Something to prop up her sagging mood and divert eyes from her weary smile. She decided on a vintage Gucci satin blouse and velvet trousers, both in her signature indigo shade and updated the look by adding steampunk-inspired lace up boots. She was ready for the production company car that ferried her from home to the stylist who'd agreed to be up in the wee hours of the morning to weave wispy milkmaid braids out of Jennifer's black curls. Then they were off to the hotel.

It was the last day, she kept reminding herself. That it was several weeks before she left for London to do the initial table reads on a feature-length movie was beginning to loom large. She was looking forward to matching wits with a legendary sleuth out to prove her a murderer, and she would spend time on solo work with the script. But until then she had only a few commercials and a small voice part in an animated feature to occupy otherwise empty days.

She had never thought of downtime in her schedule as empty before.

At least her ego felt better for the heads that turned as she walked the hotel lobby. She supposed that made her shallow, but at that moment she didn't care. She was right in the middle of the expansive marble and gold registration area when a toddler stumbled into her path.

She squatted down to help the child get back on his feet. "I fall down sometimes when I walk too."

A breathless father caught up to them. "I'm so sorry. He takes off all the time."

The little boy seized her finger and gave her the look of having decided he had found a new friend. Masses of kinky black hair and a flawless golden tone under brown skin made him absolutely gorgeous.

"No worries at all," Jennifer said.

"I hate to be that guy, but could I..?" He gestured with his phone.

"Sure." She put her head next to the little boy's and made him laugh with a snorted *oink*.

The father showed her the picture. "Is it okay for me to share it? And it'll be in Adam's baby book."

"Go right ahead." To the little boy she said, "Don't run away from Daddy. It makes him hurt in his heart." She waved bye-bye and looked up to find the perpetually worried Kelsey waiting for her. She'd been a trouper for the entire trip.

"He'll be a fan for life," she said while guiding Jennifer toward the interview room. "I hope the picture is a good one."

"I'm sure it's fine."

Sibo hugged her in his usual effusive way of greeting. He was letting his thick black hair grow out and was sporting a trimmed beard that made him look closer to thirty than twenty. "I can't believe this is the last day, can you?"

"Normal life won't seem normal," she told him, then realized it was certainly the truth for her. Normal didn't feel normal anymore.

"I'm back to Princeton in four weeks, so I can't wait to start my backpacking trip." Cliff was already perched on one of the bar-height director's chairs. He turned his phone toward them, displaying a gorgeous photo of the Sierra Nevada high country. "This is gonna be my view tomorrow morning."

"I should have planned a vacation," Jennifer admitted. "I have a table read about three weeks away. I could have gone to Spain. Or..." She let her voice trail away. She hadn't been back to Spain in years.

Their personal assistants were clustered in the back of the recording studio, waiting for the first interviewer. Jennifer set down her bag and excused herself briefly from the boys, signaling Kelsey toward her.

"It's hard to believe it's all over," Jennifer said. "Before we get started for the day I just wanted to tell you that you've been great to work with and if you need a reference feel free to list me. I don't tell everyone that."

"Th-thank you. That really means something, I appreciate it so much."

"I brought you something." She pressed a small jeweler's box into the young woman's hand. She'd noticed that Kelsey wore a different pair of earrings every day even if her jeans and black production company staff shirt didn't vary. "Wear them in good health."

"Miss Lamont! How sweet of you." She cracked open the box and gasped with delight. "These can't be real."

"Of course they are. Nothing about me is fake." She winked and left her to marvel at the diamond studs.

Cliff looked nervous. "I haven't done this before. Are we supposed to give the P.A.'s gifts?"

Jennifer kept her smile to herself. She'd been young once too. "Look at it this way. We're going to make more today than they've made the entire time they've been waiting on us hand and foot for this entire trip."

They both looked stricken and she took pity.

"Voyeux on Rodeo Drive will deliver. Cuff links never go out of fashion and sooner or later in this industry they'll need them. And they'll think kindly of you." She lowered her voice. "Don't be cheap."

She left them with their noses in their phones and settled into the chair on the left. The first interviewer was a blogger for the USC Film School and he was a nice way to start the day—no camera to worry about.

With the temporary set draped in black and no windows Jennifer lost sense of time. The morning seemed endless. Their answers grew increasingly punchy, though they steadied after a lunch break. Cliff was the first to get the sillies again. Some of the interviewers appreciated their high humor, others didn't. It didn't really matter—it would all be over soon.

"You're penultimate," Sibo told the second-to-last appointment. "I love that word, it's a five-dollar word, don't you think?"

This time there were two interviewers. Jennifer glanced at their cards. Ugh, *Buzztastic*. It was a nasty gossip machine and the site's comments were unmoderated, which meant they were a cesspool of threats and spam. If she had her way they'd never be treated like press.

They seemed more interested in Cliff's romantic life than the movie, or either her or Sibo. Just as she was musing that she might not have to say much, she realized she'd been asked a direct question.

"What's next for you?" the smaller of the two men repeated. He dripped with a kind of superior malice, as if the actors were adversaries and they needed to understand he had all the power in the room. His colleague with the complexion of whipped cream seemed to put great stock in *ennui*, as if he'd spent his entire day in a dark room under hot lights, smiling through repetitive questions, and it was all just too, too much for him.

She explained about London and the project there, but they didn't seem very interested. The other man found the energy to stir himself, almost cutting her off with, "We have a minute or two left of our allotment. Mind if we ask some general questions?"

Cliff immediately said, "Not at all."

Jennifer could have shot him. "As long as we can stipulate what's off the record."

There was a shrug of agreement, and they asked Sibo about his feelings regarding an anti-Muslim statement made the day before by a politician. He answered briefly but eloquently about believing America was better than what had been said.

Just as Jennifer relaxed, thinking it was all over, the smaller man asked her, "Didn't you do a guest shoot on *Baghdad by the Bay*?" At her nod he continued, "Quite the bombshell, wasn't it?"

"I'm sorry?"

"The shocker about Amy Lebeaux."

Hiding her alarm, she said, "I guess I haven't seen that."

"She was caught in lip-lock in a San Francisco ladies' club. The kind that is all ladies all the time." His smirking, smarmy tone set Jennifer's teeth on edge.

"I don't see why I would need to comment on that." Amy Lebeaux had gotten caught in a gay club?

"You worked with her."

She shrugged. He was clearly trying to goad a comment out of her. Her mind was in a whirl. Poor Amy, what was going to happen?

"She plays a sex kitten man-eater. How will that fly? Who'll believe it now that she's been outed?"

Sibo said, "Remember that show *How I Met Your Mother*? Everyone was happy with the gay actor playing the ladies' man. It ran for years."

Small Man ignored him. "Some people are saying she'll be replaced. She can't play the part anymore."

"Don't be ridiculous," Jennifer said.

There was a throbbing in her ears. The air around her seemed to crackle and she thought she smelled electricity. It was hard to make out what he was saying, but she heard "Sapphic sister" and "boycott by concerned moms."

There was an epic crapstorm aimed right at that cute little girl with the adorable nose and by the likes of this guy, who would rip up Amy Lebeaux's life to sell ads.

She realized that this guy was the guy she'd been afraid of all along.

And he was a *nothing*.

She had given him, and the likes of him, power over her. When she was younger, less experienced maybe it had been true. But she was not a scared twenty-year-old. She could do what Amy Lebeaux and everyone like her couldn't.

Pause before an important line. Enunciate. Project.

"It's absurd to think that gay actors can't play straight characters. I've been successfully doing it for years."

Deep down inside a part of her began to laugh hysterically.

CHAPTER FORTY-EIGHT

Suzanne toggled between two teleconferences she was monitoring to accept a chat from Annemarie. The connection steadied but before she could say a word Annemarie asked, "Have you seen it?"

"What?"

"The news. It's all over the freaking news up here. Maybe because it's filmed here and it's San Francisco, but Amy Lebeaux—"

"I saw that this morning." The trending headline had flicked past in her LGBT news feed.

"But you didn't see what happened a couple of minutes ago?"

"I'm on two calls and another starts in a three minutes."

"Sending you a link."

She tapped the URL. "A gossip site? Seriously?"

BUZZTASTIC EXCLUSIVE # #

Zip it up boys, Luscious Lamont goes for the girls. After years of making eyes at the guys, she admitted in our exclusive interview at the swanky Four Seasons that girls have been her go-to all along. If she can make us all think she loves the boys, she doesn't see why

Amy Lebeaux who got caught in a Sapphic snog can't do the same. Coincidence that L stands for Lamont, Lebeaux and—well, you do the math. Poor Hyde Butler, did he know it was all an act? #LamontLebeauxLesbian

Annemarie forwarded URLs from *People* and *Us*. "Everybody's picking it up. What is she doing?"

"How would I know?" The magazine sites were only posting about the speculation, saying nothing was confirmed. Even as she closed one article at *People*, another appeared with the headline. "CONFIRMED! Jennifer Lamont Exclusive!"

It was video even. Jennifer looking poised and on a director's chair, as if she was doing interviews for her movie, except the black curtain behind her was empty of design. Suzanne sped up the playback until Jennifer was speaking.

She was waving one elegant hand dismissively. "I wasn't going to let some gossipmonger be the one who decides that a talent like Amy Lebeaux should be marginalized. She has delightfully, humorously convinced us all that her *Baghdad* character is straight. I only pointed out that I had achieved the same thing. It's called acting."

The interviewer, a calm brunette that Suzanne recognized but couldn't name, sat opposite Jennifer with a notebook. "What would you say to people who believe that if it's not politically correct to cast straight actors to play gay parts, then why is it okay to cast Amy Lebeaux—or you—in the role of a straight character?"

"Nobody believes that straight actors can't play convincing gay characters, but too many think the gay actors can't play straight, or they can't even play parts where sexuality isn't mentioned. This is the truth of Hollywood—it you're straight and white you're up for every role that comes along. It's the default of the system. Everyone else has to prove themselves capable of playing against their supposed type."

"Do you think you'll have to prove yourself?"

"Yes. I'm a woman. I've had to prove myself for any part that didn't include cleavage and helplessness."

"As we know, at least one critic thinks women aren't convincing as smart characters."

"He proves my point, doesn't he?"

"Did your co-stars in *Rope* know you were gay?"

An elegant shrug followed a shake of the head. "It was a short shoot schedule, with not a lot of time to talk personal lives. Besides, they're both young, talented men getting their first flush of fame. I don't think my private life is of much interest to them." She laughed. "I have to say I'm not interested in theirs either. Only what they bring on the set. Only that when the director calls 'action' we are all there to do our best."

The video cleared and the interviewer took over, speaking solo to the camera. "So there you have it, America, in her own words. Stay tuned for the interview with Jennifer Lamont and her co-stars about the fascinating movie *Rope*."

"Hello? Earth to Suzanne!" Annemarie was waving her hand in front of her webcam. "This is bizarre. I mean, why would she do this after all these years?"

A vision of Jennifer, standing in front of the elevators at CommonTech, as bedraggled as Suzanne had ever seen her, preoccupied Suzanne's mind. "I really don't know."

"You're going to find out, aren't you?"

"You're the one who has brought it to my attention."

Annemarie looked chagrined. "I knew you'd care. For your sake, I hoped not too much."

"I don't know what to think. But let me think."

She waved and disconnected. Suzanne quietly ended her two other open screens and calendared a postponement for the next one, and the one after that.

She didn't have Jennifer's phone number or private email. She wasn't going to call her publicist or agent and leave a message.

A few clicks and a short conversation with a receptionist later, her video screen was filled with Selena Ryan's smiling face. "To what do I owe this honor?"

"Believe it or not, you were on a call list for next week. I thought in view of events of the day that I should call you sooner rather than later because I need a favor. That makes me a bad person doesn't it?"

Ryan's smile broadened. "It depends on the favor."

"Jennifer's phone number or address or any way you can think of that I could privately contact her."

"Oh. You've seen the news." Selena's expression reflected some of the confusion that Suzanne felt.

"Indeed I have. She came to see me a few weeks ago and I'm afraid I threw her out."

Somehow Selena didn't look surprised. "So you were counting on the fact that lesbians never let go of their exes?"

"If that were true I wouldn't need her phone number from you."

"Touché." Selena took a deep breath. "I know that she probably wouldn't mind. But I have a rule…"

"I get it." Damn. "It was inappropriate for me to ask."

"I could get her a message." Selena looked as if she couldn't believe she'd made the offer.

"No, that's too much to ask."

"Believe me, being a go-between for Jennifer and another woman was *never* on my bucket list. But like I said, I don't think she'd mind." She held up her index finger. "One message. Make it good."

"Thank you. Just give her this email. It's the private one family uses." She spelled it out to her and Selena read it back. "She can decide if she wants to get in touch. I know I really shouldn't care because she's a big girl and has proven that many times. But that's a long and lonely limb she's climbed out on."

"I know. People who've worked with her have started posting support. That's all fine and good, but just what the cost is will take years for her to figure out."

"I appreciate it. And maybe you'd like to hear why I was going to call you anyway?"

The tinge of nostalgia left Selena's expression. "If you can make it quick."

"Okay, I'll skip ahead in the long speech I have about the arts—books, film, theater, television—being the most powerful form of cultural influence at our disposal in the battle for hearts and minds. Would you be interested in serving on a steering committee for a project aimed at normalizing the presence of women in every aspect of production of the arts? Film, for example?"

"I'm intrigued."

"Good. I'll give you the long speech another time. In fact, find an open evening in your schedule and we'll talk over dinner."

"That sounds great. I'll tell my admin to work something out."

She sent a note to Annemarie saying she'd made initial contact with Ryan Productions about their Women Everywhere idea.

Annemarie would no doubt correctly assume why Suzanne had made that call this afternoon.

She didn't know what to do with herself. She should have kept her calls, but instead she was pacing around her office, through the great room, out to the warm tiles and the late afternoon sun where she could picture the dangerous flash in Jennifer's eyes when they'd been bidding against each other on the sculpture.

Jennifer had come out, looking as cool and collected as she always did, as if it were a decision of no more consequence than deciding which pair of shoes to wear. At least that was what most people would think. Suzanne had known even from her days as a model that Jennifer excelled at making very hard things look simple.

Her phone beeped with an email from her father.

Except it wasn't him. The sender was JLMT. The email contained an address and apartment number in West Hollywood and just the words, "If you can."

She heaped all blessings and good karma on Selena Ryan's head. Then it occurred to her that it was five p.m. on a weekday. It was at least a hundred and twenty miles to the northern end of the Los Angeles basin. With the weekday commute under way, a four-hour drive.

She didn't want to sit in traffic and what was more, she didn't have to. After all, what was the point of being filthy rich if you couldn't hire a helicopter on the fly? She did it for business because it made sense. Well, it made sense now.

She laughed at herself as she threw a few things into a messenger bag. Where was the quiet, submissive amanuensis to clear every obstacle in her path? Where were the minions to call in favors and wave credit cards while arranging the impossible? She and Annemarie had laughed once about learning to use nostril flares to order people around, like rich people in movies. A snap of the fingers and a helicopter would appear, lower a rope ladder and she'd be flown to her destination. While wearing a tux.

Her life was not like a movie. There were too many boring parts in it. Like waiting for a taxi to take her to the helipad at the university. Like being on hold while she played the rich donor card that had the chancellor's assistant arranging clearance to land for her helicopter service without the usual advance notice. Boring like waiting for another taxi in front of the luxurious Hollywood hotel where the helicopter company had landing privileges.

Sunset in Los Angeles, the sky a browned blue at all the edges and the air heavy with the scent of jacaranda. Honking cars, boulevards that moved at a snail's pace. The rising glitter of white and gold lights.

All of it boring until she knocked on the apartment door and Jennifer opened it, a tissue to her blotchy nose, eyes rimmed in red and impossible words on her lips.

CHAPTER FORTY-NINE

"All I needed was you." The words burst out of Jennifer with a painful twist in her heart. Maybe that was what truth felt like. She couldn't think of anything else to say that could possibly matter.

She let Suzanne cradle her close. It was like an infusion of strength and solidity. *This is okay. I can lean on her for a while.*

"I'd tell you everything will be fine," Suzanne murmured. "But I don't know that."

Jennifer had already cried herself out. She'd kept the lights off and curtains drawn, and finally, after sending her address to Suzanne, she'd turned off her phone. She'd cried in the dark, afraid, and cursing the tradeoffs of loving her solitude, of her pride in self-reliance, and the reality that there was not a single person she could ask for something as simple as a hug.

Any other day, getting an ex's private message giving her another ex's personal email would have been the winner for surreal moments. Today it hardly rated. Why Lena had done it, why had Suzanne even cared...

"I didn't mind if people thought I was a bitch. Or if they were afraid of me, or intimidated. As long as I didn't hear sarcasm in their voice when they called me an actor, I was safe. I had the career I'd worked for. And now that might all be gone."

Suzanne's arms tightened. "Have you had something to eat? Can I pour you some wine?"

"No, I—not hungry. I didn't even finish the glass I poured for myself." Jennifer stepped out of Suzanne's embrace in an attempt to pull herself together. And she didn't want to get snot on Suzanne's shirt. She wiped at her nose with a shredded tissue. "I don't know what to do with myself. I feel like there is a massive rock about to fall on my head but I'll never see it coming."

"I don't know what's going to happen, but I know you'll survive it."

"Thanks." If only she believed that. She got another wineglass from the cupboard and set it next to hers, which was still almost full. She picked up the wine bottle and thought to ask first, "Do you want some?"

"No, actually. I'm fine for now."

Her hands were still shaking as she set the bottle down again. "Have I been a fool?"

"Yes. Which time do you want to talk about?"

She knew Suzanne was trying to be funny but it stung. "Today."

"Were you a fool today? You tell me."

"I hardly know Amy Lebeaux. She's very vibrant and has comedic timing like a dream. Thinks I'm a lot nicer than I am. It was fun working on their set."

"Then why?"

"Good question." She paced across the room as Suzanne settled into one of the armchairs. "If I was going to just throw it all to fate, why didn't I do that nine, ten years ago? Twenty years ago?"

"You'd have led a different life. You'd be a different woman."

"I wouldn't be a mess." She mopped at her eyes with a fresh tissue.

"Do you want me to fight with you about whether you're a mess or not?"

"No. I don't want to fight." She stopped pacing to face her. "Thank you for getting a message to me. I'm sure Lena was thrilled."

"She made the offer."

"If there's one thing Lena is, it's a shrewd judge of character." Realizing how that sounded, she went on, "Another testament to my acting. I fooled her completely about my character until it was too late for her."

Suzanne raised her hands in a helpless gesture. "Do you want me to pile on here?"

"No. Why are you here?"

"You asked me to come."

"You sent me your email through my ex so I could ask."

"I figured you could use a friend."

"We're not friends."

Suzanne studied her loafers. "That might not be the right word, but we're something."

"Whatever you want to call it, you were right." She sniffled and tossed the tissue into a wastebasket. "Maybe fresh air will help."

"It is a little…close in here."

"I just wanted to crawl into a cave." Jennifer pressed the open button on the remote and the curtains rolled back. "My agent is probably having an aneurysm. The *Rope* people are freaked, the personal assistant was sure she'd be blamed for everything even though I sent the producers a note saying she'd been great, and who knows, there might be so-called 'scheduling conflicts' in my inbox already, calling off deals."

Suzanne joined Jennifer at the windows, her gaze fixed on the skyline. "Maybe. All of that could happen." She unlocked the sliding glass door. "Your view is stunning."

"As you said about Santa Cruz, location, location, location." Jennifer led the way along the southern balcony, loving the feel of the warm stone against her feet. She really ought to have changed out of her satin and velvet clothes though.

"It goes all the way around to that side? You can watch the sun rise and set?"

"Yes, and that's Sunset Boulevard." She pointed. "Beverly Hills, Santa Monica…"

"Come here." Suzanne guided her to the patio bench where Jennifer had only ever sat alone in the past. "Let's just breathe for a while."

The hot summer night held no hint of cooling even though the sun had faded. The sparkling lights, some in neat rows, others random sprawls of twinkling silver and blue, were calming. The fresh air eased the sting in her eyes. "Thank you," Jennifer murmured. "I just don't know what to do."

"Go on doing what you've been doing."

"If I'm allowed to."

"Who allows you to be you?"

"I'm an actor. By definition, it's a collaborative life." She didn't think Suzanne could understand. "I'm not a hermit and I do need other people to be successful."

"I know. But actor isn't all you are. You stood up for someone today. That wasn't a script you were reading. That was you."

"I don't know what I was thinking. We were two interviews from done with the entire media trip and all those mind-numbing press days. After those rat bastards from *Buzztastic* left I thought I was going to faint. Sibo and Cliff—the two young men in the movie—they were great. Mostly they were all 'wow, didn't know, it doesn't matter.' The last reporter in was a woman from *People*. She had no idea what had just happened. She asked the same basic questions everyone asks and then it was a wrap. I realized—I just couldn't stand the idea that those bottom-feeders would be the only source for the story."

"You could have denied it. Said they were malicious asshats, which would have been true."

Jennifer cocked her head. "I never even thought of that, and it wouldn't have worked. Sibo and Cliff shouldn't have to lie for me. I just threw myself on the *People* woman's mercy. Offered her an unplanned exclusive."

Suzanne spread her hands. "She took it of course. Who wouldn't?"

"At least she would have video. People would pay more attention to that I hope. Rather than that smug summary by the rat bastards."

"You saw what they published?"

"Yes. Sapphic snog and all. Assholes." Tension was draining out of her body and she realized she was exhausted. "I saw that after I got home. Then I got Lena's message while all the social media on my phone blew up." Her throat tightened. "All I could think was that I'd jumped off the roof and if you were near enough you'd catch me."

"It was the second bravest thing you've done."

"Second?"

"Yes. The first was backing yourself. Choosing you when nobody else would. Even me."

She gazed up into Suzanne's lean face, wishing the light were better. "I don't know what you mean."

"You believed in yourself. You put yourself first. I gave you reasons not to. The whole world gives women reasons not to, like we're not good women if we don't put everyone else first. You stood up to all of it and chose yourself."

Damn it, she was going to cry again. She didn't know why Suzanne was being kind. "I was afraid to come out, you were right about that."

"I shouldn't have called you a coward for being afraid—reasonably afraid—that you'd lose your job. I didn't have to worry about losing my income, and I wanted to pretend you were afraid of nothing because—because it made it easier to be angry at you instead of a situation I couldn't fix." Her short laugh was rueful. "That doesn't happen to me a lot, not being able to fix it."

She took a long, shuddering breath. "If I'd chosen us instead, we wouldn't have spent all this time alone."

"Instead, we spent all this time becoming who we wanted to be. Both of us. Surely you've noticed all of my successful, committed relationships of which there are none?"

Jennifer exhaled a half laugh along with a sniff. "Don't call me Shirley."

"Made you laugh."

"Carina Estevez seemed like a successful relationship."

"It had something, but we drifted too easily apart. The sex was good."

Jennifer rolled her eyes. "At least you were having sex. After you… Let's just say that I've been responsible for my own orgasm for a really long time."

Suzanne laughed. "See, that makes me want to ask if I can watch."

Jennifer felt the familiar stirring of the desire that had never gone away. "Maybe if you're good."

"That's not why I came here."

"I know." Jennifer sensed an abrupt stillness in Suzanne. Wariness, perhaps? Who could blame her? "This is the worst booty call ever."

She laughed again, harder this time. "I could look at this view for hours."

"I know." Jennifer took a deep breath and made herself get up even though her legs felt like lead. "How about a tour? It's too hot out here."

She left the curtains open and set the air conditioner down a few more degrees. "I think my entire apartment could fit on your patio." She flipped on more lights as she led her down the short hallway. "Yes, this is an entire room devoted to my clothes. This is my wall of shoes. Don't judge."

Suzanne ran fingertips lightly over the toes of a pair of suede boots. "Organized as always. Even your place in New York was organized." She picked up a pair of white platforms with chartreuse polka dots. "Okay, now I'm judging you."

Jennifer lifted them out of Suzanne's hands. "I keep those to remind myself that sometimes haute couture is ridiculous. And for when I'm going as Disco Diva to a Halloween party."

She stopped outside the office door. "This will make you laugh." She gestured Suzanne to enter ahead of her as she turned on the light.

"My, my." Suzanne gazed down at the table scattered with plastic bricks. "Excuse me, but is that the Limited Edition Master Set Ghostbusters Headquarters with ECTO-One, reboot mini figures and proton paks?"

"Why yes, King of the Geeks, yes it is."

Suzanne plopped into the chair and bellied up to the table. All the lines of tension eased from her face. "This is way excellent."

"Well, you never know when you're going to have a hot date."

She looked up from the mini figure of Jillian. "You're just a geek magnet, aren't you?"

"I tried meditation. I tried Hot Yoga. I tried the full bottle of wine. But nothing is more Zen than Legos."

"Told you."

"I knew you'd say that. But I don't have any It's-Its."

"Then what good are you?"

Jennifer laughed and stooped to kiss the tip of Suzanne's ear. "Thank you for coming. I hope you didn't have to like, drop a company off the edge of the planet or call off shipping a new gadgety I-probably-can't-even-appreciate-how-cool-it-is geektronic thing."

"Just a couple of meetings. One of them was about geektronics." She hummed slightly as she sifted through the bin of red bricks.

"I really need a shower. You could work on the garage door." Her voice wavered with sudden shyness. "Or you could join me."

Suzanne's hands stilled as Jennifer was jolted by the memory of those fingers caressing her skin. "I'm not sure that's a good idea."

"Okay." Jennifer backed away. "I'll just—"

"Jennifer." Suzanne had scrambled to her feet. "Let's not make the same mistakes."

"I get it." She backed into her desk, then fumbled her way out the door.

Suzanne followed her. "I don't know if this is unfinished business or a new agenda."

"You and your sexy talk." Jennifer ended up against the hallway wall. "Maybe it's both?"

"We know what's easy for us." Suzanne was standing close enough for Jennifer to see that over the years the blue in her eyes had become lighter and softer. "It would be very easy. But we have to work on the hard stuff. If."

"If." Jennifer looked down at her feet. "If anybody ever gets around to asking for more."

"If," Suzanne echoed.

For just a moment she thought Suzanne was going to kiss her, but instead she closed her eyes for a moment. "Go take a nice, hot shower."

The steam felt wonderful to her sore sinuses and stinging eyes. What had possessed her to ask Suzanne to join her? A flare of desire, a need to be held, that was all. The way this day was going she'd end up with soap in her eyes and inhaling shampoo—sure, that was erotic. So, so sexy. She found soft sweats and an old Actor's Equity T-shirt and discovered Suzanne fitting pieces while reading something on her phone.

"You're multitasking," she accused. "There's no multitasking with Legos."

"I have a few things you'll want to read. If you feel like easing back into the world tonight."

"I don't know." At the best of times it wasn't easy to merely dip in a toe when it came to the web.

"Friends. Always check out the friends first. Everyone else can wait."

"Better your phone then," Jennifer said. "Mine's off and I'm keeping it that way for now. I'm so in trouble for ducking my agent."

"Start here." She held out the display.

"Always knew it was an act because that's what actors do," Jennifer read aloud. "Always knew @realJenniferLamont was exceptional. Hashtag still what smart looks like. From the real Hyde Butler."

"Is he really the stand-up guy he seems to be?" Suzanne took back her phone.

"Yes, he is. Really. Another one?"

"Amy Lebeaux says thank you, in all caps, and has a row of kisses, gratitude and tears-of-joy emoticons."

Jennifer reached over Suzanne's shoulder to scroll, and was startled by the sudden buzz of the building intercom. "Damn. Probably my agent demanding to come up."

The desk guard was apologetic. "I'm sorry to disturb you this late, Ms. Lamont. But I thought you should know that a news van is setting up to do a live broadcast at the front door. I think you're our news-maker of the day."

"Thank you. I do appreciate knowing." Well, it was better than BeBe.

Suzanne had joined her in the living room. "I have a thought."

"Just one? How much do they pay you?" When Suzanne gave her a narrow look in response, she added, "Sorry. My sarcasm button has no off setting at the moment."

"You finished your commitments, right? What are you doing tomorrow?"

"Nothing. I have a voice-over recording next Tuesday, and that's it. I have some scripts. I'm behind on workouts. I need to start working on a Finnish accent. Right now I sound like the Swedish Chef on the Muppets."

"It's not a part that's supposed to inspire laughter?"

"No. If they haven't found a way to dump me." Her gaze fell on her darkened phone. "I really should check it. At least call my agent. BeBe will be… So. Very. BeBe."

"Who says you have to stay here? You should be on your planned hiatus."

"You mean I should run away."

Suzanne leaned against the wall, looking as if she hadn't a care in the world when Jennifer could only imagine what she'd abandoned to get here so quickly. "You're being so literal."

"Where to?"

"I'll tell you in the car. We'll have to take yours. I'll drive."

Escape. It sounded welcome. She didn't want to do a bunch more interviews or take calls from reporters. She needed a little time and space. Right now it didn't feel like her feet were even on the floor. "What should I bring?"

Suzanne bounced on her toes. "A hat and dark glasses. Anything else we can buy. I can loan you socks."

"We know how well that works." She looked out at the skyline, not entirely sanguine about the idea of running away. But BeBe would want to pull out all the publicity stops, as if her admission were no different than a wardrobe malfunction to be handled and possibly exploited.

It only took a few minutes to put her toiletry kit into an oversized shoulder bag and add some jeans and tops. Her sense of urgency increased as she thought of BeBe's hand-wringing and manipulations.

Fine, she was running away.

She confirmed with the front desk that there was no one in the parking garage and the exit at the back of the building had no one hanging around. Hat and glasses firmly on she gave the car keys to Suzanne. It's Los Angeles, she told herself. Everybody wears sunglasses after dark.

She expected at any moment to hear someone call her name, but they made it to the car, out of the garage and around the corner onto Sunset without anyone seeming to take notice.

Reclining in the passenger seat, leaning her head back, the last thing Jennifer remembered was Suzanne quietly saying, "Why don't you have a nap?"

CHAPTER FIFTY

Jennifer was completely out. Her body was limp in the reclined seat and though Suzanne tried to take the curves through the Tehachapi Mountains carefully, her head lolled as the car swayed, occasionally settling into a position that caused breathless little snores.

Once they were clear of the notorious Grapevine it was a beeline drive along stretches of freeway with only 18-wheelers for company. It was a tedious stretch of road any time of day, and one of the reasons she preferred to fly. Even at night the temperatures on the interstate were unpleasantly high. She could feel heat pulsing from the asphalt and warming the bottom of the car. Fortunately, Jennifer's Lexus had excellent air-conditioning. The dashboard display told her she'd have no trouble reaching her destination on the battery charge and gas in the tank.

Jennifer finally stirred when they left the interstate for a windier, slower highway. "Where are we?"

"Halfway to Santa Cruz."

"Santa Cruz? You still have the house there?"

"I had no reason to sell it, and my dad and I both like to go there for quiet space."

"You're taking me to Santa Cruz." Jennifer's voice was soft and unfocused.

"It'll be a hell of a lot cooler than LA right now."

"In more ways than one." Jennifer stretched and fished in her bag and came up with her phone. "Let's see how bad it is."

Suzanne couldn't hear the messages Jennifer was listening to, but she gathered that her agent had left the majority of them.

"Tell me they made it up, blah blah blah, we should have had a plan, blah blah blah. I'm her favorite client." Jennifer turned off the phone display with a jab at the screen. "She was a little less convincing than usual on that last part."

"You could always change representation, right?"

"I could. I might." She took a deep breath and made a phone call. "I know the direct to voice mail trick." She paused, listening. "BeBe it's Jennifer. I can't meet with you because I'm not home. I took off on a planned hiatus for a few days and I'll be off the grid, completely unplugged. I'm exhausted and have got to have some time for myself. We'll talk when I get back."

She disconnected. "Did I cover everything?"

"You know better than I do. It's your rodeo."

"She'll try to hunt me down, but she doesn't know about you. Or Santa Cruz."

"If I take a couple of calls tomorrow I can stay through the weekend. If we're lucky my father left some barbecue in the freezer. He won't mind if we eat it."

Jennifer was quiet for so long Suzanne wondered if she'd drifted off again. Finally she said, "I know there are going to be people who think that because I was silent I left everyone else to do the hard work. And now that we have marriage rights and it's a little bit safer, I'm cashing in."

"Do you think that's true?"

"Yes. And no. Somewhere in between, like most things. I can't go back and change it. I guess, like all my other choices, I'm just going to have to live with it. I know better, I'll try to do better." She pulled her knees up under her chin. "I'm scared. But it's a different kind of scared."

The miles slipped away and it was still before dawn as Suzanne turned off the highway toward the house. The coastal winds were coming in hard off the water. She expected the house to be cold and she wasn't wrong. She turned off the alarm and opened the garage and Jennifer pulled the car in carefully.

"The cold air feels delicious," Jennifer said. "I don't have words to describe how hot it was in Dallas."

Suzanne fussed with the heat. "It'll take the chill off in a while. It's practically breakfast time. There's always pancake mix in the cupboard. Just add water."

"You must be exhausted," Jennifer said suddenly. "I'm sorry, I've been selfish. Do you want to crash?"

"I'm too wired." Even as she said it she felt her eyelids droop.

"Come on." Jennifer pulled her along to the master bedroom. "Let's curl up. Don't worry, your virtue is safe."

Darn, Suzanne thought. She was not at all convinced she wanted safe virtue. It had seemed very mature to refuse the offer to share a shower, but now she was regretting not listening to her lizard brain.

Shoes kicked off, they opted to get under just the comforter. Jennifer snuggled close behind, one arm over Suzanne's hip.

"I love the sound of the waves. And the moonlight." A gentle kiss on the back of her neck melted Suzanne in all the places no one else had ever warmed.

Sleep rose up for her in a wave.

Sunlight in her face woke her. Jennifer was gone.

And then she smelled pancakes.

CHAPTER FIFTY-ONE

"This is the part where we mess up." Jennifer tied her hair back before stepping out into the windswept backyard. She'd learned to go out the sliding glass door back first so nothing on the plate she carried blew off. "I have to be in LA day after tomorrow. You have an empire to run."

"It's too big not to run itself most of the time. But I have meetings I can't cancel tomorrow. From here it makes sense for me to go on up to San Francisco and fly home later."

"So today's the last day we get to hide out."

"The trick is not to start a fight." Suzanne reached the picnic table first, and put down the bag of fragrant pumpernickel rolls and her plate of smoked ham and fruit salad. From her jeans pocket she withdrew a light blue box.

Jennifer froze at the sight of it. There was no mistaking the light robin's egg blue. Only one thing came in that color box. For a moment she wrestled with the same feeling she'd had years before, that Suzanne was buying her. Maybe it was the soft, worn Fury Road T-shirt, the coastal sun on the spiky hair, or something in Suzanne's smile that chased the anger away. "Is that the same Tiffany's box?"

"The same one."

She took her time getting out one of the rolls, splitting it open with her thumbs and slathering it with a shrimp and avocado mustard spread she'd become deeply enamored with the day before. The box seemed to glow in the noon sun. She told herself it was only a piece of jewelry, not a symbol of capitulation or submission.

After a restorative bite, during which Suzanne watched her every move, she lifted the top and unwrapped the tissue-swaddled item inside.

No diamonds. No pearls or gold.

Instead she was holding a bracelet of tiny Lego pieces. "I said you were trying to buy me with this. Why didn't you tell me?"

"Because by then I was angry and so were you, and I was afraid you would open it and you'd be charmed. I'm fatally charming, you know."

Jennifer ran a finger over the pieces as she blinked back tears. "So I've heard."

"And it would have only delayed the inevitable. I knew deep down we couldn't last. I wouldn't have paid a price at all, while you would have given up nearly everything. I'd have hated keeping it secret, you would have always been afraid of being discovered. No matter what, I had precious little to lose. But you would not be you. And you deserved to be you."

Suzanne looked up from the table, fixing Jennifer with an open gaze. "I didn't have a right to expect you to abandon your life plans just because the sex was good and we looked good together, and I could buy you lots of stuff."

"I knew it was more than you just wanting to buy a pretty girl."

"I don't know. Conquest was on my mind a lot."

"And now?"

"We've both leveled up. That changes the nature of the game."

Jennifer was finding it hard to breathe. She looked at the bracelet again. The little bits of brightly colored plastic were orange and yellow and blue and strung together with thin elastic thread. "I can't wear this."

"I really didn't expect you to. It was just..." She shrugged. "A silly something I bought in New York, thinking I'd see you any minute. I kept it. Kind of like the pajamas."

"No, I mean, I'd have to take this one off." She pushed up the sleeve of her sweatshirt. *I am Unforgettable* glinted in the sunlight.

"You still have it."

"I've always carried it in my makeup kit. I found it this morning."

Suzanne ran a fingertip over the silver links. "I want to see you. Date you."

"That's not a question. A question is 'Will you date me?'"

"Okay, will you date me, Jennifer Lamont?"

"I asked you first."

Suzanne rolled her eyes. "So that's how it's gonna be?"

"That's how it's gonna be." Jennifer twined her fingers with Suzanne's. "This has been magical. I haven't felt this disconnected from the world and refreshed in forever. If this were a movie we'd just walk on the beach into the sunset. Or I'd call a press conference and we'd clinch on the red carpet."

A hint of wariness edged into Suzanne's voice. "We're not those people."

"It seems a lot more fun to get caught snogging in a Sapphic hot spot."

Suzanne grinned at the idea. "I know of a bar in the Castro." Her expression changed to apprehension. "I'm going to have to tell Annemarie."

"She's really not my biggest fan."

"No. But give her time. She doesn't know what I see in you."

"Well, it would be kind of weird if she did, wouldn't it?"

"I hadn't thought of it that way."

Jennifer finished her bread and avocado salad with an appreciative sigh. She could eat that every day of the year. "So you didn't answer my question. About dating."

"Didn't I?"

"No, you didn't. I was paying attention."

"What does dating mean to you?"

"I'm kind of a Luddite about these things, but I've heard there's a thing called Sharing Calendars."

"Oh, now who's doing the sexy talk?"

Jennifer preened. "The goal would be to make a Venn diagram with all the times I am free and all the times you are free and what overlaps in the middle is us, dating."

Suzanne paused with a bite of ham halfway to her mouth. "Holy tennis balls, I love you."

Her laughter faded. "No you don't."

A slow smile crossed Suzanne's face. "I think I do."

"I think I love you," Jennifer said. "I think I always have, but it wasn't enough to change the last twenty years. So what do I know about love?"

"I do know that it takes failure to succeed." She reached across the table to stroke the back of Jennifer's hand. "And I'd rather think about the next twenty years."

All the air went out of Jennifer's chest. "Okay. That's not dating, that's more like commitment."

"In that case…" Suzanne pulled the twist tie off the bag of rolls and wrapped it around her thumb to make a circle. She held out the result. "There, I'm putting a ring on it."

Jennifer gestured at the Tiffany's box. "Well, with these riches I'd be a fool to say no."

"To what?"

Jennifer played back their conversation in her head. "I lost track. Dating?"

"Commitment."

"Commitment." She let Suzanne slip the twist tie onto her ring finger. "You know, I really don't care, but if word gets out you landed me with a Lego bracelet and a twist tie ring, you're going to be hashtag *Suzanne Mason is cheap*." She touched a knuckle on the back of Suzanne's hand. "But I know I can have you for the price of a hot dog."

Suzanne turned Jennifer's hand over and traced a line along her palm. "Now that we've at least started the hard part what about the easy part?"

"God yes. For the record, I really love it when you ask."

Suzanne's eyes narrowed. "I would really like to take you to bed."

Jennifer licked her lips. "Maybe I like it even better when you tell me."

"I remember that about you." Her grip tightened on Jennifer's hand as she pulled her to her feet. "Leave the dishes."

The moment the door was closed Suzanne kissed her with tenderness and rising heat. Jennifer hadn't forgotten the feel of Suzanne's lips on hers and how quickly they ignited her passion. She pushed Suzanne away long enough to strip off her own shirt.

"You really know how to make me crazy."

Jennifer's laugh was weak with desire as Suzanne's hands swept over her bare back. "Whatever it is we're doing here I'm an absolute virgin. It feels like I've never done this before but I make sense with you." She hissed as Suzanne's touch grew firmer.

"You know this isn't just about your body." Suzanne's hands slipped down the back of Jennifer's jeans, sending fireworks of shivers up her spine. "But right now, it's about your body."

Jennifer snaked her fingers into Suzanne's hair and pulled her mouth down for a hungry kiss of half-spoken words and shared air.

By the time they reached the bed Suzanne had only her shirt on. Jennifer swatted away Suzanne's hands as she tried to pull Jennifer down on top of her.

"Not yet." Jennifer's fingers went to Suzanne's buttons. "I'm not going to be the only one naked."

"You still have my gigantic sexy socks on."

"Do you want me to take them off?"

"I want everything off," Suzanne said hoarsely. "I love you naked in my bed. I want to hold you tight and hold you down and enjoy the way you feel against me."

Jennifer brushed her lips at Suzanne's ear. "Yes."

"I'm afraid I'm going to hurt you."

"You know I'm not fragile." She pulled Suzanne's hands to her breasts. "You've always wanted me to be strong."

"Yes," Suzanne said. "Show me. Show me how you're strong."

EPILOGUE

Eight Months Later

Selena Ryan's voice seemed to come from far away. "This is the life," she said with a sleepy but heartfelt sigh.

Suzanne shaded her eyes so she could see her. Basking in the sun in shorts and a tank top, Lena looked about to doze off. Suzanne herself wasn't far behind her. "I told you so. You didn't have to wait until we were announcing Parity in Film's first grant awards to make the drive."

Lena shifted slightly on the chaise lounge. "Now you're not going to be able to get rid of any of us."

A child's shriek of laughter was accompanied by a loud splash and Suzanne rolled her head the other direction to look toward the pool. Hyde Butler, standing in waist-deep water, scooped up his eldest daughter and tossed her back into the pool a few feet away from him, then waded over to make sure the water wings she wore brought her to the surface quickly. Both of them seemed to have endless energy.

At the nearer end of the pool, where the awning provided shade, Suzanne's father was supervising the middle girl as she bobbed up and down in a toddler-sized floater. The Butlers' nanny was reading a book and keeping a watchful eye on the infant tucked into a portable playpen while Hyde's wife, Emma, was having a much-needed nap.

Winter breezes off the coast of La Jolla were cool and damp, but February had been a month of sunshine. The hibiscus in the garden was in glorious bloom, and Suzanne loved that the poppies were already showing their golden-orange blossoms around the base of the nearest cypress tree. The patio's terra-cotta tile was still cool underfoot, but the sun was trying to make up for it.

The large awning that filtered the sunlight let through enough to warm Suzanne's skin and make her drowsy. But every nerve in her body woke up when she heard the light *tap tap* of sandals. Jennifer was home.

She swung up out of the chaise just as Jennifer tossed her phone onto the table with all the others as her entrance fee to the pool area. Emma was on to something with the Phone Quarantine Zone.

Jennifer, already clad in a swimsuit and cover-up, snuggled close for a kiss. "Hello you."

"Was the drive awful?"

"No, and the last loop is done. After all the issues yesterday we got it in two takes." Her crimson bikini, as far as Suzanne was concerned, made life worth living. "Clementine called while I was on the road and she's bringing a package with her this afternoon to the hotel, ready for signature. *Australian Zombie Hunters* here I come."

"Congratulations!" She hugged her close. Jennifer's decision to sign with Clementine Molokomme's agency had freed her from the endless anxiety that BeBe LaTour had fed. She personally loved Clementine's respectful, pragmatic style and Jennifer was certainly pleased that voiceover and animation work had gone up, not down. "That and the remake of *North by Northwest* means you're going to be a busy woman."

Jennifer squeezed Suzanne's arm as they walked toward the cluster of chaises. "It's enough." She made a show of stepping around the tile that had tripped her into Suzanne's arms not quite a year ago. "It's finally enough."

Annemarie appeared from the direction of the kitchen with a plate of strawberries and a bottle of wine, which she handed to Suzanne. Her gaze on Jennifer she said, "Open this before something bad happens, like a corkscrew slips and cuts someone's head off."

Jennifer's voice was sticky sweet. "Bitch."

"I know I am but what are you?"

"Language!" Lena called. "There are small people here."

"I'm sorry," Jennifer said. "I meant to say 'Bless your heart.'"

Annemarie laughed and Suzanne relaxed. The more time the two of them spent together the less wary Annemarie seemed to be. Having a foundation to run where Annemarie got to do whatever she wanted made Annemarie a very happy woman.

Jennifer dropped gratefully onto the lounger next to Gail, who wanted a recap of her experience with a director Gail would be working with in the fall.

"You know it's really not fair," Annemarie said to Suzanne. "All that *and* she's happy?"

"I happen to think it's totally fair."

"You would."

Suzanne set the unopened bottle on the sideboard and pointed at the lovely chardonnay that was already uncorked. "We can't finish this before we have to leave. Drink what's open."

"You are so cheap. I should tweet about how cheap you are."

"We're about to give away ten million dollars, and I'm taking it out of your wine budget." She wagged a finger at Annemarie as she returned to her lounger.

"Somebody else made that decision, but I thought we were an autonomous collective," Jennifer was saying to Gail. "I thought we all took turns acting as an executive officer for the week."

Gail immediately continued the *Holy Grail* riff. "But all the decisions of that officer..."

Suzanne murmured to Lena, "They're adorable, aren't they?"

"Agreed. You've certainly increased Jennifer's Nerd Quotient."

"Is that a compliment?"

"Up to you." Lena swiped a finger through the condensation on the outside of her iced tea and dabbed the cool drops onto her forehead. "I may end up in the pool after all. Oh, been meaning to ask you a question."

"Go for it."

"So what do you think the real truth is about that thriller that recast Jennifer's part?"

Suzanne sighed. "Exactly what everyone else thinks—three days after she comes out the star of one of the surprise hits of the summer isn't 'the right direction for the part'? Please. But their loss. And the superhero franchise's gain." She didn't bother to hide a gloating smile.

Lena stretched and shifted onto her side. "I'm not saying she didn't earn the part because she'll make a badass bad guy, but I know the producer and he was happy to make his feelings about discrimination clear one more time. He'd already threatened to boycott an entire state, though, so it wasn't like he needed to boost his credibility with anyone. Jennifer was a great cast for them. As you say, their gain, and the producer seemed to appreciate that."

Suzanne grinned as Hyde settled his daughter on his shoulders and they played sea monster. "Be careful," she called out. "It starts to get deeper right about there."

"We are invincible." Hyde added a roar but it ended as a yelp when the little girl grabbed a handful of his hair to keep her balance.

Lena had turned her head to watch Gail and Jennifer chatting like the best of friends. "Wonders never cease. Must be the sunshine and the hospitality. Thanks again."

"What's the point of living in something the size of a small hotel if you can't fill it with people you like?" Somewhere in the last few months the house had gone from her preferred place to spend her nights to simply "home." It had been easy to make room for Jennifer, though they spent a number of nights at her place in LA. If they wanted to quickly and easily disconnect from everyone and everything, the house in Santa Cruz was waiting, and there was always some of her dad's barbecue tucked in the freezer.

Emma Butler was shaking off a yawn as she emerged from the cabana. "Time to feed Bethany. I'll be back in a while." The nanny immediately scooped up the infant and the two women disappeared into the house.

Annemarie sat down at the nearest edge of the pool and dangled her legs in the water. "So how much did you love that *Variety* article calling you Jennifer Lamont's girlfriend Susan Macy?"

Suzanne burst out laughing all over again. "It did not hurt me in the least." She closed her eyes and listened to the rise and fall of Jennifer's voice as she chatted with Gail. It held no bitter notes, no anxious undertones or looming shadows.

A while later the kids were both reluctantly pulled out of the pool, and sat drying wrapped in towels, eating peanut butter and jelly sandwiches.

Even as Suzanne thought she ought to retrieve her phone and check the time, the anxious party planner, who had proven to be once again very good at her job, appeared with her tablet. "I'm sorry, but you all need to start getting dressed or the press conference won't start on time and that will push back the dinner service. I'm leaving for the hotel now."

Lena got to her feet and settled a towel around her neck. "It was too good to last."

"Time for sea monsters to get dressed," Hyde informed the kids. "If you're quick about it there'll be time to look at Suzanne and Jennifer's new Lego room." Hyde lumbered toward the house with a giggling daughter on each hip.

"I'll be ready in time," her father called from the pool. He began a lazy last lap now that the water had settled.

They were alone in their bedroom when Jennifer observed, "Lena likes you better than she ever liked me. What were you two conspiring about?"

"We were just talking shop. You know, I just realized you're going to be the first character played by an out lesbian who's an action figure. I think you're the first anyway. I could look it up."

Jennifer slipped out of her bikini. "Later. We need to get in the shower. A gaggle of entertainment reporters and media watchdogs want news, sure, and they want their dinner." She quickly opened and closed drawers in the large bureau and a small pile of undergarments and hose quickly formed on the bed. "Trust me, though. If the bar opens late it'll turn ugly. So get naked, Geek Girl."

"Yes ma'am." Suzanne followed Jennifer's every move with her eyes. A deep ache of pleasure made it hard to breathe. In moments like these Jennifer was simply...Jennifer. With practiced competence she twisted her long hair into a knot on the top of her head, used duck pins to hold it in place and walked into the shower—and she made it all look like a dance.

One of the joys of being home at the same time was taking showers together. There was enough room in there to reenact Gene Kelly's splash dance in *Singin' in the Rain*, though that wasn't the kind of dancing she had in mind.

Jennifer had just finished lathering her skin. She pointed a warning finger at Suzanne. "I can't get my hair wet. I don't have time to dry it."

Suzanne gestured at the other end of the enclosure. "I'll shower over here then."

"Don't you dare. I've been gone for four days."

With a fond laugh and a sigh of pleasure, she spooned behind Jennifer under the hot water, wishing they had all afternoon. Her hands roamed up Jennifer's slick body to cup her breasts. "I can't help it if things get a little damp."

Jennifer steadied herself with a hand on the nearest wall. "That's cheating."

"We don't have time for all the ideas I have." She turned Jennifer to face her and pushed her back against the cool slate.

Jennifer used one muscled leg to pull Suzanne even closer. "Just what did you have in mind?"

"This." Her fingertips teased along the crease of Jennifer's thigh.

A soft sigh in her ear encouraged her as did the way Jennifer wound her fingers into her hair.

"Something to tide us over," Suzanne whispered and they moved together until both of them were shaky and pleased.

Jennifer buried her face in Suzanne's neck. "I can't believe my heart can hold all of this."

Suzanne rocked her close, happy to be breathing and holding Jennifer in her arms. "You're amazing. We're amazing together."

With a sigh of regret Suzanne found gratifying, Jennifer pushed her away. "We're going to have to speed it up or we'll be late." Jennifer toweled herself mostly dry then disappeared into the depths of their closet. She called out, "Which little black dress works for a press conference and handing some deserving women envelopes with checks?"

"I'm sure you'll pick something outstanding."

"You're wearing the new Armani, aren't you? Can I pick your tie?"

"I wouldn't have it any other way."

When Jennifer emerged with a dress over one arm and a silk tie dangling from her fingers, she finally spotted the bow-topped box in the middle of her dressing table. "What's that?" she asked warily as she draped the clothes across the foot of the bed.

"A present. I'm buying your affection."

Jennifer said, "We really don't have time," even as she picked up the small box with the Lego logo. "I already have a Rey *Star Wars* figure."

"I know."

Jennifer's look was appropriately suspicious. She upended the box over the bed and a Tiffany's bird's-egg blue ring box tumbled out. "You're so sneaky."

"I just thought we should make it more official than a twist tie."

They both glanced at the lampshade on Jennifer's side of the bed where the silver bracelet and twist tie ring dangled together.

"Okay," she said softly.

Suzanne slipped her arm around Jennifer's waist as she opened the box.

A trillion-cut rose diamond centered in a band of glittering smaller white diamonds set in platinum. To Suzanne the sparkle, elegance and strength represented everything that was Jennifer. "I hope you like it."

Jennifer gazed at for several moments before throwing her arms around Suzanne for an exuberant kiss. "It's beautiful!"

"I was hoping it was simple enough. Not...not like a costume."

"It's perfect, you're right. I could wear it most of the time, except on camera." Jennifer's eyes glittered with tears she blinked away. She tilted the ring into a sunbeam, casting prisms of rainbow light across her own face and the ceiling above her. "Truly beautiful."

"I'm so glad you like it." Suzanne finally relaxed. She'd carefully studied Jennifer's jewelry and taken notice of what Jennifer chose to wear when it wasn't for a public occasion.

"You're right of course." Her voice took on a slightly mocking tone. "You and Annemarie and Selena are making speeches about supporting projects that pledge fifty percent participation by women. When Hyde and I make our little speech it would be nice to flash your ring at the world. But I'm not putting it on."

She'd relaxed too soon. What had she missed? "Why?"

Jennifer took a step back. With her hair still piled on top of her head and her body wrapped only in a towel, she put the box in Suzanne's hand and arched an elegant, meaningful eyebrow.

Somebody had to do the asking. Suzanne didn't hesitate to kneel.

"Jennifer Lamont, will you marry me?"

"Yes." Jennifer's lips curved into a full smile. "I suppose I should admit that you beat me to it. Your ring isn't ready until next week."

A wave of pleasure filled Suzanne so completely that she had to resist the urge to cry. "I look forward to it."

The ring fit Jennifer's finger better than the twist tie. Suzanne kissed it and then Jennifer's palm. "Let's go change the world."

"I think we should get dressed first."

"Spoilsport."

The End